Passing Through (The Sixties)

by Robert E. Maurer

Printed by CreateSpace
Charleston, SC

www.CreateSpace.com/6028907

www.PassingThruTime.com

ISBN-13: 978-1523728275

ISBN-10: 1523728272

Cover Design: Stella McKeown
Author, *Some Ways Art Happens*,
Gallery exhibited Artist,
Junior High Art Teacher, Illustrator

For Zoelle

My life, my wife,

For Eternity

CREATIVITY consists of Arrogance,
believing one has
something important to express,
and Humility,
believing one's craft is not
yet expressive enough.
In the cooking together of the two
come the calories to place
words on a page,
paint on a canvas,
notes on a score.

But ART has more ingredients
than these two.
From Living come the spices
to season the meal.
A bird, wings outstretched,
turning on a current of air,
a family member's suicide,
a lake's refreshing chill,
a newspaper headline,
an alcoholic's rant,
a secret,
a sunset,
a stallion.

--Robert E. Maurer

Table of Contents

Acknowledgements

Every author requires one person whose belief in their labor is constant. My wife, Zoelle Montgomery Maurer, is that person in my life.

Zoelle's experience of the 1960s was far, far different than mine. Her perspective proved critical for my attempt to portray the period honestly. As my friend and confidant, her encouragement and faith were vital.

Libraries and librarians were a rich resource, especially the Burlington County, Evesham, and Vincentown Libraries here in South Jersey. As "knowledge" goes digital, it is so very important to future generations that librarians continue to enhance and transform the library's essential community roles. Librarians are cornerstones of our democracy, promoting the love of learning, a commitment to accuracy and free expression, and the public's right to know.

I also appreciate the librarians at two specialized Michigan State University collections for inviting me to transfer my personal papers. The African Activist Archive is being digitized, and can be found at www.africanactivist.msu.edu. The American Radicalism collection is currently cataloguing my contributions.

This novel hopefully portrays accurately a portion of the American activist generation of the 1960s. But the novel does not speak for every activist. Every person's individual story is vital to understanding the whole of this generation's rising up and challenging Authority wherever it exerted itself.

Beginning largely in 1960 on northern college and university campuses, spreading to their surrounding communities and the entire society, activists did not end a war or *apartheid*, or eliminate discrimination based on gender or sexual orientation. Their impact, however, shook a nation to its core. The progressive changes they spawned are still manifesting today.

A decade earlier, beginning largely with young adults in southern small towns and large cities, spreading north and west, activists did not eliminate racism or achieve economic justice. Their impact, however, also shook a nation to its core. The progressive changes they spawned are still manifesting today.

i

Preface

I had expected to quote portions of song lyrics at the beginning of each chapter. In the second half of the 1960s, these lyrics were either highly popular, just released, or evocative of the emotions during the time period covered.

Identifying which agencies owned the print rights to license lyrics for quotation was arduous. The projected out-of-pocket fees were prohibitive. Therefore, each chapter begins only with song titles and related information.

As a "preface" for the entire novel, lyrics from two songs would have appeared in their entirety. The tone of a generation was amplified by singer-song writer Eunice Kathleen Waymon (aka Nina Simone), sixth child in a preacher's family born in Tryon, North Carolina, in 1933, and Robert Allen Zimmerman (aka Bob Dylan), an only child in a Jewish family born in Duluth, Minnesota, in 1941.

Nina Simone wrote and recorded *Mississippi Goddam*, released in the album "Nina Simone in Concert", 1964.

Bob Dylan wrote and recorded *The Times They Are A-Changin'*, title track of the album by the same name, released in January 1964.

The tone of a generation was also amplified by the English poet, William Butler Yeats, who presaged not only the Nineteen Sixties, but also the current age, by writing the following in 1919:

> Turning and turning in the widening gyre
> The falcon cannot hear the falconer;
> Things fall apart; the centre cannot hold;
> Mere anarchy is loosed upon the world,
> The blood-dimmed tide is loosed, and everywhere
> The ceremony of innocence is drowned;
> The best lack all conviction, while the worst
> Are full of passionate intensity.
>
> From, *The Second Coming*

CHAPTER 1 – MEETING (LATE FALL 1965)

Universal Soldier, covered by Donovan, written by Buffy Sainte-Marie (1964), released in the United States, September, 1965.

Paths of Victory, an old gospel song (also known as *Deliverance Will Come* and *The Wayworn Traveler*), re-written by Bob Dylan (in 1962 or 1963) and covered by Odetta in her 1965 album, *Odetta Sings Dylan*. The original gospel song may have been written in 1836.

The notice, thumbtacked to a bulletin board outside the university's cafeteria, had carried only a few hand-printed words.

"Viet Nam Discussion. Monday, December 6.
63 Tiemann Place. Apartment 10. 8 o'clock."

Daniel had almost overlooked it among the dozens of other thumbtacked notes about looking for roommates, selling used textbooks, requesting a ride to Chicago for Christmas, and the like. Was this "Discussion" the answer to his predicament? He could go to the meeting and hand out copies of the letter. That just might fulfill the promise he'd made to Ellen.

Although he'd grown up on Long Island, Daniel was familiar enough with Manhattan to know that Tiemann Place, a short block, truncated between Broadway and Riverside Drive just below 125th Street, marked one of Manhattan's racial and economic boundaries. Walking south of Tiemann on Claremont Avenue would take him to Morningside Heights, a white promontory on an increasingly multicultural island. Walking north instead would lead to Harlem, a black, middle- and occasionally upper-class valley.

The sun had set at about 4:30 that afternoon, and an early winter breeze had replaced the sidewalks' daytime heat. Daniel zipped his coat up to his neck and put his fingers in the tops of his front pockets. He'd decided, after changing his mind about it, to attend the meeting. Preoccupied as he was about whom he'd see there, and what he would say, Daniel passed Tiemann Place without noticing the street sign. After walking a few more blocks, and sensing the changing hues of the faces around him, he turned around just before reaching 125th Street. He walked more quickly, smiled more often, and dug his hands deeper into his pockets.

Where was the damn street, he wondered. He did not want to miss this meeting and have to come out again to another one. As he hurried his way through foreign territory, he wondered to himself why the hell had he made that promise to Ellen several weeks earlier?

"I can't think of a better person to do it, Danny, you've got to do it for me," she had pleaded, lowering her head so that her eyes locked on his. "I'm so upset. I can't do it. He would have wanted you to."

"No, no, I'm not the right person."

"Danny boy, you must help me. Peter's life, everything he stood for, everything he fought for, everything he believed in, has been erased by his death. That obituary never mentioned any of it. I can give you some details. Someone has to tell his story."

"No, please, Ellen. Find someone else. I don't even write that well."

"Come on, you've got to do it, Daniel, please!"

"Oh, alright, Ellen. I'll write something. I promise." Daniel had agreed, just to quiet her. He'd even gone ahead and written the letter-to-the-editor. But he hadn't been able to get it published, and he knew he had to try something else. If he went to this meeting, he figured, he'd be off the hook. Ellen would have to acknowledge his efforts, even if nothing came of them.

Then Daniel found Tiemann Place, and the right building. He rang the bell below the mailbox just inside the first door and pushed through the second door after hearing the buzzer. There was no elevator so he started to climb. It was the first time he had climbed a set of stairs in an apartment building in his life.

Rounding the landing to the foot of the last flight of stairs, Daniel's right knee buckled as his left foot rose toward the step. He almost fell. Shielding the copies of the letter next to his belly, he righted himself, thought about turning around, and then thought about Ellen. Puffing heavily as he reached the front of the door to the fifth floor apartment, he started to rehearse what he would say. He pushed the doorbell button. Before he had time to collect his thoughts the door was opened by a smiling young woman.

"Hi!" she said, "My name is Christie. Come in, come in. We're expecting *many* more people. What's your name?"

"Daniel," he answered. She motioned him inside.

"How nice of you to be on time."

He entered a spacious room with folding chairs spread out to form a circle stretching from either side of a faded brown couch at the back of the room. Three people stopped talking and looked up at him. Walking through a gap in the circle, Daniel sat down in the empty chair nearest the door and glanced at his watch. Eight fifteen. The notice had said the meeting would start at 8 o'clock. Was his watch fast, he wondered. Daniel lowered his head to study the letter he had brought with him.

"May I offer you some coffee?" Christie asked Daniel. "I just made a fresh pot."

Daniel nodded.

"Cream and sugar?"

Daniel nodded again. When she came back into the living room and offered him the mug, he thanked her and took a quick, large gulp, scolding his mouth. Now he'd have to finish it, he thought, before he could leave.

After he silently read the letter over several more times, Daniel focused on making an inventory of the room. Some of the folding chairs were wooden, others were metal. Daniel concluded the collection was borrowed from different sources. A metal table with folding legs, on which the lamp stood, leaned against a sidewall. A wooden, straight-back chair was pushed underneath, as if its owner were keeping one possession off limits to her guests. A bureau stood next to the metal table. The only other furnishings in the room were two tall lamps, standing at either end of the couch, and a table lamp a few chairs away. These three lamps provided the only sources of light in the room. A shard of fear shot across his mind. If people couldn't make out the light print of the letter, would he have to read it out loud?

He watched Christie fluffing the only pillow on the couch, then removing a few papers from the top of the bureau and pushing them out of sight into a drawer. She reset a chair in the circle, the same one she had reset a moment before. She kept glancing at one of her guests and then looking away. The last person to enter the apartment had called him William, but no one was talking to him. Standing near the couch with a wide stance, his back ram-rod straight, William had his arms crossed and he kept looking down at his watch. Christie turned to go into the kitchen. Daniel saw that her hair was braided in a circle around the back of her head, in just the same way his grandmother braided her white hair. How odd, he thought, for a young and pretty girl to wear her hair like that, so old-fashioned.

By 8:30 seven people were there, including Daniel and Christie and William. Daniel noticed Christie silently counting the empty seats. Seven. She looked up with a smile and crossed the room to open the front door, but no one was there. She kept moving, offering the coffee, cream, and sugar to her guests. She then talked cheerfully with the group of three people who seemed to know each other. Smiling at William, he did not ever smile back at her.

Daniel did not meet anyone's gaze, even when a young man sat down opposite him and sent a friendly "hello" across the space between them. The longer he sat, the more certain he felt that he would not entangle himself in any conversations because, after the meeting ended, his departure might be delayed by others' attempts at chitchat.

Counting the empty chairs, Daniel grimaced. How many more people did they expect? Eight copies of the letter were all he'd been able to afford at the copy shop, and he wanted to keep one for himself.

Daniel then noticed that Christie was folding a few empty chairs and leaning them against a wall in the hallway. A good sign the meeting was about to begin, he concluded. But then he watched as William strode quickly over to her, and whispered something. Christie rapidly reset all the folded chairs in their original places.

Why wasn't the meeting starting? Were they waiting for someone? The longer he sat the more determined he was to slip out as soon as the meeting ended, maybe even before it ended. He glanced at his watch again.

It was almost 40 minutes past the announced starting time. Maybe he should just give up and leave now. As he considered this, William sat down and signaled to Christie. She took her place next to him, pad and pen in hand.

"Has anyone attended a meeting about Viet Nam before?" William asked. No one raised a hand or nodded.

"Ok, fine. Let's have everyone introduce themselves, and say where they're from."

Nicki had been the last to arrive, and was the first to speak. When she'd come into the apartment she'd started toward one chair, then changed direction in midcourse toward another. The drape of her open coat and maroon dress, the sort of dress Daniel had seen in the windows at Saks Fifth Avenue and Henri Bendel's, made a pleasing swishing sound as she'd walked across the room. She pushed her hand through her hair and started to talk.

"I'm Nikki. I'm from Cambridge. No, not England. Massachusetts."

"My name is Steve. I come from a small ranching town in Montana you've never heard of."

"I'm Ed. I was born and raised a few blocks away. I'm here because a priest introduced me to Dorothy Day's Catholic Workers Movement."

"I'm Charles. Born and raised in Los Angeles."

"My name is Bob. Bob from Bangor. Maine, that is."

"My name is Christie. I grew up in Hopewell Township, New Jersey."

"I'm Daniel. My hometown is Babylon, Long Island."

"My name is Marvin. I'm from St. Petersburg. That's Florida, not the Soviet Union," he said, looking at Nikki.

"And finally, my name is William. I'm an American citizen, but was born and raised in Ottawa, the capital of Canada. My father was a diplomat, stationed at the US Embassy there. He's still with the State Department. So, Ok, fine, now that we're all acquainted, let's get to the heart of the matter. What do we each know about the subject at hand? What does anyone know about Viet Nam?"

"I've read some really good books," Nicki said, "Bernard Fall's *The Two Viet-Nams*, for instance. I found it very informative and I strongly urge everyone to read it."

"I'm wrestling with a moral dilemma," Ed said. "How can I be a good citizen and yet follow my conscience, which tells me the war is

5

immoral?"

"The draft is the issue that will unite the country against the war. I know it," William said.

"I have a friend who went to Mississippi," Christie remarked. "She taught in one of those freedom schools there."

"Well, that doesn't have anything to do with the war," William countered. "Let's stay on topic, OK?"

"Does anyone know why one million refugees went south after the Geneva Accords cut Viet Nam in half?" asked Charles.

"I don't know about that," responded Bob, "but I do know that Vietnamese Buddhists have been speaking out against the war."

"William, I think there is a connection with Mississippi and--" Christie began.

"Now, look, everyone," William interjected, "we just can't go on like this. We've got to come up with a plan, take some action."

"OK, William, how about the Gulf of Tonkin?" Ed offered. "Maybe we should start with that."

"I don't think so," Marvin argued. "Who really knows what happened? We've got to research French colonialism, and see the roots of the war from that perspective."

"You know, don't you," said William, who kept changing the topic at hand even though he continued to criticize others for doing so, "that President Johnson sent the first American combat troops to South Viet Nam only last March, and yet 30,000 showed up for a teach-in at Berkeley two months later. I thought you'd like to know." For a moment no one said anything.

Daniel finished the mug of cold coffee, and set it next to his chair on the floor. He drew his legs underneath and sat forward to relieve an ache in his back. He kept trying to come up with a clever way to get their attention, hand out the letter, and be done, but the conversation, like a ping-pong ball in play, shifted to a different spot every time he was about to open his mouth with a well-considered remark.

Eventually the students started to slow down and listen to each other, instead of listening to themselves speak, and the talk started to take focus. Then it speeded back up again as they began to throw out concrete suggestions for actions. Nicki suggested writing letters to their Congressional representatives, Marvin thought they should draw posters for school bulletins boards. Ed wanted the group to research how the U.S. had gotten involved in the first place. Christie suggested contacting other groups in the Morningside Heights area and circulating a list of books and articles and creating publicity to attract more people to the next meeting. Someone else thought it would be a good idea to invite an Asian scholar to speak at a school forum. Each new suggestion for action rose like a hot-air balloon, was batted about the room for a while, and then drifted to the floor. By 10:30 the only accomplishment was Steve's. He'd managed to get Nicki's phone number during a break.

Christie quickly glanced again at William's face. Like a cheerleader after each play on the field, she had broadcast affirming smiles to encourage everyone. But there was still no decision about a concrete plan of action, which everyone knew was William's goal. A plan would keep them going, give them a reason to meet again. Christie leaned away from William, toward the center of the circle.

"Daniel," Christie said, "You haven't said anything all evening. I bet you know what we should do next."

"No, er, that's OK." He'd decided an hour ago that he would tell Ellen about the meeting. It wasn't his fault, he would say, that he had not made anyone interested in the letter he'd written. Daniel had mostly stared at the middle of the threadbare rug. He was imagining the route back to his dormitory, so that he would not get lost, when Christie's question interrupted him.

"But you must have some idea," Christie pleaded. "You brought some papers with you. What are they?"

"OK, but, well, I don't know where to begin," Daniel said, now the center of attention. "This letter," he looked down at it. "It's a letter I wrote. It's a letter about Peter Hunting. About who he was. He was killed in Viet Nam." Daniel paused and took a deep breath.

"Don't stop," Christie urged. "Was this Peter a soldier?"

"No, not a soldier. He was the first American civilian, as far as I know, to die over there, as a result of this war you're all talking about."

He stopped, looked down at the mug on the floor, and waited. All at once the others started asking questions. Then Nicki stood up, put her hands on her hips and called out, "OK OK OK everyone!" until the room was quiet. She sat down and looked at Daniel.

She asked gently, "Was Peter a friend of yours?"

"No, not really. We went to college together, in Connecticut. But no, he wasn't really my friend. He was a year ahead of me. But I know someone who knew him very well. His girlfriend, actually."

"So how come he was in Viet Nam?" Ed asked.

"The last time I saw him, he was living in Washington, D.C.," Daniel began. "He said he was in training with the International Voluntary Services. Peter told me that he was going to teach English to the Vietnamese peasants."

"I didn't even know there were American civilians over there," Charles commented.

"Me, neither," Steve said. "So, was this Peter mistaken for a soldier or a spy by the Viet Cong?"

"*The New York Times* article said he was led into an ambush, maybe by Viet Cong agents. But somehow I don't think that's the whole story," Daniel said. Looking around the circle, he noticed everyone listening attentively. He moved forward to the edge of his chair, his back straight, and then he held up the letters, shaking them.

"I wanted the world to know more about Peter, I promised his girlfriend that I'd help tell his story. So I wrote this letter, to the editor of *The New York Times*. But they never published it."

"So let's hear it," said Christie. "Will you please read us the letter?"

Without answering her, Daniel started.

"Dear Editor,

"Your November 13, 1965, edition carried an article on page 3 under the headline, 'Vietcong's Ambush of U.S. Aid Worker Laid to 2 'Friends'.' The article went on to describe the death of Peter Hunting, a regional supervisor for the International Voluntary Service [sic] serving his second two-year term. The article described how Peter was shot because two of his 'friends,' riding with him in a vehicle in the Mekong Delta, may have been Viet Cong agents who led him into an ambush.

"Although a separate, short article mentioned Peter was a Wesleyan University graduate who had studied Chinese and French, both articles omitted important details about his life and mission.

"Peter arrived in Viet Nam in July, 1963, to study Vietnamese. One of his first assignments was to build a bicycle parking lot. He went on to dig wells and build windmills, as well as teach English to locals and officials.

"Peter and I were in the same fraternity, Alpha Delta Phi, at Wesleyan. He graduated a year before me. He came from rural America, growing up in a home surrounded by woods in southeastern Missouri. How he came to be interested in the Chinese language I have no idea, but he was good at it. He was a good young man who wanted only to do good things in the world. As far as I know, he had never been out of the country before, but International Voluntary Services (with an "s') represented the same values in which he believed.

"Peter Hunting died, in my opinion, because of the presence of the American military fighting against the Vietnamese. Were it not for American soldiers killing Vietnamese, Peter would be alive today.

"Sincerely,

"Daniel Gens"

The room was silent for a few moments. Ed was the first to speak.

"I like your letter. It really captures the irony of our involvement in the war."

"Yes," Nikki agreed. "It tells Peter's story well, and it also challenges anyone reading it why they should still support the war."

"I have a *great* idea," Christie announced. "Daniel, why don't you put a copy of the letter in every student's mailbox?"

"Great idea!" Marvin echoed.

Christie turned toward William. "Isn't this what you wanted? An agreement by the group to take an action?" Everyone waited for William's reaction.

"Yes, yes, splendid idea," William said, after a long pause. "I'll put a note at the bottom of the letter, saying, 'distributed by the Ad Hoc Student Committee Against the War in Viet Nam.' Christie, you can do posters saying, 'Read about the first American civilian killed in Viet Nam. Check your mailbox.' We can even add at the bottom of the poster an invitation to our next meeting. How about it, everyone?"

There was immediate agreement.

"I'll start on the posters right after class tomorrow," Christie said.

"I'll help you," Nicki offered.

"Hey, I'll find out the best places to tack them up," Ed volunteered.

"And I'll talk to some classmates who might chip in to pay for copying enough letters for everyone," Bob said.

"Nice meeting, William," several said as they left.

"Yeah, well done, William, a great success," others said as they patted him on the back.

One of the last to leave, Daniel lingered for a few moments in the hallway, and then went back to the apartment.

"Did you *really* like the letter?" he asked Christie.

"Yes, I *really* did."

Walking south on Broadway, Daniel waited to cross at a light. What had happened, he asked himself. Without a second thought, he had nodded in agreement when everyone else agreed he should distribute copies to the entire school! Now there was so much more work ahead than he had ever intended. At least Ellen would be proud of him, wouldn't she, he thought. They all seemed to like the letter, didn't they? Even Nikki came up and said he was doing a good thing, didn't she?

He took a left onto West 122nd Street toward his dorm building, smiling as he recalled Christie's assurance.

CHAPTER 2 – MOTION (CHRISTMAS EVE 1965)

Ballad of the Student Sit-Ins, words and music by Guy Carawan, Eve Merriam, and Norman Curtis, early 1960.

His foot relaxed a bit on the gas pedal, easing the speedometer back from 72. Daniel reminded himself that he was running a marathon in this borrowed car, not a series of hundred yard dashes.

"Hey, slow down *more*," Ephraim said.

"It's OK," Daniel responded, "I've got it under control."

"No, no, we can't get a ticket," Ephraim implored. "Do you know what I went through to get this car! If you get a ticket, my father'll really know I lied to him."

The car had never been used to drive in New York City. It was preserved for special occasions when the family had piled into the 1958 Plymouth to relax at a resort in the Catskills. Driving at a painstakingly slow speed, Joseph, Ephraim's father, had been certain that Joe E. Brown or Jerry Lewis would wait until he had arrived before they went on stage.

"You know, I never knew this old buggy could do more than fifty," Ephraim said. "But you've got to go more *slowly*."

"Hey, look, I've driven long distances a lot. I know how to spot a speed trap, OK!"

This late winter afternoon, Joseph's car was not headed west toward its traditional vacation destination. Rather, it was roaring south on the New Jersey Turnpike headed to a place it had never been before.

Daniel and a series of traveling companions intended to proclaim their conviction, right in front of the White House, that the 30-hour bombing halt, announced to begin on Christmas Eve, should be extended. Surely, the President and his advisors, Daniel assured himself, would seize on the spirit of the Season to seek a settlement. How could the leaders of a nation, which gathered in churches and synagogues to celebrate peace, rededication, and miracles at this time of the year, not support the termination of a reign of death from the sky?

> **Munsee rides across the Raritan River bridge next to the Plymouth, leaving his traditional territory behind. His bow is slung across his back like a guitar. Munsee benevolently observes Ephraim's conflicted spirit. Neither Ephraim nor anyone else sees Munsee who heads toward the capital of broken treaties.**

For Daniel, this night would seem to last a lifetime. It was as if he and the others were on a pilgrimage traveling to the seat of political power, each person having his own tale to tell, enduring the test of winter's bitter cold, all for a holy cause.

"How's it going back there, guys?" Daniel asked. "Got enough heat?"

Sean, Norman, and Jacques in the rear seat chimed in: "OK, yeah, *tres bien.*"

"Have I ever told you about my driving across Kansas when that woman bookkeeper picked me up--" Daniel began.

"Yeah, yeah, about an hour ago!" Sean replied.

"Oh, sorry."

"Daniel, please slow down! Either you'll kill me on this road or my father will kill me when I get home," Ephraim declared. "Why did I ever let William talk me into this?"

"Yeah, you never told me. How did you meet William?"

"On a bus going to D.C. We sat next to each other."

"Why were you on a bus together?"

"You remember that Quaker fellow, Norman Josephon, who burned himself to death in front of the Pentagon? He was protesting the loss of life caused by the American military in Vietnam."

"Vaguely."

"Well, his act of conscience sparked, oh God, I should use a different word—moved many of the tens of thousands who came to D.C. on that Saturday of Thanksgiving weekend, just a month ago."

"Yeah, I heard about that."

"So, I would never have met William any other way. We're from such different backgrounds. My family lives on Hester Street in Manhattan, two blocks from my father's kosher butcher shop on East Broadway. But there we were, not knowing anyone else, so we stuck together for hours, listening to speeches, some of them pretty boring, and chanting our heads off. We never once asked each other where we were from, or what our fathers did. Anyway, he rang me up two days ago, and convinced me to get my father's car, and meet you this afternoon at the address he gave me. I like him."

Daniel fell silent.

"Why are *you* going?" Ephraim asked.

"I love to drive," Daniel responded.

In the days following the anti-war organizing meeting in Apartment 10, students and a few faculty had congratulated Daniel on his letter-to-the-editor after reading the copy they found placed in their school mailboxes. Even though Daniel had continued to be acutely aware of his failure to have the letter published in *The Times*, this burst of recognition, plus the money raised from a dozen classmates to pay for the copies, had allowed him to feel more at ease among all these strangers. Like a shopkeeper who appears from behind the back room curtain whenever the bell atop the door announces a customer, Daniel was beginning to learn how to project self-assurance, chat with the public, all the while knowing that he could not permit anyone to approach his curtain, behind which he maintained all the records of his faults.

Daniel had had unexpected help, of a sort, in the art of socialization. Associating himself with a student whose name, with one stuffing of all the mailboxes, was now known throughout campus, William had seized the opportunity to shepherd Daniel around, introducing him to social circles he could never have entered on his own.

"Here's the member of my committee I've been telling you about," William had begun every introduction, as if he had discovered Daniel. "Remember that great letter about a civilian killed in Vietnam? My committee Ok'd the text before distribution."

Christmas parties had provided William with Daniel's classroom. Several of William's social circles had offered invitations to cocktail parties hosted on campus by faculty and off-campus by liberal organizations. The cocktail party, William instructed Daniel, presented the perfect opportunity to schmooze and ingratiate himself with many people in a short time. William counseled Daniel to hone in on the hostess who knew everyone else, and was more than delighted to make introductions.

At his first cocktail party, Daniel had remained in one place a few feet from the nibbles table, in a corner where no one could approach him from the side or behind. He had smiled faintly as guests passed by, relieved they were more focused on food than on him. He had observed William, half-envious how at ease he seemed, half-afraid William would parade him on yet another round of introductions. He noticed that William had rarely taken sips from his glass of gin and tonic, whereas Daniel had quickly drained one glassful and was near to draining the next. Once, he had steeled himself enough to stumble a few feet to the nibbles table, refilling his plate with cheese and crackers. Returning to his corner, Daniel had looked for William again, but he wasn't where he had last seen him. In fact, with practically everyone in motion, Daniel observed that no one remained with another long enough to get to know them. How clever, Daniel had thought.

"Daniel, you must circulate," William had ordered as he swooped in for a refill.

"But I don't know what to talk about. Everybody's talking."

William had laughed.

"Oh, Daniel, it's not that hard. You just have to have three things at the ready. Some inane remarks about the weather, the name of the leading scorer in last night's basketball game or some other sports' highlight, and a question like, did you see that article in *The Times* on XYZ? That's all you need."

At the next cocktail party, Daniel had looked fondly at first for what he hoped was *his* corner. He had noticed, however, that a somewhat ill-kempt student occupied the safe area. Keep moving, Daniel had said to himself, trying to emulate William. He had sipped more alcohol than he wanted, but had managed to talk about Willis Reed's rebounding during the Knicks game with a professor and about the frigidly cold weather with the hostess who had seemed more eager than Daniel to move on to the next person. For an hour, Daniel had *circulated*. At times, he had been abandoned by someone who left him before he could leave them, but, overall, he was beginning to understand how he could maintain a façade, which had allowed no one to penetrate it, all accomplished by keeping in motion.

As Daniel gripped the wheel of the Plymouth with both hands to assure Ephraim, Daniel thought again of William, and how grateful he was for the social mentoring. But then he also recalled the second and third meetings of the anti-war group in Christie's apartment.

"Ah, good, I see you're going to become a regular," Christie had said as she ushered Daniel into her apartment.

"And I *would* like some coffee," Daniel said, grinning.

"You're learning fast!"

"It's good to be here. If there's anything you or the others want me to do, just name it."

At its second meeting, the group had expanded to eighteen, re-naming itself the "Morningside Heights Student Committee Against the War in Viet Nam." William had suggested it needed a formal structure.

"Every committee I know about has officers," William had declared. "You know, a president, vice-president, and so on."

"Absolutely right," Ed had echoed. "I suggest William for president."

"Thanks, Ed. And I suggest Ed as vice-president and Christie as secretary-treasurer."

"Shouldn't the post of secretary-treasurer be split into two, to give more people a chance to serve?" Daniel asked.

"No, no, we're not *that* big, yet. One person can handle both jobs. All in favor of the officers nominated?"

William had taken the few hands raised and the silence of the rest as an affirmative vote. Daniel had said nothing more.

The Student Committee's third meeting was on the evening of Wednesday, December 22nd. Daniel learned that William had received a phone call earlier that day from Father Phillip Ryan in Washington, D.C., who told him that the White House had announced a halt to the bombing over North Vietnam, which would start two days later. Since the White House had also announced that the bombing halt would last only 30 hours, William explained to the group that Father Ryan had asked for a continuous stream of people to come to Lafayette Park and conduct a non-stop vigil across the street from the White House, asking for an extension to the bombing halt. The priest had said he did not know how many people could be found at such short notice during the Holiday break to walk around in the bitter cold, but he had wanted at least a few people conducting the vigil round-the-clock.

"So, Father Ryan is counting on us, and a few others who live in Washington, to keep the vigil going continuously through its first night until more people can be mobilized for the next day," William had explained.

"I'll drive," Daniel had volunteered. "It's all I really want to do to help out."

Daniel paid the toll at the far end of the Delaware Memorial Bridge, and was accelerating away from the booth.

"Why are you looking at the speedometer *again*?" Daniel asked.

"Look, Daniel, if we get stopped, who do you think will be mailed the overdue notice if I can't pay the ticket? And how do I explain to my father that his car was not on Route 17 heading toward Ferndale, but instead on Interstate 95?"

"We'll think of something. Stop worrying."

"Stop worrying! What if one of us leaves one of those burger wrappers, what're they called, McDonald's, under the seat, and my father finds it. We observe kosher!"

"OK, OK, I'll take it slower. But I've got to get a good feel for this car. Remember, once I drop you and the others off, I head back to New York for another load."

"Oh God, that's right."

As Daniel emerged from the Fort McHenry Tunnel, he looked over at Ephraim, asleep with his head against the window. The other three were asleep, too. Daniel felt pleased with himself. His smooth driving, virtually the same 65 miles-per-hour to keep Ephraim at bay, never braking too rapidly when approaching a tollbooth, had given his passengers the sense of safety and security needed for them to sleep like babies. Daniel smiled like a proud father at evening's end. Relieved that he did not have to engage in any more conversations, he was the sole pilot now.

Daniel nearly missed the turn off from Interstate 495 onto the Baltimore-Washington Parkway, however. He had failed to look for road signs overhead because, falling into a trance-like state, his eyes had been fixed only on the illuminated part of the road ahead. He had forgotten the advice of the Kansas bookkeeper about looking elsewhere into the distance to relax the eye muscles on a long night's trip.

As a result of his crossing America by thumb, after graduating high school, often driving strangers' automobiles, Daniel had learned a fundamental truth about self-change: the courage to embrace a new experience rested solidly on carrying an old, familiar one into it. Driving was one of Daniel's now familiar experiences, which supported his likelihood of going to a new place until that new place also felt familiar. On this Christmas Eve, he was taking his first step on an unanticipated path, which could result in radicalization.

"Bathroom break!" Daniel called out as he stopped the car by the side of the parkway.

Daniel opened the door, glad to stretch his legs and feel the cold air slap him on the face. He walked around the front of the car and up a slight incline until he found himself surrounded by bushes. As the wind provided a few moments of false refreshment, Daniel enjoyed watching the steam rise from the yellow stream.

Sean became quickly wide-awake at the cold's touch on his face, hands, and elsewhere, as he stood at a considerable distance upwind from Daniel.

"Where are we?" Sean shouted.

"I guess we're about an hour outside Washington," Daniel shouted back.

"I can't see a friggin' thing in these bushes," Sean announced.

As Sean started back to the car, his foot was snagged by part of a bramble, and he almost fell down. "What the hell am I doing here?" Sean muttered.

He quickly took stock of his situation, as Sean often did when he questioned a previous decision he had made. He had learned to become a realist, gathering all the facts, weighing pros and cons, until he could calculate the odds as to which course of action was the most promising, and therefore, likely to succeed.

"Oh hell," Sean shouted in front of the car's headlights, "my shoe is soaked with urine!"

"That's a good one," Norman exclaimed. "You've got to watch your aim in this breeze."

Norman was an experienced traveler, having already been to Europe three times, once as an exchange high school student living with a French family. He had been to Paris, Rome, London, Berne, and other European capitals, but had never entered his own nation's capital. Neither had any of the other pilgrims.

Until a few days ago, Jacques had not seen Norman in six years, ever since Jacques' family near Amboise had hosted Norman for a year. Jacques thought of himself as an idealist, believing the world of ideas contained solutions to the world's problems, if only one stuck to one's principles. He had graduated from the Sorbonne, and was now immersed in the study of international law.

"This is ridiculous." Sean made a new calculation after all had returned to the car. "We're not going to make any difference. No one will know we were even there. I'm tired, hungry, cold—and wet! Let's go back."

Ephraim quickly supported Sean, if only because he figured the odometer would have registered fewer miles than if they continued.

"Hey, guys, I've never seen Washington," Norman countered. "We're not that far away. Let's at least look around. What'ya say?"

How could he face the next meeting of the Student Committee, Daniel thought, and tell them he never made it to Lafayette Park? Sean and Ephraim continued pestering Daniel to make a U-turn at the next parkway exit.

What'll I do, Daniel wondered. Maybe I could get everyone to promise to say that we had walked around Lafayette Park for awhile, but left because of the bitter cold. Yeah, that might work. But, oh no, what if the priest talks with William? Then William will know I was lying.

Daniel just kept driving, ignoring the debate raging around him.

Sean and Norman, on either side of Jacques, kept bending forward, glowering at each other, arguing more and more acerbically.

"Look, Mister Know It All," Norman, now leaning across Jacques, said directly to Sean's face. "We all agreed on this little adventure and I for one am going to see it through."

"OK, Mister Bleeding Heart, let me ask you this," Sean shot back. "If you were on a train and someone yelled out it was going to crash, would you still stay on?"

"Yeah, I would, especially if I didn't believe the person who yelled out!" Norman countered.

Jacques bent forward, using his forearms to push both combatants back into their corners, like a referee separating boxers. He then asked Daniel what he wanted to do.

"Oh, God, I'm not sure." He was often so uncertain of which way to shade his response to please everyone that he often ducked behind his curtain.

"Daniel, you must tell us what you think. You are the driver," Jacques insisted.

Yes, that's right, Daniel thought, I am the driver. I like being at the wheel, having others in my care.

"I want to drop everyone off at Lafayette Park," Daniel finally said, "and then go back to New York and get more people and keep doing that a few more times."

"I guess it's two-to-two," Norman announced. "How do you vote, Jacques?"

Jacques said that he thought a vote would be meaningless since, in whichever direction the car would head after the vote, there would be two people who did not want to go in that direction.

"I believe in a democracy where the minority has to be protected from any harm the majority's decision might cause them. So I don't think putting two of us out of the car, to walk in their desired direction, is the solution," Jacques discoursed. "And we can not cut the car in half to satisfy us all, can we? *Mon dieu*! No, we all knew at the beginning of this journey the destination of the car. So it was like agreeing to a pact. We even each gave twenty dollars US for gas and tolls, did we not, as a further sign of our commitment to the pact? Therefore, there is an invisible web, which weaves us together, whether we know it or not, or even if we dislike it or not. Pacts can not be voided just because a few of the parties, even a majority of them, change their mind unless all agree that the underlying circumstances leading to the pact have substantively altered. And they have not changed, have they? The pact binds us. So we must all continue to support our original agreement and go to Lafayette Park."

The matter was settled. After a short silence, as if it took a brief respite for the young men's hormones to regroup, Norman spoke first.

"You know, guys, you probably never heard of Gerdes Folk City in The Village, but I caught Bob Dylan there."

Sean chimed in, "That's nothing. I saw Peter, Paul and Mary at a recent hootenanny there."

Ephraim countered, "So all you two did was sit in the audience! After the set, I got Art Garfunkel's autograph when he and Paul Simon performed there a few months back."

The one-upmanship briefly continued, until sleep leveled them all.

Daniel turned right onto Route 50, which eventually became New York Avenue. Then, after a slight right, he drove a short distance on Pennsylvania Avenue. He stopped in front of Lafayette Park. The five got out of the car. Ignoring the slightly lightheaded feeling of having gone without dinner or the faintly surrealistic sense of being a stranger in a strange land, Daniel was now looking across the street through the high fence--at the White House! He glanced at the other four. Together, it was as if they were standing before the All Powerful, in awe of the majestic scene before them, affected in a way none of them could have anticipated. Frozen to the spot, they forgot why they had come. Transfixed by the simplicity of the beauty before them, these pilgrims suspended their belief for a few moments that anything evil could emanate from this White Basilica set against the black sky.

"Are you boys the New York contingent?" Father Phillip Ryan asked, looking at the license plate. "I am so glad you are with us. Counting yourselves, you can see we are now twelve. Though we're small in number, where your cause is just, well, forgive me, it's probably more important to say we have some hot coffee for you," as he pointed to several thermoses sitting on a small table.

Driven by the biting wind, snow had laced the red-toned faces of seven supplicants who had begun the round-the-clock vigil at sunset. At the outset, Father Ryan, a Jesuit priest, had asked permission of the seven to read from the Book of Psalms on this Christmas Eve. He had of course known there could not be a processional or a reading from the Gospel or a musical rendition of the Magnificat. But he had sensed, as it was evening, that he was officiating a form of Vespers. When no one had objected, the priest read a portion of Psalm 23: "Even though I walk through the valley of the shadow of death, I fear no evil; for Thou art with me; Thy rod and Thy staff, they comfort me."

The seven had doggedly kept each other moving in a circle. A few had tried sporadically to sing "I Ain't Marching Anymore" by Phil Ochs, or "Lyndon Johnson Told the Nation" by Tom Paxton. Most had known the entire chorus, but only a few words of a few verses. The singing attempts had eventually petered out. The seven had walked slowly, each seeing the back of the other straight ahead and, glancing across the circle, the face of another coming toward them—the same back, the same face--for hours on end. Were not the seven a medieval processional, braving a quest, which tested their fealty to an unseen lord? Why else would they keep constantly circling, without food, in the bitter cold darkness?

Cars had passed, but drivers could not see the snow-soaked signs hung loosely around their necks with string. Their message could not be received, and yet they had continued to walk, four young women and three young men, believing that the President of the United States would be convinced by their vigil to extend the bombing halt permanently. Why would the most powerful man on earth do this? Because the seven, now twelve, were morally right, they fervently and innocently believed.

The five from New York had almost finished all the coffee in the thermoses by the time Daniel decided to head north to pick up the next load, scheduled for 1:15am on Christmas Day. He sensed that Sean and the rest needed him back as soon as possible.

The old Plymouth took on a new life under Daniel's guidance, free of Ephraim's fears. It sped away from Lafayette Park with pep and confidence. Daniel felt such a heightened sense of awareness from a combination of coffee, cold air, and fatigue that he absolutely knew, once he hit the Parkway, he could easily cruise at 75-80mph.

Daniel soon experienced the Parkway, however, as if in a partial hypnotic trance. Looking straight ahead at the road in front of him, his mind's edge was dulled by the monotony and ease with which he performed the few simple tasks needed to guide the Plymouth. The darkness itself masked the different contours and textures of the scene before his eyes, which in day light would have provided variety in his field of vision. The different shades of darkness falling across the highway provided an almost dream-like beauty. The unbroken white line near the shoulder of the interstate to his right and the broken white line dividing the lane to his left were mesmerizing. These lines were the only points of contrast in his field of vision. Daniel experienced increasing difficulty keeping his attention focused on what he was doing. He blinked his eyelids frequently to try to moisten them because his eyes were burning. His ability to remember why it was that he had only one hand on the wheel diminished. Then, as if a collar around his neck were violently jerked by someone next to him, for a few split seconds of terror Daniel realized, as he returned to something resembling the present moment, that he had become disconnected from the fact *he* was driving.

As Daniel took the entrance ramp to I-95 North from the Washington-Baltimore Parkway, the stimulating effects of the caffeine from his three cups of coffee began to wear off, leaving a kind of unsettled, slightly nervous edge. He could not stop yawning. The Plymouth drifted a few feet into the other lane. For the better part of a second or two, driving at 75 miles per hour, Daniel was simply not mentally inside the car. The vehicle proceeded "safely" because no steering or speed adjustment needed to be made during those few seconds. There were no other cars around him, fortunately. His eyelids grew even heavier. His eyes were fixated on nothing. Something deep within him violently jerked the collar again. He was "wide awake" once again, fully attentive to his responsibility behind the wheel, or so he thought. But a diabolical miscalculation was in play. It would be with him tonight and, in various guises, with him for years to come.

Tonight, the miscalculation took the form of his fatigued body, desperately wanting rest, continuously trying to convince Daniel's mind that it actually took *less* effort to drive, or rather, that *less* was, in fact, actually what was *normally* needed to accomplish the driving task. Convinced now that less effort was all that was required, the mind gave its blessing to the body to rest, even sleep, because the body had deluded the mind into believing there was virtually nothing to do to complete the trip safely.

Stretching his eyebrows, eyelids, and eyes as wide as possible as he went over the Delaware Memorial Bridge, Daniel convinced himself that he had won the war to stay awake all the way to New York. He had not. He had been lucky. The diabolical miscalculation had only retreated—this time.

"Hey, Jeff, are you still going to Washington?" one of the demonstrators asked, as the tiny group started to disband.

"I guess so. I told them I would. But after walking around here, my feet wish I hadn't!"

"Don't stretch yourself too thin," the demonstrator cautioned. "Take care."

Jeff walked to a coffee shop just north of the United Nations on First Avenue where he had agreed to wait for Daniel. Near-by, he and three others, with signs protesting the United States government's unwillingness to impose sanctions on South Africa, had been picketing that evening outside the apartment of Arthur Goldberg, the US representative to the UN. Jeff had been impressed with how his newfound friends conducted their business.

Anishinaabe looks through the window of the coffee shop at Jeff. She travels twelve hundred miles as the crow flies from Minnesota to Manhattan, reversing the trek of her Turtle Island ancestors. Wearing turkey tail feathers in her hair, she cares for a large drum. Not seen by Jeff or anyone else, she mounts her horse and heads south.

Two months before this Christmas Eve demonstration, on October 22nd to be precise, Jeff had been persuaded by a fellow graduate student to attend what was then only the fifth meeting of the Committee on Southern Africa. He had known little about *apartheid* or colonialism, but soon realized how well informed and serious, though few in number, the committee members were.

Drawn to the building itself where they had met, directly across from the United Nations, Jeff had liked the simple yet beautiful lobby and the ever-so-peaceful chapel inside the building. He had looked forward to sitting in its darkened quiet, remembering the tranquility of his Minnesota boyhood farmland. Jeff had paused inside this sanctuary each time before taking the elevator to the sixth floor conference room, to separate himself from the city's horns, sirens and trucks' backfire, to be in touch in his imagination with the beauty of country meadows, and the person he thought he still was.

Throughout his first meeting, Jeff had merely listened to the proceedings. Pleasantly surprised by how orderly it had been, Jeff felt as if he were attending a session at the United Nations itself. The minutes from the previous meeting had been distributed. They had noted the exact time at which the meeting began and was adjourned. (Jeff had appreciated the members' sense of respect for time.) Every member had an area for which they were responsible, he had learned. Elaine had reported on the meeting with a high official of the National Council of Churches and Frank had reported on the program planned by the Consultative Council on South Africa, called Emphasis Week, to commemorate the sixth anniversary of the Sharpeville massacre (March 21, 1960). Shirley had reported on a memo from the Institute for Policy Studies listing members of the important Africa subcommittee of the House of Representatives. Others had reported on the planned demonstration organized by SNCC and SDS to be held in March, and about the people doing research on South Africa at Harvard University, and on a December conference jointly sponsored by Lincoln University and Bucknell College. With the exception of a white man from South Africa, all the other participants had been white American men and women.

Jeff had also appreciated everyone's sincerity and efficiency. One after another, reports had been given, commented upon, decisions made on what would be done next, who would contact whom, what new information would be incorporated in a new mailing. It all appealed to his sense of responsibility, as if each person--heard, respected, dependable—were like the members of his own family.

Daniel had already picked up Sharon and Jill, sisters, and Jim at Morningside Heights University. Pulling up to the coffee shop, Daniel described Jeff, a fellow graduate student in his religion class, so that Jim could find him inside.

"No, thanks, I don't need coffee or a danish," Daniel told Jim as he left the car. "I'm good."

By the time the Plymouth had entered the New Jersey Turnpike, three of Daniel's passengers, despite promises to stay awake, were fast asleep in the back seat. By the energetic way she was informing Daniel why she was visiting New York, however, Daniel felt he could count on Sharon in the passenger's seat to keep him awake all the way.

"How do you know Jim?" Daniel inquired.

"We're all from Savannah, Tennessee. Grew up there. Jill's my younger sister by two years, and Jim, he's two years younger than Jill. He's on Christmas break from Vanderbilt."

"You know, Sharon, I've never had, er, any interest in being in the South. Just a lot of rednecks and hillbillies, right? What about all those Selma marchers being clubbed last March? Ignorant white people and poor Negroes are about all I see in the South."

Sharon smiled. She had heard it all before from northerners.

"Hey, Daniel, that's your name, right?" Sharon asked.

"Yep."

"So you and your Jewish friends own New York and the rest of the North, right?" Sharon asked.

"First of all, I am not Jewish. And, second of all, that's a stereotype. Sure, there are wealthy Jews, but I grew up with a lot of Jewish friends whose parents weren't wealthy," Daniel countered.

"And I know lots of progressive whites who are intellectuals and lots of middle class Negroes who can afford to send their children to college. So there!" Sharon shot back.

"I've traveled a lot in what's called Middle Tennessee," Sharon continued. "Some of it's like the Deep South. Some of it isn't. You'll find all kinds of people there. Just like in the North, I guess. After all, Senator Albert Gore, Sr., is from middle Tennessee, and he thinks we should end the war by negotiations. And, anyway, have you heard of Anne and Carl Braden from the Southern Conference Education Fund in Louisville or Myles Horton from the Highlander Research and Education Center in Knoxville? I've spent time with all three."

"No, I never heard of them."

"Look, do you want to know what's going on in my neck of the woods?" Sharon asked.

"Sure," Daniel answered.

"I have a childhood friend, Joyce, and she attended a meeting in Nashville in the spring of 1964, along with some 40 other students. Most were white, a few black. They wanted to discuss what they could do in a racially divided South. The white students wanted to emphasize their southern consciousness. In other words, they wanted to show that their collective history was not only different from that of northern whites, but that their solutions on issues of civil rights, war, and labor justice would be peculiarly southern. They didn't want to be swamped by northern civil rights folks coming into the South. And, very important, Daniel, they didn't want to preempt or tread on any black organizing efforts in the South. Are you following?"

"Sort of."

"So those forty people decided their main statement of purpose would be written by a member of SDS who had been one of the authors of the Port Huron Statement written two years earlier, and that SDS, in recognition of that southern consciousness, would not organize chapters in the South. Those forty, including my friend, Joyce, named their new group the Southern Student Organizing Committee, and submitted their proposed organizing program to SNCC for its approval. A white southerner, George, who had worked for SNCC on a grant from SCEF, would represent SSOC."

"Sharon, tell you what. Why don't you get some sleep. I can handle the driving just fine."

"You sure?"

"Dead sure."

Daniel could not keep up with the acronyms, let alone the differences among the organizations. And he remembered how he liked being the solo pilot on the first trip to D.C., as others slept.

How could Daniel be expected to know at this moment, from this one encounter with Sharon, that he was being introduced to the most important kind of communication characterizing this newest activist age? It was going to be face-to-face communication, between and among travelers. Motion would be the coinage exchanged for information. Frequently cars and chartered buses, infrequently trains, planes, and commercial buses would interconnect the expanding consciousness of a generation of young activists.

All across the country, in tiny groups, attitudes toward Authority were beginning to change, strategies and tactics were being discussed, research was being done on the "establishment," all accelerating at a pace faster than letters could communicate.

Within these tiny groups there was the matter of building relationships, finding trustworthy people to carry out tasks, attracting the resources to sustain it. Frequent meetings among members built trust and solidified expectations. Opposing a far away war, ending segregation, *apartheid* and colonialism, however, were challenges far outstripping the influence of any local group.

Travelers, like honey bees, had already started going from place to place. What they learned in one group was deposited in the next. Gathering and sharing information, these ceaseless travelers turned motion into blooming national movements.

The sun, not yet visible, was sending a faint light over the eastern horizon as Daniel turned onto Pennsylvania Avenue and drove the short distance to Lafayette Park. As if he were in a bubble created by himself, his ears received sound as if through a filter, distorting it. The bubble's surface seemed tinted, so his eyes received images as if imbued with the gray fuzziness of a rain-soaked windshield. Daniel thought he had stopped the car. He doubted himself. He pumped the brake again, to make sure.

The light over the horizon surely must be "dawn" or the "false dawn," but he wasn't sure of that—or of anything else. He was someone all right, but not himself.

The Plymouth emptied quickly of warm passengers, and quickly re-filled with frozen demonstrators.

"Remember, I'm watching the speedometer," Ephraim said.

"How could I forget," Daniel replied.

"Turn up the goddam heater," Sean barked. "I'm not going to thaw out until next summer!"

As the back car door slammed shut, Jacques called out, "Where's Norman?"

"Oh, yeah," Sean answered, "he hooked up with a chick on the line, and they went off somewhere. I haven't seen him since. Let's get outta here!"

CHAPTER 3 – HOLIDAYS (WINTER 1965/66)

Those Three Are On My Mind, words and music by Frances Taylor and Pete Seeger (1966), following the murders of Andrew Goodman, James Chaney, and Michael Schwerner (June 1964) by members of the Ku Klux Klan, near Meridian, Mississippi. Harry Belafonte also covered the song.

On this Friday morning, the last day of the year, Daniel was just another cipher comprising the massive holiday exit, but he was excited at the prospect of being pampered back in his suburban family home. Daniel daydreamed about watching television all evening, especially after his parents went to bed, and sleeping all morning.

His Long Island Railroad train pulled into Jamaica Station, a bustling hub where many trains paused, as if to rest after traveling beneath the noise and dirt of New York City before heading further eastward.

Generations upon generations earlier, railroad tracks, like pairs of giant scissors, had been laid, slashing through the bucolic land once occupied by the first inhabitants and their descendants. Trains had pierced the day and night like slow-motion bullets. Their loud noise had disturbed the air. Animals had scattered. Waterways had disappeared. As more iron fingers sliced eastward through forests and meadows, more and more people had plowed the land into potato fields and then hammered those fields into housing tracts. The first inhabitants had been herded into small parcels of land near the easternmost end of the iron fingers. Daniel had never been interested in learning about the first inhabitants. In fact, he had always rooted for the cavalry every time they showed up on TV to rescue the wagon train with its cargo of white women and men.

By the time his train had passed through the tunnel under the East River and pulled into Jamaica Station, Daniel had shed his coat, the one he had recently bought in the city. The warmth of the railroad car's heater had transported him to an earlier, untainted, placid time inside the only home he had ever known. Daniel moved his hand slowly, almost affectionately, along the worn smoothness of his blue corduroy shirt.

"This train is making stops at Valley Stream, Lynbrook, Freeport, Rockville Centre, Baldwin, Merrick, Bellmore, Wantagh, Seaford, Massapequa, Massapequa Park, Amityville, … , Babylon … ," the conductor intoned over the scratchy loudspeaker. The names were as familiar to Daniel as if they were his siblings. Each one meant he was coming closer to home.

As he passed through Lynbrook, Daniel thought of his grandmother who had lived one town away in her tiny Malverne home, with all that acreage stretching down to a stream. Daniel had called her "Gra'ma" as a child because his ears had not picked up the "nd" sound in the middle of the title. He had always been told that she had packed all her belongings in a steamer trunk and left Zurich when she was 17 years old and arrived in America alone through Ellis Island. With Papa, whom she met and married a year later, she had raised chickens and grown grapes on that Malverne land. Their chicken and egg business had even drawn customers from Brooklyn and the Rockaways, considered a far distance to drive in those days.

"There is Grossmann's farm across the road, and McIlvoy's farm down the road," Gra'ma had proudly told her young grandson often. "We all get along here. In life, you've got to get along."

As the train pulled into Babylon station, he pictured his mother in the Plymouth directly across the street from the station's entrance. She was always there, waiting, in the same spot.

> **Opposite the station, Montaukett squats and watches Daniel cross the street. No one sees Montaukett, not even Daniel. She can roam the earth at will, but prefers the old territory from Jamaica to Shinnecock and beyond. Her ancestors originate near a**

29

stream in an area centuries later thought of as Green Mall by an English-born land developer financed by a chemical company. In harmony with what unsullied Nature still exists around her, Montaukett watches and feels all that Daniel does and feels.

As Daniel walked toward the familiar parked car, he unzipped his jacket. The unusual temperate breeze reminded Daniel that he had missed, for the first time, raking the leaves at his boyhood home.

"How do you like graduate school?" his mother, Rebecca, asked him soon after they left the station.

"I guess it's OK," he answered. "Lots of strange people. But, Mom, it's really good to be home."

"I'm really glad you're home, too," Rebecca responded. "I have all your favorite dishes for the big feast."

"Oh, Mom, I can't wait. And I can sleep in every morning?" asked Daniel, knowing the answer.

"As long as you want, dear."

"And we'll be going to church like we always do?"

"Yes, we will."

They passed block after block of familiar homes, frozen in time, their appearances doggedly maintained and unchanged year after year. Daniel recalled how everyone on every block had seemed to agree in advance to pile fall leaves next to their curbs at the same time. The scent of burning leaves, no matter how far away, had evoked in Daniel an almost religious feeling of contentment and tranquility. Like funeral pyres awaiting the torch, which sent souls toward heaven, these piles of leaves, when lit, had sent the sparks of a season's end skyward. A lit match touched to one end, then the other end, and finally tossed into the center of the pile had caused a heat, which seared the face and hands of all those transfixed near-by. More than leaf fights, more than belly-whopping into a pile of leaves or a hot cocoa afterwards, Daniel had loved to stand at the fire's edge, watching its red/orange knife blade tearing into the leaves, rapidly spreading in all directions. It was as if the flames were purging the impurities in his body. Soon the cold of winter's approaching would return to his face and hands as the fire expended itself, but the exciting memory of the hot, fiery glow, which rapidly transformed his world, had remained with Daniel.

"Hi Dad, how was work?" Daniel asked soon after his father entered the living room and sat in the recliner, handing him the *Daily News*.

"The same. Nothing much changes," Edwin responded.

"Say, son, I want to ask you," Edwin began, just above a whisper as Daniel sat next to him. "Was the real reason you weren't home for Christmas because of your studies?"

"Yes, er, yes. I had papers to write. So I had no choice. That was the only reason. No other. I *had* to use the entire vacation."

"You know your mother was heartbroken. It's the first Christmas without you. Even when you were in college, you came home every Christmas."

"I know."

Edwin, a clerk in the county courthouse, had been so proud to be able to buy his new bride their first home in 1939 that he took out an ad in the local newspaper announcing the gift. Over the years, Edwin had transformed the attic into the couple's bedroom to accommodate his mother's moving into their former first floor master bedroom. He had also half-finished the basement, which became Daniel's new bedroom when his former first floor bedroom had become too small for him. His mother now had more room to spread out in Daniel's old bedroom where she worked as the bookkeeper for her brother-in-law's Manhattan optical and cutlery firm. Edwin had also finished a small area of the attic with a dormer window for his daughter's bedroom. Even in the midst of these physical changes to the house, the routine remained unchanged over the years. Daniel knew the precise time of day or evening by when his mother woke him in the morning for school or asked him to set the table for dinner.

"Mom, I brought home some laundry. I hope that's OK?" Daniel said, less as a question and more as a placeholder in the domestic rhythm of the household.

"Yes," his mother called out from the kitchen, less as an answer and more as an addition to her list of chores.

As he crossed his left ankle on top of his right, looking down at the worn sneakers he had had since sophomore year in high school, Daniel made the short emotional trip back to his boyhood days when all his physical needs had been met almost instantaneously, without his doing a thing to put food on the table, hang laundered clothes in his closet, heat the home in winter. More than physical comfort, growing up in the same community had meant stability. John, the station owner, had pumped the gas or fixed the car every time the Gens family pulled into the Sunoco station. Jack, the supermarket manager, had not only greeted his mother and him, but had also frequently bagged their groceries. Roberta, the bank teller, had always been the one to enter Daniel's small deposits into his savings account. Change had happened, but glacially, as if it waited for everyone's permission.

The next morning, Saturday, was New Year's Day. The family slept in, having stayed up to watch the ball drop at midnight on television. Daniel was the last to shower, hot water running cold before he was finished. Wearing his bathrobe and slippers, Daniel returned to the warm basement to dress, and then went upstairs to the kitchen.

"I can't wait for dinner tonight, Mom," Daniel said. "What're we having?"

"Oh, nothing special," Rebecca replied, winking.

New Year's Day dinner was one of the very few exceptions to the metronome-like punctuality of the running of the Gens household. Everything about it was different than almost any other meal of the year. Its preparation started earlier and its enjoyment lasted longer. Its serving did not commence at 6 o'clock, as other dinners did, and the dishes were not cleared just before 7 o'clock so that the television could be turned on, as on other evenings. The unfolding of this carefully choreographed ritual draped itself over the face of the family clock on the kitchen wall.

Small franks stuck with toothpicks were served along with celery stalks smeared with creamy bleu cheese. Puff pastries filled with chopped spinach and crumbled feta cheese completed the main *hors d'oeuvres* offering. Small cut-glass bowls, one filled with olives stuffed with pimentos and the other with mixed nuts, added the final, mouth-watering touch.

Edwin asked everyone to bow their heads. After reciting his usual short prayer, he announced with great fanfare, "Let's eat!"

Daniel waited patiently as his father prepared for the next ritual. Edwin uncapped two bottles of Rheingold beer, reserved only for special occasions, as he had done since Daniel turned sixteen. Tilting each of the two tapered beer glasses in turn, he poured the liquid down the side, leaving only the slightest "head" when he finished. Edwin then extended the first glass to

Daniel, as if he and his son were the only pair in the world to share this patriarchal moment.

"Here's to the prodigal," Edwin toasted. "Our home is again complete, at least for a few days. Be thankful for all that we have."

Father and son tilted their glasses towards each other, and then towards everyone else around the table, and took small sips.

"Dad, you know what?" asked Daniel.

"What's that?"

"There's a guy at school, and he and his Dad drink Rheingold, just like us. Isn't that neat?"

Edwin leaned back in his chair, his shoulders dropping as he let go of his beer glass. He looked out of the window for a moment, as if trying to see the basketball court he had built years ago for his son. Then he said to no one, "That's nice, son."

After the first course Rebecca cleared the dishes. Offerings not seen since last Thanksgiving dinner appeared as ceremoniously as bells ringing in the church steeple on Sunday morning. Yams with melted marshmallows on top, pearl onions in a cream sauce, potatoes *au gratin*, string beans with almond shavings, all in dishes also not seen since last Thanksgiving, surrounded platters holding the turkey filled with chestnut stuffing and the ham festooned with pineapple slices.

The main course loosened everyone's tongue, as conversation shot across and around the table immediately following the silent passing of all the dishes across and around the table. It was as if no one were permitted to speak until everyone's plate was filled. With Time suspended, all three generations sensed the relaxation of hierarchy, the disappearance of boundaries set by age and gender. Funny stories were shared, the parents updated their children on neighbors' doings, and cousins were mentioned. All joined in. Then, Daniel asked what he thought was a friendly question.

"Gra'ma, I saw your steamer trunk last night when I went to bed in the basement. Would you let me open it and see what's inside?"

His grandmother's hand trembled as she put down her fork on the table. She picked up her napkin slowly to pat her lips, looking toward her son at the head of the table.

"Why would you want to do that for?" Rebecca interjected.

"Look, all I know is that your mother, Mom, came from Holland, but you've never talked about your family, except something about some English blood, whatever that means. And you came from Switzerland, Gra'ma, but I don't know anything about your life before I was born. Or about your ancestors. It's all a blank, on both sides."

"This is a festive occasion," Rebecca responded. "Isn't there something in the Bible about the dead burying the dead? Let's forget about the past for now. We're all together here as a family. That's what matters."

"But, Mom, I don't get it. Ever since I was born, you've kept scrapbooks filled with everything I've ever done, it seems. And yet, all I've ever seen of you and Dad before I was born is your wedding picture. And I've never seen any photos of Gra'ma and Papa. Maybe they're in the trunk."

"Son, there's no point on holding on to the distant past."

Daniel had often wondered if the Great Depression had not stripped the two families of their sea-going hopes for a bright future in America. An empty steamer trunk, one family photo, and a half-dozen unmailed postcards bore witness only to meager survival, through a span of time from the first affordable automobiles to the first affordable television sets.

After the main course dishes were cleared, this time by Daniel and Edwin, dessert was served. Three kinds of pie and two kinds of ice cream. Plus after-dinner mints in case there was an ounce of room left in anyone's stomach.

All the family now enjoyed cordials, even Daniel's sister, Lynn, who was three years younger. Cherry Herring, Grand Marnier, and Crème de Menthe were the selections. But there was more to come.

Ever since his parents had left the Episcopal Church, with its High-Church bishop insisting that everyone kiss his ring, and joined the Congregational Church, the New Year's Day meal ended with a ritual suggested by their young minister. While holding hands to form a circle around the table, each one in turn said aloud the thing for which they were most thankful.

Gra'ma was always the first to begin: "I am thankful I have a roof over my head, that I am safe, and that I am with my family."

Edwin was next: "I am glad my son is home, and that our table is blessed with such abundance."

Rebecca and Lynn mentioned family and health and friends, and then it came Daniel's turn: "I am thankful for this home and for everyone around this table. May it always be."

At the end, taking their time, each looked another straight in the eyes, fixing their gaze until each had silently expressed thanks for the other's presence. Daniel felt like a boy again, protected, loved, and pure, until it came time for him to look at his mother. He lowered his eyes at first, then forced himself to look straight into hers. She smiled. He could not.

That night, well after everyone else was asleep, Daniel turned off the television, and went downstairs to the basement. Before he changed into pajamas, he looked at the steamer trunk. What secrets did it hold? What didn't his parents and grandmother want him to know about their past? He kept looking at the trunk, hoping it would open by itself, so he could not be accused of violating their trust. But it did not. He inspected the clasps that held it closed, and saw there were no locks. How easily he could open it, and take until dawn to examine its contents. He held either side of the lid with both hands, and raised it slowly, as if to signal any ghost inside that he was friendly and meant no harm. He paused, unable to go further. Then his hands let the lid go, and it fell back into place. He quickly closed the claps and covered the trunk with a nearby blanket, the one his parents had purchased at an Indian crafts fair, as if to hide that even his fingers had ever touched the trunk.

Daniel slept uneasily that night in the basement.

> *Surrounded by woods. I walk along a path. Come upon a waterfall. Crystal clear. Lost in the woods. Find the same path again. Come upon the same waterfall. Color of water now brown. I am lost again. Same path. Same waterfall. Color of water now dark red.*

On Wednesday, Daniel walked to Tom's Sports shop in the center of town to buy athletic socks. Frigid air had entered Long Island the evening before, sending residents to their storage bins for scarves and gloves. Ignoring the cold, Daniel looked up at the crystal blue mid-winter sky as he walked.

Tom's had not been his favorite store at first. On his eighth birthday, Daniel had been encouraged by his parents for the first time to pick out his own baseball glove. Try as he might to hold onto the worn mitt they had given him on his sixth birthday, it would not do, they said, for the upcoming

Little League tryouts. Daniel had eventually come to love the smell of the place, however. Over the years a wonderful memory was created down each aisle. There was the rack from which he had selected a football for the many touch and tackle sandlot games he played. From another rack he had selected his basketball for the outdoor court his father had built for him. There were the lacrosse sticks, reminding him of the neighbor's boys tossing that impossibly hard ball between them. And there were the cans of tennis balls, recalling the countless stickball games he had played, drawing each time a rectangular strike zone with chalk on an abandoned concrete wall.

As he left Tom's and turned down another street filled with stores, his eye caught the F.W. Woolworth sign. He stopped on the sidewalk and pulled his jacket's collar tighter around his neck. What was it that day, years ago, that had prevented him from joining the demonstration, Daniel asked himself. After all, it had been his high school buddy, Ira, who had phoned him. He had invited Daniel to join him, his dad, and others to walk around in front of Woolworth's. It was the first time he had learned that Woolworth's stores in the South did not permit blacks to eat at their lunch counters. My God, Daniel now calculated, that was sometime in the spring of 1958, two years before those four black university students had sat down at the segregated Woolworth's lunch counter in Greensboro, North Carolina. I could have been a part of history if only I had joined Ira. What was so important that I had not joined in, Daniel asked himself.

He remembered he had just obtained his learner's permit. It had been a big deal at 16. Did he have a driver's education class during that warm afternoon when, he had learned much later, a small group of adults, Jews and Gentiles, whites and blacks, some with their teenage children and some from the local NAACP, had walked in a circular picket line, chanting "2,4,6,8, Woolworth's must integrate" in front of the five-and-dime store?

He did not exactly lie to his friend, Daniel rationalized. He remembered he had wanted to go when first invited. So why did he not join Ira that warm spring day?

That night, Daniel again slept uneasily in the basement.

> *In a warehouse. Many boxes on shelves behind me. I look through one box to try to find typewritten page 100 of my novel. Four young white men surround me. Will not let me walk*

*around. Menacing. They want to harm me. I can
not find page 100. I shove a box at them to ward
them off. They say I lie. Page 100 not in that box.
I shove other boxes at them as they walk around in
front of me, still calling me a liar. I am terrified.*

The following Sunday morning, while waiting for the processional, Daniel looked around the familiar church. The same hymn board with four hymn numbers. The same multi-colored flowers at the foot of the stairs leading to the choir loft. Daniel picked up the hymnal. He just stared at the cover. He knew the organist would strike the first chord, signaling everyone to stand, but he could not open to the first hymn as he had always done, to study the first line, then to stand and sing out the first note.

He was remembering all those years ago when his Sunday school teachers had constantly admonished him to tell the truth. At some moment during his teen years, Daniel ignored that lesson and had become accustomed to carving out his own truth, in whatever shape suited him at the moment. He had no qualms, when a college classmate asked him if he had seen the movie "Jules and Jim" or "Never on Sunday," about answering, "Of course!" After all, why should he deflate the enthusiasm of a fellow human being who was sharing his excitement over seeing a film? It was easier to shade the truth than to have others feel uncomfortable, Daniel had rationalized over and over again. Or was it that Daniel had not wanted to draw attention to himself by being different from others? He had yearned for others' respect, but his way of earning it, if it could be called that, had been to get along with others, agree with them, bobbing and weaving through conversations without giving anyone cause to land a blow on his self-esteem. Laugh even when he had not heard or understand the punch line, nod "yes" when he had guessed that a question was being asked whose tone suggested a positive response.

Still sitting in the pew as others rose for the processional hymn, Daniel wondered, was that why he had told Ira he would *definitely* go to the Woolworth demonstration?

It was a short walk from the Nassau Street railroad station in Princeton to the stop where Christie boarded the bus for the last leg of her trip to the Borough of Hopewell. Soon the bus passed many large homes, set far back from Carter Road, heading northwest toward a less elegant time. Christie watched out the window as the old homes disappeared, replaced by small farms, which stretched out on either side of the road, the first ones hewn from a stubborn wilderness over two and one-half centuries ago. Old barns, slowly disintegrating as each season did its best to hasten their end, stood near new barns freshly painted, as if the land itself wanted to hold onto the past as long as possible while building the future.

Christie knew that Hopewell's earliest white history was based on a fraud. She had learned that a settler, becoming an agent for The West Jersey Society of England, had been granted the power to sell land for the Society's financial gain. He had described the tracts as being fertile farmland. Many settlers from colonies to the east and north had been drawn to Hopewell. Even the name had promised a better life. What they found had been far different than what had been advertised. Angered by what they had purchased – acres of untamed wilderness – the settlers had taken the matter to court. The long trial had ended with the settlers' defeat. Christie had heard the story over and over again as she grew up. It had sharpened her sense of how con men, frauds, and hypocrites, greedy for gain, preyed on unsuspecting people.

> **Lenni-Lenape sits astride her horse, her buckskin leggings protecting her as she gallops alongside Christie's bus, unseen by anyone, even Christie. Lenni-Lenape roams a vast area, knows its rivers, streams, hills, animals, and birds well. She allots land according to the needs of her extended family. Watching Christie look out the window, Lenni-Lenape feels tenderness toward her.**

Christie's bus stop was the last, at the corner of Princeton Avenue and West Broad Street, across from Judd's General Store. She walked a few blocks down West Broad, turned right onto North Greenwood Avenue, crossed the railroad tracks, and made another right, just before Highland Cemetery, onto Washington Avenue. Outside her father's church a sign announced Sunday's sermon title: "Can Sinners Be Thankful on Christmas?" Christie wondered how her father would answer that one as she crossed the church lawn and walked inside the parsonage next door.

"Hello, Grandfather," Christie said, as she entered the living room and walked toward a man dressed in a white shirt, red tie, dark brown cardigan sweater over his shoulders, black dress pants, and slippers.

"Cristabel, how was your journey home?"

"It was OK, Grandfather."

"OK? What do you mean, OK? I despair for your generation. The same monosyllabic response to every question."

"Yes, Grandfather," Christie walked out of the room, greeting her father as he entered the room.

"Sermon ready for tomorrow, son?"

"Yes, it is. I believe it delivers a sound message for Christmas."

"I hope, son, that your sermon includes the message that it is better to give than receive. The church needs a new roof!"

Grandfather had been assistant pastor at the Park Avenue Presbyterian Church in New York City. It was largely through his influence that his son, Rev. Calvin, Jr., had been admitted to Princeton Theological Seminary after his lackluster college days. Grandfather's frugality, coupled with his success in the stock market based on tips from a few wealthy parishioners who also served his congregation as ruling elders, meant that his family had never lacked for physical comfort in New York. Rev. Calvin, Sr., had kept his good fortune a private matter, certain that God frowned on vulgar ostentation.

His son, however, had been less fortunate. Rev. Calvin, Jr., had never been invited to serve even as an assistant minister in a large urban congregation because he lacked his father's charm and wit greatly adored by upper class church women who, through influence on their husbands' position on the local presbytery, made the hiring decisions. Rev. Calvin, Jr., had hewed his life with an austere religious auger, disdaining the finely tailored robes with colorful, often royal purple trimming, which his father had frequently worn. He excused his father's allowing himself what was considered a tasteful show of his station in life. The son's choice had been a plain black robe worn over a black suit and black tie.

Christie unpacked her clothes in the front bedroom, the only one she had ever known until she left for college. Then, remembering what her mother would have asked her to do, Christie left the parsonage and walked back to Judd's General Store. Inside, she reviewed all the varieties of Indian corn, which were always the centerpiece for the Christmas dinner. So many different combinations of colors, she found it hard to choose among them. Christie finally bought a dozen, and returned to the parsonage.

"Ah, good, I see you have provisions for tomorrow," Rev. Calvin, Sr., exclaimed. "You know we will be eight for dinner."

"Yes, father forewarned me," Christie replied.

"Good, I want you to be prepared. Ah, dear granddaughter, your legs are so much younger than mine. Would you fetch me my copy of the *Westminster Confession of Faith*? Spiritual nourishment, you see."

When Rev. Calvin, Sr., could no longer negotiate even the short walk from his Park Avenue apartment, which his congregation had subsidized, to the nearest delicatessen, he had reluctantly accepted his son's invitation to live with him in Hopewell. The two-story frame house, though large enough to be comfortably furnished, could not hold all of his belongings. It had broken his heart to see so much of his fine furnishings carted away. Leaving friends of importance behind as well, Rev. Calvin, Sr., had moved to this small rural town where no one knew how important he had been.

Even his beloved *Institutio Christianae religionis*, the 1559 Latin translation of John Calvin's major work, lay in one of many cartons in his son's damp basement. His books had been his favorite children. Now, unable even to navigate the stairs into the basement, and with no extra room on the first floor where his bedroom was situated, Rev. Calvin, Sr., could only request that a favorite child be brought to him.

"Here is your book, Grandfather."

"Thank you, my child. You are such a comfort to me. How are you getting on with the festive dinner?"

It was Rev. Calvin, Jr.'s, habit to invite some of the "less fortunate" members of the congregation, as he called them, to share Christmas Day dinner in his house. Christie would be cooking not only for her grandfather, father, and younger brother, Paul, but also for a struggling farm family of four. The meal's preparation had begun on Friday, the day Christie arrived home, when she had gone into the basement and gathered mason jars filled with a summer's canning accomplishments. Stewed tomatoes, pickled beets, peaches, and strawberry jam as topping for homemade ice cream had been brought to the kitchen. Her mother had taught her well, especially how to pour hot liquid paraffin carefully into jars just after they were filled almost to the top to protect the canned vegetables and fruits.

Saturday morning, Christmas Day, Christie rose early to decorate the table with the Indian corn and red holly berries. She cooked the hunk of venison shot by a parishioner and given to her father instead of an envelope in last week's collection plate. The turkey was freshly slaughtered by another parishioner. Just about everything on the table was raised or grown near-by.

After hours cooking in the kitchen and then setting the table, Christie was ready to serve. The eight gathered around the table, with grandfather at the head. After a lengthy blessing delivered by Rev. Calvin, Sr., as if he were still in the pulpit, Rev. Calvin, Jr., asked his guests how they were faring. Jonah, the father, ticked off a list of misfortunes.

"You remember all those rainy days last spring? Well, they pushed back my planting time, and that caused a low yield on some crops at harvest time. Pushing back that planting time meant more opportunity for those voracious mice to get into some of my seed sacks. Well, that reduced the number of rows I could plant. And then there was a dry August."

Just as father was about to sympathize with Jonah and his troubles, Rev. Calvin, Sr., said in a stern, stentorian voice:

"God's will. He had it planned out for you. He knows what you need to make you stronger. Have faith in His plan for you, my boy."

"What my father means to say, Jonah, is that you can rely on God's grace," Rev. Calvin, Jr., said softly, as much to himself as to his guests. "It will help you to turn your bad fortune around."

"I do not mean to say that, son. I do not mean to say that at all," grandfather snapped, his voice rising. "God has determined what will happen to the poor boy and his family. That is how I read my Bible. And that is the way God wrote it."

Looking across the table at Jonah and his family, Christie felt their bewilderment as they listened to the ongoing theological debate between father and son. For her, this was the latest of many dinners during which both men argued over predestination and free will. The debaters and their captive audience ignored the forks on the table.

"Why don't we enjoy this meal," Christie said, almost to herself.

The debate continued, however. Christie left her fork on the table, too, unwilling to interrupt her elders.

Taking many religion courses in her first two years at Smith College, Christie had been trying to decide who was right between these two men in her life. Finally, instead of choosing between them, she had decided to escape their divisions and retreat to the distant past, studying the Sumerians and other "first cultures" as she called them, to seek pre-Biblical truths about man and his gods.

But now, sitting at the table, Christie continued to stare at her father and grandfather, locked in theological arguments, ignoring everyone else. And here was the food, growing cold on their plates. She finally grabbed her knife and fork, cut off a piece of venison, and began chewing vigorously. How *selfish* of them, she almost uttered aloud, surprising herself by the vehemence of her feelings.

Four months earlier, as Christie had prepared for her first term at graduate school, death had come unexpectedly almost to her doorstep. Standing on the front porch, she had seen the cars of a funeral procession parked across the street next to the cemetery. The coffin had borne a boy she knew in high school who had died in a far away place in Asia. The boy had not gone on to college, as Christie had. She had not known him well, even though they had graduated in the same small class, but, seeing the coffin lowered into the grave with military honors, Christie had started to cry. Uncontrollably. She had not known why. She had not cried when her mother died. But on this hot, humid August afternoon it had been as if her tears flowed from an unexplainable sense of loss, an empty place in her soul where innocence had recently resided.

On Monday morning, as Christie walked over to her old grammar school past the cemetery, she thought again of the boy in the grave. Perhaps his death had provided the reason why Christie so readily agreed to hold the anti-war group meet regularly in her apartment.

She purposely arrived at the school an hour before she was to meet her former college roommate, Alice, whom she had called the week before. She knew no one would be in the playground. She wanted to feel the solace that a familiar place can bring when it's devoid of any activity. Sitting on a swing for a long time, Christie remembered her teachers. She wanted to tell them she was considering becoming a teacher herself. In fact, she had almost volunteered a year and one-half earlier to teach for the summer, but she knew she would have had to disobey her father.

"Christie, there you are," Alice exclaimed. "It's really good to see you again." The two hugged, with Christie holding on longer than Alice.

"How long has it been?" Alice asked.

"I remember exactly," Christie announced. "It was a year ago June. Don't you remember? I waved good-bye to you as you boarded the bus for Oxford, Ohio."

Christie and Alice had gone to a rally in the spring of 1964 where they had heard two Yale students describe how canvassers and teachers were needed that summer in Mississippi. The canvassers would register Negroes to vote. The teachers would conduct classes in something called Freedom Schools. Christie had been drawn to the teaching project. If she had been honest with herself, she did not want to spend another summer in the same home in which she had spent summers for the last 21 years. But more than that, there had been something about the speakers themselves, their honesty in describing the rudimentary classrooms, the lack of books, and their own sense of confidence that somehow, someway, with everyone working together, they would succeed in focusing a national searchlight on southern intimidation and violence. In the end, Alice had attended the training school held at Western College for Women, led by veterans of the Student Nonviolent Coordinating Committee.

"Your letters didn't tell me much," Christie began.

"No, they didn't, on purpose. You never knew if you'd be stopped on the way to the post office, and searched. And, rightly or wrongly, you were suspicious of everyone in town. Maybe someone at the post office would steam open your letter, and share it with the sheriff."

"Weren't you scared all the time?"

"In the beginning, yes. I lived in a shack with seven other people. We were all scared. But, love them, the SNCC folks taught us what to do, what not to do. They gave us the courage, just being with them, learning what they'd been through, how they handled it."

"Were you ever threatened, physically I mean?"

"No, never. One of our cars was burned, though. It turned out other townspeople and police in Mississippi were far more aggressively violent than in Mileston, where I was. Anyway, we just sang a lot. That kept us together and chased the fear."

Getting off the swing, walking next to her veteran friend of the Mississippi war, Christie decided that she did not need to have her father's permission to find a mission greater than her fears. Alice's example gave her the only permission she required.

CHAPTER 4 – RECONNOITER
(EARLY SPRING 1966)

You Don't Own Me, covered by Dusty Springfield in her 1964 debut album, *A Girl Called Dusty*, originally sung by Lesley Gore in 1963.

Adapted from a traditional American folk song, *We Shall Not Be Moved* was performed by the SNCC (Student Nonviolent Coordinating Committee) Freedom Singers throughout their 1963 fund-raising tour.

Although it was March, normally still a time of chill and frost in upstate New York, stray warm winds blowing for days and steady sunshine had teased crocuses from their wintry hiding places. Exposed and vulnerable – not knowing if it were the right season to grow – these hearty plants nevertheless pushed through the earth in bright colors of lilac and yellow, ready for anything.

Crocuses adorned the entrance to the church campgrounds, which were being readied for the conference by an advance party of twenty-five. Individual letters of the alphabet were thumbtacked to the doors of outlying cabins while room numbers were posted on doors inside the main dormitory. Metal folding chairs were offloaded from a truck and stacked in a large hall inside the administration building. Foodstuffs, enough to feed 175 people, were delivered to the kitchen just off the large hall.

Choosing the conference site had been contentious. Some organizers had wanted a "constitutional" assembly, which resulted in the drafting of a national strategy agreed by elected representatives, meeting in plenary, from organizations invited to attend. Others had wanted only workshops so that anyone hearing about the conference and deciding to attend could get to know one another and share experiences. Still others had wanted to hold the conference in Washington, D.C., so that it could finish with a demonstration against Johnson's war.

In the end, the leaders of the main sponsoring organization, University Movement, had decided on what would later turn out to be a risky plan. They had taken an organizational step backwards by holding a *retreat*. The theme would be encapsulated in two headings: "Who We Are" and "Where We Are".

The planners had intended that people coming from across America would share their stories and build relationships. There would be as many workshops with as many differing issues as time would permit, and a final plenary session to discuss national strategy, but the primary focus would be on "free time". Long breaks after workshops, and no workshops scheduled for the evenings would allow participants to talk informally with one another, in whatever combinations they chose. It had been the decision of the organizers to break from established patterns, a deliberate and distinct contrast to academic forums with their tedious presentations of scholarly papers and panel discussions, and to constituent assemblies with their parliamentary maneuverings.

The retreat had been deliberately scheduled to begin two days after the Second International Day of Protest Against the Vietnam War. Retreat participants could first attend the march down Fifth Avenue in New York City on Saturday, March 26th, and then take a leisurely drive to the church campgrounds just outside the rural town of Wappinger, a place far distant from everything familiar.

"Hi, we're here from the Morningside Heights Student Committee Against the War in Viet Nam," William stated emphatically, as if the woman behind the registration desk were already familiar with the name.

"OK, that's nice. Glad you're here. Do you want a bunk bed? That's five dollars a night. Or a camp site? That's free."

"We each want a bunk bed," William said, pointing to Daniel and Christie.

"And how many nights are you staying?"

"We're here to the end. So, three nights."

"That'll be forty-five dollars altogether, for all three of you. The meals are free. You'll see a price list for snacks when they're put out. The 'Name Tag Walk About' begins at 4pm today. Please print your full names on the tags. Oh, yes, here's the workshop schedules. The first ones begin tomorrow morning."

Jeff and Mildred from the Committee on Southern Africa soon arrived with Ephraim from the Socialist Party. None of the six had ever attended such a large conference. Daniel and William had been to a few citywide meetings, but Daniel, not known by anyone outside his university, mostly sat in the back rows and remained silent. Here, however, he was determined to mix in, apply his cocktail party social skills to meet people, tell them his story of how he transported dozens (actually twelve) to Lafayette Park, making sure they understood how he had sacrificed his Christmas holiday to do so.

As Daniel walked around the large hall with the name tag stuck to his chest, he overheard various conversations, but found it still difficult to enter any.

"Don't I know you?" Carl, originally from Akron, now residing in Ann Arbor, asked Judith, originally from Peoria, now residing in Chicago. "Didn't we talk on the phone when I called your social action group?"

"Yes, of course, I remember you. You were doing some kind of research," Judith responded.

"Yeah, yeah, Robert," said Leon, originally from Copperhill, Tennessee, and now residing in Manhattan, "I remember your name on our subscription form. It's great to meet you. Wow, a subscriber. We only get about one a day."

"I love your newsletter," Robert, originally from Scarsdale, now residing in Mexico City, declared. "When are you coming out with the second one, Leon?"

"Who knows? We sent in a bulk mail application to the post office ages ago. I don't really think they want to give it to an organization like ours."

"Hey, Carol, over here," Everett from Jackson, Mississippi, currently residing in Nashville, called out. "Remember me from the march on

Washington last April?"

"Oh, yeah, how are you?" Carol, originally from Denver, now residing in Boston, answered. "Yeah, I remember hiding behind you when the TV camera panned the crowd, so my mother wouldn't see me because I told her I wouldn't go."

"Say, excuse me, but Phil over there said you worked in Cleveland two years ago," Michael, originally from Orange, New Jersey, currently residing in Iowa City, inquired.

"That's right, with the Economic Research and Action Project," Ray, originally from Austin, now residing in Pittsburgh, responded.

"That's great. I read an article on how you're creating an interracial movement of poor blacks and poor whites."

Daniel, rather strangely he thought, did not feel alone as he wandered around the large hall. He sensed the room was energized by the vibrations of more than a hundred different strings, each tuning to the vibration nearest them, if only for a few moments, before heading to the next vibrating string. People who had not even previously exchanged names, now talked excitedly, like campers returning for another summer.

It was the first time for this entire group of participants, but not the last time, that individuals, feeling like outsiders back home, were connected and rejuvenated by the power emanating from a mass of seemingly like-minded people, happy to be together, wanting to believe they were working for the same causes, anticipating that larger and larger numbers would translate into course-correcting impacts. Hardly a symphony, now or later, but, like cicadas at the hottest part of the day, excitedly tuning up.

Participants came from every part of America. Virtually all were under thirty years of age – most under twenty-five. Those from the South seemed already to know one another well, having attended each other's local meetings and small demonstrations. Those from the West were mostly Californians who packed into Volkswagen buses and drove toward a coast their parents and grandparents had abandoned many years before. The Midwest was represented by people from Chicago, some from that city's Hyde Park neighborhood, and small colleges in Iowa and Ohio with names like Grinnell and Antioch. The majority came from the closest large metropolitan areas: New York, Boston, Philadelphia, and Washington, D.C.

On Tuesday morning, the first full day of the Retreat, Christie decided not to stand in the line forming to await the ringing of the lunch bell. Instead, she walked toward Wappinger Lake.

> **Lenni-Lenape watches Christie from her canoe beached on the shoreline. She nods her head once. She has witnessed many times before the squall line thinly dividing resistance from change.**
>
> **Lenni-Lenape looks along the shoreline, and sees the empty canoes of Montaukett, Munsee, and Anishinaabe. She smiles. How fitting, she thinks. The Algonquian family is together again on the land of the Wappinger confederacy.**
>
> **Later, after several hours of talk about their lives, the four Original People agree to take as long as it takes to reach a plan for their four wards.**

"Christie, wait for me," Sharon called out, coming down the hillside behind her. The two women had only met for the first time at breakfast, sitting across from one another at a long table. They had barely exchanged names and where they were from. Instead, Christie had wanted to discuss with Daniel which of the six workshops they might attend together. She had not wanted to be without a man whom she knew among all these strangers. Sharon had sat next to Jeff, recalling their trip to Lafayette Park last December.

"I was so looking forward to this conference," Christie began to admit to Sharon, "to be in a new environment, but a few men in the American Imperialism workshop just kept arguing with one other about Manifest Destiny. Each one was so intent on being *right*. Their bickering felt all too familiar."

"I'm with you," Sharon sympathized. "In my workshop white men were arguing over the merits of integration versus black power, as if they were certain about what was good for black people."

The two women sat next to each other on a log at the edge of the lake, watching the water rippling gently. It was a beautiful, spring-like day, so neither woman needed to wear the sweater carefully tied around her waist. They welcomed the soft, warm breeze with its hint of spring, touching their faces. No one said anything for the moment, enjoying the silence, lost in her own thoughts.

"You know, I was just thinking about my father," Christie said, looking down at the lake's edge, as if talking aloud to herself. "He asks me to do things sometimes which he could easily do for himself. I never thought of it 'til now."

"What kinds of things?" Sharon asked, looking at Christie.

"Like getting his pipe, even though it's six feet away from him on a table," Christie responded, without looking up. "I mean it's not like he couldn't get up from his chair and get it himself," Christie said softly. She suddenly felt ashamed, talking so openly to a stranger about her father. She adored her father, except when she felt he allowed grandfather to belittle him. Christie wanted to stop talking, not say another word about her father, get up and walk back to the lunch line, but Sharon's next question riveted her to the spot.

"Do you think he has the *right* to ask you to get his pipe?" Sharon asked, leaning over so that Christie could not help but see Sharon's face.

"I don't know." Christie's voice was almost inaudible. She looked away from Sharon. The question had startled her. She had never given it a thought. All those years of serving her father and grandfather and parishioners and visitors—the weight of all those years bore down on her now, as if she did not have the strength to call into question what had always seemed to her as a God-given obligation.

Sharon now crouched in front of Christie, seeing tears well up in her eyes. She took Christie's left hand in her right.

"Maybe it's none of my business, but maybe your father and my father are not all that different. Mine's a good man, but he's blind in one eye, psychologically speaking I mean."

Not looking at Sharon, Christie nevertheless listened intently.

"It's so natural for him, like breathing this air around us, to exercise his authority over me that he never questions it. Not once. And 'cause I've always felt that his authority feels so natural for him, I've never questioned it either, not 'til now. I've never questioned a whole lot of things 'til now. Do you understand what I'm saying?"

50

"I don't want to understand what you're saying, Sharon," Christie snapped back. "All I know right now is that I don't know what I'll do when my father asks me to get his pipe the next time."

They heard the ringing bell from the campgrounds, summoning them for lunch.

"Probably rung by a man!" Sharon quipped. They both stood up, turned toward each other, looked into each other's eyes for the first time--and burst out laughing.

Jeff attended the morning workshop on Vietnam, which drew the largest number of participants. The discussion centered on a paperback book issued only the month before, titled *Vietnam: Between Two Truces*, by a Frenchman, Jean Lacouture. Jeff had not heard of the book. Those few workshop participants who had read it were teaching the others what they knew about the cultural and religious intricacies spawned by Vietnam's one-thousand year history. Jeff noticed that no one took the lead in this form of teaching. Each contributed what he or she could. Questions just kept floating past Jeff. Was President Ngo Dinh Diem, a Catholic, supported by the US government due to a few influential American Catholics led by Francis Cardinal Spellman, as *Ramparts* magazine contended? Who were Generals Nguyen Khanh, Nguyen Cao Ky, and Duong Van Minh, or for that matter, Madame Ngo Dinh Nhu? And why did the Buddhist monk, Venerable Duc, burn himself to death? Like a blind man feeling his way around a room for the first time, trying to connect the relationships among the objects he encountered, Jeff first absorbed as much as he could about each Vietnamese notable, and then haltingly tried to connect each one to an historical narrative, which most Americans, including the United States government, faintly understood.

Folding chairs had been neatly placed inside the large hall around two dozen very long tables, in preparation for the participants' first dinner. The seating arrangement had been purposefully designed so that no one would feel there was a "back" of the hall or a "front" of the hall. There was definitely not a "head table", or at least not one so visibly designated. This physical arrangement was in keeping with the organizers' announced intent of creating a "participatory" atmosphere, mimicking many activists' intention to forge a new American Left, which would reconstruct the nation through decisions taken by all citizens, from the "bottom-up" and no longer from the "top-down."

In one corner, however, there was a table beginning to fill with what were coming to be known as University Movement "heavies," which comprised the Retreat organizers. Their bylines frequently appeared in left-wing publications. The few mainstream press reporters covering "campus unrest", as it was now sometimes called, sought quotes from them. The heavies, mostly men but a sizeable number of women, had already dispersed themselves throughout all the day's workshops so that they could reconnoiter over dinner to assess the Retreat's progress.

While inching forward on the long line leading to the buffet, Daniel, now eager to meet everyone he could at the Retreat, engaged the person in front of him in conversation. Randy stated he was an assistant minister in a United Methodist church in Newark, New Jersey, and had graduated from Union Theological Seminary.

"Where did you grow up, Randy?"

"Mobile. And where are you from?"

"Babylon. That's on—"

"Long Island."

"Yeah, how did you know?"

"My wife, Dorothy, went to school there. Maybe you knew her, Dorothy Sanders?"

"Knew her? We went to elementary school together. Does she still run like the wind?"

"She has to," Randy chuckled. "We have three young daughters. But how is it that you remembered her?"

"I thought I was the fastest runner in the sixth grade class until one day, this skinny girl named Dorothy challenged me to a race. She ran like the wind and beat me by a mile!"

Not far away, in a corner opposite the organizers' table, Christie and Sharon found empty seats, but did not immediately sit down. As they spotted other women entering the large hall, Christie and Sharon tried to catch their eye and motion them over to sit with them. Only two women joined their table. While many other women noticed their invitation, they were either looking for their current boyfriends (a few for their husbands in the dining hall) or were hoping to meet a future one.

Arthur almost turned back after being pulled over by the police on Route 1 near Aiken, South Carolina. The locals called it Jefferson Davis Highway. He had been warned by friends to go slowly in that state. So he had. However, traveling 40mph in a 50mph zone was almost always judged as exceeding the speed limit by white officers whenever they spotted a black driver.

"You've got outta state plates," one officer, bending over to look through the driver's open window, declared, "so whata ya'll doin' in South Carolina? Plan to stay long?"

"No, officer, just passing through," Arthur answered.

"You belong to any nigra organization?" the other officer, bending over to look through the passenger's open window, asked.

Arthur did not respond to the question. He knew all about this kind of grilling. He had grown up just outside Albany, Georgia. In the fall of 1961, when he was a freshman in high school, he had accompanied his older brother to the Bethel AME church to listen to a SNCC field organizer talk about overcoming fear through non-violent resistance. His older brother had been jailed over that Thanksgiving holiday for defying the local police chief when he and others had been ordered to leave a former "whites only" bus station waiting room, which had been desegregated by a ruling of the Interstate Commerce Commission only a few weeks earlier. Arthur had also witnessed the bravery of his older brother who stood up to the dean of his brother's historically black college. The dean had tried, during that Thanksgiving demonstration, to herd the protesters into the formerly "colored only" waiting room.

When Arthur thought the officers had finished their grilling, he asked a question of his own.

"Sir, I was going 40 in a 50 mile-an-hour zone. Why did you pull me over? Was it because of my skin color?"

"Hell, no!" the officer shot back, caught off guard by the frankness of the question and offended that his authority had been questioned. There was a long pause. Both the officer and the driver waited in silence, each keenly aware a new script for this kind of scene was trying to be written and tested by authors unknown. Then the officer chuckled, looking knowingly at his partner. "Hell, no," he repeated, softer this time, without the edge of defiance. "We pull over pretty white women, too. Look around. Do you see anything happening around here?"

"I truly understand," Arthur said, sympathetically. "I do."

"You don't understand nothing, *boy*," the officer shot back. "I'm gonna give you a ticket. It's a warning ticket. And if you're caught speeding in South Carolina again, we'll have your black ass in jail. You understand *that!*"

Proud that he had maintained his dignity while, at the same time, not giving any cause to be assaulted or arrested, Arthur was also apprehensive about what he should do next. Turn around and go back to his home in Albany? Or chance another ticket? Maybe different jurisdictions did not cross-reference speeding tickets, he wondered. Sitting in his car by the side of the road, Arthur fantasized how defeated he would feel if he had to tell his friends he did not go to the Retreat. At the same time, images of being thrown into a jail cell, kicked in the stomach during the night by a drunken white inmate, unnerved him.

Arthur's purpose in attending the Wappinger Retreat was to figure out not only if blacks and whites could work together, but if blacks themselves could work together. He had witnessed the rivalries among representatives of different black organizations there in Albany and the disagreements over tactics even though, publicly, everyone spoke of one "Albany Movement". And then he remembered his older brother, standing shoulder to shoulder with his fellow protesters and supporters, singing "Ain't Gonna Let Nobody Turn Me Round" at the top of his lungs in Mt. Zion Baptist Church. Arthur had not known all the words then, but he had sensed the strength and unity, which singing gave the group. Sitting alone in his car, Arthur smiled, knowing he knew all the words now.

Instead of driving all day and resting a few hours at night as he had planned, Arthur decided to pull off the road behind some bushes, and wait for dark. He knew he would lose a half-day or more, but he wouldn't be spotted as easily driving all night and resting during the day, at least until he crossed the Mason-Dixon Line into Pennsylvania from Maryland.

As lunch was ending, Arthur arrived at the campgrounds. He grabbed a tray full of food and sat down at a table where people were just leaving to attend the Tuesday afternoon workshops. He quickly looked around and saw a few soul brothers at a distance walking away. It was not his fault he was late, he wanted to shout, but there was no one to listen nearby. He ate the food quickly, and then walked alone to the anti-colonialism/anti-*apartheid* workshop.

Arthur was surprised by the small number of participants—he counted 15—and even more surprised that he was only one of three blacks. Surely there would be more of his people attending, he thought. He sat down next to a black man who, Arthur noticed, was wearing a dress shirt with a button-down collar and a tie.

"Mildred is one of the founders of the Committee on Southern Africa," Arthur learned as he listened to Jane, one of the heavies, introduce the leader of the workshop. "I've always admired her self-assurance, whether it was with African liberation leaders or State Department officials."

After a review of the workshop's agenda, Mildred asked Jeff to talk about the recent demonstration in Newark. Arthur leaned forward in his chair, wondering why he'd not known about a demonstration in an important northern city with a predominantly black population.

"I think you will remember that the New Jersey regional chapter of the National Conference of Christians and Jews presented Charles Engelhard with their Brotherhood award last month. Well, can you imagine, their Brotherhood award! So we mobilized about 200 protesters and stood outside the Robert Treat Hotel there in Newark."

Jeff reminded those in the room that the guest of honor's empire extended not only to exploiting blacks in South Africa through Engelhard Minerals and Chemicals, but that he had also spun a web of influence to protect his financial interests, which included the US and foreign governments, the New Jersey state and national Democratic Party, international educational institutions, foundations, and securities markets.

"Even though we felt such disgust at Engelhard's being director of the South African Chamber of Mines, which set wage and working conditions for African workers, we held a peaceful and dignified demonstration. Even when the police formed a cordon around Engelhard, we opened up a path through our picket line so he could enter the hotel. So you know what? We really stuck it to him when one of our demonstrators held a sign calling Engelhard 'Mista Charlie.'" Few of the demonstrators had understood the full significance of the reference, however, including Jeff.

Arthur could not believe why Jeff and the other protesters had not staged a "sit in" on the steps of the hotel, preventing the award from being given in the first place. Why weren't they more aggressive by standing in the way of the police who were escorting Engelhard into the hotel, getting arrested for civil disobedience? Was he actually witnessing, Arthur wondered, the story of how white folks placed politeness and manners above the injustices and crimes endured by people of color at the hands of other white folks?

When Jeff finished his account by naming some of the newspapers, which had covered the event, all the participants applauded enthusiastically, except Arthur. A placard with "Mista Charlie" on it, how bold, thought Arthur, that'll convince him to change his ways, rubbish.

At the break, Arthur turned to introduce himself to the black man seated next to him, but Dzimba was swiftly making his way to congratulate Jeff on his presentation. For a large man, Arthur noticed that Dzimba carried his weight and height with great dignity, as if he had been groomed for leadership by generations of royal ancestors.

Dzimba was on a mission today to clear the way for his brother, Mabwe, to come to the United States to study. Both brothers had been born in Bulawayo, second largest city in the former Rhodesia, but called Southern Rhodesia since 1964 by most except its white rulers. Dzimba had come to the United States on a US government-funded scholarship, studying at Kendall College in Chicago beginning the same year as the Albany Movement, of which Arthur's brother was a part.

Southern Rhodesia was still under the control of Ian Smith who had unilaterally declared independence from Britain the day before Peter Hunting died in Vietnam. Dzimba feared there would be tough times ahead for his brother and others as the white minority was determined to maintain control, through force, if necessary.

"Jeff, may I have a few moments of your time?" Dzimba asked.

"Of course," Jeff responded.

"I am hoping to bring my brother to safety here in the United States. As you know, a family here must sponsor him. I will also look for a school that will accept my brother for admission. In this way, the State Department will give Mabwe a student visa. Will your committee look for a sponsoring family?"

Jeff was reluctant to get involved. He knew of needy individual cases, but they often took up so much time, time away from work devoted to the big issues of ending both *apartheid* and Portuguese rule in Angola and Mozambique.

"I would appreciate whatever assistance you can provide, no matter how small," Dzimba said softly.

Jeff asked for his address and phone number in DeKalb, Illinois. Jeff was about to end the conversation with a polite, "I'll see what I can do," when Dzimba said, "I do not know how I will be able to thank you well enough, but I pray that your blessings will be manifold." Dzimba extended his right hand.

"I will do everything in my power to help your brother," Jeff said firmly, shaking it.

The workshop reconvened. There were reports about the upcoming Emphasis Week preceding the anniversary of the Sharpeville Massacre. A pamphlet titled, "Witness to the Mozambique Revolution", was distributed with participants being asked to publicize the guerilla war whose existence colonial Portugal had denied. Participants were urged to write their Congressmen supporting US sanctions against Southern Rhodesia, especially at a time when most letters sent to the State Department were against imposing sanctions.

Everyone seemed pleased with himself or herself that so much ground had been covered and there was support for all the activities mentioned. All except Arthur. He caught up to Dzimba on the way back to the large hall.

"Excuse me, brother. I'm Arthur. And I've just got to talk to you."

"Fine. Why not sit under that tree," Dzimba said, pointing to a bench next to an oak tree.

"I don't understand you, man," Arthur began, after they sat down. "I was sittin' next to you, right? And I saw you smiling at the white folks talking about all those saccharin things, like handing out pamphlets, and writing Washington. What's with all that?"

Dzimba paused for a moment, looking out across the meadow.

"Arthur, how shall I begin? Arthur, I am African ..."

"OK. You are my brother from the Motherland, but you don't act ..."

"Arthur, I hope you will not take offense, but we are not from the same family, or even from the same tribe. And, in addition, I am a guest in your country."

"Yes, OK, but I feel me and my people are treated as less-than guests in my so-called country, treated like a piece of meat whose been chewed for all its nutritional value by whites so they can survive, ever since my great-great grandparents were kidnapped from Africa. So, you see, you *are* like me. An outsider. Why aren't you *militant*?"

Dzimba paused again. He felt the sincerity of the question, but a half-century and more of oppression in Southern Rhodesia had taught him a certain reserve, a cautiousness about discussing political beliefs with strangers. His caution came also from his learning that the Smith government had spies in his own community back home, who would sell information for a few pounds. He also suspected there were American spies hired by right-wing reactionaries with deep ties to the chrome industry in Southern Rhodesia. He feared these American spies might try to provoke him into actions designed to get him expelled from the US and sent back to Southern Rhodesia.

"Are you not hungry, my American friend?" Dzimba asked. "We can talk of all these matters another time. But now let us satisfy our bodies. Agreed?" Dzimba smiled broadly with feigned warmth toward Arthur.

"OK, let's eat. We've got lots of time to talk later, right?"

"Correct."

After the afternoon sessions ended, the organizers gathered near the main building, congratulating themselves on a good day of workshops. Convincing themselves that there were so many similar themes and approaches voiced in the Tuesday morning workshops, they decided three of them should draft a strategy statement, which would be read out and approved at the Thursday morning plenary. This decision, taken in the enthusiasm of the moment, risked undoing the original purpose of the Retreat.

Prior to Tuesday evening's dinner, the emphasis on "free time" encouraged many participants to gather in various small camps throughout the grounds, as if each participant were on a reconnaissance mission, gathering information, not as soldiers do about the terrain in order to evaluate the strength of an enemy, but as the educated do in order to analyze commonalities and differences among themselves.

Outside Cabin #8 a small group of white and black, male and female activists from the South, some from Louisville, Kentucky, were discussing how to counter the attacks on them by anti-communist organizations. Although this group was the most integrated and aggressive of all the camps, Arthur did not feel at home there.

On the steps of Cabin #6, a group mostly comprised of seminarians was sharing stories about their first summer in southwest Georgia as part of a student inter-racial ministry. They discussed how they could make sure they would be seen strictly as volunteers this coming summer in support of a black agenda rather than bringing their own "project" with them to implement. Christie liked everyone in this camp, but did not see how she could fit in.

Several self-declared Marxists were gathered in a corner of the large hall, discussing a recent article by Martin Nicolaus called, "The Professor, the Policeman and the Peasant," about the role of the Michigan State University Group in South Vietnam and its relation to pacification programs. Ephraim made sure he got everyone's contact information and promised to keep in touch.

The upcoming trial of Bram Fischer, the Afrikaner anti-apartheid lawyer who had eluded capture by South African police for ten months, was discussed by a small group in Cabin #2. In the 1930s Fischer had joined the South African Communist Party as the only non-racial party then functioning. He had defended Nelson Mandela and others at the Rivonia Trial in 1964. Jeff was glad to learn more about this distinguished lawyer.

A substantial number of those meeting in separate camps could have, for an all-too-brief window of camaraderie, comfortably exchanged places with each other. They might not know the particulars of any given event or region, tacked to history's bulletin board by such place names as Sharpeville, Greensboro, Saigon, Orangeburg, but most believed that the alliances within and between the financial (New York) and political (Washington, D.C.) capitals of the world were conspiring to extend the elite's power over multiple institutions in multiple countries, including their own. Daniel had read about the huge influence of such families as Cabot, Rockefeller, Morgan, DuPont, Mellon, Hanna, Harriman—and of such investment firms as Dillon, Read & Co., Lehman Brothers, Kuhn, Loeb & Co., Goldman, Sachs—in a book which he had bought in a tiny, second-hand bookstore in Greenwich Village.

Next to his teenage books by James Fenimore Cooper, Daniel had placed his newest acquisitions about the super-rich.

After Tuesday's dinner, twelve people met at a pre-arranged spot. They made certain no one else knew where they were meeting. Their secrecy was not to hide any shame over what they were about to do. Not at all. They simply cared to protect their privacy. Most had done it several times before. They did not want any interruptions to what was fast becoming an anticipated practice across the country whenever two or more gathered.

As if walking inside a church, without talking, the twelve entered an empty cabin near the perimeter of the campgrounds. They carefully adjusted themselves in sitting positions, nodding to each near-by congregant, making sure he or she settled in comfortably. The community was now gathered. Its members fully sensed the occasion, and had prepared accordingly.

Norman brought the pot. He had once traveled with his father to Mexico where he had discovered the joys of smoking marijuana. Now, inside the cabin, Norman set the stage. He took his task seriously. He smiled at each person sitting on the floor in a circle, as if to affirm their individual importance, and ascertain their readiness to proceed. The circle was a required part of the ritual, as much to focus participants on the life-affirming activities inside, as it was to erect a barrier, protecting the twelve from the hostile world outside. These newest pioneers instinctively claimed the unpredictable space they had created around them as their own, however temporarily, exchanging worn out conventions for the new ones they were forging.

Jeff lit several candles, as if he were an acolyte. Sensing a tranquil mood had been created, Jeff nodded to Norman.

"I know there are a few newcomers," Norman began. "I just want to assure you that you don't have to be nervous. We were all first-timers once. I'll explain how you do it. Everyone else will help, too."

The protean sense of interconnectedness inside the circle, intensified among friends, born for the first time among strangers, was based upon a keenly honed awareness that, unless every congregant felt pleasure, no one would. A "bum trip" for anyone "brought down" everyone else. Rather than the old ethic of the survival of the fittest, a different ethic was emerging through a new custom, which assured the value of every member of the *entire* community: the weaker were helped by the stronger, every one of them.

"If some of us have more experience with marijuana than you do," Norman explained, "and we sense you are having difficulty getting off, we will show you how to breathe, how to let your mind relax, listen to your responses, relate to your fears, encourage your joys, help shed your anxieties. I believe this is the only way our collective communion is possible, and through our collective communion comes the very incredible but very real experience of glimpsing what the Kingdom is like and what America still can be."

There was no priest present in the circle to officiate. No one trained through years of careful instruction into the mysteries and meanings of ritual. None was needed or wanted. If a title were required, Norman would have had difficulty choosing one. In any event, no one saw the need for a title. In just a few short months, authority itself and the hierarchy on which it rested had been repeatedly challenged, either frontally or by being ignored. Like a glacier whose initial melting occurs out of sight, the momentous dissolution of authority had commenced drip by drip almost without notice by the outside world. And while it would never occur to anyone in the circle that the Magnificat should now be sung, a rhythmic ripple of call and response did indeed faintly echo not only throughout this evening, but also throughout the nation. It was based on an ancient reprise: "He casts the mighty from their thrones, and raises the lowly."

Norman took out several pieces of cigarette paper and a plastic bag from his knapsack. He carefully rolled a bit of the contents from the plastic bag between his fingers, to refine larger bits into smaller ones, and eliminate any small twigs. Then he laid the refined marijuana along the length of a cigarette paper. After rolling the paper around the marijuana completely, he licked the thin strip of glue along the edge of the paper, and sealed it, twisting one end tightly and the other end loosely, so that nothing would fall out. Norman rolled several more joints, placing them carefully next to each other in front of him. He looked around, making sure he had everyone's attention. No one spoke. The novitiates felt the thrill of being on the verge of entering a dimension of consciousness whose existence was passed down from one century to the next by wise ones.

Norman put the tightly twisted end of the first joint between his lips and lit the other end. The flame flared at first as the loosely twisted paper provided the fuel. He sucked on the joint, taking as much smoke as he could into his mouth. The hot smoke scratched the back of his throat, almost compelling him to cough in order to relieve the slight pain. Norman was familiar with the smoke's way of teasing the throat to expel it. He did not allow any diversion from the mission, however. He took the smoke now deeply into his lungs, tracking the slight burning sensation all the way down. He then stopped breathing, holding the smoke in his lungs for as long as he could, moments of silence, nothing happening, the absence of motion, nothing flickering across his mind. Then, as slowly as he dared, Norman exhaled the smoke out of his lungs, through his throat and out of his nostrils, ever-so-slowly, more slowly still, as he felt the upper portion of his head expand, some ethereal part of his mind expanding like a balloon beyond his scalp, filled not with air but with bliss. With his breath fully expelled, for an infinite moment, Norman again did nothing, not even breathe.

He passed the joint to the person sitting to his right, and on it went, around the circle, Norman lighting new joints, the elders helping the novitiates, until he knew it was enough. Everyone, to differing degrees, had been touched by the genii in the marijuana. Calm and happy. The genii worked its magic not only in each one of the twelve, causing each to lose all sense of earth-bound time, destroying the internal clock, which indicated demarcations, blotting out worries with their due dates stamped on them. The genii also created interconnected entities out of solitary ones, uniting individual minds into a group mind. When one part of the group mind laughed, all the other parts laughed, too. When one part of the group mind announced it was hungry, every other part nodded vigorously in agreement.

Well before entering the cabin, the twelve had already begun to reject the rituals they had been taught as children. Those traditional rituals were supposed to assist them in coping with pain, grief, suffering, confusion, guilt, and loss. They assuaged nothing anymore. The twelve, and so many of their kinsmen and women, were entering an extraordinary time of paranoia, fear, dislocation, doubt, and testing. This new ritual, doing dope, carried the heavy burden of not only assisting in the formation of uniquely new communities, but also coping with intense emotions rarely experienced before. The twelve had put into their lungs the breath of life, creating amongst them a burgeoning community soul hopefully strong enough to protect each one from the abrasive confrontations and denunciations in their new political lives, or so they thought.

Jeff smiled across the circle at Norman. Only a few months before, on the evening of Christmas Day, after Norman had rejoined the Lafayette Park demonstrators following his early morning affair, Jeff and Norman had shared a ride back to New York City with Daniel at the wheel. Although they had walked past each other repeatedly for several hours in the bitter cold, and then sat next to each other—or rather, slept next to each other—in the Plymouth, Jeff and Norman had not exchanged more than a few words. And yet, here in this cabin, without having said a further word to each other, they now felt a love between them, and the same love for everyone else in the circle, which was beyond physical and emotional love—a pure love talked about by great beings.

It would be gone before sunrise.

CHAPTER 5 – FISSURES (EARLY SPRING 1966)

The Ballard of the Green Beret, written by Barry A. Sadler, Steve Amerson, John C. Campbell, and Robert L. Moore, Jr., performed by SSgt Barry Sadler, #1 on Billboard's Top Ten, March 28, 1966.

Kill for Peace, written by Tuli Kupferberg, performed by the Fugs, *The Fugs Second Album*, 1966.

Overnight, the temperature sank precipitously. Arctic air blanketed the campgrounds. Creeping stealthily into every cabin and tent, the cold's penetration was not deterred even by jackets laid on top of blankets and sleeping bags. Water, which over the last several days had rested undisturbed in the cracks of many rocks in the area, expanded as it froze, causing the cracks to expand slightly as well.

At Tuesday's dinner, the organizers and workshop conveners met to review the day's events. Although most of the conveners reported there was a general spirit of cooperation and cordiality among the participants, a few reported rather sharp, though short-lived, debates among some participants in several morning and afternoon workshops. Those conveners mentioned that a few participants did their best to cover over disagreements by using recently learned phrases from a new minor growth industry, called Sensitivity Training: "I appreciate the point you are making, and I see merit in it, but ..." On the whole, however, the debates were disturbing news.

"We can't take any chances," Leonard, an organizer, observed.

"Yes, maybe you're right," Jane, another organizer, responded. "Remember, all of you conveners have to devise an action strategy and it has to be approved by your workshop participants. And then all the strategies will be woven into a grand strategy by three of us, and presented to the Thursday morning plenary for approval."

"That's right," Leonard continued. "And I'm concerned that many of the participants, who traveled a long way to get here, may be tired, and some are overwrought."

"Yes, and on top of that, when you think about it, many of them have experienced fatiguing demonstrations, late night newsletter collations, non-stop meetings, cross-country road trips, confrontations with faculty and administrators, handing out flyers on street corners, and a lot more."

"So, we need to increase the odds for a successful outcome," Ted, an organizer, suggested. "Let's send our own representatives to the remaining workshops. Their mission will be to hammer out compromises should disagreements arise during discussion of any action strategy."

"It's too manipulative," Frank countered.

"Nonsense," Ted said. "We're just assisting the participants to make decisions, not have an endless debating society. How about it?"

"Agreed," each of the organizers, in turn, said, except Frank.

Twelve representatives, Jeff among them, were instructed that evening by the organizers neither to tell anyone in their respective workshops who had sent them, nor their role, but rather use their negotiating skills to suggest wording that everyone would support.

Jeff felt honored to be asked. He was not assigned the "Southern Africa" workshop, where he would already have worked with just about everyone, but to the "Working with Liberals" workshop. Other Wednesday afternoon workshops were on "American Imperialism and the 3rd World," "The University, Defense Contracts and The Draft," "Civil Rights," "Working with Communists," "Art and the Movement," "Violence vs. Non-violence," "Community Organizing," "Welfare Organizing," "Electoral Politics," and "Labor and Marxism." Working diligently since New Year's Day to write and circulate papers on all of the workshop topics, the organizers had wanted participants to digest and discuss them in their own local groups before coming to the conference.

Just after the Wednesday morning workshops broke for lunch, by chance Christie and Daniel passed each other on the same path. Christie was walking quickly in the opposite direction from the dining hall, her head down, toward the lake.

"Hey, where are you going?" Daniel called out after her. Christie did not answer. He turned and ran to catch up with her.

"I don't want to talk to anyone," Christie said, not turning toward Daniel, but loud enough for him to hear.

"Wait a minute. Slow down. What's the matter?" Daniel pointed to a bench by the side of the path. "Come on, sit down here, and tell me about it. What happened?"

There was something in Daniel's voice, sincerity perhaps, genuine concern perhaps, and his persistence, which persuaded Christie.

Sitting next to her on the bench, Daniel saw that Christie was trembling. He thought she was cold, so he put his arm around her shoulder.

"Stop it! What are you doing? Don't do that!" Christie screamed, moving quickly away from him down the bench.

"I'm sorry. I thought you were cold. I was only trying to help," Daniel said apologetically.

"I'm sorry, I'm sorry," Christie said. She crossed her arms in front of her chest and bent forward, face pointed to the ground, as if to huddle inside a protective ball.

"What's wrong?" Daniel asked gently.

"Everything's wrong. No, no, it's not just wrong, it's evil," Christie said emphatically. "I wasn't going to tell anyone. My Grandfather always told me to talk only with God and the family about personal things. I don't know, I really have to tell someone. I don't know why, but may I?"

Since their first meeting four months ago Christie had noticed Daniel gaining stature and respect in their anti-war group. She liked the way he took on tasks and responsibilities without bragging about what he planned to accomplish. But it wasn't his emerging authority in the anti-war group that prompted her today. Rather, over the months, she had sensed a kindness in Daniel. She now relied on this quality.

Haltingly, with Daniel prompting her with frequent questions to move the story along, Christie confided that William had asked her to sit next to him last evening around a campfire.

"I had agreed. I know he can be very bossy sometimes, but I had enjoyed sitting near campfires when I was fourteen or fifteen."

"Where was this?" Daniel asked.

Christie told Daniel that for a week each summer for three summers her father had sent her off on the church bus, which took her to Rushford Academy in the northwest hills of New Jersey. At night, scores of mid-teenagers from churches across New Jersey and New York had gathered around a giant campfire, singing "Kum ba yah" and "We are Climbing Jacob's Ladder".

"I never felt so close to God in my life, not even in my father's church. He was somewhere near me, and I felt His protection from any harm. I yearned for that experience again."

As the embers of the fire were dying last night, Christie continued, and everyone else had left, William had put his right arm around her, closing the space between them. Christie had liked the feeling of the warmth of his right arm around her, and the sense of protection it signaled. But William had other ideas, Christie related. He had lowered his face next to hers, and, not saying a word, had lifted her chin to kiss her on the mouth. Startled, Christie had pulled her head back. William had quickly moved his right arm slightly higher, catching the nape of her neck in his elbow, preventing her head from moving, and tried to kiss her again. At the same time, he had reached across her chest with his left hand, feeling her breasts. Christie, feeling deeply violated, had broken free from his grip, and had run back to her cabin, sobbing.

"I can feel him now, even as I tell you," Christie continued, "clutching me like I was his prey. How could he ever think it was OK? What did I do to bring this on me?"

"Nothing, Christie, you did nothing. You never told William you liked him, right?" Daniel reasoned with her.

"No, never," Christie responded. "Not even a look. All I did was whatever he asked me to do for the meetings. He's never even asked me on a date. Why did he attack me like that?"

Christie confessed again and again to Daniel how guilty she felt, as if she'd somehow signaled to William that she was interested in him sexually, causing him to want to kiss her.

"I am so ashamed. There's something impure in me that attracts him."

Daniel comforted her, reassuring her again that she had done nothing wrong.

"Maybe you're right, I don't know," Christie said. "You think I did nothing wrong?"

"Nothing wrong."

"Thanks for listening to me. I didn't intend to take up so much of your time, but I just couldn't keep it inside. It hurt to keep it inside. I've so often felt ashamed, for things I thought I did wrong. I can't begin to tell you," Christie went on, the words tumbling out as if a generation of secrets, stored deep below, had suddenly found a pathway to come swiftly to the surface.

"Thanks, Daniel." She had stopped crying.

Christie talked of many other things with Daniel. In fact, they talked animatedly through the lunch break. It was as if each were touching in the other a loneliness they both had tried to paper over with reams of anti-war documents and scores of activities.

As they were about to head off to their respective afternoon workshops, Daniel confided to Christie that he'd been selected by the organizers to ameliorate any disagreements which might arise during the "action strategy" discussion in the workshop to which he had been assigned. He asked her to keep it a secret. Christie told him that she was pleased that he had been recognized and valued. But she did not respond to his request for secrecy, keeping to herself her dislike of the heavies trying to manipulate the workshops' outcome.

Christie arrived at her workshop a few minutes early and sat in the back.

"What are *you* doing here?" Christie asked, as Jeff sat down next to her. "Shouldn't you be at the Southern Africa workshop?"

"Ah, well, you know, I thought I'd learn something new in this workshop. We rub against a lot of liberals, so I thought I'd just sit in, you know."

Paul convened the workshop, "Working with Liberals." It had attracted many more participants than the organizers had anticipated. More folding chairs were brought in.

"The goal of the workshop is to clarify our relationship with liberals, as individuals and with their organizations," Paul began. "After all, we've been working mostly on campuses and in poverty communities, and we've found ourselves mostly cooperating with religious, peace and civil liberties groups, but--"

"The name of the workshop must be changed," Ephraim, standing at the back of the room, interrupted. "It should be called, 'Working *Against* Liberals.' There are liberals everywhere, everywhere you turn. In trade unions, too. I know, they sell the working man out!" Ephraim stated loudly, for all to hear. As Ephraim tried to continue with a diatribe on co-optation, and how liberals used "our" slogans to promote their programs to re-legitimize class divisions, Jeff stood up and was quickly recognized by Paul.

"If we spend all morning discussing the title of the workshop, we'll never get anywhere," Jeff intoned. "Let's just agree that, as we discuss the topic, some of us who have had a good experience working with liberals will tell us why, and those who feel we should not work with them at all will explain their position."

Paul asked if everyone in the group agreed with Jeff. Seeing no objections, even from Ephraim, Paul continued the introduction. He explained that most everyone at the Retreat had come from middle class backgrounds, and had continued their middle class orientation by attending college and then, for many, continuing with graduate work or post-student jobs, living near campus. And yet, Paul pointed out that many had studied the writings of Third World progressives or immersed themselves in poor communities, which had a "third world" status within America.

"We now know the war on poverty just tinkers with capitalism around the edges, but does not fundamentally change power relationships between rich and poor."

It was natural, Paul continued, that many would feel comfortable working with religious and civil liberties groups because their orientation was middle class, too.

"But where does their power and legitimacy come from?" Paul asked rhetorically. "Aren't they just the reformist extension of the ruling class which encourages liberals to mollify the extreme injuries caused by capitalism, but dissuades them from questioning the systemic basis for the ruling class' power?"

Paul concluded the introduction by asking more questions.

"On whose behalf are we working, or ought to be working? Should we try to radicalize these liberal middle class people and organizations? Or just work with the oppressed? Either way, how can we stay radicalized ourselves in their midst?"

Paul asked for each participant, when they spoke for the first time, to give their name, where they were from, and describe one radical action, if any, in which they had participated. He also asked each participant to stand so they could be heard.

At first, the participants were reluctant to talk about themselves. They had been taught all their lives that the spotlight should never be on them, but on others less fortunate. Some in the workshop had learned that lesson earlier in life when, as teenage pupils in their suburban Sunday school classes, they had been taken to a sister church in the "ghetto," as their white teacher had called the urban neighborhood, seemingly very far from where they lived. The teenagers had brought used clothing, donated by church members. Dressed in their Sunday best, the teenagers had been instructed to set an example of good manners, and show interest in their instant playmates' daily lives. Convinced by parents wanting their children to set the proper example and by teachers looking for student tutors, these teenagers had often been reminded that, if you had a "good brain", you were expected to help others selflessly—and certainly not boast about it.

After the first few participants provided only name and location, Paul coaxed everyone to provide an example of their experience with liberals.

James introduced himself as an anti-war activist living in Detroit.

"I often drive to Toronto and stop by the Student Union for Peace to pick up copies of a pamphlet called "Escape from Freedom, or 'I didn't Raise my Boy to be Canadian'". Before this, I was a member of a peace group made up mostly of older adults, but it seems all they did was to hold candlelight vigils and write their Congressmen. I didn't think what they did was irrelevant. I just wanted to have a greater impact. So now I talk with American college students who are thinking about going to Canada to avoid the draft. And the only reason I join in with older liberals is to find young men in their midst, to recruit them as potential draft resisters."

Sam spoke next. He said he had helped to set up the JOIN Community Union's first storefront office in Chicago one year ago, and was helping poor whites.

"You've got to address each individual's specific problem, like health issues and unemployment, and then build awareness that, by joining together as a community, the causes of those issues can be changed."

Sam was now working with VISTA volunteers who were thinking about organizing a rent strike. He explained that he had also worked with welfare mothers, which created the basis for developing a welfare union.

"Empowering the people, rather than offering handouts as the liberals do, is the basis for lasting solutions to the problems of poverty," Sam concluded.

"Hi, everyone, I'm Susan. I graduated from Yale in 1963 and the next year I became a rent strike activist."

She recalled how she had participated in a demonstration supporting Harlem residents' anti-rat and rent reduction campaign, standing with local residents in freezing weather outside Mt. Morris Presbyterian Church as a member of the Northern Student Movement (NSM).

"I discovered that sometimes radical change can only occur when legislators change the law. And for that, we needed a coalition of liberal organizations to lobby their representatives to create federal legislation for affordable and safe housing."

Biding his time, William had deliberately waited to follow a participant whose story reflected someone working positively with liberals. Sitting in the front row so that when he spoke he could turn and face the entire room as if he were a guest lecturer, William stood and identified himself as a student from New York City. He had decided to conceal that he was president of the Morningside Heights Student Committee Against the War in Viet Nam for fear that there might be a government agent planted in the room taking notes, which would somehow find their way to his father at the US consulate in Toronto. He had given his father the impression that he was playing a much bigger role in the anti-war movement than merely being the head of a small student committee.

"Before coming to this retreat, I organized a large contingent of demonstrators for last Saturday's march down Fifth Avenue. There must have been thirty-thousand," he trailed off, leaving it vaguely hanging in the air how many he actually brought to the march.

"I happen to *know* that President Johnson and his advisers, particularly McNamara, have taken note of the growing protests. I know that if we keep marching, we will give liberal representatives in Washington, who are on the fence, more of a reason to feel comfortable in joining with the Senator from Alaska, Ernest Gruening, in speaking out against the war. We must push for a negotiated settlement."

There were a few audible groans in the room, but William ignored them.

"We can and we must work with liberals within the establishment to change public opinion. When the polls show that the public is turning against the war, influential moderates inside and outside government will follow suit, and urge the President to sue for peace."

Christie fumed, shaking her head from side to side.

Cindy rather shyly introduced herself as a former student at the Free University of New York where she had taken a course on dialectical materialism taught by Lyn Marcus. She recounted that she had been very excited about the courses at the Free University because they were not part of the mainstream liberal curriculum taught elsewhere, but she had left the "university" when some of the other teachers, like Staughton Lynd, resigned because of the rigid control exercised by its founders.

"I am glad, however, to have learned about an ideological approach, which envisions a new communist movement creating a mass party of the working class."

Ephraim immediately stood, and was hesitatingly recognized by Paul.

"I am trying to get a new job and become a trade unionist. I hope to find contacts through the Jewish Labor Committee. Labor unions need to become far more militant than they are, challenging the class struggle head on. I believe I can radicalize union members."

Labor unions, Ephraim continued, could then become a channel for welfare support, which would not demean the recipient as liberal coalitions of citywide church and synagogue groups did in their welfare programs. What these coalitions did, he described, was to bend at the waist, and extend a so-called helping hand, which was actually thrust downward.

"That hand never pulls the recipient up to their lofty level. On the contrary, that hand, unintentionally at first but nevertheless effectively, actually keeps the people in poverty. It never points to the powerful corporations and agencies, which keep them poor through disincentives, law and order, wage manipulations, and fomenting racial and cultural tensions.

These do-gooders organize themselves into Societies," Ephraim continued, "but the only society they yearn to keep is the social circle of their major wealthy contributors."

Pulling her jacket around her shoulders for warmth and comfort, Christie stood and waited patiently to be recognized.

"William," Christie began, "why didn't you tell everyone the name of the group we belong to. Aren't you proud of all the activities we've accomplished in such a short time! And why didn't you tell everyone how you think you know McNamara cares a fig about what we're doing? *How do you know that, William!*" Christie raised her voice, punching out the words of the last sentence as if hitting a wall with her fists.

"You musn't get excited," William responded in a calm voice, standing up and turning to face the group, looking at everyone but Christie. "I just know. You'll have to take my word for it."

"You mean like Westmoreland asks us to take his word about the body count?" Christie shot back. The room erupted in laughter. "I'm beginning to think that you can't trust the military, you can't trust liberals, and maybe even you can't trust some people in this room," Christie said in an even tone, looking straight at William.

"I don't know what you mean," William responded, looking again around the room at the participants. "But I can tell you this. Liberals see themselves as people who can bridge divisions, especially in a time of increasing political polarization. They hold the important middle together, where democracy thrives, while the extremes flail at each other."

"So *you* say," Christie answered in a mocking tone. "If you want to know the truth, I think liberals are by nature *hypocrites*! Oh, they'll work alongside you most of the time, and you sincerely come to believe that liberals are your buddies in the cause. Then, one day, out of the blue, they'll turn on you. And never explain why. In fact, William, I don't even think they realize how much *hurt* they cause by their *disrespect*!"

Jeff immediately stood up and was just as quickly recognized by Paul.

"We've got some important work to do in our workshop. We've heard a lot of different experiences with liberals and opinions about them. Our task now is to agree on a written action strategy, which will become part of the overall strategy read at tomorrow morning's plenary session. So I've drafted something and I'd like to read it."

"Go ahead," Paul said.

Jeff's statesman-like attempt not to offend anyone with his draft statement sparked a debate that had been brewing below the surface for months. It was as much about each participants' self-identity as it was about strategy and tactics. Jeff ran out of ameliorating suggestions for compromise language as each objection was voiced. A half-hour later, the workshop broke up without an agreement on how to work, or not work, with liberals.

The hubbub in the dining hall increased markedly during Wednesday's dinner. Participants leaned forward to hear, and also leaned forward to be heard. But the decibel level was not the only difference in the atmosphere from the evening before. At some tables, the air was rent by quick verbal reactions, like the sound of two rams battering their horns, not the quietly considerate reflections as had been the mood twenty-four hours earlier. Though still involving only a small minority of the diners, sharp exchanges peppered with uncharacteristically impulsive remarks outmatched and overwhelmed the calmer, more contemplative tone of the majority. Nervousness was underfoot.

Opinions fragilely formed over the last few months were now more frequently presented as established fact—and defended passionately. And yet, such newfound certainty was the assertive face of a newly felt uncertainty. Who was she becoming? With whom has he joined? Some were grabbing tightly onto a word or slogan or idea as if it were a life raft, asserting an identity they had only recently tried on for size. "Who We Are" was becoming less and less clear. The purity of a simple protest against injustice was beginning to give way to a fissured Movement intent on justifying, differentiating, and defending itself. But which justification, what differentiation, how to defend? The sound in the dining hall was cacophonous: more John Cage than John Lennon. Unpredictability and randomness, producing unexpectedly clashing vibrations.

The air of discord in the dining room also reflected a tinge of fear, as if the cacophony represented an attempt to drown out a shared nervousness that some participants were not heading down the same path everyone had expected to find.

Daniel skipped dinner. He walked along a pathway, which skirted the lake as the sun was starting to set behind the tree line. Yes, he thought, he had agreed to be a representative sent by the organizers to seek compromise language, but the participants had been so far apart in the "Violence vs. Non-violence" workshop that Daniel did not know where he stood, let alone offer points of compromise among the differing sides. Walking slowly with his head down, Daniel almost ran into the bench on which Arthur sat.

"You startled me!" Arthur exclaimed.

"I'm sorry. Really. I didn't see where I was going," Daniel replied. "Mind if I sit down?"

"If you must," Arthur said.

Moments of silence passed, and then Daniel spoke.

"I didn't see you at the Name Tag Walk About."

"The what?"

"Oh, sorry, at Monday afternoon's registration, when we were supposed to get to know one another."

"No, I didn't make it. Got delayed coming here."

"It all felt so together. Everyone seemed genuinely excited, making new friends, exhilarating really. It all seems a distant memory, now."

"Yeah, a lot of things feel like distant memories, now."

Arthur and Daniel watched the darkening lake as the sun disappeared behind the trees. The cold pecked at their faces and hands, but neither seemed to want to move off the bench. Arthur was the first to speak.

"You know, it feels so peaceful here. Just watching the water."

"Very peaceful."

"I don't know. It's tough to admit this, but I'm not sure where I belong anymore."

"You, too!"

"It's like the ground's shifting and I don't know where to stand. There used to be common ground, but I just feel I'm on my own patch, all alone."

"What do you mean?"

"OK, it's like this. I'm from Georgia. I used to hang out with white Southerners. Went to their parties. We protested together. But now I think desegregation won't benefit my people."

"But why not?"

"I'll give you an example. I went to a segregated high school. I excelled in sports. Would I have been voted the most valuable player on the football and baseball teams if my school had been closed and integrated into the nearby white high school? No way, no matter how well I played."

"You know what, in the workshop this afternoon, there was such sharp disagreements on whether non-violence was the way to change things or not. I don't know what to believe anymore."

"For me, and I mean no offense, but from now on I'm only hanging out with folks that believe in Black Power. It appeals to me."

"OK, but where does that leave me? I mean, you don't really think I'm supposed to hang out with the Rockefellers and talk about White Power?"

Arthur and Daniel looked into each other's eyes for the first time--and burst out laughing.

The organizers' dinner table was empty. They had decided to adjourn to one of the cabins after receiving disturbing reports from their intermediaries sent to Wednesday's workshops. Only two workshops, on "Southern Africa" and "Art and The Movement," had drafted and approved "action strategies." The other ten workshops had not.

The organizers were in a bind. They believed to a person in participatory democracy, but they had invested months of work to achieve the anticipated outcome of a publishable statement reflecting a common purpose arrived at by an overwhelming majority of all the participants.

"Here's what I think we should do," Leonard began. "We'll write a general statement of purpose, which mentions no strategies of action. We'll read this statement aloud at the end of the plenary session as a 'reflection' coming from ourselves, not the participants. In this way, we'll have our publishable statement without having the participants discuss and vote on it."

"I don't know," Frank responded. "It's like masking all the disagreements we're hearing about, rather than debating them."

"I like the idea of the statement," Jane affirmed. "We don't have the time to hammer out all the disagreements, or risk a split if we tried."

All the organizers agreed, except Frank.

This "solution" was not the only public mask being created. In ways far too subtle for all the participants to understand fully at this stage—or, in fact, for the next two years—some activists had begun to fashion masks through which they presented themselves. In fact, some invented several masks, depending on the environment. One mask was deployed whenever a participant felt most comfortable and relaxed within his or her own identity grouping. That mask was displayed only to people who had passed a certain test or met a specific criteria. A different mask was crafted when he or she left the safety of that grouping, and encountered a possibly hostile world. It was as if some activists were becoming like phases of the moon, showing only what they chose to be shown in the light, and hiding the rest in darkness. A few became adept at being a face, which was not seen to be there at all because all that they really knew themselves to be was hidden. The original excitement of making instant new friends, sharing one's story openly and unreservedly, and counting on others to do what they said they would do— all that would be replaced for an increasing number of people by caution and probing.

That evening during "free time," some participants gathered in various cabins or braved the chilled air under the stars or met elsewhere. Even since the Retreat began, most of these participants had been cautiously probing to find and talk with like-minded people.

Outside the perimeter of the camp grounds, at a back table in a nearly empty coffee shop, four young men, who had at first guessed and then later confirmed each other's sexual orientation, met together for the first time.

"Last fall, I thought it was very brave for a representative of the Mattachine Society to come on campus," Sean began. "He had put up posters around campus announcing the event. Only a tiny group showed up, but there he was, dressed in a suit and tie, along with a member of a lesbian group in a dress. Both told us they were just as normal as anyone on campus, except for their sexual preferences, which they felt was normal for themselves. But then, at a break, I left with the girl I had brought with me so no one would suspect I was a homosexual."

Sean looked at each of the other three at the table, and then said: "I left because I couldn't handle the fear and the secrecy and the shame I was feeling."

Inside the camp grounds, Frederik, a white Afrikaner who had moved to the United States a decade earlier, sought out Dzimba, the black Rhodesian, with whom he had talked during the Southern Africa workshop. Frederik had thought of himself as a close friend of the white Americans with whom he worked in the anti-*apartheid* campaign. He had identified with them, and wanted for himself the same American career and societal positions he envisioned them attaining. But tonight, as he and Dzimba talked of the Africa they knew and loved, of the British colonial legacies still very prevalent in their respective cultures, Frederik realized that even though they were both a half-a-world away from their ancestral homes, he had found a true and lasting friend in his African brother, something he had not found even with his best American friend.

"Let's skip dinner, and go from table to table inviting women to get together in Cabin #5," Sharon suggested to Christie.

"I'm with you."

After a dozen women agreed to meet, Christie asked Sharon, "What are we going to talk about?"

"Darned if I know, but I can tell you this," Sharon said. "Without men present, we'll find plenty to talk about."

Mildred and Jeff were still sitting next to each other in the dining hall, even though most had left hours ago. After yesterday's workshop on Southern Africa, Mildred had suggested to Jeff that they meet for dinner the next evening. She had told him she would bring him up-to-date on FRELIMO and the MPLA so that he could better understand these two liberation movements fighting Portuguese colonial rule.

Jeff liked the quiet, but confident way she talked about their leaders and histories. Even though he had by now attended a dozen Southern Africa Committee meetings, he appreciated the chance to receive such detailed accounts of events in Mozambique and Angola from someone who had been to Africa several times. He felt relaxed and comfortable with her. As the hours passed, he asked about her personal life, but each time Mildred steered the conversation quickly back to Southern Africa. She did the same whenever Jeff tried to share stories of his growing up in Austin, Minnesota.

The next morning, Thursday, the plenary was scheduled to begin at 9am. The dining hall had been transformed overnight. Except for a row of tables at the head of the hall and tables for the buffet breakfast, all the other tables had been removed. Folding chairs had been set up side-by-side in rows, facing the head tables, with one long aisle down the middle. Hierarchy had been resurrected.

Only one-third of the participants arrived on time, despite written and verbal announcements that breakfast would still be available at the start of the plenary. By 9:30am, not many more participants had arrived, so one of the organizers rang the dinner bell with authority, its clapper rapidly sounding as if it were an emergency.

The plenary was finally called to order at 10am by Leonard. As the first order of business, he announced that the total number of registrants stood at 227, from 22 states and the District of Columbia. He did not know that forty-five had already left the Retreat either the night before or early that morning, seeing no point in attending the plenary.

Leonard called on each workshop convener, in turn, to stand in their place and provide a 10-minute summary of the main points addressed in their workshop. Leonard did not mention that the convener was originally to have presented a consensus "action strategy" for discussion and vote. Since the time allotted for plenary discussion had now been scrapped, the morning plodded on wearily with summary after summary after summary, noticeably boring virtually all the assembled, except the organizers, separated from the body, behind their tables.

At 12noon when the last summary had been presented, a 15-minute break was announced, to the relief of the body. The heavies understood all too well by now that the high spirits present at the beginning of the Retreat were dormant, if not dead. They knew that familiar ground had indeed been reconnoitered as they had anticipated, but they also realized that cracks, uncovered in what had previously been hoped was a solid, unified, radical political undertaking, were now all too visible. The organizers had hardly expected, on this last morning, to be faced with a sour mood, a Retreat of a different kind altogether.

"I have second thoughts about reading the reflection," Jane offered during the break. "Everyone seems so quiet, even depressed."

"Yeah, I think you're absolutely right," Frank continued. "There's no energy, no enthusiasm left."

"Reluctantly, I'll have to agree with you both," Leonard admitted. "So what'll we do?"

When the plenary was called back to order 30 minutes later, forty participants did not return, preferring instead to get an early start for their next destination.

One of the organizers then stood up. He walked some ten feet from around the back of the organizers' tables to stand directly in front of the body. Like an orchestra conductor, he paused just long enough to make sure he had everyone's attention.

"I think some of you know me, but for those who don't, my name is Al. I went to Natchez, Mississippi, to work on the Freedom Election in the fall of 1963 and then organized a community union first in a white Cleveland neighborhood and later in a black neighborhood. That was in 1964 and '65."

He told his story, not in a boastful way even though he was one of the most experienced activists in the room.

"I was nervous each time I was in a new situation, but I always found strength and support from the people around me. I've been in Berkeley and Boston, Nashville and New York, Chapel Hill and Chicago, Seattle and Santa Fe.

"Students like yourselves and others, here and there in tiny numbers, have been steadily turning up the heat on a stove large enough to boil the entire country. We all share a vague sense that America is off course overseas in Indochina, just as it's way off course at home in the South. A mismatch, that's what it is. Peasants versus the United States military. Negroes versus the sheriff and the Ku Klux Klan. It's un-American to have such lopsided contests. Un-American to slaughter the other side."

His talk was not in the program. His speaking was not even discussed by the heavies during the break.

Al was certain he had to raise the vibration of his congregation to a higher frequency. Even though a white boy from a wealthy New Jersey suburb, like a black preacher in a rural wooden southern church standing alone in the middle of great tracts of pine trees, his voice reached the sides and back of the large room and beyond. As if fashioning a great quilt of many colors, warming and comforting his listeners, Al hoped he was knitting them together, reviving their spirits, intending that his energy energize them.

Standing now almost toe-to-toe with those in the front row, Al then took out a piece of paper from his pocket.

"When I stood to speak a few moments ago, I wasn't sure if I'd read what was on this paper, but now I will."

He stepped back a few feet toward the tables.

"You see, it was written by a couple of the people you see behind me. And it was written because most of yesterday's workshops couldn't agree on strategies. We, the organizers, were going to publish this statement as if it were a true reflection of this retreat, under our own names. But in reading it to you now, I want to see if you, each one of you, can embrace it as your own statement. And, after I've finished, I'd like you to signify if you agree with it by standing up. Here goes.

"We do not see ourselves either as a federation of organizations or even as a coalition of individuals. Rather, we see ourselves as participants in an autonomous, organic and living body. We dedicate ourselves to a radical reorganization of society itself. Although we mostly live in or near college campuses, this radical reorganization goes far beyond academia, and includes the work place, government, the non-profit sector, and other institutions, all within an international context. As a living and growing body of people, we base our unity not on hierarchy or ideology, but on our belief that rebellion against calcified and deaf authority will forge an inclusive society in which every person participates in the decisions influencing his or her own destiny. Our mood of rebellion flows directly from the Free Speech Movement, the Vietnam protests, sit-ins, teach-ins, civil rights marches, and so on. We do not believe that the two major political parties, as currently constituted, offer the means for the reorganization we seek. We intend to be where the action is. We intend to continue to research and expose the powerful connections, which unite the rich and how they maintain their privileged positions. We unite around many slogans. Here's three of them: 'Let the people decide.' 'There's a change gonna come.' 'Don't just stand there, do something!'"

As Al was reading the statement, he slowly walked backward until his body touched an organizers' table. As he ended, he paused, and then asked loudly, "Who agrees with this statement?" He waved his arm enthusiastically, inviting participants to stand.

A few immediately stood, most in the front rows. Seeing them stand, others wondered if they should, too. After all, they had come far distances, spent now four days in discussions, and sensed there should be some kind of finale. A dozen more stood while others looked around the room to see if any of their new, instant friends were standing. More than half of the assembled remained in their seats, not convinced every part of the statement spoke for them.

Al stepped toward the first row again. He was about to encourage a stronger affirmation when a note was given him, which he opened and read. Believing he now had in his hand the catalyst for a roaring finish of solidarity and commitment, he read the note aloud.

"Earlier today, David Paul O'Brien and three others burned their draft cards on the steps of a courthouse in Boston. We ask that you pass a resolution of support and comradeship for our four brothers."

One-half hour later, the Retreat ended. No resolution of support for the draft card burners was put to a vote. Some of the participants, though sympathetic, opposed the burning of draft cards as it might turn liberals away from contributing to anti-war organizations. Others said that, since 1964 the burning of draft cards was becoming more prevalent, this act of conscience should be supported even though it meant destroying government property. The participants were clearly divided. The flow of energy Al had generated was dissipated not only by the debate, but also by the participants' desire to get on the road. No final "reflection" was adopted, either.

It was still early days for this movement. So many people attracted to it who had not yet clearly thought through who they were and where they were in relation to the issues of the day, even by the end of the Retreat.

It was still a movement that had within itself as many fluid identities and embryonic positions as, sometimes, there were people in the room.

CHAPTER 6 –– INDEPENDENCE (SUMMER 1966)

Red Rubber Ball, written by Paul Simon and Bruce Woodley, performed by Cyrcle, Number 3 on Billboard's Chart for the week of July 4, 1966.

This Little Light of Mine, a traditional song adapted by Zilphia Horton for the civil rights movement.

Rev. Calvin, Jr., walked slowly next to his father the short distance from the parsonage to the church early, well before eleven. The elderly man, decked out in his best silk suit, leaned with both hands tightly gripping his walker, barely raising one foot after another as he made his way, tortoise-like, down the aisle. When they reached the front pew, his son took the walker, folded and hid it behind the pulpit. Rev. Calvin, Sr., would not be given the walker again to depart the church until after every parishioner had shaken his son's hand and left the vestibule.

On this Sunday before next day's Fourth of July holiday, Rev. Calvin, Sr., looked forward to celebrating the birth of the nation. He was certain God had blessed America like no other people on earth. As the old man thumbed through his worn pocket Bible, he knew God would show him which passage to read. Stopping at chapter 8, verse 9, in *The Book of Daniel,* he read silently to himself: "To us, O Lord, belongs confusion of face, to our kings, to our princes, and to our fathers, because we have sinned against thee. To the Lord our God belong mercy and forgiveness; because we have rebelled against him, and have not obeyed the voice of the Lord our God by following his laws, which he set before us by his servants the prophets." Rev. Calvin, Sr., was uncertain how to interpret "confusion of face", but he felt confident that he had obeyed God's laws all his life. How could he not feel grateful, he thought, for the life God had predetermined him to live? After all, his large block of stock in Middle South Utilities had done well over the years. His rich life-style in New York had been supported by its dividends and appreciation.

Rev. Calvin, Sr., prided himself on his knowing that God had allowed him to pay his own way, even now in his humbler circumstances. The secrecy and subterfuge he sometimes employed to help others was also a source of pride. He even had a secret arrangement with a parishioner who, each Sunday, placed three hundred dollars inside an unmarked envelope into the collection plate. The mechanics of the deception had been as much a particular point of pride for the father as the money itself. Before every service began, the parishioner had walked over to the benefactor, bent over as if to shake his hand, and was given a signed bank withdrawal slip, which the parishioner during the week brought to a bank officer who knew of this arrangement, but was not told the money's destination. Every Sunday the parishioner had sat in a different part of the church so that the ushers, when opening the envelopes after the service, could not guess from whom the anonymous and generous weekly donations came.

The organist played a Bach fugue as the first worshippers arrived. Christie assumed her duty of seating parishioners, trying to ignore their looks of surprise at what she was wearing. She had learned from her mother to escort parishioners to the front pews, then the middle ones, leaving pews in the back open so as not to have latecomers experience the embarrassment of being seen by those who had arrived on time. Valuing punctuality as had her mother, Christie did not condemn, as her mother had, the souls who missed the opening hymn. When the organist began the processional, Christie vacated her usual position at the back of the church and took a seat on a side aisle. It was the first time she had ever abandoned her post.

As was his custom, whenever Rev. Calvin, Jr., entered the church proper at the start of the processional, he looked for Christie in the back to send her an affectionate fatherly smile, as if it were thanks for her ushering duties. It upset him today that he could not find his daughter in her usual place.

Christie tugged at her miniskirt several times, trying to lengthen it as far as she could over her bare, crossed legs. She even opened a hymnal and placed it facedown over her knee, but decided it looked silly. She would just have to bear the stares from people who had known her all her life, she thought.

> **Lenni-Lenapi looks around the church, and through its walls to the countryside beyond. She senses conflict everywhere, evaporating from the wooden floor and from the land, feels the gnashing of cultures, one against another, and worshipped gods bashing each other with blade and word. She knows the disputes she, and others very like her, have settled in the past, with hospitality and diplomacy. One of the first to make treaties, Lenni-Lenape is tuned to the discomfort Christie experiences.**

Saving money from her part-time job as a bookstore clerk, Christie had asked Nicki, still a member of the Morningside Heights Student Committee Against the War in Viet Nam, to go with her to Gimbel's to pick out new clothes just after the Wappinger Retreat. She could not afford Saks where Nicki went, or B. Altman's, but she had relied on Nicki's fashion sense to guide her.

Over the years her mother had bought most of Christie's clothes from second-hand shops, accepted hand-me-downs from parishioners, and even charitable parcels from the wives of ministers serving wealthier churches. By dressing Christie in clothes already many years old, she had assured herself that she was protecting Christie from modern temptations, like impulse buying or manipulation by trendsetters. Christie had come to appreciate the quality and durability of the clothes her mother selected. Now, her mother's absence had left Christie both an opening to venture out on her own and uncertainty as to which additions to choose for her wardrobe.

It was Nicki who had insisted that Christie buy the woman's suit with the black jacket and matching miniskirt, and the white blouse and black heels to complete the ensemble. During their first shopping foray three months ago, Christie had nearly warmed to the idea of wearing a denim miniskirt and peasant blouse on school days, but exposing her bare legs in church or on any other formal occasion seemed blasphemous. Nicki had continued to point to women much older than they, who wore skirts, which dropped below the knees.

"It's so last century," Nicki had repeated often, in a tone, which suggested that Christie could not possibly still be interested in continuing to dress "so last century."

"Don't you want to break from the past, make a statement about who you're becoming?" Nicki had asked.

"Well, yes, but does it have to be so radical?" Christie had responded.

"Christie, stop a moment. Take a good look at your reflection in that shop window," Nicki had commanded.

"You're attractive. You are, Christie. You really are. But you are not free. Dressed like you always dress, there's no glow coming from you, no liveliness.

"Now, take a good look at me. It's not just the clothes. It's how these clothes make me feel. I feel daring sometimes. Other times I feel sexy. Sometimes it's just that I feel good. And you know what it all adds up to, in a strange way, I guess. A feeling of power."

On their third trip to Gimbel's, Christie had bought the denim miniskirt and the peasant blouse, the black suit with the miniskirt, the white blouse and the black heels. Accustomed to wearing her denim miniskirt in New York these last two months, she had come to feel part of a small but rapidly growing club of young women who often only noticed each other walking down Broadway or between classroom buildings.

Sitting now in the seat nearest the side aisle, Christie did not feel powerful. She did not feel blasphemous either. Still tugging at her skirt to lengthen it, not daring to cross her ghostly pale knees again, she did not regret, however, her choice of clothing for this Sunday service. It was here in her hometown, in her father's church, during *this* Sunday service that Christie had decided to assert to herself and others who she was becoming, even if she was unsure who that new person was. She knew her conscience would not allow her to lead a dual life: freedom could not be practiced in New York and denied in Hopewell.

Christie resumed her seat at the conclusion of the first hymn. Familiar prayers were repeated and Biblical passages read, but her attention was not on the service. Rather, she replayed in her mind the long conversation she had had with Alice a few days before, again in her elementary school yard.

"A lot has happened to me since we last talked here," Christie had begun. "I've thought a lot about how I was raised."

"And how was that?" Alice had asked.

"As far back as I can remember, I've reproduced without thinking the pattern of unquestioning service I first observed in my mother. She taught me to yield to the authority of my parents and Grandfather as God's servants on earth. I was repeatedly instructed that birth's purpose was to await death—and God's election."

"That's awful," Alice had responded.

"I see that now, but, as if to prepare me daily for a heavenly journey, my mother bathed me twice a day when I was a young child, scrubbing my skin vigorously, the same way she polished furniture."

Her mother, Rachel, had wanted Christie to glow with cleanliness, a glow she had often seen in paintings of the Madonna and child in an art book she had kept in a dresser drawer.

"You said a lot of things have happened to you recently," Alice had said.

"Yes, I'll give you some examples. Following the Wappinger retreat I told you about, I made some important decisions."

Christie had then described to Alice how, knowing that Ed wanted to become president of the group one day, he had willingly agreed to Christie's request to host the Morningside Heights Student Committee's weekly meetings at his apartment. She had also asked Daniel to take the minutes.

"I now see my mother's training of me in a new light. Perhaps it was not based on how I was to perform a God-ordained role at all, but rather on how a woman, dependent on her husband's earnings and career, curried favor so that neither she nor her daughter and son would be abandoned. But I don't see myself as a person who always needs to please others, like being a hostess, a coffee-maker, a chair arranger, or needs to worry about the successful outcome of every anti-war meeting."

Rev. Calvin, Jr., began his sermon. Its theme, tailoring his theology to the holiday, was on the false independence felt by sinners when they become arrogant and stray from God's will.

Christie would not listen. She was thinking about death. The death of her high school classmate. The letters arriving from New York with news of the death of grandfather's friends. But especially about the death of her mother.

When Christie was barely in her teens, she had witnessed how Rachel kept running here and running there, without complaint, no sighs or groans indicating that anything was misaligned, all parts seemingly functioning perfectly, until, one day, without a sound, her short-machine-like-life-of-endless-errands-to-please-others had simply stopped running, given out, ceased moving.

Christie had taken no comfort in her father's eulogy that her mother had been one of the "elect". He could not know that, Christie had angrily said to herself when she heard her father's veiled attempt to placate his own guilt. She had known well enough, from her grandfather's Sunday school lessons, that only God knew whom He had chosen to be saved from eternal damnation.

As was his practice while preaching, Rev. Calvin, Jr., having trained himself to glance down at the text, quickly absorb the next two or three sentences, then look up to speak them as he slowly panned the congregation, now seemed to address each person directly. Each time he raised his eyes from the text, he focused on a different section of the congregation, so as to leave no one out. More and more frequently, however, he looked to the back of the congregation at a woman dressed in black, sitting next to a side aisle. On this hot summer morning, the color of her jacket stood out, among the summer florals worn by many women and the light-colored jackets worn by some men. His eyes kept returning to this woman in black. He wondered who she was, and what kind of loss she had experienced.

William turned his radio dial to a station to which he had never listened. He had heard that a British mathematician, who had teamed years earlier with William's academic hero, Alfred North Whitehead, to write an important book, would be addressing the American public. William listened intently as WBAI in New York City broadcast an appeal by Bertrand Russell on this Monday, July Fourth, at five in the afternoon.

Russell's upper class British accent reverberated with centuries of a rich civilization William profoundly admired. This Anglophile had read Shakespeare avidly in college, and loved to listen to recordings of Churchill's wartime speeches. In fact, at the beginning of the broadcast, William thought he had detected Churchillian intonations in Russell's ninety-four year old clear and confident diction.

Having been raised in one of the Commonwealth countries, he was thrilled to see Queen Elizabeth II when she visited Ottawa in 1957 and again in 1959. His father had briefly been posted to London when William was in his early teens. Quickly mimicking a British accent more articulated than the original, William had continued this affectation for years after he returned to Canada.

He turned the radio volume louder.

Daniel had told his mother not to pick him up at the railroad station. He looked forward to walking home, getting some exercise, he had told her. This reason was only partly true. He wanted to postpone as long as possible his parents' seeing how long his hair had grown. It touched his shoulders.

At first, Daniel had convinced himself that he could not afford regular haircuts. Then, as his hair had grown out, he liked what he called his "Buffalo Bill Cody" look, hair flowing over his ears and neck. He had noticed other males his age with long hair. A few had tied their hair with a rubber band, as young women did when they had made pony tails in high school, but he thought these young men appeared rather silly. As more and more men grew long hair, Daniel felt he had joined a growing band of renegades.

Walking again toward his boyhood home, Daniel remembered that as a teenager he had meticulously explored, first his immediate neighborhood and then the entire town, atop his Roadmaster bike. Thirsting for every scrap of knowledge about his high school classmates, Daniel had eagerly looked up their street addresses in the telephone book, tracked down their blocks on a map, and then set out to ride past their homes. Every free afternoon after school had presented the opportunity for another reconnaissance in his campaign to amass a secret cache of facts about his classmates' residences — color of the trim, flower boxes under the windows or not, cement or slate walkway to the front door, dormer windows or a full second story, make and model of the automobile in the driveway. It had been as if this growing stockpile of details provided ammunition to protect his inner, insecure, poorly constructed fortress.

Each outing had not only snapped more pieces of his town's geographical puzzle in place, so that previously explored roadways and intersections were fitted into newly discovered ones. His travels had also served to piece together Daniel's view of his own social standing in the community.

When he had first seen Andrew Jacob's columned two-story mansion on Hathaway Road, he had a clue as to why he always felt so awkward in the company of this son of wealth. Another day, when he discovered Prescott Williams' ranch home on South Avenue in the poorer area of town, he had a clue why he felt at ease in his presence. Keeping the accumulated observations to himself, this treasure trove of facts had allowed Daniel to feel superior in his own fantasy world. It was as if he had built a wall around himself, always peering over it, secure in the knowledge that he could see his surroundings whenever he chose, but no one could look inside his wall. Of course, Daniel had to venture out, walk his high school's hallways, and participate in class. He could not always avoid feeling socially ill at ease and nervous around many of his classmates, even when a small group had self-selected themselves, Daniel included, as "our crowd," in reaction to the formation of several large social cliques. But he had never been more himself, in control of his destiny, than atop his Roadmaster, pedaling full speed down the middle of a new roadway, no cars ahead or behind, fingers locked across his stomach, head held high in the breeze.

During the weeks before this July 4th holiday weekend Daniel had called former high school classmates to see if they would be in Babylon. He had wanted to talk movement strategy and tactics with people he'd known for years. At last he felt that he had status, a record of achievement he could show his former classmates to earn their respect.

"Hello, Muller, is it really you?" Daniel had begun with one of his best high school friends with whom he had not communicated in several years.

"Yeah, yeah, Gens, it's me."

"Oh, man, it's been five years since we graduated, but you sound the same."

"I do?"

"Yeah, yeah. Remember on those hot summer days, when we went to firemen's field and played stickball?"

"I sure do. Let me see. Wasn't a home run if you hit it over the tree and a triple if it went into the tree?"

"Yeah, yeah, and a double was over the pitcher's head, and a single under the pitcher's head. Loved those days."

"So, what are you doing now?" Muller had asked.

"Oh, man, I've been so busy. Got out a spring mailing of our newsletter to update everyone on the war and picketed the South African consulate in June. Did you know that over 400,000 migrant farm workers in the US got paid last year an average of only $1,362 from all sources of income? But no more about me, how about you?"

"Daniel, I was hired right out of college by Lehman Brothers. My wife and I live in Scarsdale, and we have a child on the way."

"That's nice."

"I've taken up golf. Can you believe it?"

"Really? Hey, I'm sure you remember that secret sign our crowd had in high school?

"No, not really."

"You must remember. After each class, as we walked down the hall, we'd take out one shirt tail, and let it hang outside our pants, and then stuff it back in as we walked into the next class. That's about as rebellious as we got in the Fifties!"

"No. I don't remember. Seems really long ago."

"Have you kept up with any of our classmates, especially in our crowd?" Daniel had asked, hopefully.

"No. Not really. I did run across Turner, and he's in his father's insurance business. Doing very well. All my friends now are financial analysts or neighbors in Scarsdale. What else are you doing?"

"Oh, you know. The usual. Studying."

"My company's sending me to London. They want me to learn about the derivatives market."

"The what?"

"Derivatives. Very complex. But very profitable if you know what you are doing. Could be the next big step in my career. Anyway, Daniel, I've got to run. We can do lunch one day. I'll call you."

Daniel had hung up the phone. He felt as if Muller, in his clipped, business tone, had been saying at the end of the conversation, "Good-bye, it was nice knowing you."

After a similar conversation with another one of his best high school classmates who was deciding in which hospital he should take his residency, Daniel had quit calling anyone else.

As he walked along Lakeview Avenue from the railroad station, Daniel wondered if he would run into someone he knew, at least to see if someone recognized him. Maybe if he could talk face-to-face with an old pal, he could feel the closeness of "our crowd" again. But what about the long hair? He always had a crew cut, military style, like his cousin who had volunteered for the Army. But even if they recognized the old "me" under this hair, Daniel thought, what would we talk about? Is there anything we have in common anymore, except memories, Daniel wondered. He could think of no one from his past who had shared the same path he had chosen to walk.

Passing by so many familiar houses on Brower Avenue, he questioned whether anyone behind those front doors cared about what he cared about: Viet Nam, South Africa, Harlem, Farm Workers, the South. He had learned of so many injustices during the Wappinger Retreat. He wanted to ring doorbells. He wanted to shout: did anyone know how devastating the local "urban renewal" program had been to black families and their communities? He wondered if there had been any demonstrations against the war in his hometown. Would there ever be any demonstrations? Would anyone take an hour or two from mowing their lawns or finishing their basements to find out what was going on in the world? He didn't even know one radical in town, now that his high school friend Ira had moved out.

Daniel quickened his pace. He walked the short blocks of St. James Place and Tarence Street. He wasn't concerned anymore about his parents' reaction to his long hair, or what they might say about the tear in his dungarees where he had scraped his right knee. He was rather proud of that tear. Running to catch up to a small group of students heading toward First National City Bank two months ago, he had tripped and fallen as he approached the corner of Broadway and West 111th Street. Although Daniel had not actually had an account at the bank, he wanted to support Jeff and the others who were closing theirs to protest the bank's financial support of South Africa. He had left the wound unattended for a week, as if to share symbolically the suffering of South African political prisoners he had read about.

As he walked further, Daniel began to notice some changes in his hometown. More cracks in the sidewalks than he remembered. More tree roots pushing up sections of sidewalks, breaking pieces of concrete, which he thought had been joined solidly together for the last quarter century. Weeds in flowerbeds, and brown patches in lawns. He was certain the grass had been much greener as he sped past homes atop his Roadmaster bike than it was now. From a place deep within, Daniel experienced first a feeling of isolation and then anger as he had never experienced before. Why had his hometown deteriorated so? Why hadn't any of his former classmates taken the path he had taken? He was not an oddball, was he? They could damn well have their well-paid careers, Daniel scoffed.

Knocking on the side door of his parent's home, even though the door was always unlocked, had been Daniel's life-long habit. It had been a ritual of respect so that his entrance would not surprise them. His anger now stayed the ritual. He flung the door open. Without saying a word, Daniel walked past his mother seated in the living room and headed for the basement stairway. The old familiar furniture now looked so faded. The rug almost threadbare.

"What's the matter?" his mother called out.

"None of your damn business!" Daniel shouted back, and went downstairs to his room.

The next morning, Daniel slept in. He had always relished these extra hours of sleep, as if they could totally refresh and restore body and mind after months of punishment. He knew his mother would have a delicious breakfast for him whenever he emerged from the peace and quiet of the cellar. As he dressed, however, the wash hung the evening before along ropes near his bed seemed to hem him in, restrict his movements more than ever. The sun light coming through the cellar window seemed dimmer than he'd remembered. Forgetting where the light switch was, Daniel had to maneuver around shirts, underwear and socks hung by clothespins to find it. Even his old toy chest had been moved by his father to the back of the basement to create more space for a workbench in what was once Daniel's exclusive area. Other people's things were encroaching more and more on what little cellar space his parents now defined for Daniel's existence. He felt more and more a stranger in this home.

After breakfast, he returned to the basement. The steamer trunk was still unlocked. Without hesitation this time, he opened the hinged lid and let it rest upright against the cellar wall. His eyes tried to adjust to the darkness inside. Soon, he felt inside the trunk. Nothing on the top or in the middle. He felt closer to the bottom, as his eyes had seen nothing but blackness. His hand came across an old doll. Taking it out into the light, he saw that its mouth seemed permanently open, as if always talking or screaming. His hand went deeper, until it touched a case on the bottom. Lifting it into the light, he surmised there must be a tiny lock thwarting his effort to open it. He felt around the bottom of the trunk, but his fingers never discovered a key. Daniel went to his father's tool bench, selected a flathead screwdriver, and slipped it between the front edges of the case. Twisting it from side to side, he forced the screwdriver deeper inside, until the case popped open.

Inside the case he felt a piece a plastic, a sleeve of some kind, with a photo and a piece of paper inside. Taking it out to the light, he saw the photo was of two young girls on a beach, but he did not recognize them.

The paper had an official-looking raised seal on it. A death certificate. With the name, Mathilda Weidmann, on it.

That's Gra'ma's maiden name, but not her first name, Daniel thought. Who's "Mathilda?" Could that be her sister? Only once, Daniel recalled, did his grandmother speak of her having a sibling.

Daniel abruptly replaced the photo and certificate inside the sleeve, then placed it inside the case. The lock snapped back in place. Nothing would look as if it were disturbed, Daniel thought, as he closed the trunk's lid. Nothing, except the pulsing in his heart.

Early that afternoon, with time moving so slowly for him that the clock's hands seemed glued to its face, Daniel suddenly pressed his father for the keys to the family car.

"Have you apologized to your mother for your outburst yesterday?" Edwin inquired.

"Yep."

"After all your education, that's all the answer you can give?" his father retorted.

"Dad, I told her I didn't mean anything by it. And that was that."

"Just make sure it does not happen *again*. You know how happy you make your mother feel when you're home." His father's words skated over the top of Daniel's mind as if they never touched his conscience below. "Where are you taking the car?"

"Jones Beach. For a swim. I want to relax. Just be with myself for a while."

"You've earned it, son," his father's voice mellowing. "Your grades were pretty good last semester, you said, and you have that job washing dishes in the cafeteria. Go ahead, son, enjoy yourself, you've earned it, but be back by eleven, no later. You don't want to worry your mother."

Daniel grabbed the keys and was out the door before his father could say anything more.

For every summer he could remember, a family trip to Jones Beach had been the high point of many a Saturday. Archery, pitch-and-putt golf, roller skating, or just walking along the boardwalk were diversions everyone had enjoyed, even Gra'ma, who watched. After spreading several blankets on the hot sand, anchoring them with sneakers and picnic baskets, each member of the family had laced themselves with sun tan oil and lay down to roast, the women in beach chairs, the men stretched out on blankets. Whenever the summer sun became unbearable, each had waded gingerly into the ice-cold ocean's surf, soon letting the salt water buoy them as they floated on their backs.

Daniel drove as fast as he dared on the Meadowbrook Parkway. It was an exhilaration he always enjoyed, by himself in the family car. No one to watch the speedometer, or to tell him to keep in the slow lane. He gripped the steering wheel tightly, as if to drive out all emotions except the feeling of speed. At the end of this ride would be the ocean playground he had loved as a child.

Daniel pulled into the West End parking field, which his family had always used. It was mid-afternoon. Heat and humidity were at full-throttle. Many bathers, who had arrived in the cool of the morning, were now packing up, hoping to beat everyone else to the roadway leading out of the state park.

Daniel walked the long distance from the parking lot to the archery area, rented a bow and 20 arrows. He remembered how accurate he used to be years ago. His form soon came back to him, sighting down the arrow's shaft toward the target's bull's-eye. The bow was, however, heavier than he remembered. He needed more strength than he first thought to pull back the string. The first arrow fell short. Daniel realized he would have to get more tension into the bow, so he pulled the string back further. With the next three shots, however, as he released the slightly quivering bow, the taut string hit him on the inside of his left forearm, stinging the skin. Only one arrow hit the target, well below the bull's eye. With the fifth attempt, the taut string scraped the skin, drawing a droplet of blood. He quit. The remaining arrows were given to a youngster who was having no trouble hitting the bull's-eye.

> **Montaukett puts her hand in her pocket as she watches Daniel leave the archery area. She feels no wampum there. She is glad she has nothing worth stealing or worth being captured. She values what the land and sea can produce, and knows there's enough for all.**

Next, Daniel rented roller skates. As he listened to the pre-recorded organ coming over the loudspeaker, he was glad they were still playing the same music they had played when he was a child first learning to skate. After practicing an entire summer on his neighbors' sidewalks, he not only had kept his balance on the rink then but also sped around its outer circle, gliding effortlessly on one foot and then the other. This afternoon, however, the skates did not feel secure on his size twelve shoes. Afraid to let go of the railing, Daniel pulled himself along hand over hand, trying to reconnect his feet to the childhood memory of the rhythm of the motion, which would propel him forward. After picking himself up for the third time, he quit.

The late afternoon summer air hung like a damp blanket over Daniel. He could not remember such mugginess at the beach. Seeking refuge, he spotted a restaurant he had never seen before. Unlike the old, outdoor concession stand where bathers had sat in wet suits and kids had carried their sand pails and shovels with them, the new indoor restaurant posted a sign at the entrance disallowing bathing attire and bare feet. Through the window he could see plastic menus being given by a waitress to the diners. How times have changed, Daniel thought, recalling fondly the one large signboard listing all the offerings and their prices above the old concession's ordering counter.

He paused, unsure of what awaited him through the door. Since he had not stripped off his pants or shoes to take a swim in his bathing suit underneath, he declared himself properly attired and decided to go inside to survey this new world. Daniel ordered a drink to ease the transition. It was no longer a Rheingold beer. A friend of his, Jake, had introduced Daniel to the Rusty Nail, a potent combination of Scotch and Drambuie. He had begun drinking Rusty Nails as a kind of reward, stopping off at the West End Café on Broadway late at night after a meeting, before he returned to the dorm. He knew Tiger would be there, at the head of the oval bar, greeting him enthusiastically. Other regulars would also be there, for talk and laughter. After only nine months in graduate school, Daniel had felt more at home in the West End Café than he did yesterday afternoon walking along familiar Babylon streets and entering the house he had known for eighteen years.

After his third Rusty Nail, a hamburger and French fries, Daniel stumbled out of the restaurant, to a near-by bench on the boardwalk. He sat for a long time, watching the sun set at the end of the ocean. The liquor released his mind from all concerns, even the death certificate. He wallowed in the pleasure of being disconnected, freed from a past, which no longer knew him. He and his alcohol dreamed of a fuzzy future, all possibilities open.

On the bench, it was simply Daniel, the moon protecting him high overhead, a cool breeze lapping his cheeks, the ocean stretching his soul to infinity. It was well after midnight before he felt sober enough to drive back to the basement.

This afternoon, however, as William continued to hear Bertrand Russell's appeal to America's conscience, he was shaken to the core by the eminent Englishman's indictment. Russell was announcing his establishment of a tribunal to hear evidence of war crimes committed by the United States in Vietnam! At first, William could not believe that Johnson, Rusk and McNamara were being called "criminals". William tried to argue in his head with Russell's case and with his parallels to Nazi Germany, but he could not keep pace with the numerous and detailed allegations, let alone refute each one. He was stunned by the assertion that a ruling "elite" in the United States was bent not only on exploiting the world's resources, but also keeping millions of Americans in poverty.

Early on, he heard Russell say:

"Many of you may not be fully aware of the extent to which your

country is controlled by industrialists who depend for their power partly upon great economic holdings in all parts of the world."

And then:

"When we consider that the fantastic sums of money spent on armament are awarded in contracts to the industries on whose boards of directors sit the generals who demand the weapons, we can see that the military and large industry have formed an interlocking alliance for their own profit."

And then:

"The [American] poor carry the burden of taxation and the fighting of colonial and aggressive wars."

And finally:

"The battle-front for freedom is in Washington, in the struggle against the war criminals—Johnson, Rusk, McNamara—who have degraded the United States and its citizens. Indeed they have stolen the United States from its people and made the name of a great country stink in the nostrils of people the world over."

As his horse galloped across the meadow, Jeff's thigh muscles ached with his effort to squeeze its flanks and remain in the saddle. He tried to notice the familiar trees and banks of flowers, but his concentration was on staying upright.

At the beginning of the ride, as he had done many times before on this route, he had relaxed the reins to give the horse his head. Ever since Jeff and Sally had befriended each other in the fourth grade, this was the horse Jeff had chosen from his father's stable to ride over to her house. Although the horse was moving at the old speed, he was taking Jeff faster than he wanted to go today.

Jeff and Sally had both attended Shaw Elementary School and then Central High School in Austin, Minnesota. When Jeff had enrolled at Macalester College, Sally had followed a year later. At the end of his graduation ceremony, she had vowed not to date anyone else, and asked Jeff to agree to do the same. Sally had understood that they would wait for each other until she had graduated from Macalester. That fall Jeff had gone to New York.

Now, a year later, Sally was going to enter nursing school in St. Paul. She expected this July 4th holiday weekend to be the time when Jeff would ask her to marry him. After all, he could continue his graduate studies at the University of Minnesota, Sally reasoned.

The sun had barely risen above the power lines when Jeff reined in his horse next to hers, and bent toward Sally for their traditional morning kiss.

"Ah, Jeff, it's simply swell seeing you again," Sally began, and then talked about her family and what fun she had had with them all summer.

"You remember Samuel, my brother, of course you do. Well, he's playing clarinet in the upcoming Fourth of July parade. We've simply just got to watch him in his uniform. And do you know what? Right after graduation, Dad bought me a new car so I can drive to nursing school, and, would you believe, a new gasoline station opened around the corner. That's simply marvelous, isn't it?"

"Yes, yes, it is."

"And you remember Bert and Harry from your high school class? They moved away to Chicago. Well, would you believe, they came back. They missed Austin so much. And Meredith and Frida from my class were hired right out of college by Hormel Foods."

"Ah, Sally--"

"I am as sure as I'm talking to you that when I graduate nursing school, St. Olaf Hospital will hire me. I just know it. So we'll have two incomes and--"

"Sally, the sun's up. Why don't we ride a bit?"

"Sure. It's just that I haven't seen you since last Christmas."

"I know."

They headed toward Cedar River. Riding behind him, Sally could see that Jeff was unsure of himself in the saddle. She called out to slow the pace to a trot and she caught up with him. Jeff's unease was so unusual, she thought. He had always been an excellent horseman. But, of course, she rationalized, how could he have known a horse in New York City? It had been almost a year since he had ridden, Sally figured.

Jeff held the reins tightly now, shifting in the saddle, trying to find a position which did not pain him. He bent slightly toward Sally, straining to listen to her. He had always been charmed by her enthusiasm. The prospect of returning one day to Austin, its pace of life, and the good people he knew had never been far from his thoughts. But as they trotted along the edge of the river, Jeff held on to the saddle horn tightly, fearing he might fall into deep water. He thought back to the promise he had made to himself that morning, to tell Sally about New York. Hearing her call to him how much fun she was having, he decided he could wait a day.

> **Anishinaabe sits in her canoe. She knows the experience of being trapped. She looks at the water, remembering the beavers swimming here. She also remembers the military jail in which she stayed for months, and then escaped. Anishinaabe knows Jeff's soul as he tries to avoid the deep water.**

Two days later, Jeff still had not told Sally about New York—and Mildred. They spent the morning at the annual "Spam Town USA" Freedom Fest. Ever since they were kids, it had been their solemn pledge that one would never go on a ride without the other. On this Independence Day, however, Jeff became nauseous after the third ride, which was on the Ferris wheel. It must be the cotton candy, he convinced Sally. She assured him that she would not go on any other rides without him, but Jeff persuaded her to go ahead anyway. He watched as Sally and her younger brother enjoyed bumper cars, and then the rocket ride and merry-go-round, which had always been Sally's favorite ride with Jeff. He recovered slowly. In the back of his mind, he kept thinking that he was leaving the next day to hitchhike to California to meet with Southern Africa activists. He was anxious to get away. He sensed the West Coast would open a new phase in his life, one he was consciously deciding to write in his own style.

Finally, he was recovered enough to ask Sally if she wanted to play a few games with him at the arcade. That had never been her favorite portion of the Fourth's Festivities. She didn't enjoy the competitive aspect, winners and losers, but she agreed, wanting to be with him.

They played skeet ball, milk bottle knockdown, and high striker. The fun they had always enjoyed together, on the rides and at the arcade, vanished for Jeff. He wanted, however, to make it up to Sally. Picking up a rifle at another stand, he aimed very carefully. Again and again he hit targets, knocking them down. He was so pleased with himself that he could win a small teddy bear for her. Sweating now, only partially from the sun, he nervously smiled as Sally affectionately hugged the bear, instantly naming it, "Jeff".

Every Fourth of July they had gone together in the afternoon to the free ice cream social at one of the several local Lutheran churches. She had always chosen strawberry and he pistachio. It had always been a memorable and intimate time for them. Jeff would begin their anticipated ritual by giving Sally a spoonful of his pistachio. She would lick her lips in great delight after swallowing. She would then give him a spoonful of her strawberry, and he would repeat the lip-licking ritual. As they grew older, lip-licking became more and more erotic, heightened by their doing it in a church.

This afternoon, after they had been served their favorite ice creams, Jeff took Sally up to the choir loft where he knew they would be alone. He did not offer her, however, any ice cream on a spoon. He just sat next to her. He looked her way several times, but said nothing, wondering how to begin.

Maybe this was the moment, Sally hoped. How thoughtful and appropriate, she smiled inwardly, in this church they knew so well. Sally hugged her teddy, and waited patiently.

William turned the radio off. He went to the refrigerator, took out a bottle of beer, and removed the cap with some difficulty, his hand shaking as he brought the neck to his lips. He tried to steady himself by leaning against a nearby wall, but its support offered him no respite. He felt disoriented. If Russell's case were true, William asked himself, how can you negotiate with a military-industrial caste who continuously rules America regardless of who is elected President or serves in the Cabinet? How can you exert moral pressure against immoral criminals? What good is rallying constituents to write their Congressmen when the industrialists' lobbyists are writing the laws and regulations?

William had always counted on his ability to think two steps further ahead than any of his peers. He had already resigned as president of the Morningside Heights Student Committee to become an unpaid East Coast regional traveler for a coalition of anti-war organizations. He was on the rise. After being a regional organizer for an appropriate amount of time, he desired to move up again and assume a national role in what William figured was the most important issue of his day. For the first time, however, he was uncertain what to do next. And his uncertainty was refueled a few weeks later by two friends, one in Lexington and the other in London. The former, a student at the University of Kentucky, telephoned to say that students there had announced their support for Russell's International War Crimes Tribunal. The latter, a graduate of the London School of Economics, mailed William a copy of the July issue of the Clare Market Review *containing the text of Russell's "An Appeal to the American Conscience."*

William had always seen the arc of his life as gaining entrance to powerful circles by being invited as a contrarian to join their councils, proving how "democratic" they were. Now, his good friends, who previously worked within the system to change it, had become avid supporters of the unofficial equivalent of the Nuremberg trials. Moreover, his friends now desired to abolish the very system in which he felt destined to rise. The ground had not just shifted, it had parted beneath his feet. Not knowing where he stood, William kept hidden his sudden uncertainness, bordering on panic, about how to oppose the war and the industrialists who wanted it.

Ephraim deliberately chose the holiday weekend of July 4th to move out of his parents' apartment. Fearing his father's reaction, he had not informed them. He waited until they left for Saturday services.

He had only told his older brother of his plans. Ephraim hoped that Shalom would not only help him move, but also give him his blessing. Ephraim was shocked by Shalom's reaction.

"I'm not going to let you move to your new place, Ephraim." Misunderstanding him, Ephraim replied that he did not need his brother's help and would move himself. After all, his cramped room did not allow space for many things, so it would require only a few suitcases and boxes to pack. He would use his sleeping bag in his new apartment until he could afford a bed. Moving far to the North energized Ephraim, as if an ancient and recurring force was accelerating his life.

"No, no, Ephraim. What I mean is, I forbid you to move uptown," Shalom commanded. "Move a few blocks away, certainly, as I did, but stay in the neighborhood. If you move uptown, we'll never see you. You will be destroying the family. You will break our father's heart."

Munsee knows what it is to be forced out, to move to a strange land, without roots. He watches Ephraim, intently. Munsee senses his need to leave, but fears something inside Ephraim may become extinct.

Ephraim sat down in the nearest chair, stunned by his brother's truculence. Was not this the brother who had covered for him by saying to their father that he was working in Shalom's clothing store when he was actually attending Socialist meetings and demonstrations?

After barely graduating from the Little Red School House & Elisabeth Irwin High School in Greenwich Village, Ephraim had gone straight to work in his older brother's second-hand clothing store on Orchard Street. He had been glad for the job. The long hours had meant Ephraim could stay away from his father, whose demeanor always seemed to be questioning his son's religious beliefs every time they met. As a bonus, his brother would give him time off whenever he had asked to serve as a volunteer organizer for the Socialist Party.

"Destroying the family," Ephraim shot back in a mocking tone. "Don't make me laugh. You lied often to father to protect me."

"So, all this time you thought I was protecting you. No, no, little brother, I was protecting father. That's right. If he knew you were active in left-wing politics, like his murdered father, he would have had a stroke."

Ephraim had known of his grandfather, Sergei, only through family photos and his mother's stories. Ephraim had noticed that Sergei always stood in the photos, looking proud to have family members seated around him. During the October Revolution of 1917, Ephraim had been told that Sergei was in Kiev as a Menshevik and then as a member of the White Army. His grandfather had been on the wrong side of history, Ephraim had learned. It was said that his grandfather had to hide his Jewishness as much as possible due to the White Army's anti-Semitism, but that on several occasions he had stood up for himself and his religion. He had been killed during the Russian civil war.

Ephraim's mother once explained to him that her husband had fled to America a year after Sergei's death, vowing never to become involved in politics. Even when he had become a citizen, Joseph had never voted in an election due to a paranoid fear of reprisal.

So deep was Ephraim's fear of being discovered as a Socialist organizer by his father that he had a recurring nightmare in which his father discovered his secret, and, in a violent rage, cut off his head with a meat cleaver, and then threw him into the same grave as his grandfather.

When Ephraim was twelve, polio had caused his left leg, shorter than his right, to bend slightly at the knee, even when standing. His constant and deep-seated fear of his father seemed to travel throughout his body, exaggerating Ephraim's childhood deformity in other places. The fingers of his left hand were often bent at the second knuckle, as if he were forever holding a small, invisible ball in the palm of his hand. The best protection from his father's wrath, Ephraim calculated, was to keep on the move.

"Shalom, you are telling me you gave me a job in your store not for my sake, to help me out, but for father's?"

"How could I keep the peace in the family, Ephraim? How could I? I love you, and I also respect everything father has done for us. He left a tyranny to give us a future."

"You mean, Shalom, what he did *to* us!"

"I could not stop you from getting involved in your left-wing politics, much as I wanted to. In some ways, I admire you for it. But you do not understand. If you move uptown, I know you will never come back. A hole will be torn in the fabric of our family, and it will never be mended. You and I will go our separate ways, and we will not know each other, not speak the same language. Maybe you can not see this, Ephraim, but I am older, I know, I *plead* with you, find a place in our neighborhood, and remain in our family. Maybe you will even come to synagogue occasionally?"

Ephraim had never attended services at Beth Hamedrash Hagadol, even for the High Holy Days. This synagogue was central, however, to his father's Russian Jewish orthodoxy, which ranked religion first in his life. Although the synagogue had been founded by Eastern European Jews, their orthodoxy and his father's matched well. Joseph had often walked the five blocks to Norfolk Street several times a week. Even on Sunday afternoons, he had been one of the first to arrive for Rabbi Ephraim Oshry's popular lectures. Joseph had admired the Rabbi's courage and endurance during the Holocaust when he held services in secret and helped prepare *matzos* for Passover, risking his life to do so. Out of respect, Joseph had named his second son after the Rabbi.

Ephraim tried to be as different from his father as he could, in beliefs, dress, avocations, even food whenever he did not eat at home. He was now away from the family apartment most of the time, and even when he was inside the apartment, he avoided his father by staying in his room. And yet, incessantly trying to evade his father while still bedding down in his father's house only increased his desire to have a place of his own. After all, Ephraim had seen his older brother, Shalom, move into his own apartment around the corner on Essex Street a few years before. He liked his brother even though he kept kosher and went to the synagogue almost as often as their father. Shalom had been named in memory of the Rabbi who not only first welcomed Joseph to Beth Hamedrash Hagadol, but also served as kosher supervisor over butcher shops.

Ephraim has also been effected by the Retreat. He had met so many new people and engaged in so many conversations with secular Jews, lapsed Catholics, religious Protestants, practicing Buddhists, and devout atheists. Although he doggedly and aggressively defended his socialist ideology, even to the point of his being described by some as headstrong and haughty, Ephraim felt bathed by their outpouring of energy and laughter and responsiveness. Also during the Conference, after several encounters, Ephraim finally realized that a *goy*, Patricia, would sit deliberately next to him at every meal, seeking him out not so much to change his mind about the role of the proletarian masses, but asking him questions about what he liked and his plans for the future. He surprised himself by loving the attention. Ephraim realized he enjoyed the absence of the weight of his heritage when they were together.

Choosing an apartment on the Upper West Side meant that Ephraim was joining many second generation Jews who had also moved out of the Lower East Side, trying to distance themselves physically and emotionally from their parents' Orthodox culture and religious rituals—and their poverty. Ephraim had witnessed his father keep the kosher butcher shop open longer and longer hours for fewer and fewer customers. While he admired his father for bringing meat to a few elderly women trapped in their tenement apartments by poor health, and charging them nothing, he also despised his father's tyrannical rule over his own family. Stroessner in Paraguay or Papa

Doc in Haiti certainly had nothing over his father, Ephraim was certain, as far as controlling his family through fear.

Ephraim knew the front of his father's hand on his cheek as a child, and the leather strap on his buttocks as a teen-ager. How could a man so generous with virtual strangers be so cruel to him?

His mother never challenged her husband's authority. She was thankful to him that he had given her two sons because, when Joseph had married at forty, he told her he did not want to have any children.

"I am moving out today, Shalom. And that is final."

Independence was being celebrated all over the country this Fourth of July. Beneath the traditional arc of pyrotechnic displays in the sky were the stirrings of another Revolution, this time against the modern representatives of Kingly authority.

In four contrasting sections of America, Christie, Daniel, Jeff, and Ephraim watched fireworks this Monday evening as they had since childhood, but they pondered other things.

Daniel in suburban Long Island stood alone on a corner across the street from the entrance to the local Country Club, wondering whom he could organize to protest the Club's exclusion of Blacks from membership. Jeff stood alone on the carnival grounds in the rural Midwest, wondering if the local Hormel Foods executives controlled his town in the same way as Charles Engelhard controlled company towns in South Africa. Christie stood alone on the commons of Hopewell Borough, wondering how she would go about researching the interrelationships among corporate and political centers of power. Ephraim stood alone in New York City's Battery Park as the Macy's pyrotechnics in the night sky awed the crowds below, wondering how he could awaken the masses to the bread-and-circus diversions staged by the powerful.

It was dawning on each of the four, and thousands more, that they desired separation for themselves from the authorities they had known, and freedom for others from the authorities that oppressed them. Flight from the familiar.

Standing separately this night, the four would become interconnected by threads they were just beginning to weave, each in their own style. They could not know how strong the threads would become. But they knew that History would no longer be written by their parents, or by the authority figures their parents honored. Now, these four, and thousands more, would pick up pens and start to write their *own* history by *making* their own history, their first collective steps on a path toward radicalization.

At this moment, on this Fourth of July evening, their first page contained only a few, brief, scribbled notes.

Independence would come with costs. It shredded time-honored familial and social sinews. It turned worlds upside down, all guideposts lying prostrate, silent on the ground. Would the familiar points of the compass, now being rendered pointless, be replaced? And by what?

History waited expectantly for an answer.

CHAPTER 7 – MOVEMENT (EARLY FALL 1966)

Where Have All The Flowers Gone?, first three verses written in 1955 and recorded in 1960 by Pete Seeger, with two verses added by Joe Hickerson in 1960.

Ain't Gonna Let Nobody Turn Me Round, adaptation of a traditional song by members of the Albany Movement.

"Did I wake you?" Daniel asked on the phone.

"Ah, no, I'm still up. Who is this?" Greg asked.

"It's Daniel. From the New York group."

"You're still coming, aren't you?"

"Yes, yes. It's just that we went to borrow a car, and it had a flat tire. I'm afraid it's too late to find a garage to plug it."

"Well, look, we don't start until 12 noon tomorrow anyway," Greg said hopefully. "And Baltimore is what, four hours from New York, so maybe you'll make it on time."

"I hope so, but, look, start without us, if we're late, OK?"

"Yeah, OK. Good luck in getting the tire plugged."

"Thanks."

Greg put the receiver down, and returned to his tiny work area in the living room of his apartment. He stared at the mimeograph machine, which was poised for renewed action on the card table. Just prior to the phone call, his ink-stained fingers had again adjusted the stencil against the drum, eliminating, he hoped, every small wrinkle. Now anticipating that the first page of the first issue of his first newsletter might finally look its best, Greg once again cranked the mimeograph's handle. As he did so, he uttered a few encouraging, though blasphemous words at the machine. A roller squeezed a sheet of paper against the stencil as the ink-filled drum turned. Ink was pushed through the stencil, onto the first page, which was deposited in the tray. Greg looked at the first page as if it were a newborn baby. He waited a moment. He cranked the handle again, completing another 360-degree rotation. Out came another copy of page one. He waited again, for the ink to dry.

His mailing list numbered only a few dozen, so he figured it would not take long to hand write the names and addresses on the outside of the newsletter, fold them in half and staple them shut. It was Wednesday evening, two days after Labor Day. He aimed to finish the print run and addressing before the groups arrived late the next morning.

Choosing to print on both sides of the page to save not only paper but also postage resulted in the ink on one side bleeding slightly through to the other side. Fortunately, it left only a faint shadow of itself. Toward the end of the press run, the middle of the letters "b" and "d" in some words wore away. The ink pushing through these mutated letters left solid black spots on several pages. Greg cursed the spots, but was too exhausted even to think about cutting a replacement stencil.

The five stencils Greg had cut earlier today on his Remington typewriter were a chore. His hunt-and-peck typing method, if it could be described by such a lofty term, had resulted in typos he painstakingly fixed with fluid dabbed onto the stencil at the point of the incorrect letter. The fluid had filled in the cuts made by the typewriter key. After the fluid had dried each time, he typed the correct letter onto the congealed fluid. It had taken Greg five hours to complete the five stencils, preceded yesterday by ten hours of research and an hour drafting the text. Thirty minutes were added to the process today because Greg had had to call around to friends to find one with a bottle of Liquid Paper, after he had forgotten to replace the cap on his own bottle, resulting in the liquid inside partially solidifying. Luckily the friend lived close by.

To prepare for the research/action meeting, which would involve twenty-three people, Greg had approached a Unitarian-Universalist church to secure a place. He had also arranged for friends in Baltimore, nine of whom were attending the meeting, to provide sleeping bag space in their apartments or dormitories for the out-of-towners. Every participant would chip in for pizza and sodas for lunch and dinner, and eat breakfast the next morning at their hosts' apartments. The church had agreed to supply coffee, lots of it, throughout the two days.

After only a few hours' sleep, but just in time to walk over to the church, Greg finished stapling the last one of the batch of newsletters he wanted to distribute to the participants. He almost forgot to take his extensive notes on Thomas Steele Nichols, former president of the Mathieson Chemical Corporation and a Johns Hopkins University trustee.

After walking the twenty-four blocks from North Calvert Street down St. Paul, Greg turned right onto West Franklin, and entered the First Unitarian Church of Baltimore. A few of the local participants were chugging their first cups of coffee. The activists from Philadelphia, Minneapolis, and Washington, D.C. had phoned Greg before leaving their respective cities, saying they expected to arrive by 11:30am or soon thereafter. Just before the pizzas were ordered to be delivered for lunch, the New York contingent arrived, the plugged tire holding for the entire trip.

Over lunch, Greg and Christie sat next to each other.

"Of course I do," Christie responded to Greg's question whether she had remembered him from the Wappinger Retreat.

"How is your friend, Alice?" Greg asked.

"Just fine. Of course, now I remember how you know Alice. You told me at the retreat you had participated in the Mississippi Summer Freedom Project and then I told you about Alice. She's raising money now at Oberlin to support Cesar Chavez."

Ephraim, sitting across the table and reaching for another slice of pizza, interrupted.

"You're talking about Alice? Remember, Christie, I told you I knew her cousin who had shopped at my brother's clothing store on Orchard Street. And through that cousin, I met Alice at a Socialist Party rally. I'm glad to hear she's helping farm workers to form a union."

"I saw Alice just this past Fourth of July," Christie remarked. "She didn't tell me she was a Socialist!"

"No, Christie, she's not," Ephraim responded gently. "She's not into ideology, but she does support the farm workers against the growers, and that's fine with me."

Multiple fast-forming personal inter-connections among activists were solidifying in order to learn about, track, and confront the personal and professional inter-connections formed generations ago among the wealthy and powerful.

"Has everyone had their fill of pizza?" Greg stood and asked. "And remember, we're grateful to the Unitarians for all this coffee. We've got a lot to accomplish, and little time to do it.

"You'll all remember, when I sent out the letter inviting you to this research/action meeting, that the idea came from a chance encounter I had with Daniel after our workshop on 'The University, Defense Contracts and The Draft,' at the Wappinger retreat.

"In our guts, we knew we needed to paint a bigger picture of the establishment's centers of power and influence. So, a few of us decided on three major areas of research: Olin Mathieson Chemical Corporation; Johns Hopkins University; Baltimore. Within those three major areas, as you know, then seven of you and me were assigned major sub-topics to research over this past summer. For example, under Johns Hopkins University, there's its president, Milton Eisenhower, and its Applied Physics Laboratory with its DoD contracts and its Washington Center for Foreign Policy Research. For another example, under Olin Mathieson Corporation, there's the Badger Army Ammunition Plant. We also decided to look carefully at Baltimore's new Inner Harbor project and its connections with James Rouse, a developer who served on an important housing committee appointed by Dwight Eisenhower.

"Now, all of us are here today not only to discuss the results of the research, but also to agree on several direct actions to expose and confront these interconnected center of power, one of which we'll carry out this Sunday."

The twenty-three activists sitting around long tables cobbled together were part of a movement engaged in tedious, old-fashioned research. These "radical researchers" had ferreted out primary sources, clipped articles from domestic and international newspapers, stuffed three-cut manila folders with documents and xeroxes of documents and 3"x5" index cards baring every relevant and possibly relevant fact, cross-referenced wherever possible. Discovering the utility of the "Clip It" gadget, some individuals with a few comrades had started clipping services, xeroxing page after page of neatly cutout articles, organized by date and sometimes by subject, distributing the results to a growing number of other individuals and organizations, saving the latter much time and, importantly, subscription money.

Greg had already thought of a practical way how twenty-three people, using their academic skills and insights to unearth reams of connective tissue within the ruling body politic, could exchange, discuss, clarify, and then agree on plans of attack, all in one and one-half days' time.

Large, white cardboard, poster-sized sheets of paper were spread on several long, rectangular tables arranged side-by-side-by-side. At the top of each sheet, Greg had hand-printed the title of a major research area, for example, "Olin Mathieson" on three sheets and "Johns Hopkins University" on three more. Greg also wrote the date on each sheet: Thursday, September 8, 1966. Each researcher then wrote his or her sub-topics on sheets below the appropriate area, in outline form. Having completed this exercise, the sheets read:

A. Olin Mathieson Chemical Corporation

    1. John M. Olin, honorary chairman and director
    2. Thomas Steele Nichols, chairman, executive committee
    3. E.R. Squibb & Sons, subsidiary in South Africa
    4. Badger Army Ammunition Plant, Baraboo, Wisconsin
    5. Winchester Division

B. Johns Hopkins University (Baltimore)

    1. Applied Physics Laboratory
        a. Terrier, Tartar and Talos missiles (Navy contract)
        b. Oscar (Navy Navigation Satellite) satellite contract, locating aircraft carriers in the Gulf of Tonkin

   c. Board of Visitors: Admiral John Sides (Ret.), Vice President, Lockheed Aircraft Corp.

2. Institute for Cooperative Research
  a. Biological warfare study of effects of associated diseases (Department of Defense contract)

3. Milton S. Eisenhower, university president
  a. National Brotherhood Award
  b. Board of Visitors, U.S. Naval Academy
  c. Latin America
   1) President Dwight Eisenhower's personal representative; special ambassador
   2) Member, U.S. Latin American Affairs Committee
   3) Argentina
  d. Director, War Relocation Authority (WW II)

4. Johns Hopkins University's School of Advanced International Studies
  a. Washington Center for Foreign Policy Research
   1) Contract with US Air Force to study future military alliances in the Pacific
   2) Roger Hilsman, Research Associate, and former Assistant Secretary of State for Far Eastern Affairs
    a) Assistant Chief, Far East Intelligence Operations, Office of Strategic Services (OSS), forerunner to CIA
   3) Professor of Government, Columbia University

5. University Trustees
  a. John M. Olin
   1) Joined his father's firm, Equitable Powder Manufacturing Company, renamed the Western Cartridge Company; then became   president and director,

Olin Industries (the successor corporation)
    b. Thomas Steele Nichols
        1) Former president, Mathieson Chemical Corporation, president and chairman of the board, Olin Mathieson Chemical Corporation
        2) Donor, private residence for the president, Johns Hopkins University
        3) Member and benefactor, Rognel Heights Methodist Church
        4) Pimlico and Bowie racetracks
    c. Benjamin Griswold III (stepped down as Trustee last year)
        1) Director, Olin Mathieson Chemical Corporation
        2) Director, Rouse Company

C. Baltimore

    1. Inner Harbor
        a. James W. Rouse, President, Rouse Co.
            1) Member, President Eisenhower's Advisory Committee on Housing Program and Policies, chairman, subcommittee on rehabilitation, redevelopment and conservation
            2) Founder and member, executive committee, Greater Baltimore Committee
            3) Influential in developing national urban renewal program

    2. Thomas Steele Nichols
        a. Director, Maryland National Bank, Bigelow-Sanford Carpet Company, Fruehauf Trailer Company, Western Maryland Railroad
        b. Member, (W. Averell) Harriman Mission to London
    3. Benjamin Griswold III
        a. Partner, director, Alex. Brown & Sons, first

investment bank in the US, founded by his grandfather, Alexander Brown.
1) Brown Brothers Harriman & Co., another investment bank, was formed when Brown Brothers, which can trace its roots directly back to Alexander Brown, merged with Harriman Brothers and Company.
b. Director, Central Savings Bank, Fidelity and Deposit Company of Maryland, Maryland Life Insurance Company

4. Milton Eisenhower
a. Director, Commercial Credit Corporation

Greg then took a red magic marker and circled key words, all of which related to the "military," wherever they appeared on any of the sheets. Similarly, he took a blue marker and circled words related to "university", a yellow marker for "South Africa," a green marker for the names of multinational "corporations," a purple marker for the names of "individuals" who served on multiple boards of directors, and an orange marker for references to Baltimore's "inner city" programs and projects. Finally, he took a pencil and carefully drew arrows between interlocking entities, for example, "Milton Eisenhower", "US Naval Academy Board of Visitors", and the "Navy Navigation Satellite" contract with "Johns Hopkins University". And "John M. Olin", "Winchester Division" of Olin Mathieson Corporation, "Johns Hopkins University", and the "Badger Army Ammunition Plant". As the meeting proceeded, many more topics (and bullet points under them) would be added.

Myla was first up.

"Badger Army Ammunition Plant was the largest ammunitions manufacturing plant in the world when it was built during World War II. It is located 42 miles north-north-west of Madison, Wisconsin. It's named for one of Wisconsin's nicknames—the badger state. Although the plant has been owned by the US government, its prime contract operator since 1951 is the Olin Mathieson Corporation. I understand another researcher will present Olin's long history as a gun and ammo manufacturer, so I'll just say here that it was a natural fit for the Truman Administration to pick Olin to

115

manage Badger. I have yet to find if Clark Clifford, first as a Truman Administration naval advisor and then as Truman's White House Counsel, had any role in selecting Olin. All three, Truman, Clifford and Olin, have Missouri in common, but I'll have to keep digging. In any event, in January of this year, Olin started preparations at the Badger Plant to manufacture ball powder, which is used in the Army's M-16 rifles for fighting in Vietnam."

Myla currently lived in Minneapolis, and had been raised in a Quaker family. While she no longer attended the weekly Meetings, she still identified herself as a pacifist.

Myla then wrote down the bullet points in her presentation on several posters under the topics: "Olin Mathieson", "US military", "Vietnam," "Madison, Wisconsin."

"Thomas Steele Nichols," Greg began, "was made president of the Mathieson Chemical Corporation in 1948. Nichols and John M. Olin, son of the founder of the Equitable Powder Company, which had grown into Olin Industries, became hunting and fishing buddies. Both men also loved thoroughbred horses, raising and racing them. By 1954, John Olin had become president of Olin Industries. After some initial doubt and opposition, both men decided to merge their two companies, creating the Olin Mathieson Chemical Corporation. Their combined companies had 35,000 employees, 46 domestic and foreign plants, making it the 5th largest US chemical company with corporate headquarters moving to New York City.

"Now, as we have discovered, finding out the private clubs these powerful men join can be one of the keys to unlocking their public relationships. Nichols and Olin have been members of the Metropolitan in Washington, D.C., Fifth Avenue in New York, The Links, Brook, Maidstone in Easthampton on Long Island, and National Golf Links of America next door in Southampton on Long Island."

Greg then added many bullet points under various topics, including the men's names under "Johns Hopkins University," as both were current trustees.

"Nichols," Greg continued, "lives near Baltimore and has deep connections with this area. For example, he donated a substantial sum in 1956 to construct a new private residence on the central campus of Johns Hopkins University, presumably to help persuade Milton Eisenhower, whose brother, Dwight, was President of the United States at the time, to serve as

University president. Nichols was also especially generous when it came to his late mother and her family, the Merediths. For example, he had constructed a seventeen-foot cross at Rognel Heights Methodist church in Baltimore as a memorial. It consisted, in part, of stones from all states, three federal territories, six continents and various Holy Land sites, all for the commemoration of Methodism and Christian brotherhood."

Greg then added more topics and bullet points, including Bowie and Pimlico racetracks, to the sheets.

"We're going to need more tables and blank poster paper for all these interconnecting relationships!" Daniel observed.

"Don't worry," Greg responded, "we've got back-up. Jeff, you're next."

"I'm going to tell you about John Olin and his family's history, but I also want you to keep in mind that Olin Mathieson owns E.R. Squibb & Sons, a pharmaceutical company, which has a subsidiary in South Africa.

"After graduating from Cornell University, Olin came to work immediately at his father's Western Cartridge Company. During World War I, Olin's father made a fortune. Then his father acquired his rival, the Winchester Repeating Arms Company, in 1931, and the son was named head of the new Winchester Division. You might know that Winchester's motto is 'The Gun That Won the West.' During World War II, Winchester, still headed by John Olin until 1944, made another fortune. The Olins became one of the wealthiest families in America.

"John Olin is today the honorary chairman and director of the company which bears his family's name. His brother, Spencer, was also a director. Spencer was very active at the highest levels of the Republican Party, as its national finance chairman during the last two years of the Eisenhower Administration, and the National Republican Committee's treasurer during the first two years of the Kennedy Administration.

"John Olin also owns the Nilo Plantation, which is approximately 10,000 acres immediately south of Albany, Georgia. 'Nilo' is 'Olin' spelled backwards."

Jeff added more topics and bullet points to the sheets.

Matthew from New York City was up next. He was fast becoming national authority on the many Department of Defense contracts currently held by universities across the country, and to the extent to which all parties wanted to keep these DoD contracts either secret or at least below the radar.

"Let me give you some background first," Matthew began. "Johns Hopkins' Applied Physics Laboratory, or APL, was founded in 1942 to develop a fuse, which could detonate a warhead near its target. The Lab was first located in a rented garage with its 'used car' sign left in place as camouflage. Currently, APL has a contract with the Naval Ordnance Systems Command to research, develop, test and evaluate surface missile systems, ballistic missile systems, and propulsion systems. The Applied Physics Lab is now in Howard County, Maryland, with approximately 2,500 employees.

"It has worked on the development of a series of surface-to-air missiles. The missiles are nicknamed the 'Three-Ts'. Developed in turn, the Terrier, Tartar, and Talos missiles are grouped by the Navy under the name, 'Bumblebee Project.' These missiles were among the earliest used on Navy vessels, and are seeing action in Vietnam.

"Serving on APL's Board of Visitors has been Admiral John Sides (Ret.), Vice President, Lockheed Aircraft Company, who had served as the commander-in-chief of the United States Pacific Fleet until his retirement a few years before. Sides is known as the 'father' of the guided missile program. Ten years before, Lockheed had begun development of Polaris, a submarine launched ballistic missile. A year before, Sides had been appointed by Lyndon Johnson to the President's Foreign Intelligence Advisory Board which had been created by former President Dwight Eisenhower. The Advisory Board had been chaired since 1963 by Clark Clifford, the highly influential Washington lawyer mentioned earlier by Myla. By the way, Clifford was also influential with John Kennedy who had originally appointed him to the Advisory Committee in 1961.

"The Laboratory was also instrumental in developing over 30 satellites circling the globe, the first one reaching orbit in 1960. Of particular importance to Navy pilots on bombing raids over North Vietnam today is a satellite nicknamed 'Oscar,' which is used to locate aircraft carriers.

"In the early 1950s, the liaison between Johns Hopkins University and APL was D. Luke Johnson, chairman of the Board, Maryland National Bank. Luke Johnson was also a university vice-president and trustee as well as APL's business director."

Matthew added his many topics and bullet points to the sheets, squeezing them in wherever he could.

Another researcher, Henry, lived in Washington, D.C. Having served as a Congressional intern, he had become disillusioned with Congress' failure to question President Johnson's case for the Gulf of Tonkin resolution, whose passage became the Administration's green light to send combat troops to Vietnam. Henry focused on the Washington Center for Foreign Policy Research, created in 1957 by the Johns Hopkins University's School of Advanced International Studies.

"The Washington Center is a collection of scholars, former government officials, business executives, journalists, diplomats, politicians who exchange ideas on important international issues of the day. Roger Hilsman, Jr., is currently a research associate, having been with the Center since 1957. Hilsman had first been the director of the Bureau of Intelligence and Research at the State Department, and then Assistant Secretary of State for Far Eastern Affairs in the Kennedy Administration. The record shows, I believe, that Hilsman had been an influential player in the years 1961 through 1963 in constructing policy, which led to the Vietnam War. Then Hilsman had butted heads with the Pentagon by advocating that a counter-insurgency strategy, or 'winning the hearts and minds' of the local populations in Vietnam, could be successful rather than a traditional military strategy."

More topics and bullet points were entered on the sheets by Henry.

Clarence, now living in Center City Philadelphia, had grown up in a wealthy Bucks County suburban town where he had joined the local chapter of the Young Republicans. After Barry Goldwater had been nominated as his party's candidate in the 1964 Presidential election, Clarence's political views changed. His presentation focused on Milton Eisenhower, younger brother of the President.

"Milton Eisenhower is the current president of Johns Hopkins University. The Board appointed him president in 1956, so he obviously had direct access to the highest American governmental circles during his older brother's second term as President, beginning ten years ago. As a director of the Commercial Credit Corporation, which was a pioneer in consumer finance, Eisenhower has been at the center of this important growth industry. Milton has also been mentioned in earlier presentations, and will be again. I want to tell you about a little known fact. Milton was appointed by FDR as the first director of the War Relocation Authority, charged with creating internment camps for Americans of Japanese, German and Italian descent soon after US entry into World War II. Although Eisenhower was director for only a few months, he did narrate a 1942 film, *Japanese Relocation*, which sought to explain the need for the camps. In that film, Eisenhower stated: 'Neither the Army nor the War Relocation Authority relished the idea of taking men, women, and children from their homes, their shops, and their farms. So the military and civilian agencies alike determined to do the job as a democracy should: with real consideration for the people involved."

Clarence added more topics and bullet points.

Christie focused on Milton Eisenhower's international role as she provided an overview of United States investment in Latin America.

"Milton Eisenhower served as the President's personal representative and special ambassador to Latin America during his brother's eight years in office, the last four years of which, as Clarence said, Eisenhower was Johns Hopkins University's president. He was also a member of the U.S. Latin American Affairs Committee.

"Let me give you a little background on the evolving US investment strategy in Latin America. It began as a purely "colonial" extraction of raw materials and produce from Latin America for American consumption, such as copper, tin, bananas, oil, and sugar. Then the strategy became the development of internal Latin American markets to absorb the increasing exports of American manufactured goods for Latin American consumers. Agrarian reform, diversification, and common markets were the concepts promoted by David Rockefeller, head of the Chase Manhattan Bank, for example, in an article I read in *Foreign Affairs* a few months ago. To return to Milton Eisenhower, he was also a successful fundraiser for Johns Hopkins, especially from the Rockefeller and Ford Foundations."

Additional topics and bullet points were entered by Christie.

"We have one last major area, dear to my heart," Greg said. "It's about my hometown. After its presentation, we'll take a break."

"There is a gigantic urban renewal project called the Inner Harbor, which is planned for Baltimore," Ephraim began. "The project will clear a 110-acre site of everything on it except for a few landmark companies like the McCormick Spice Company and a Lutheran church. A developer, the Rouse

Company, has an interest in developing a section of the Inner Harbor. One of Rouse's directors, Benjamin Griswold III, is also a Johns Hopkins University trustee and an Olin Mathieson director, as well as director of several banks and an insurance company. James Rouse, the founder and president of the Rouse Company, had been a leading spokesman for the Baltimore Plan, aimed at removing large slum areas in East Baltimore in the early 1950s. Rouse was then appointed a member of President Eisenhower's Advisory Committee on Housing, chairing its subcommittee on rehabilitation, redevelopment and conservation. He was a principal advocate of the then new national urban renewal program."

Daniel almost jumped out of his chair. "My god, so that's where it all began, that's where the idea came from which leveled part of Babylon's black neighborhoods. Damn it. We've got to do something!"

"We'll get to that, Daniel, don't worry," Greg said, "but first, as Ephraim puts his topics and bullet points on the sheets, I think we all need a stretch break, say ten minutes."

When the meeting resumed thirty minutes later, Greg, with the help of everyone around the table, drew many more arrows between and among topics and bullet points on the various sheets. A single arrow meant that the person or entity at the arrow's beginning had influence on the person or entity at the arrow's tip. A double arrow, both parallel to each other but going in exactly opposite directions, meant that the persons or entities at both ends of the arrows had mutual influence on each other. The array of arrows vividly highlighted major strands of a gigantic and complex spider web stretching from Baltimore, Washington, D.C., and New York to Vietnam and places in between. The participants also knew, from research they had done on other universities, industries, and military contracts, that there were multiple spider webs which stretched across the United States to Latin America, Europe, Africa and Asia. The participants now coined the term, "the military-industrial-university complex," to describe these webs of interlocking centers of power, deliberately and ironically echoing Dwight Eisenhower's famous dire warning about the military-industrial complex in his presidential farewell speech.

Once all the arrows, first drawn with pencil, and then confirmed by discussion, were blackened by magic marker, the group decided on three direct actions to be discussed in their late morning session the next day. The largest action would be in Baltimore on Sunday. A second action would be planned for Olin Mathieson's corporate headquarters in New York City, and headed up by Daniel. A third would be staged in East Alton, Illinois, where John Olin's father started the Equitable Powder Company, forerunner of Western Cartridge and Winchester, if willing activists could be found in the St. Louis area. The meeting broke for dinner.

The next morning, Friday, precise details of the Baltimore demonstration were worked out to the last second, involving three scout cars on Saturday and eleven picketers on Sunday, all designed to confront Thomas Steele Nichols.

There were only two lights, a floor lamp in the far corner and a table lamp just inside the door, illuminating the large living room of the old, Victorian house a few blocks from Johns Hopkins University's administration building. This house, with rooms added over the years at slight angles to each other, so that no one floor exactly met another without a riser or steps, was fun central. News of the Thursday night party had spread far and wide throughout Baltimore's growing, but still relatively small, radical community. The out-of-towners were also eager to attend.

Dancing spilled out of the living room and onto the front and side porches. No piece of furniture was immune from an accidental kick or shove, or spill from a drink as the partygoers in tightly packed rooms tried to avoid slamming into one another. In fact, not a few partygoers were pleased with themselves after completing a walk from one room to another with their glass still holding the same amount of liquid as when they had replenished it.

There were seven permanent residents in the house and, on any given evening, one or two transients in sleeping bags on the floor. One couple, three single women, and two single men, all sharing the rent equally, occupied the six bedrooms. Theirs did not constitute a commune, as most cooked their own meals or ate out, did their own laundry, and kept their own money. The seven understood themselves more as boarders, coming and going as they pleased, rather than as a quasi-family with defined obligations to one another. (Communal arrangements in large numbers, with agreed rules on equality, property, and shared chores, refined through residents' meetings, however, were on the horizon.) Their prime economic rule was that, if one of the renters were about to leave permanently, they would have to find their replacement so that the rent money could always be paid on time, thus avoiding an excuse for the landlord to toss them all out. The original seven named their home "The Queen's Palace" in honor of the long reign of Elizabeth I. They fancied the idea of its continuous occupancy by radicals for many decades to come.

Parties, whether impromptu or planned, were as much a part of the radicals' culture as had their parents' parties been for the post-World War II culture, but for far different reasons. Each generation had fun, but it could be said that the newest generation's parties were a deliberate rebellion against the rules and customs of their parents' parties.

In their parents' day, party games and favors had been on the menu as much as pigs-in-a-blanket and high balls. For example, a popular game had consisted of a ping-pong ball being passed from guest to guest by means of tucking a plate with curled edges under one's chin, balancing the ball on the plate while moving to the next guest, cautiously tipping the plate so that the ball would roll onto the adjacent plate also tucked under that guest's chin. Intimacy had not been the goal of such fun-filled activities. Even passing an orange, without a plate to support it, by tucking it under one's chin and tilting one's head sideways so that another guest could, with head tilted sideways in the opposite direction, grab it under his or her chin, had much more the flavor of fun and oddity than an attempt at sly sexual communications.

Men dressing as women, with full make-up, earrings, padded bras, skirts, and high heels (optional), and women dressing as men with long pants, dress shirts and ties, had never been intended to send any sort of signal about re-orienting gender preferences. Quite the contrary. "Turn-about" parties had been such fun precisely because each gender felt secure in its own identity, and could therefore vamp the opposite.

There had been a strict common factor on who was allowed to come to a Fifties party. It might be members of the "Friday Nighters", a small group of men who knew each other from work or were college chums, and their wives. Singles either had not been welcomed, or usually chose not to attend. The owner of the home where the party took place, always on either a Friday or Saturday night, had automatically been "the host," usually the wife, greeting guests at the door, taking their hats and coats in cold seasons, and offering them a drink either from a well-stocked bar (with a mirror behind to amplify the show of prosperity) manned by her husband or a punch bowl with cut glass cups grasped by an index finger through their circular handles. Virtually all the guests had arrived either at or soon after the announced starting time, normally 8pm.

Introductions had not been necessary as a rule, as the membership of the group rarely varied. The host would make sure the canapé plates remained well supplied, and, as glasses were emptied, had asked if the guests wanted their drinks refreshed. Later in the evening, there would be a customary signal from one of the guests (never the host)—a quick glance at the watch followed by, "Oh, I didn't realize how late it was getting"—to alert the others that it had been time to leave. Coats and hats had been retrieved by the host from either a bed or, if large enough, the hall closet, who then, arm-in-arm with her husband, waved good-bye at the front door as, herd-like, the guests walked to their cars.

After the hardscrabble years of the Great Depression and Second World War, the prosperity, which had reached its zenith at the end of the Fifties and early Sixties, and the implied societal rules about how that prosperity had been created and should be demonstrated, was precisely what was now being challenged at off-campus parties throughout America, like the one at The Queen's Palace.

Anyone hearing about the party at The Queen's Palace understood that it required *only* the hearing about it to attend. That was "invitation" enough. Not only activists, but any of their near or distant acquaintances were welcome. Arrival time was anytime during the evening, or occasionally early the next morning. Some knocked on the front door, waiting for it to be opened, but most, hearing the music inside or seeing others gathered outside, thought either was permission enough to open the door and walk in. On cold evenings, coats were left on the backs of chairs, piled into a corner, or laid on any available bed, by the participants themselves. There was no liquor bar. If a punch bowl were visible, it had been filled at the beginning by the residents, and supplemented throughout the night with whatever partygoers brought. Paper cups for an army sat upside down around the bowl. Nibbles, like potato chips and pretzels, might or, more often, might not be set out by the residents. The residents rarely considered it a party requirement to "feed" participants.

There were no parlor games, no attempts at feigned intimacy. Intimacy occurred naturally during the evening, sometimes openly, sometimes in a darkened hallway or by a tree outside. Later in the evening, sexual intercourse would happen for some, often between strangers. A Victorian house it may have been, but the mores and customs of that long ago era, propelled into the twentieth century by the public posturing of a hypocritical wealthy class and aped, without examination, by an aspiring middle class, were fast being trodden underfoot by the hip-swinging, arm-waving, head-bobbing dance gyrations of this newest generation, the very first to watch their contemporaries exhibit dance "moves" on television.

Those attending the party were hardly "guests," in any sense of the Fifties' word. There was no "host." In fact, most partygoers did not know who actually lived in the house. Even if a resident wanted to act as host, making sure everyone was well cared for, such an attempt was impossible, given random entrances and exits, sometimes multiple times by the same people throughout the evening and early morning.

Most couples, whether formed through marriage or just going together, entered the Queen's Palace side-by-side, but then throughout the evening normally danced with multiple "partners," if any pairing on the dance floor could be described with so formal a term. Some participants reclaimed the same space, either standing or sitting, after every dance or trip to the punch bowl, while others wandered from room to room. Many went upstairs, just to check it out, and found that one of the rooms had a sign posted on the door: "Do Not Enter." Women asked men to dance, men asked women to dance, individual women danced by themselves, as did individual men, women danced together, men danced with two or three women. The social order of the Fifties was being reconfigured. With all the movements, gyrations, twists and turns, the casual observer was hard-pressed to tell who was dancing with whom. Finally, it really did not matter. What mattered was the beat of the music, individualized movement of any kind, spastic or rhythmic, in the midst of all the other individualized movements occurring simultaneously. Rapid motion to a pounding beat caused a kind of blurred vision, which lessened distinction and differences among near-by, even near-distant, physical forms. What one was wearing, how one coiffed her or his hair, who was dancing with whom and how close they were dancing—all points of attention during their parents' parties—melted into one large collage whose pieces had indistinct outlines, no clear edges, no beginnings and no endings, only varied colors-in-motion. Even the "right steps" and "right body movements" learned from earlier television shows did not matter as the evening wore on. It mattered not how gracefully one moved. There was no hierarchy of dance performers as in their parents' day—some executing the perfect dip or others doing the tango as most watched. Movement, no matter how fluid or jerky, was all that mattered.

The teenage boy leading the teenage girl during the lindy hop on American Bandstand had yielded to the new times. Few men led; fewer women followed. Both genders had a new way of expressing themselves. There was no "dance floor" either, as dancing occurred, or not, anywhere the loud music could be heard. Boundaries were challenged, easily yielding to new configurations, or, more frequently, disappeared altogether. Differences vanished. No one felt a stranger.

Some participants brought their favorite "45s" and albums. They danced to "Summer in the City" by The Lovin' Spoonful and "You Can't Hurry Love" by The Supremes and some listened intently in order to understand the words of "Yellow Submarine" by The Beatles. Some sang out enthusiastically as Stevie Wonder's version of "Blowin' in the Wind" played. All lyrics, however, seemed so very less important to this newest generation than their parents', when phrasing was king. Tonight, at the Queen's Palace, the beat, full-throated volume, and brain-numbing arrangements governed.

On Saturday morning, September 10th, three cars departed from 2809 North Calvert Street and headed north, taking the first left onto East 29th Street. The first two cars then turned left onto St. Paul Street while the third car headed west onto Druid Park Lake Drive. Inside each of the three cars were scouting parties, timing the lengths of their planned routes to the minute, routes they would take again early the next morning to their assigned destinations.

The third car turned off Druid Park Lake Drive and onto Liberty Heights Avenue, which turned into West Liberty Road. The car pulled onto the

Baltimore Beltway north and then the Northwest Expressway to Owings Mills, Maryland. Inside the car, Daniel and Ephraim noticed how quickly neighborhoods changed in character as they crossed major boundaries, like interstates, rivers and railroad tracks.

"It's as if a master hand had drawn invisible lines, dictating who lived where," Daniel remarked to Ephraim.

Not knowing the Owings Mills geography, Jack, the driver, asked a local for the location of Rolling Ridge Farm, and then drove along a country road until he found a sign marking its entrance. It had taken exactly 35 minutes from North Calvert Street. They paused to talk about what to do next.

"I'm not sure we should just go down that long driveway into Nichols' estate," Daniel offered. "I can't even see his house from here."

"But how will we know what kind of car he drives, so we can spot him at the church tomorrow morning?" Ephraim asked.

"But the car is probably in his garage, so we wouldn't see it anyway," Jack countered.

"And it's equally true it just might be parked in plain sight in front of his mansion," Ephraim argued.

"Let's wait here, and maybe we'll catch sight of his car coming towards us on the driveway," Jack suggested, trying to resolve the dilemma. "I don't feel right going onto his property."

"How protected the wealthy are by the natural environment surrounding them," Ephraim opined, "as if distance from the main thorofare itself was all that was needed for their privacy and safety."

After another thirty minutes of Ephraim providing a diatribe on property rights interfering with human rights, the scouts, seeing no life along the driveway, decided to move on. From Rolling Ridge Farm, it took them 23 minutes to drive south on I-695 and then east on Baltimore National Pike, before finally turning left onto Walnut Avenue.

By knowing the driving time from North Calvert Street to Rolling Ridge Farm and then to the church, the scouts in the third car now determined how early they would need to leave North Calvert Street the next morning in order to be in time to follow Nichols' automobile from Rolling Ridge to the 11 o'clock church service. Any car that left the estate at about 10:30am and headed toward the church, they reasoned, would have to be carrying Nichols. Since no one had been able to find a recent photo of the man, the only way to identify him as he entered and left Rognel Heights Methodist Church was to follow his automobile, alert the other scouts by flashing their parking lights as they neared the church, to spot Nichols leaving his vehicle.

An hour earlier, after heading south on St. Paul Street, the first two cars had turned right onto West North Avenue, and then right onto West Franklin Street, and eventually right onto Walnut Avenue. It had only taken them fifteen minutes to go from city to suburb. The two cars then stopped at 810 Walnut Avenue, in front of the Methodist church, built in 1949, at the corner of Colborne.

"Will you look at *that*," Myla exclaimed. "It must be two stories high."

"Wow, you can see that cross from blocks away, I bet," Clarence asserted.

"It's just where we thought it would be, on the front lawn of the church," Greg reasoned. "Nichols' memorial to the Merediths. What an icon. We've got to do a drawing of it for our flyer."

"Good idea," Matthew confirmed. "Say, looks like the church is empty, so, while we're waiting for Daniel and the others to get here, let's leave our cars and investigate the neighborhood on foot."

"Ok," Greg responded. "Christie, Cynthia, and Jeff, why don't you head down Walnut. Clarence and Myla, you can head down Colborne. Matthew, Henry and I will go over a few blocks, and see what's there. Meet back here in about fifteen minutes."

When all had returned to the two cars, they decided on which was the most strategic location to intercept the highest number of parishioners walking to the church's front entrance after parking their cars.

When the third car finally arrived at the church, they all declared their reconnoitering a success, and quickly left so as not to draw any more attention to themselves in so quiet a neighborhood.

Back at the North Calvert Street residence, after downing pizza and cola, the eleven demonstrators debated whether or not to disrupt the church service itself. The eight had already agreed that, as parishioners arrived, they would walk in a circle with their placards on the sidewalk corner formed by Walnut and Colborne, so that most every parishioner would have to pass by or near the circle to enter the church. They reasoned that church officials would not ask the police to remove them, especially because they figured the sidewalks were probably public, not private, property. Some argued that the genocidal use of napalm in Vietnam, plus the implicit support of the South African government's oppressive policy of *apartheid* by an American corporation's presence in that country, justified a confrontation inside the church during what they felt was a hypocritical service anyway. Others argued that the confrontation itself would be so provocative that the focus on the war and racial divide would be lost, and only the disruptive action would be publicized and remembered. Eventually, one idea gained majority support. On a normally quiet Sunday morning, the unexpected presence of demonstrators in front of a suburban church was provocative enough, but would not overshadow the issues raised on the placards. It was also decided that the demonstrators would place leaflets describing Nichols' connections to Vietnam and South Africa under the windshield wipers of every parishioners' vehicle both before and during the service, so that they would each have a fuller explanation of the demonstrators' causes than the placards could present. It was further decided that Greg and Daniel would seek to engage Nichols in a conversation after the service as he walked back to his car.

The suggestion of sending out a press release in advance of the demonstration was quickly shot down. These activists did not trust the traditional media to stick to the embargo, figuring the press would alert the church and Nichols to the planned protest.

That afternoon, the placards were hand printed with lettering which read, "Nichols cares more for his horses than for the people of Vietnam and South Africa," and "Get Olin Mathieson's bullets out of Vietnam" and "Are Methodists War Mongers?" Instead of punching holes in the upper right and left hand corners of the placards to attach string and hang them around their necks, the researchers/demonstrators stapled them to thin sticks so that they could be held aloft and better read by parishioners and passers-by.

Also that afternoon and late into the evening, Greg typed, cranked and cursed, producing 175 flyers, printed front and back. A condensed version of the research about Olin Mathieson's Winchester Division ("The Gun That Won The West"), the Badger Army Ammunitions Plant and Vietnam appeared on one side, and E. R. Squibb's & Son's as well as major

American banks' support for South Africa and the effects of *apartheid* on the majority population, appeared on the other side.

The flyers were signed, "Baltimore Radical Research Action Project."

Precisely at 10:30am on Sunday, two cars carrying eight demonstrators parked near the corner of Walnut Avenue and Gelston Drive, two blocks south of Rognel Heights Methodist Church. A few demonstrators had to be awoken upon arrival, as they had slept only a few hours, preferring to party again. Carrying twenty flyers each, seven activists fanned out in the immediate neighborhood on pre-designated streets, placing flyers under the windshields of every car parked along any street, which could be taken to the church. The seven assumed that the parked cars closest to the church would be those of choir members who had arrived early to rehearse, and ushers putting the announcement sheets inside the church bulletins. One demonstrator surprised a few joggers taking a break in Gelston Park, giving them flyers.

Then the seven, including Greg, Myla and Clarence, gathered at the corner of Walnut and Colborne, where the church stood. They were joined by the eighth activist who handed them each a placard. The seven, in turn, gave Jeff their remaining flyers, and formed a circle, walking the corner silently. Jeff then eyed arriving parishioners as they walked toward the church. He was by now practiced in the etiquette of handing flyers to passers-by. Smiling at each one, he sought to make eye contact first. A jovial "good morning" followed. Then, taking one step toward his target, Jeff thrust out a hand holding a flyer, saying politely, "Please take one." Most did. Good manners provided Jeff at least this one advantage. Some, seeing the placards and either personally knowing, or knowing of, Thomas Steele Nichols, whom they greatly admired, refused to take the flyer. Nevertheless, during the service, every still vacant car windshield received its flyer.

Trailed by the third car, Nichols' Sedan De Ville pulled up to a small stretch of curbside marked with a yellow line in front of the church. Officials had long ago persuaded the city to leave this part of the frontage for handicap drop-offs and pick-ups, or limousine parking for weddings and funerals. The De Ville stopped and two men got out of the back seat. Nichols glanced down the sidewalk at the circle of demonstrators, but did not stop to read the placards as he walked calmly to the front steps of the church.

"Hey, guys, I didn't expect that," Daniel exclaimed excitedly, as Jack tried to find a curbside space to pull into.

"Me, neither," echoed Ephraim. "I thought the chauffeur would have gotten out and opened the door for Nichols."

"Now we won't be able to see either of those men's faces," lamented Daniel.

"You think that's a bodyguard with Nichols?" Jack asked.

"No, he's too well dressed for that," Ephraim replied.

"Hey, look, the De Ville's pulling around the corner. Let's see where it parks," Daniel suggested.

Julius leaned against the side of the De Ville, glad for the peace and quiet surrounding him on this clear, cool, crisp, September Sunday. Dressed in a black suit, black shoes, white shirt and silk black tie, Julius always chose to wear his chauffeur's cap both inside and outside the car. He was a proud man, proud of his eight years serving the Nichols' family. They had been generous to him: paying for a daughter's braces, giving him an unexpected, extra week of vacation, and picking up the tab for a family jaunt to Disney World. No matter what time of day or night, even when it meant giving up a half-day on his day off, Julius gladly served any family members' transportation needs. His loyalty was returned by the family in a way far more significant to Julius than monetary gifts. Respecting Julius, never once did a family member ask him to drive someone outside the family, like a friend or business associate. He knew of other chauffeurs who were expected to drive such "freebies", some of whom would abuse the man behind the wheel, thinking of him as just a driver rather than a member of a profession with a long, distinguished lineage. Julius had heard stories of how some "freebies" would disrespect the chauffeur by fornicating in the back seat of the limousine or cursing him when drunk. Julius' boss was a good and kind man, in his eyes.

It was decided by the three that Daniel would approach the chauffeur, pretending he was a college kid interested in earning some part-time money. Ephraim would accompany him, but let Daniel do all the talking. Daniel was thrilled to see that the chauffeur was an African-American. Surely, he would be sympathetic to their causes, and provide juicy details about his boss on which they could build future direct actions.

"How is it driving someone around? I mean, how are you treated?" Daniel asked after some pleasantries, and telling Julius about his feigned desire to be a part-time driver.

"Real fine. I have no complaints." Julius responded.

"No complaints? But aren't you at their beck-and-call twenty-four hours a day? How can you have any time for yourself, to be free from their control, and do what you want?"

"Oh, you don't understand. I like my job. They let me know in advance when I can take days off, especially when the boss is traveling."

"Sound like exploitation to me," Daniel stated rhetorically, thinking a more direct approach would entice Julius to spill some dirt.

"I don't know what you mean? Look here, the family treats me with respect, that's all I know. The boss is a good man."

"But your boss is a war monger. He makes ammunition so that black soldiers can kill brown peasants in Vietnam. He supports the exploitation of black South Africans."

"Look, I don't know who you are, and I don't care. You don't even know him, do you? You college kids are all alike. You think you know everything, but you don't. And if you want my opinion, I don't think you should think about becoming a chauffeur, either."

"Ok, OK, but here, you should read this. It'll help you to see your boss for what he really is," Daniel retorted as he handed Julius a flyer.

"Please, go back to your campus, son. This is not your world here."

Julius watched as Daniel and Ephraim joined the circle of demonstrators. He crumpled the flyer and, not wishing to litter, stuck it in his pocket. He had no intention of reading it, or showing it to Mr. Nichols.

Julius pulled around to the front of the church at precisely 12 noon. He waited. Inside, the old friend with whom Nichols had entered the church showed him the flyer, which had been given him by an attentive usher. Nichols read it rapidly, smiled broadly, and handed it back to his friend. He joked about being the center of so much attention. His friend laughed with him, patting him on the back as they both headed for the exit.

The pace of the two men down the church's front steps quickened as they saw Julius opening the back door of the De Ville. Nichols was annoyed by the prospect of having to walk through a knot of demonstrators to find safety inside his car, but showed no outward sign of agitation.

Not knowing which of the two men was his target, Daniel called out, "Mr. Nichols!" Nichols turned his head toward Daniel, slowing down a bit, which allowed Daniel to block his path. Nichols stopped, but the other man continued into the De Ville.

"We are part of the Baltimore Radical Research Action Project, Mr. Nichols. Why don't you close your Squibb subsidiary in South Africa?" Daniel almost shouted at him, surprised suddenly to be not only face-to-face, but almost nose-to-nose with "the enemy." As he sensed parishioners were also now standing near the demonstrators wondering what would happen next, Nichols decided to defend his company's record. After all, he knew had nothing to apologize for.

"Do you know how many scholarships we've provided to black South African students, so they could go on to university? And how many people who have jobs in our facility?"

"All to ease your conscience, no doubt, Mr. Nichols. The taxes Squibb pays to the South African government means more police to arrest and torture those scholarship students, doesn't it? How many of your employees have been detained due to the Pass Laws?"

"We are guests in South Africa, just like every other company. We cannot and do not get involved in politics. No company does."

"And yet, due to those Pass Laws, you condone the practice that no black employee can rise to a position higher than the lowest white employee? How naïve do you think we are? Your presence strengthens the economy, legitimates an economy based on *apartheid*."

"With all due respect, you and your friends do not understand that American companies have a moderating influence. If we pull out, there will be a blood bath in South Africa. Do you want *that* on your conscience?"

"How many Vietnamese peasants has your ammunition killed today, Mr. Nichols?"

Nichols had had enough. He looked at his watch, told Daniel he was late for an appointment, and would Daniel let him pass. Despite all his pent-up anger toward the enemy standing so close to him, the man whose name he had written on some of the placards now held aloft, Nichols' simple request to let him pass, politely delivered, disarmed Daniel. Daniel stepped aside. Nichols passed by. Daniel looked directly at Julius, as if to salvage some sign of support, possibly a slight nod of the chauffeur's head to acknowledge his boss might not be a good man, but Julius closed the back car door after Nichols entered, opened the front door, and glided into his seat without a sideward glance.

The other demonstrators, not letting the opportunity pass, thrust as many flyers into as many parishioners' hands as were in the immediate vicinity. A few parishioners crumpled them up, tossing them forcefully to the ground as if to bury them. Most folded the flyer neatly and stuck it in their pocket or purse to be disposed of later. Other parishioners had been impressed by the demonstrators' sincerity and seriousness, and saved the flyer, wanting to learn more about the man they had always assumed was good, kind, and generous.

The De Ville headed northwest, soon entering a scenic route inside Gwynns Falls/Leakin Park. Nichols relaxed in this bucolic atmosphere. He joked with the man sitting next to him, recalling the old days when nineteenth-century industrialists like Thomas Winans, then one of the wealthiest men in America, had their thousand-acre estates in Baltimore and summer homes in Newport, acreage and locations whose geography by themselves protected their privacy. Still, Nichols was pleased with himself, feeling his real audience, the parishioners near him, had been re-assured by his performance. The De Ville continued to speed along country roads, taking Thomas Nichols and his long-time friend and business partner, John Olin, to a private hunting lodge where they planned to shoot pheasants.

Three aging cars—one a Volkswagen beetle—headed east toward crowded downtown Baltimore. Excited and drained, the demonstrators bucked each other up with examples of the successes they had achieved.

"We passed out every one of those flyers, didn't we?" Clarence boasted.

"We sure did," Myla echoed. "And how about some of those neighbors, coming out to see what was going on. We even got them flyers."

"All that cranking sure didn't go to waste," Greg joked. "And what about some of the church goers, mostly women but some men, thanking us for being there."

"That was incredible," Cynthia said.

"Yeah, and those joggers in the park. They promised to read the flyers," Henry continued.

"And Daniel, you really went toe-to-toe with Nichols," Christie gloated. "You really nailed him!"

"Well, thanks, Christie, it really felt good."

It would no longer be their parents' history driving the future with new names maintaining old connections. It would not be religion's history with new creeds reformulating old doctrines. No longer would the analysis of a singular historian, pouring over original source materials to discern trends and motivations based on how the leading personalities of the day shaped events, result in accurate history. History itself would now be the residue of many poorly recorded bursts of energy and action. These eleven, joined by thousands more, would write a group history. True history would be written on the backs of napkins, in the margins of school notebooks, hinted at in the under linings of key passages in Camus, Sartre, *Siddhartha*, Nietzsche, Hegel, Emerson, Burke, Nabokov, Barth, Baldwin, Styron, scribbled notes on the backs of flyers, in countless unminuted—and poorly minuted—meetings, referenced, but not fully explained, in fewer and fewer personal letters. Even the Movement itself could not keep pace with recording, let alone understanding, the *political* history it was making.

It would not last long, this euphoric moment of a generation waking up, fomenting a direct, targeted, and sustained challenge to Authority in private and public arenas, creating its own, unique history through sheer energy and action.

It would not last long, but for the eleven returning to downtown Baltimore, it seemed as if their moment of triumph could and would be repeated again and again. So many targets to research, so many direct actions to take.

Joking around now inside their respective vehicles, the eleven felt they had all the time in the world to make their revolution.

CHAPTER 8 – PRESSURE (LATE FALL 1966)

Eleanor Rigby, written by John Lennon and Paul McCartney, performed by The Beatles, released August 6, 1966, both as a single with *Yellow Submarine* and on the album, *Revolver*.

Oh Freedom, first recorded as *Sweet Freedom* in 1931, recorded by Odetta on her "Odetta Sings Ballads and Blues" album (1956) as part of her medley, titled "Spiritual Trilogy.," Also covered by Joan Baez. Sung by members of the Student Non-violent Coordinating Committee.

> *Figure in penny loafers walks down an endless corridor. Looks down at books held by the left hand, pieces of paper held by the right hand. One after the other, passes classroom doors on the left and right. Many young people, talking to each other, not noticing the figure, pass in both directions. The figure stares at one piece of paper. How many college credits are typed on it? Uncertain how many. Can not see numbers clearly. Enough to graduate? Squints for long time at paper. Cannot see total number of credits needed to graduate. Not sure figure is even typed on the paper.*
> *Figure turns slightly to the right at a bend in another endless corridor. Looks at more books clutched in the left hand, more papers clutched in the right hand. Unable to figure out if German is required or not. Did I even take German? I can not remember. Is German required for one year, or two? Who do I ask? Where do I go?*
> *Figure's steps quicken. Books fall to the corridor floor as the left hand trembles. Eye-lid blinks rapidly. Unable to*

read the few papers remaining in the right hand. Fingers weaken. Which way to the registrar's office? Stands at the junction of two endless corridors. No one to ask.

A steel band tightens around the forehead, encircling the entire head. Figure cannot see who is twisting it. Feels increasing pain. Looks around, then whirls around to find the culprit. Sees no one, but itself in a reflection in a windowpane.

Walks through classroom door. No books in left hand. No papers in right hand. Is this my German class? Is a German class even on my schedule? No one in classroom. Wait for someone. Wait.

Figure looks through classroom windowpane. Sees procession. Everyone in cap-and-gown entering large field.

Do I have time to get my cap-and-gown? Did I order my cap-and-gown? Do I have enough credits to graduate? How many credits do I need to graduate? How many credits do I have? Is German a requirement? Did I take German? Do I have time to take German? Who do I ask? Where do I go?

Figure, standing, immobilized by ropes pulling equally on different parts of the body in four directions. North, East, West, South.

Figure dissolves.

Daniel exited his dorm room with books held tightly in his left hand, pressed against his hip. He walked a route he had before, but now was not certain if he were headed in the right direction for his eight o'clock morning class. He turned down corridors as if in a dream, passing by other students, some of whom he recognized, but certainly did not know in which of his courses they sat.

Traveling back from demonstrations, either on the subway when in the city or in someone else's car when out of town, then trying to keep awake while reading textbooks well past midnight, sitting in stiff library chairs until dawn more often dozing than writing a term paper, Daniel easily and often overcame any obligatory reflex to attend classes. In fact, so often did he miss class that most classmates could not recall his first name or even what he looked like. Trying to keep up, Daniel thought about approaching classmates to copy their notes, but often found no time to do so, much less decipher their handwriting.

Yesterday, he had persuaded himself to head to the Registrar's Office to ask about the relationship between attendance rate and graduation. He had walked passed the door, however, fearing that he would be exposed as a fraud, a student in name only.

As he sat down in the back row of his 8 o'clock class, he surmised there was no quiz or test this morning. Everyone seemed relaxed and chatty. He also noticed that no one was holding a term paper. Daniel slumped in his chair, feeling the familiar pang of hunger in his stomach. Even though it was part of his meal plan, he had long ago forsaken breakfast in the cafeteria to get an extra half-hour in bed. Sometimes he had been so tired at night after a long direct action strategy meeting that he did not bother to undress, except to remove his shoes.

Midway through the class, professor Rickard Schwinn commanded Daniel to stand up, asking him, as if he did not know, what Daniel's name was, sarcastically joking that he had never seen the student now standing before him.

"You *know* my name!" Daniel shot back, hands on hip.

"Yes, Daniel, I do. But when I take attendance for every class, I would like you to be present. Do you have a problem with that?"

Daniel had adopted an aggressive strategy of concealment whenever he did attend class. He had asked his professors pointedly challenging questions, as if the queries flowed from an extensive base of acquired knowledge, thereby hoping to avoid the professors' calling on him to answer a question about material he had not read. His increasing self-confidence in organizing street demonstrations had translated into an arrogance during verbal jousts with his professors, challenging them on their interpretations of presented facts, not on the facts themselves of which Daniel knew very little. He had honed a fiendish tactic, a kind of pact with his devil, which he prayed would see him through. On the one hand, Daniel had keenly sensed that his professors relished the intellectual combat. On the other hand, he had known he was just bluffing his way through these encounters, pretending he had lots of goodies to show his academic customers in the public part of his shop while he knew for sure he had very little on the shelves behind the curtain inside the private part of his shop. He had prayed he would not somehow slip up, and be the cause of his professors' shredding the curtain, revealing the near emptiness inside.

"When you teach something relevant," Daniel replied to Professor Schwinn, "let me know. I'll sit through your rotten class," and walked out.

It had been very different in high school. Daniel had been the model student: always on time for every class, straight home after soccer and basketball practice, homework assignments completed before watching "I Love Lucy" or "Dragnet." An unspoken hierarchy of authorities had been accepted by Daniel as the natural order of things. Parents, aunts and uncles, teachers, administrators, Little League and high school coaches, ministers: older people were respected, listened to, appreciated for whatever knowledge and guidance they bestowed. The unexamined natural order of things had never been challenged by questions, pecked at by doubt, or upended by comparison with alien systems. Every day of his ordered life in high school, Daniel easily accepted his place in it, pleased to be praised by those in authority.

His ordered life at home included agreeing with his father's request to go door-to-door with campaign flyers supporting Dwight Eisenhower's campaign for a second term. Being in the front row of a large crowd gathered along a main street in Garden City, Long Island, as the President, standing in a convertible, waved to his supporters was all Daniel needed to secure his loyalty. After all, his father was a Republican committeeman, and the Republicans seemed to do a good job running the county and the country.

It was two weeks after he had abruptly walked out of Professor Schwinn's Old Testament class that Daniel again took a seat in the back. He shifted in his chair as the professor strode back and forth in front of the classroom, as if king of his own domain. Then Daniel heard these words.

"Everyone, clear your desks. I am handing out the blue books. Then I will hand out the mid-term exam questions. Use pen only. You will have 40 minutes to complete the exam."

Why the hell, Daniel lamented, did I pick this morning to return? Suddenly nauseous, Daniel felt as if a bear trap had sprung around his foot as he was wandering aimlessly in a forest. Didn't the unseen hunter know that Daniel could not possibly be the right target? How could this professor have such control over his life, Daniel thought, and do so little to earn that status.

Not knowing about the mid-term, or even caring enough to track down a classmate who might have warned him, Daniel wondered if failing this exam would mean failing the course. He cared deeply about the Old Testament, believed it had great wisdom, but not this professor, who treated his students like children. He wanted to pound the desk, break the bones in his hand, anything to relieve the searing pain in his head.

Daniel glowered at Schwinn, walking up and down the aisles, distributing the exam questions, which Daniel knew would expose him as a fraud.

Conjurors, Daniel now called them, professors using tricks to claim or exude authority, rather than earn it. Early morning professors catching students with half-opened eyes and embarrassing them before their classmates. Some relied on deep voices or elegant English to project authority while others dropped the names of colleagues whose papers were just published as if they were in the same league. They controlled students, Daniel observed, kept them in their subservient place. Calling students by their first names always. Dividing the class into competing groups by favoring the brighter students and subtly denigrating the others. Emphasizing their upper class associations by discussing in which countries they'd spent their sabbaticals or on which lake was their vacation home. They read from lectures written five years before and read every year since, at least the laziest among them did. The careful student smelled staleness wafting off the professor's soul. This method of academic presentation, if it could be called that, allowed little of what was happening outside the classroom to intrude on their carefully prepared lesson plans. Life was not allowed in the door. The king controlled the court.

Daniel read through the exam questions quickly. Relieved, all could be answered with short essays. He was confident he could bullshit his way through--again.

Daniel began to notice how he asked questions, lots of questions. At first, asking "why" had occurred here and there, but now it occurred obsessively. His constant questioning often bordered on rudeness. An answer would come back. Not satisfied, more sharply this time, he asked another "why" in response to the answer, and then "why" again and again, in response to each new answer, as often as necessary, until he sensed the bedrock of truth was within grasp. Even then, he often distrusted the factum and its source.

From questioning the basis for his professors' authority, it was an easy leap for Daniel to question the role and authority of the academic institution itself. Why did it exist? What was its true function in society? What allegiances did the members of its board of directors have? Why were there no students on the board? Was his institution like John Hopkins University, signing contracts with the military? What else did his institution do besides trying to teach students?

From academia, it was an easy leap to question every sector of society, beginning with government and multi-national corporations, and moving on to religious institutions, foundations and charities. Daniel saw hypocrites everywhere. He saw people in authority spewing forth answers, thick with pretense and pretentiousness, as if lecturing a passive people who never asked "why." He saw people in authority playing the part of conjurors, with magic tricks to entertain, distract, and deceive, all the while maintaining a public patter meant to convince the audience that they were in charge, commanding the stage, no one need worry how the act would turn out, all was well in the kingdom.

At this moment in his life, Daniel could only ask the questions. He understood correct answers would come only after hours upon hours of research and investigation. But how many hours were in his day? He had to stay in school to get his degree so that he could translate it into a job to support himself, which meant spending a few hours each day going through the motions of being enough of a student to graduate. But he was also needed on the streets, distributing flyers, strategizing at meetings, contributing articles to newsletters, mimeographing calls to action. He wanted to spend time with Christie, but when could that happen? His old high school pal, Jordan, would be in Babylon during Thanksgiving, but Daniel thought would he even want to travel to Long Island and visit his parents, let alone Jordan? How could he continue to work part-time in the cafeteria washing dishes, to earn the extra money he needed for books, subway fares, and an occasional movie, now that he had promised to help organize an anti-war march?

Daniel no longer had anything so much as resembling a schedule. There was only a constantly lengthening list of tasks. Cross out three as completed, and add six more "to do." He laughed at so-called experts who talked about time management and needing to prioritize. Everything was a priority! Daniel could not even find the time to organize his time. If he had worn his last pair of clean socks for the last three days, and they now stunk, that was a sure signal it was time to do laundry. If there was no more food in the refrigerator, it was time to shop for the snacks he relied upon whenever he had no time for the cafeteria. Was researching Richard S. Perkins, First National City Bank's chairman of the Executive Committee, and his connection to the Metropolitan Museum of Art, more important than writing a paper on Benedict Arnold for his American Studies class? No, Daniel concluded, he had to do both. He had first to research if there were other Metropolitan Museum board members connected to the support of *apartheid* in time to crank out a flyer about First National City's and Chase's revolving loan of $40 million to the South African government, and then join Jeff and a few other demonstrators on Fifth Avenue at 82nd Street to hand out flyers to lunch-time Metropolitan Museum visitors, and then complete the Arnold paper by the late afternoon extended deadline. In the early evening, he'd drop by the Thalia at West 95th Street and Broadway to see a foreign film. Or he'd check in with Ed to see if there was a planning meeting that night for an anti-war lobbying campaign in Washington. Daniel already knew he would not get to the laundromat this night, so he washed his socks in the sink before turning in for a few hours' sleep, hoping they would be dry when he woke up. They were not, but he wore them anyway.

For the first time in his life, the hum of anger seared his waking moments. He was not conscious of it, as anger, however, for a very long time. Sometimes it would show up masked as exaggerated annoyance over trivial things, like pounding his fist on the top of a desk when he had simply dropped a ballpoint pen on the floor, or slamming down the phone when, after dialing, he heard a busy signal.

This constant hum of internal anger grew louder in public. Watching in exasperation as the subway door closed in his face before he could board, Daniel screamed curses at the train leaving the station. His questioning of professors became more like a defense lawyer's inquisition of a prosecution's witness in a capital case than the previous jousting. He abruptly ended phone calls with his mother by saying how busy he was, chafing under her reminders to take good care of himself and get plenty of rest. It deeply annoyed him that she looked forward to seeing him at Thanksgiving, so stated by her as if it were an accomplished fact.

Relishing Sunday mornings when he could steal a few more hours of sleep, he now damned them because Christie insisted on their going to a nearby progressive church. He grew hoarse on picket lines, shouting at the top of his voice over and over again even though none of the corporate powers in their 40th floor executive offices could hear him. Daniel beamed a laser-like anger skyward, like a wolf howling at the moon, toward a universe that no longer had a place for him in which to feel at peace.

He ate less, ate on the run, snacked at late night parties instead of eating dinner or even lunch, all to have more time to complete his lists of tasks scribbled on napkins, scraps of paper, sometimes in a notebook he always carried but rarely opened otherwise. It was not just his sense of obligation that spurred him on. Daniel knew without doubt he was not only a first-hand witness to history, but also a creator of history. He had no right to quit. He had no right even to take a break. Every day, evidence of the struggle from every corner of his neighborhood to every corner of the globe was all around him. True, the other side had more money, more influence, more power. All Daniel had was the hope that devoting his every waking moment to the struggle would, in the end, result in a different outcome than if he did nothing.

Daniel literally carried another kind of history under his arm, every Saturday night, after stopping at the newsstand on West 96th Street and Broadway to spend $1.25 for the Sunday *New York Times*. He read this thick, heavy edition for information to be used against the other side, and for any glimmers of hope that reporters, columnists, or editorialists were finally understanding and printing the movement's message. He found only snippets, here one month, there another, indicating the nation's newspaper of record barely understood that many bubbles had reached the top of the stove and were about to boil the country.

Daniel believed it was only a matter of time—and enormous energy on the part of thousands of brothers and sisters—before the legitimacy of so many institutions would be questioned and confronted so seriously and extensively that their pronouncements and actions would no longer carry weight, and indeed would fade into the dustbin of History. And so it was, Daniel knew, with the House Un-American Activities Committee, a once powerful institution, which had seriously disrupted the lives of some and the attention of many. When HUAC was finally discredited, it was no longer able to write the histories it once wrote. Daniel was not sure how it would happen, but he knew he was involved in a movement which sought nothing less than to shift the weight of the world from the shoulders of the elite to their own collective shoulders, fashioning a just and peaceful world in which "the people" made the decisions affecting their lives. Daniel suspended his judgment about the kind of world he wanted, for to imagine a new world would be like becoming a Morgan or Rockefeller, a master manipulator of other people's lives. Shifting the weight of the world was more than enough for now. Leave it to "the people" to fashion their own society with everyone's participation.

How could he stop, Daniel asked himself? His comrades, as he had begun to think of them, male and female, did not stop. How could he even think of letting them down? If he did not show up with the flyers, there would be nothing to give to the passing public in the hope a few would understand, and join the next demonstration. If he did not collate the fundraising appeal letter, there would be no stipends for his friends to help pay their rents and buy a few groceries. If he did not accept the invitation to speak before the Action Committee of a downtown church, he would not be paid the stipend to keep him in toilet paper and shaving cream. The pieces of a new life pattern were forming with each decision. New language, habits, associations, places, content, orientation, loyalties, pleasures. There would soon be no reference points from the past guiding him into his new future.

Except for Sunday mornings when he was in town, finding time to be with Christie was difficult, even though Daniel wanted to be with her often. They would *rendezvous* at odd times and places. One mid-afternoon, as had become their occasional custom, they met in a lounge area in the foyer of Morningside Heights University's library. Christie had just discovered through her research that both MHU's president and a board member, plus Johns Hopkins University's Applied Physics Laboratory had interlocking corporate ties with Lockheed Aircraft. In addition, MHU's president and the same board member served on the board and executive committee of the Institute for Defense Analysis, a think-tank sponsored by a consortium of twelve universities. In fact, the university board member was IDA's chairman. Christie went on to show Daniel the university's extensive real estate holdings, and the board's interlocking corporate connections among builders, banks, insurance companies, and investment firms, which supported and grew those real estate holdings.

At first, Daniel did not grasp the full significance of what Christie had discovered, so she walked him through the directories and government databases, which proved the corporate connections. Daniel already knew that insurance companies invested their policyholders' premiums in residential and commercial ventures that served to erect even stronger boundaries between urban black ghettoes and upgraded "new" neighborhoods designed to keep whites in the cities. He had heard about Morningside Heights, Inc., which included on its board representatives from all the major educational institutions in the area. Christie told him that MHI had been formed decades earlier by David Rockefeller, currently president of Chase Manhattan Bank.

Daniel was glad Christie had discovered these interrelationships, but furious that he did not know about them a few months earlier during the Rognel Heights Methodist Church demonstration. He and his fellow activists had worked so hard on the research, writing handouts, and figuring out the logistics of the demonstration, and yet here was a key connecting link, Lockheed Aircraft, which showed the arc of powerful interrelationships spreading across the military in Vietnam, university military contracts, and the containment effort to keep urban blacks "in their place". Daniel immediately grasped the powerful significance of all these links, which pointed to the university president's office not two blocks away.

He left Christie abruptly, without explanation. He could not take the time to run off a flyer, or organize a picket line, or write a letter. Daniel could not wait for anything. All the anger and outrage he had felt and expended against "The Establishment" since the Christmas Eve vigil was stoked anew. With all his faculties marshaled and focused, Daniel marched to the building, which housed his new-found enemy.

He'd think of something to say to this man, whom he had only recently still considered a good and wise man, by the time he got to his office, but say something Daniel knew he must. His new-found knowledge burning in his brain, his months of becoming bolder and bolder in confronting distant injustices, his growing confidence that he was on the right side of history, entitled Daniel, he firmly believed, to confront the president of the university and call him a hypocrite to his face. After all, Daniel was still feeling angry at himself for letting Nichols off the hook without confronting him more about Vietnam.

Daniel strode into the office's reception area. To his relief, the secretary was not at her post. On the door straight ahead, he saw the frosted window glass with the president's name and title painted on it. He flung the door open. Daniel then halted abruptly, as if to scold himself for even thinking he had the right to invade this sanctuary, but, after surveying the huge, empty office around him, Daniel told himself he had every right to be on the enemy's territory, executing a surprise attack.

Daniel stood there. He knew he must do something. He did not want to make this trip for nothing. He had to leave a mark. He looked around the cavernous office. Is that a real Rembrandt on the wall, he wondered. Picking up a poker from the near-by fireplace, Daniel swung it, smashing the frosted glass in the door, watching the president's name and title fall to the floor with a loud crash. He had no second thoughts, no regrets, as he carefully replaced the poker and walked at a normal pace out of the office, down the corridor, and out of the building, into the crisp fall sunshine. He felt exhilarated and cleansed.

His hand had struck down a tiny symbol of the powerful whom he so detested, whose power he now firmly believed was based on the illegitimate foundation of legalized political and corporate corruption. He smiled as he walked toward the dorm, at peace with his act of defiance, a smile easily mistaken by passers-by as the smile of a mad man.

That evening, alone, Daniel smoked a few joints he had saved from a party a few nights before, and drank as much beer as he felt his stomach could hold. Soon, he could not move from the chair in which he was sitting. He felt numb. Terrified to close his eyes, feeling the world would spin out of control if he did, his eyelids were nevertheless heavy, his bones riddled with fatigue. The burden of history had entered the room with him. It had sat down next to him, waiting, wondering.

He watched the traffic light outside his window turn from red to green, from green to red, again and again and again. Auto headlights made streaks of shimmering light on the rain-soaked street for what seemed like an eternity. Daniel did not move. Not a finger, not a thought. No dreams came to him. Nothing. Was this how death felt?

Christie arrived at the parsonage Wednesday dinnertime, intending to spend the Thanksgiving holiday with her father and grandfather. When Rev. Calvin, Sr., finished his lengthy prayer about all the wonderful blessings God had bestowed upon him and his family, Christie asked:

146

"I'm curious, Grandfather, you know those pretty reports you receive each year from Middle South Utilities? Do you ever read them?"

"Not really, Christabel," Rev. Calvin, Sr., replied, pleased his granddaughter had taken an interest in them. "I look at the nice pictures sometimes, and check to see if the company will increase the dividend rate, but that's about all. Why do you ask, my child?"

"So you do not read the "Notes to Consolidated Financial Statements" in the back of the annual report, or know about Middle South's labor policies, or know who the largest stockholders are?" Christie stated in a tone more as an accusation than a question.

"Christabel, there is one piece of paper and one only I do read from this company, which was recommended to me by my good and trusted Presbyterian friend, John, and that is the amount written on the quarterly dividend check. And that is all I need to know, or want to know."

"Ah, yes, your good friend, John. Did you know that your investment banker friend served as a director on the board of the Tri-Continental Corporation in New York, which owned the seventh largest block of stock in Middle South?"

"How dare you infer my friend was anything but honorable? In fact, he advised me to increase my shares over the years, and I am very glad I did."

"Then, Grandfather, you do not care that Middle South owns Mississippi Power and Light Company, and several of that subsidiary's corporate leaders are members of the White Citizens Council, which advocates white supremacy?" Christie asked, looking straight into her grandfather's eyes.

"Who is speaking such communistic dribble? One of your professors, no doubt, at that liberal school you attend! I want no more of this conversation. Son, have you finished your sermon for this Sunday yet? It's an important one. Many more people in the pews on a holiday, putting money into the collection plate after your sermon."

"No, father, but it's coming along. I thought I would—"

"Grandfather," Christie interrupted, "I did research in the library. My sources are business publications, and the kinds of magazines like *Business Week*, which I used to see displayed on your coffee table in New York."

"You do not interrupt your father, young lady!" Rev. Calvin, Sr., shot

147

back pointedly. "Show your father respect. Apologize to him," he commanded.

"With the greatest respect, Grandfather, I met with Ted Seaver, executive director of the Michael Schwerner Memorial Fund, who told me that the biggest investors in Middle South are all in Boston, like Harvard University and State Street Investment Corporation and that Middle South's corporate headquarters, on Park Avenue in New York, is a stone's throw from your old church!"

"Enough! No more. Now you will apologize to me *and* your father, or else."

"Or else what, Grandfather?"

"Or else, or else, child, you will go to your room immediately without finishing your supper," Rev. Calvin, Sr., intoned as if his word were law.

"And that's all you have to say?

"You heard me."

"Father?"

"You heard your Grandfather," Rev. Calvin., Jr., said softly, not looking at his daughter.

The next morning, her overnight bag re-packed, Christie left behind a short note for her father on the dining room table, alongside the centerpiece she had made of Indian corn for the holiday, saying she was returning to New York, and was sorry she would not be with him to celebrate Thanksgiving or hear his sermon.

When she arrived in Pennsylvania Station, Christie took the #1 IRT Broadway-7th Avenue subway uptown one stop, changed at 42nd Street to the Times Square Shuttle, then took the #6 IRT Lexington Avenue subway downtown to Astor Place. She then walked to a soup kitchen across from Tompkins Square Park in the East Village, where she had read they needed volunteers. This was where, today, on the nation's family day, she felt most comfortable, serving strangers.

Jeff had not wanted to listen to the messages piling up on his answering machine. He knew who they were from. His mother and father asking when he was coming home for Thanksgiving. Sally, chattering on about nursing school, wondering if she would ever see Jeff again. The excuses also piled up. Would cost too much to fly home. Too many homework assignments due at the end of this brief holiday period. Besides, Jeff had a more pressing matter to decide. Should he go with Mildred to meet her parents in Darien?

Jeff had convinced himself that Mildred was so different from any other girl he had ever known. Raised by wealthy parents with deep, New England roots, she had somehow managed to identify with the plight of black and Indian South Africans and still remain close to her family's aristocratic ways. For example, she shared her mother's dream that when it came time for Mildred to marry, the wedding reception would be held in the Grand Ballroom of The Plaza Hotel. And yet, Mildred was never condescending in her relations with oppressed South Africans, and, in fact, many of them regarded her as a sister in the struggle.

In the end, his parents learned in a letter from Jeff that he would stay in New York. There wasn't enough time, he wrote, to fly back and forth and also get his assignments done. He did not call or write Sally, hoping his parents would somehow get the message to her.

Mildred went alone to Darien for Thanksgiving, however. Meeting her parents was too stressful for Jeff. It would signal a significant romantic entanglement, which he was not sure he felt, although he wished he could feel in time. His ambivalence also included the fear he might not be able to cope with her parents' imagined upper class attitudes, feeling they would look down on his rural Midwestern roots.

On Thanksgiving morning, Jeff walked south on Central Park West, watching the floats and giant balloons being readied for the Macy's Day Parade. Instead of watching the parade, Jeff took the #A Independent subway train downtown, changed at 42nd Street to the Times Square Shuttle, then took the #6 IRT Lexington Avenue subway downtown to Astor Place. He then walked to a soup kitchen across from Tompkins Square Park in the East Village, where he had read they needed volunteers. This was where, today, on the nation's family day, he felt most comfortable, serving strangers.

Daniel procrastinated for days about deciding to go "home" for

Thanksgiving. He had the money to take the train. He would have the time to complete his holiday homework assignments. And, Lord knows, he desired the pampering and rest. However, there were problems.

Daniel had lied so often, especially to his father, about how well he was doing academically that he could no longer look him in the eye. In fact, he was too afraid to look any family member in the eye, particularly during their ritual at Thanksgiving dinner's end when they took turns gazing at each other, expressing thanks for the other's presence. While he was proud of his many political acts, he had kept them hidden from his family, believing they would never understand. More than that, even if he tried to explain his motives and actions, he feared his family would see him in a different light, not the same pure and respectable child they loved. Feeling the widening gap between him and them, between their response to him as the son they thought they knew, and his knowing he was deceiving them, Daniel still wanted desperately to hang on to his feeling protected, loved, and pure. By returning home, however, he imagined he could not handle the strain, and would expose himself, somehow confess in a babble of tumultuous words what they would see as criminal, but he still considered as noble acts of rebellion.

And, how could he look his grandmother in the eye, Daniel wondered. He yearned to know more about Mathilda's suicide, but how could he ask about something he was not supposed to know about?

Besides, Daniel knew that he could not make it through another four-day Thanksgiving visit without 80-proof alcohol, to which he was turning more and more as his way to reconcile all the competing masks he was now wearing.

He waited until the Tuesday evening before Thanksgiving to call his parents, and let them know he had too much schoolwork over the holiday to afford the time to return to their home. He was skewered by the disappointment he heard in his mother's voice. In reaction, he promised that he would be "home" for the Christmas break, and then lied again about someone ringing his doorbell so that he could end the call quickly.

Two days later, Daniel walked to West 116th Street, took the #1 IRT-Broadway 7th Avenue downtown, changed at 42nd Street to the Times Square Shuttle, and then took the #6 IRT Lexington Avenue subway downtown to Astor Place. He then walked to a soup kitchen across from Tompkins Square

Park in the East Village, where he had read they needed volunteers. This was where, today, on the nation's family day, he felt most comfortable, serving strangers.

CHAPTER 9 – COMMUNION (THANKSGIVING 1966)

Down by the Riverside is a Negro spiritual dating back to the Civil War. It was first recorded by the Fisk University Jubilee Chorus is 1920.

Amazing Grace was written by an Englishman, John Newton, in 1779.

Off to his right as he entered the soup kitchen, Daniel noticed an outstretched arm waving a hand in a large oval motion. Confused by his new surroundings, Daniel was heartened to see Ephraim's face below the extended arm, indicating that Daniel should negotiate his way to the end of the long serving counter and join him on the other side.

As he walked through a narrow aisle with metal folding chairs neatly tucked under long, wooden tables, Daniel noticed a line of people already forming at the beginning of the extraordinarily long counter. He also noticed volunteers bringing out large metal pans, which were slid with skill so that the pans' lips caught the edges of the open areas where steam wafted off the hot water. Daniel had not thought in advance about what he expected to find, but he was still surprised by the varied sizes and shapes, age ranges, and skin colors of the dozen or so volunteers who kept bringing out large pans of food.

He grinned at a few, trying to make contact, but they were too preoccupied to notice.

"I didn't expect you to be here, Ephraim, but I'm really glad you are."

"So, why are you here, Daniel?"

"I don't know. All my schoolmates seem to have gone home, or are visiting friends. So, I saw this notice and thought, I guess, if I could help people, well, thought it would be a good thing."

"Aha. In that case, I'll show you the ropes, but keep your eyes open, you might learn a thing or two—about yourself! This is my fourth time here. So, put these on."

Daniel easily tied the long apron with a bowtie knot behind his back, but looked for a long time at the hairnet. Finally, his fingers parted the net slightly, and he slid it onto the top of his head.

"No, no," Ephraim said, laughing. "It's sitting on your head like a crown, your Royal Highness!"

"Cut it out, Ephraim."

"Here, like I did, tuck all your hair inside the net, even if it has to cover your ears. Now, that's better."

"Do I still look foolish?" Daniel asked.

"Nah. Look, we have to be sanitary. But here's what I've also learned. True, we are giving food to people who would not otherwise be eating a dinner today. But we're also giving them our respect. That's very important."

Within the next fifteen minutes, Christie and Jeff arrived, put on their aprons and hairnets, and stood ready to serve. All three were then instructed by Ephraim to make sure they each asked the client if they want a portion of the dish in front of them—or not.

"Don't assume, just because they're in a soup kitchen, they don't have a choice as to what they want to eat," Ephraim advised.

The first in line moved eventually to Daniel's station.

"Would you like mashed potatoes?" Daniel asked, without looking across the counter, his serving spoon poised above the food.

There was no response.

Daniel looked down at the shape in front of him, expecting to see a belt or stomach. Instead, he saw the head and body of a child, who looked up at the person next to him.

"Mi hijo no entiende Inglés, Señor," a male voice uttered from somewhere in the surrounding din.

153

"What?" Daniel exclaimed.

"Discúlpeme, Señor, my son, he not understand English."

"OK."

Daniel tried to flick a spoonful of mashed potatoes onto the young boy's plate, but missed. Instead, the potatoes landed on the tray.

"Oh, God," Daniel exclaimed.

"No te preocupes," the father told his son. "Tenemos que seguir adelante. Estamos sosteniendo la línea."

"I'm sorry, I'm sorry," Daniel uttered, as the father, with a hand on his son's shoulder, went to the next station.

Daniel turned abruptly toward Ephraim.

"I really screwed up."

"It's not about you, OK. Get over it."

Daniel tugged at the front of his apron, reassuring himself that the knot in the back was still tight. As the figures passed in front of him, he occasionally pointed to the mashed potatoes, with a quizzical look on his face, to avoid asking those he figured did not know English. He was often wrong, as most of those clients asked for gravy in perfect English. Daniel was also struck by how well dressed many clients were. He had expected Skid Row bums, with runny noses and foul smells.

As each new face appeared in front of her, Christie greeted the person with a cheery "hello." After serving the green beans, she offered a "Happy Thanksgiving" with a smile, often receiving a smile in return. Jeff soon picked up Christie's manner, as he served the butternut squash. After more failed attempts at thinking, then executing how he should relate to the clients, Daniel too echoed Christie's words, and something of her spirit. Ephraim looked down the line at his rookie servers, and was glad to be with them.

As their good-natured rapport continued with the clients, and as they chatted happily among themselves, the four forgot their own families and their Thanksgiving dinners around tradition-laden tables, celebrating their good fortune of having found each other and participating in this life-giving service. And for the next three hours, they also forgot about the next pamphlet one had promised to research that night, or the next meeting another had put in his calendar for Saturday, or the newest mailing another had agreed to take to the post office tomorrow.

Even Daniel felt the honesty and directness in the simple exchanges between two human beings, one serving, the other receiving, and both looking at each other with respect, and occasionally, if he were very honest with himself—with love.

Ephraim looked again down the counter to his right, watching "his rookies" at work. He had started at the soup kitchen early in the morning, peeling and cutting, preparing the vegetable-laden soup while other, more experienced volunteers, had stuffed and basted the turkeys, and put cloves into the hams. Since he was still relatively new, Ephraim knew he would then be directed to the serving line rather than being "promoted" to the kitchen, but, now, standing with his new-found friends, he was more thankful than ever he had decided to serve.

Later that afternoon, Ephraim invited the three to come back to his place and share the evening together. On the way home, he picked up wine, and then assorted edibles for their own Thanksgiving feast. The others marveled at how high the prices were at Zabar's, but Ephraim shrugged off the expense. He was thrilled at being able to open his apartment to these new friends, and he intended it to be a very special evening, indeed.

Quickly discovering that living on his own was expensive, Ephraim had found a weekend job as a limousine driver. He had loved the intimate contact it afforded him with the wealthy and sometimes famous, eavesdropping on their conversations. It was a wicked pleasure he had enjoyed, hearing them discuss business deals over the car phone.

He had also pumped the other drivers for tips on how he could increase his own tips. The older, full time chauffeurs, in a class by themselves, had been flattered by Ephraim's eagerness and questions, and glad to have a young, captive audience listening to their anecdotes and jokes.

Although he was now making "good money," as he called it, Ephraim had known that there would be dry periods, like after New Year's Eve, when bookings fell off. Consequently, he had figured out several ways to make lots of tax-free money by hustling. After several weeks of trial-and-error, by mid-October he had figured out all the angles.

Many of his assigned jobs on a Friday and Saturday evening were pick-ups at mid-town hotels, like the Helmsley Palace and The Plaza, for out-of-towners going to Broadway shows. Ephraim had learned that, as the clock moved closer and closer to the 8 o'clock (actually 8:05) opening curtain, traffic in and around the Theatre District moved at a snail's pace, if that fast.

Therefore, the first 'hustle" of the evening had occurred when Ephraim pulled up near the entrance of his clients' hotel, ignored the doorman whose job it was to announce that a guest's car had arrived, went inside the hotel, rang up his clients on the house phone, and politely hinted that they'd better get a move on if they did not want to miss curtain due to heavy theatre traffic. He had then told the clients he was wearing a colorful scarf around his neck, and would meet them directly outside the hotel's front door. Ephraim had calculated that such a notice to the clients resulted in the doorman being effectively blocked from putting the hotel guests into his limousine, thus saving them from having to tip the doorman. Not only increasing Ephraim's chances of that much larger a tip at the end of the job, Ephraim had intended that the house call would encourage his clients to feel they were receiving very personal treatment, while preserving their anonymity because no signboard with their name on it needed to be placed in the limousine's windshield.

His honed hustler's tactics had not ended as he closed the door of the limousine, his clients safely inside. Ephraim had experienced that the window for driving at a normal rate on any street in the Theatre District narrowed exponentially from 7:35pm onward. Therefore, if he could drop his clients off at that time (hence his urging them to hurry their hotel departure), the clients would be pleased by arriving in plenty of time to get settled in their seats. More importantly, the early drop-off had given Ephraim relatively traffic-free routes to escape the Theatre District and head uptown where the tax-free money was about to be made.

In the beginning of his trial-and-error days, Ephraim had reasoned that going up Eighth Avenue, then crossing in the mid-Sixties or low-Seventies to Central Park West, and heading south on that well-to-do avenue, would allow him to beckon people, desperately trying to hail cabs, to his limousine window, saying he would take them to the Theatre District for $15. After discovering that the law of supply-and-demand had been working against him because cab drivers had long ago figured out that the shortest distance between a drop-off in mid-town and their next fare was also to take Eighth Avenue to that area of the West Side, Ephraim switched his escape route. He had now driven up Madison Avenue to the low-Seventies, across to Fifth Avenue, and then headed downtown. He had not only found more desperate people hailing far fewer cabs, but they were willing to pay $20 to

$30 (especially in the rain). So glad to be riding inside a stretch limousine to the smash hit for which they had bought tickets months ago, his pick-ups had not even objected when Ephraim picked up another desperate Broadway-bound customer, for another $20 to $30.

Whether he had taken Fifth Avenue or occasionally Park Avenue toward the Theatre District, he always crossed from there to the West Side on 51st Street, which was virtually and unbelievably deserted, and then turned left, heading downtown on Broadway and then bearing right onto Seventh Avenue as it crossed Broadway just below 45th Street. He had dropped his "customers" at the corner of the street where their theatres were, explaining that they could walk faster down the block to their destination than he could drive. Ephraim had then returned to the East Side, it now being around 7:55pm, knowing that the supply of empty cabs looking for fares was rapidly increasing, but also knowing that, since taxi drivers paid for their own gas and he did not, cabbies were less likely to cruise farther uptown, so he would find a few truly panicked people in the East Eighties willing to pay $35 or $40, even though they knew they would miss the opening curtain.

Since Broadway shows ended at different times, he could easily find a place to park on Eighth Avenue, walk to his clients' theatre, and be outside the front door, waiting to greet and walk them to the limousine. Ephraim already had in his pocket more hustling cash than the company would pay him for this job, including the automatic tip-on-the-bill, but he hoped the clients, at the end of the evening, would tip him an additional $20 at least. If he had taken especially good care of them, always opening the limousine door, having an umbrella at the ready if it rained, and knowing when to chat with them and, most importantly, when to be quiet, he might expect $50 or even $100. If he dared, Ephraim occasionally used the time his clients' were dining after the theatre to hustle, if he could stay alert behind the wheel. Not knowing when his clients would emerge from the restaurant, Ephraim had risked missing them only a few times to make even more money.

After unpacking the Zabar's treats, Ephraim hosted his guests with utmost attentiveness, as if they were his limousine clients, wanting them to feel relaxed and cared for, but without, of course, any expectation of a return. He wanted his guests to feel at home in his home. For just a moment, Ephraim thought of his father's generous gifts of food for neighbors, but quickly dismissed the comparison.

The four talked about politics, the struggle, liberation, never once mentioning either school or family or part-time jobs. After some hours, as the main dish was baking in the oven, Ephraim invited them to leave the living room and sit around his small kitchen table. He poured each a cup of wine. Raising his glass in a toast to Dionysus, the god of wine and ritual madness, then to his Roman counterpart, Bacchus, and finally to another Roman counterpart, Liber, who represented freedom, Ephraim explained that Liber also championed freedom's associated rights, especially free speech, and opposed servitude. He asked his friends to raise this first cup of wine to the gods and drain it.

"I'd like to acknowledge," Ephraim continued, "that we have each departed from a land of semi-bondage. I mean we have all left our families, we have escaped from the rules they make, and we are now tasting freedom. We would not know what it is to be free if we had not known what it was like to be under their thumb. We should rejoice in that experience of oppression because it has made us keen sensors of justice and freedom."

Ephraim then took pieces of scallion, dipped them in vinegar, and passed them around the table for all to eat. He broke off pieces of a baguette, and placed them in front of each person. He opened a window, letting in the frosty air of this late November evening, and then poured a fifth cup of wine, setting it on the windowsill of the open window.

Ephraim filled each of his friends' cups and his a second time.

"Tonight we celebrate in New York City. Next year we celebrate in a free Johannesburg, in a free Saigon, in a free Yazoo City.

"I want this night to be different from all other nights. So I ask each of you to think way back in your family history, and tell me of your people being in bondage, in slavery, as it were."

The others paused for a long time. No dictators or oppression in their immediate family trees came to their minds.

Jeff was the first to break the silence. He remembered stories of how one of his Finnish ancestors on his father's side had been interned in a camp following a brief civil war.

"He had died from malnutrition in the camp," Jeff continued. "I think he had been a supporter of the 1917 October Revolution in Russia when Russia ruled Finland. My ancestors were nationalist Finns who wanted independence from Russia. Other Finns wanted Finland to stay part of the new communist order. Consequently, both sides fought a civil war. I also have a vague memory that earlier ancestors had died during a famine under Russian rule."

Christie knew her people had come from England many generations ago, but she could not recall any persecution or other oppression they had faced.

"I do recall, however," Christie continued, "my mother once telling me that, on her mother's side of the family centuries ago, an ancestor had fled to England from France. The ancestor fled following the St. Bartholomew's Day Massacre in which tens of thousands of Huguenots were killed. The Huguenots were among the earliest Calvinists in France. My mother told me that they were aggressive critics of the dominant Roman Catholic Church in France, which persecuted them."

Not being able to recall any family history handed down to him, Daniel also could not imagine there had been any repression of ancestors on his father's side, all of whom came from Zurich, Switzerland. He was never told any details about his mother's Dutch ancestors.

"What I can guess," Daniel continued, "is that my European ancestors must have come to America seeking a better economic life."

Ephraim recalled his grandfather's death in 1917 in the Ukraine during the October Revolution.

"No one in my family knows for certain whether Sergei was killed by the Red Army during a battle, or was murdered due to his Jewishness by a fellow member of the White Army."

Ephraim continued:

"I think we, including Daniel who listened to our family stories, now all understand that there is an Eternal Flame, a spirit, inside everyone which will not let us or our ancestors rest until injustice and inequality vanish. Because we once knew oppression in our own blood histories or our friends' blood histories, we can today identify with the oppressed, and cause injustice and inequality to vanish in their name."

Then Ephraim extinguished all the candles which he had lit at the beginning, and asked everyone to think about what they just heard in silence. Then he re-lit the candles.

"We have all recently ventured into strange lands, have we not? And yet, something inside us, a spirit, has commanded us to serve others who are in bondage, whether drafted by the Army, forced to live in Bantustans or ghettoes."

Ephraim then covered each piece of baguette with the napkin at each of his guests' place, and his own.

"It is the spirit of our ancestors, once in bondage but who freed themselves, which joins our spirit of struggle for freedom and justice."

Ephraim then invited everyone to drain the second cup of wine, and he uncovered the pieces of baguette.

"And you know that the ancestors of some of our brothers and sisters gained their freedom through violence, by taking up arms and killing their enemies. We must understand that such violence is now seen as glorious and necessary."

Ephraim then recalled that many movements to gain freedom necessitated violent and bloody struggles. He recalled the American and French Revolutions as well as the more recent Algerian revolution, and the current wars of liberation in Angola and Mozambique, in Vietnam, and the freedom fighters in South Africa. He likened the riots in Watts the year before as a new sign of liberation struggle in America, perhaps the beginnings of a Second Civil War. Ephraim also recalled the history of arrogance and hypocrisy of Caucasian people, in Europe, North, Central, and South America, Africa and Australia, who conquered their lands' first inhabitants by force, and then immediately outlawed force against themselves. He talked about the guilt activists feel in the wake of unspeakable death and destruction of colored peoples by members of the Caucasian race.

"True, we would prefer the path of non-violent resistance, where we confront the deeds of injustice, but love the doer. How much better it would be for society if our appeal to conscience would awaken their consciences, have them see the light and join us, and free them from the bondage of bigotry and hate. But we cannot avoid the historical fact that winning freedom occurred when oppressed peoples had no other option given them except to take up arms. We remember Nelson Mandela's defense of violence during the Rivonia Trial when he stated: 'We first broke the law in a way which avoided any recourse to violence; when this form was legislated against, and then the government resorted to a show of force to crush opposition to its policies, only then did we decide to answer violence with violence.'"

160

Ephraim raised his cup of wine and continued:

"How blessed we are to know the difference between freedom and slavery, and know that we are free, we have choices, we have privileges, and therefore we are morally obligated to assist the oppressed to attain whatever kind of freedom they choose."

Ephraim then went to the oven, pulled out a tray of baked salmon, and set it in the middle of the table.

"This salmon, from the sea, the bread from the wheat of the land, and the scallions from under the earth, each represent a source of strength and vitality for our bodies. Nature sustains us, gives us life.

"I am going to pause now. If anyone around the table has a question about anything I've been doing or saying, or has a comment, this is the time to speak up."

"Ephraim, I'm sorry, but I am staunchly opposed to violence in any form," Christie stated. "I know that violence is often used by the powerful to undercut the political or religious aspirations of others, but I believe that even when one oppressed group successfully defeats the oppressor through armed struggle, the remaining, deep scars reinforce a 'we/they' conflict, which takes other forms, like discrimination and economic dominance."

"I think I agree with Christie," Jeff said. "I can't help thinking that if Mandela's followers had continued his initial non-violent resistance, even when he went to jail, like Gandhi, the rigid Afrikaner system of *apartheid*, with its Pass laws, would have cracked much sooner."

Daniel kept quiet for some time, thinking about his smashing the president's office window with the poker. Was damage to property considered a violent act? Was there maybe a middle ground, he wondered, destroying property as a sign of resistance against a system, but not harming anyone physically?

"I do not know if I could really and truly love the evil doer while I am marching against the evil system they are enforcing," Daniel began. "I just can't stand listening to Johnson on television defending the war, or watching those southern sheriffs with their ham hock faces defending the use of dogs against people. I don't have enough love in my heart ever to care about winning those fools over. I know what Dr. King says and I admire him for it, but that's just not me. I hate those bastards like LBJ and Verwoerd and Sheriff Rainey. But I agree with Christie on one point. One day you rise up and kill the enemy and the next day they rise up and kill you. I ask you, how do you permanently end cycles of violence and bloodshed? They certainly weren't ended in Syria-Palestine after Jesus walked the earth!"

Ephraim concluded the discussion by saying that they might not come to agreement tonight, but should continue discussing the issue in future. He continued:

"'The task of liberation is long, and it is work that we ourselves must do. As the Talmud tells us, we like Moses may not live to complete the task; but neither may we refrain from beginning it. We are about to eat; may our dinner give us strength for the work ahead! We are about to drink; may our wine give us joy for the work ahead!'"

Then Ephraim refilled his cup, and poured most of the wine into Christie's cup from his, and then indicated that she should pour part of her wine into Daniels's cup, and Daniel part of his wine into Jeff's cup, and then Jeff pour a tiny amount into Ephraim's cup.

They all lifted their cups, and drank to freedom everywhere.

Though the kitchen window remained open throughout their meal together, none of the four felt the night's chill air. The evening continued in the warmth of story-telling and joking, aided by a dessert of delectable chocolate truffles. Keeping the vibrant camaraderie going until the end, each hugged Ephraim as they departed his home.

In the elevator, Daniel told Christie and Jeff to return to the university without him, as he wanted to walk up Broadway by himself. On the pavement, he felt the crisp evening air give way to a knot of pain, as if a thousand butterflies were forcing their way out of a cocoon inside his stomach, and there was no room for them to fly. His right hand trembled, not from the cold, but from the pressure of being pulled in a thousand directions at once, as he brought his trembling hand to his face to adjust his newly purchased glasses.

Quickly stuffing his hand in a front pocket to stop its shaking, Daniel wondered, not for the first time, what would become of him.

CHAPTER 10 – ACCELERATION
(WINTER/SPRING 1967)

For What It's Worth, written by then band member Stephen Stills, and recorded by Buffalo Springfield, as a protest song in response to increasing tensions between club goers on the Sunset Strip in Los Angeles and the police enforcing a recently passed, strict curfew law, which led to the first of a series of riots in November 1966. Released as a single, January 1967. The band was playing the Whiskey A Go Go club in late November 1966.

The End, by The Doors, in their first album, *The End*, released the first week of January 1967. The Doors, with Van Morrison, was formed when two bands performed together at the Whiskey A Go Go club in June 1966.

We're A Winner, written and produced by lead singer Curtis Mayfield and recorded by The Impressions, released as a single in 1967, and #1 on Billboard's R&B Chart, March 1, 1968.

"What is this stuff about a Human Be-In?" Daniel asked Malcolm over breakfast.

"Yeah, I know it sounds hokey to some, but there's an urgent, even noble motive behind it. Let me start with the name. It's meant to echo the civil rights' sit-ins beginning in 1960 and the university reform and anti-war teach-ins beginning in 1965. Here's the way the organizers see it. Two major youth movements are rapidly diverging."

"I don't feel that in New York," Daniel countered.

"Oh, I see. How shall I put this? A lot of people who live in New

York are so parochial, they think there's nothing much to the rest of the country except a few rivers and some rocks."

"OK, OK, I get it, but let's say there are two youth movements, so what?"

"A stone's throw from this apartment is Haight-Ashbury, bordering Golden Gate Park. It's become the spiritual and symbolic home of what is known as the counterculture movement. This movement opposes the war, but they are very uneasy about the other youth movement's confrontational style. So, the Be-In this afternoon simultaneously emphasizes a spiritual focus on 'Be-ing' as a pathway to peace and love, and an aggressive political focus on 'In-your–face' tactics as a way to end the war. The Human Be-In is intended as an event to bridge the divide and bring both youth movements together, at least physically."

"I don't know about that. I truly believe confrontation is the only way to change things."

"Look, try to keep an open mind. But for right now, why don't you finish your pancakes, get a few hours' sleep, and then we'll head over to the Park."

Daniel's new-found contentment in the simple task of serving others in the soup kitchen on Thanksgiving Day, and the communion he experienced that evening in Ephraim's apartment, had been swiftly replaced by the old, hectic routines of protest. Knowing he would not travel to his parents' home for the Christmas break, Daniel looked elsewhere for a change of pace. He thought he had found it in a flyer he received in the mail in early December.

Malcolm had sent Daniel an announcement about a Peace Dance and Pow-Wow in San Francisco on Saturday, January 14th, some kind of a gathering of the "Tribes". Daniel could not imagine what the flyer was talking about. He had read in the *Berkeley Barb* of people gathering to generate enough energy to end the Vietnam War, even levitate the Pentagon building, so Daniel had figured the event was organized by those "hippies" he had read about. He couldn't take this gathering seriously, however. Probably an excuse for a humongous block party, he had concluded.

Growing up, California had been as foreign to Daniel as Indochina or Japan. He had neither friends nor relatives living there. No one he knew had ever traveled to California, or, if they did, they had never returned to talk about it. The pain, however, of his fifteen year-old heart being ripped out when that traitorous bastard named O'Malley had moved Daniel's beloved Dodgers out of Brooklyn still seared his memory. Whatever "Los Angeles" was, he had hated it from then on. Of course he had not liked the New York Giants either, arch enemies of his sainted Bums, but he disliked whatever "San Francisco" was even more for removing from the Polo Grounds in upper Manhattan a team he loved to hate.

Despite the traitorous hole in his heart, Daniel had sensed there was something *mysterious* about "California," a mystery he first experienced during that hitch-hiking trip a few years back when Malcolm had given him a ride up Highway 101 from San Luis Obispo to the Klamath River. Perhaps it had been the effects of the fog, as he tried to look back from the Presidio, shrouding San Francisco in a grey blanket of cold, damp air, which refused to yield the city's landscape, like a woman with a cape draped over her torso.

Malcolm, a stagehand for the San Francisco Mime Troupe, had met Daniel at the airport and settled him into a guest bedroom in his apartment. The Troupe had been in rehearsals for the production of *L'Amant Militarie*, its own adaptation of the Italian Carlos Goldoni's play about a Spanish invasion of Italy whose satirical wit was clearly aimed at the Vietnam War. It was not only the Vietnam War, Daniel had learned from Malcolm, which was going to draw twenty thousand mostly young people to Polo Field in San Francisco. A growing portion of Daniel's generation had also been actively disengaging from their straight-laced parents who could not stop their children's desire to, as one Human Be-In speaker would put it, "tune in, turn on, drop out." Imagining all kinds of dire consequences, parents and their political representatives had been gamely trying, though. Three months earlier, a California law had gone into effect, which banned LSD. Daniel had heard about "acid", but when he learned how long it took to get over its effects, he never imagined himself having the time to try it.

Refreshed by several hours' sleep following his pancake breakfast, Daniel found himself on this early Saturday afternoon walking around Polo Field, seeing more tie-dye shirts than he ever knew existed, passing tables filled with drug paraphernalia more exotic than he ever imagined, losing Malcolm more than once in the crowd, and listening to more poets than he'd ever heard before. Daniel became bored. He could not comprehend how this mass of genuinely appearing happy people could ever be taken seriously by the military-industrial-university complex, let alone make even the tiniest dent in that complex's control of the American government. Their merriment, and their uninhibited bodily displays set to the good vibrations of a Beach Boys' hit, utterly depressed Daniel.

He abruptly decided to walk back to Malcolm's, make a few New York phone calls to keep up with events, and wait patiently until the next evening when he'd board his return flight. Before leaving the field, though, he quenched his thirst at a lemonade stand, thanking the girl who gave him the free lemonade, and wondering why she had smiled at him like Da Vinci's *Mona Lisa*.

It was now Sunday morning, the calmest he had ever experienced since early childhood. Daniel had nowhere to go. There were no papers on a desk calling him to read, or letters summoning him to reply. The food in the refrigerator was not his to cook. Or the ringing phone his to answer. He lay prone in the embrace of the deepest sleep he had known for a year, in Malcolm's guest room bed, door tightly shut, far away from anything or anyone who could wake him. How bright the morning sun as it moved across the third story window, finally reaching Daniel's feet about noon. Angelic sleep.

All the cells in his body craved sleep. They had been so active, carrying out so many commands for countless nights and days. Now, only a few cells stirred, while the sun soothed his calves. Daniel rolled from his left side to his right, barely aware he was again pulling the covers over his shoulder and tucking them under his chin, as his legs, folded slightly at the knees, came to rest. An hour passed, and another. The sun moved up his body and stroked his chest.

The sun finally tapped Daniel on his shoulder. He woke. He lay enveloped in the room's stillness for quite some time, terrified. How in hell could he have done yesterday all those things he now vainly tried to forget, he asked himself. He couldn't shake the memory, no matter how comforting the blankets and sun were.

Yesterday afternoon, Daniel had run at break-neck speed chasing down a car on Waller Street, as he was leaving Golden Gate Park, because he had thought it carried his boyhood dog. An hour earlier, inside the Park, he had stared at a vibrant green leaf, watching it change to other pulsating colors, and then gasped as each color dripped, like candle wax, onto the branch below. He then had crawled on the ground, convincing himself that he had to keep his head low, or else a sniper would get him for sure. On his feet again after what seemed like hours lying flat on his belly, Daniel had fallen instantly in love with every girl who passed, smiling idiotically at them. And, all the while, desperately looking for Malcolm, never finding him in a sea of humanity moving in slow motion, Daniel, in turn terrified and ecstatic, had craved the assurance of someone he knew and trusted that he was not losing his mind, breaking down completely and irrevocably. It was as if his mind had been an untamed stallion, twisting and turning in unexpected directions at alarming speeds. The stallion had been relentless. All through Saturday night and even after the sun rose on Sunday morning, it had never slowed. The stallion had run and bucked for far longer than its rider ever felt he could hang on, but hang on Daniel had.

After fully waking, Daniel waited and waited, cautious not to re-ignite the hallucinations so recently and vividly gripping his mind. Any feelings within or sensations without finally evaporated in the gentle sunlight, leaving Daniel washed out, shorn of impulses. The bright sun was now diffused throughout the guest room, but only a dull gray, the color of a Connecticut's February sky, suffused Daniel's mind. The contrast was too much for him to bear, so Daniel lay back on the bed, and stared straight up at the off-white ceiling, not vacating that one spot until he felt secure enough to dress and look out the window. The city stretched before him, cascading toward the Bay. A few of the charms of its landscape revealed themselves, but these were not sufficient to hold him captivated. He desperately wanted to get back east.

A few months had now passed, as late winter turned into early spring. Daniel sat alone in their favorite back booth at the West End Café, a half-empty glass of Pabst Blue Ribbon in front of him, untouched for the last hour. Christie, Jeff, and Ephraim had left him then, completing their early morning strategy session on persuading teachers and professors by the thousands to sign an anti-war petition, to appear in two weeks as an advertisement in *The New York Times*, but Daniel had no desire to walk back to the dorm, despite April's temperate night breeze. He basked in the 3am quiet, hearing only the chink of glasses being loaded on trays by waitresses clearing deserted tables. Such moments of solitude were so rare. Daniel cherished this one, letting his mind wander where it will, without the press of demanding deadlines and trumpeting telephones.

His mind, though, had other plans. It kept returning him to San Francisco. The more Daniel concentrated on not remembering San Francisco, the more he remembered its effect on him.

Swallowing more sips of flat beer from the glass, Daniel remembered Malcom driving him to the airport for the return flight. He then collapsed in his economy seat, going to sleep almost immediately, blanketed by the motherly attentiveness of a stewardess. "California" remained a mystery, no, a nightmare. He feared that all the attention on "Love" and "Being" and "Harmony", all of which he judged as childish narcissism, would turn the media's focus away from the true struggle, which was about economic and political power. He thought the media moguls would naturally want to play up images of "hippies" pounding their bongo drums, as if they were the *real* and *only* youth movement, presenting them as curios to divert public attention away from efforts by revolutionaries to publicize the media moguls' Establishment buddies waging wars abroad and keeping peoples of color under their thumbs at home. Better to keep the print pages and television screens filled with people in sandals, Daniel imagined the moguls' intent, than give copy space or airtime to radicals focusing attention on who ruled America and for whose benefit. And what about Daniel and his comrades in all of this, Daniel wondered? How could they become influential if the mainstream media distracted the public's attention with stories of "flower power"?

As the Café's 4am closing time drew near, Daniel also reflected on the advice given by some psychologists and self-appointed pop culture philosophers. He had heard their mantras all too often: "You can not help others until you have helped yourself." "If you want to change others, you first have to change yourself." He couldn't bear these apologists for the *status quo*. Daniel reasoned, even if he wanted to change himself by removing, say, all his capitalist/competitive training he had received throughout his life, how could he then survive in America, except by living in a monastery? He could only change if he was solidly connected to a small group of people who also wanted to change, creating their own definitions of who they were and the rules by which they functioned, and then, as they were experimenting and consolidating, they were also encouraging more and more to join them while, at the same time, they were exposing and challenging the power structures, which oppressed them and others. As others joined, Daniel reasoned, the newly minted veterans would help the newest recruits during their transitions to the new definitions and rules as well as hopefully being open enough to allow the recruits to influence their collective evolution. No one can change in isolation, Daniel firmly believed. "I cannot finally be free to choose my own destiny and be happy until we have collectively freed society," Daniel said to himself as he paid the tab and left the Café.

Demonstrations, protest petitions, letter-writing, meetings, research, speeches had been occurring with such rapidity that Daniel's memory could neither hold onto it all, nor could he feel confident that any string of actions, so blurred in his memory, could be properly evaluated to determine if they caused change. Toward the end of March, Daniel decided to jot down in a diary some of the events in which he participated:

Monday, March 20th

Listened to Dr. John Bennett, president, Union Theological Seminary and leading anti-war figure, lecture tonight on six "presuppositions", or rationales, which pro-war advocates use to support fighting in Vietnam. (1) communism succeeding in one place in the world is impermissible because then it will be encouraged to succeed elsewhere; (2) it is a test case for wars of aggression – by standing our ground in Vietnam we reduce the likelihood of WW III with the Soviet Union; (3) by stopping this "war of liberation" now we will not have to fight them in the future; (4) The US must never be seen as an "appeaser", as Britain did before WW II, in the face of an aggressor; (5) the "illusion of American omnipotence" must be preserved; and (6) military success in Vietnam will put the brakes on China. Good ammunition for understanding where the hawks are coming from.

Tuesday, March 21st

Went uptown to attend a "call for action" on the 7th anniversary of the Sharpeville massacre in South Africa, held at St. Mark's Methodist Church on St. Nicholas Avenue and West 137th Street in Harlem. Heard Floyd McKissick, National Director of the Congress on Racial Equality, Dennis Brutus, former South African political prisoner, and William Booth, New York City Commissioner on Human Rights. The meeting was chaired by Percy Sutton, Manhattan Borough President. Sponsored by many organizations. Very motivational.

Daniel noticed, as he was about to make the next entry, that he had not taken the time in the last few days to write down what he had done. He promised himself to do better in future.

Sunday, March 26th

Frank called from Detroit late in the evening to tell me of the Rev. Albert Cleage's Easter sermon during which he unveiled a painting of a Black Madonna, stating, as Frank quoted from the sermon, "… the historic truth is finally beginning to emerge – that Jesus was the non-white leader of a non-white people …" Cleage was telling blacks to stop worshipping a white Jesus. I think Jimmy and Grace Boggs, social activists there in Detroit, know Cleage.

Tuesday, March 28th

Walked around in a picket line, carrying a sign, "Apartheid has a friend at Chase Manhattan." Chase's annual stockholders meeting. About 30 demonstrators, sponsored by the American Committee on Africa, among others. Some anti-*apartheid* supporters were inside the annual meeting, raising issue of Chase's loans to South African government. Disappointed by low turnout.

Thursday, March 30th

Saw film, "Civilization on Trial in South Africa," narrated by the Rev. Michael Scott of the Africa Bureau in London, hosted by the Episcopal Churchmen for South Africa. Met its leader, Bill Johnston. Shown at All Saints Church on East 59th Street. Very dedicated people.

Tuesday, April 4th

Sat in the congregation at Riverside Church. Heard the Rev. Martin Luther King, Jr., oppose the Vietnam War. He said: "A nation that continues year after year to spend more money on military defense than on programs of social uplift is approaching spiritual death." What a speaker!

Saturday, April 15th

Feet hurt. Walked from Central Park to the United Nations. 400,000-strong demonstration against the war. Heard Benjamin Spock, James Bevel and Martin Luther King speak. Malcolm called. He marched in a 100,000 strong anti-war protest in San Francisco today.

Tuesday, April 25th

Very tired tonight. Organized busloads of students and others from New York and New Jersey to support F.I.G.H.T. at Kodak's annual stockholders meeting in Flemington. On an impulse, decided to ride with Arthur to Cornell University so we could talk strategy. Very tired.

Friday, April 28th

Saw on the news that Muhammed Ali refused induction into Army.

It had only been less than a month's worth of diary entries, but Daniel abandoned the project. He was too tired at the end of many nights to write even a few lines about where he had been or what he had seen.

Three weeks before Daniel boarded his January "red-eye" flight to San Francisco, Arthur found himself once again on the road, this time with two fellow sophomores heading north on New York Route 96 between Cayuga and Seneca Lakes. In the year since he had enrolled at Cornell University, Arthur had found a few like-minded students who had also read *The Autobiography of Malcolm X*. Heading to Rochester at the start of their Christmas 1966 break, Arthur and his Cornell brothers were expecting to become volunteers in a struggle initiated by a friend of Malcolm X's.

Two hours later, they pulled up in front of Reynolds Street Church of Christ, its congregation led by Minister Franklin Delano Roosevelt Florence who had been with Malcolm X when he had spoken in Rochester. (Malcolm X would shortly be assassinated in New York City.)

Like Arthur, Minister Florence had traveled many, many miles from his Southern birth home. Both he and Arthur shared the Black Power view that blacks, not whites, had to organize and lead blacks out of poverty. As a result, they believed blacks would gain both respect and power to achieve their goals by negotiating directly with white power structures. They both wanted no more middlemen, such as white liberals, acting as mediators. Only black leaders sitting at the same table with white leaders would be the acceptable dynamic for change. For the first time, Arthur felt he had found people who believed as he did.

Upon arrival at the church, the three were assigned to Ron Jackson, an associate of Saul Alinsky. Arthur soon learned that Alinsky was a Jew born of Orthodox parents who had become the architect of how powerless communities could organize themselves and achieve their goals.

"Let me give you some background, first," Ron began the orientation for a dozen black volunteers. "There was a riot here in Rochester two and a half years ago. Martin Luther King's Southern Christian Leadership Conference had declined an invitation from a coalition of Rochester Protestant churches to help organize the black community. So Alinsky was invited. He and his Chicago-based Industrial Areas Foundation are known for an aggressive and publicly combative style against white power structures. We agreed that we would only be consultants, Alinsky's way of underscoring that blacks must lead blacks to win concessions. Whites would be encouraged to play roles only as friends and supporters.

"Rochester is a company town. Eastman Kodak and, to a lesser extent, Xerox, are major players in many aspects of the city's economic, political and cultural life. Alinsky and Minister Florence liked the name F.I.G.H.T. for a new, black community organization to confront the local giants.

"On December 22nd Kodak nullified an agreement made with F.I.G.H.T., which had been signed by a Kodak vice president only two days before. The agreement was to recruit 600 blacks to work at the company. We want you volunteers to extend F.I.G.H.T.'s reach wider in the community, to force Kodak to honor its agreement."

"Will some of the residents resent us outsiders telling them what to do?" Arthur asked.

"You don't tell folks what to do," Ron responded. "You give them the facts about Kodak's breaking the agreement, which meant jobs for them and their neighbors, and how the community is not going to take this lying down. Then listen to them. Answer any questions you know the answer to. Invite them to attend the next community meeting."

Arthur and his Cornell brothers worked night and day, going door-to-door in black communities as sub-zero winds whipped off Lake Ontario through the city streets. Residents opened their doors, at first surprised and then flattered that enthusiastic college students thought enough about their problems to spend time with them. Remembering Freedom Summer in Mississippi, Arthur dubbed their efforts "Freedom Winter," the major difference being that knocking on doors and leading meetings were now exclusively done by blacks. Arthur also felt proud that he was fighting for economic gains. He had been, of course, proud of his older brother fighting for civil and political rights, but Arthur knew that abiding respect and freedom were, in capitalist America, based on a firm economic footing. The opening up of jobs in white corporations today, Arthur reasoned, meant blacks learning skills on which their children could build their own businesses, eventually leading to whole communities not being dependent on white largesse for employment.

On New Year's Eve, Arthur finally got his chance to be with his hero. Ron had asked Arthur to drive Minister Florence to the local airport where he was to meet with visiting national church officials from New York. Arthur expected to listen to a firebrand, denouncing the treachery of whites while extolling the virtues of an organized black community. After all, it had only been eight days since Kodak had broken the agreement for which Florence had hailed the company's "vision".

"I'm so happy to drive you, Minister Florence," Arthur said.

"I'm glad you're driving. I have a lot on my mind."

"I know you're going to beat Kodak."

"Perhaps, but to tell you the truth, the more time I have to spend away from my family, the more I think of them."

"But Kodak's the enemy, right?"

"Son, there are lots of so-called enemies, but," Minister Florence paused for a moment, "but I can still remember the excitement in my young son's eyes when he opened up the Christmas present I made for him. A hobby horse. I'm sure he's riding it now. And how about you, Arthur? Do you have any brothers and sisters?"

"An older brother, but I want you to know that my Cornell brothers and I want to create a department of Black Studies."

"I like that idea."

"Yes, and we're discussing the taking of any action necessary to achieve that goal."

"Son, please remember, never push whites beyond the point of no return. They'll never sit down with you again. They'll cut you down. Always, always give them a way out."

Arthur was surprised. It was not a sentiment he expected, but he said nothing in response.

In the first week of April, Arthur spread out a map of New Jersey, but he could not immediately find Flemington on it. Knowing that F.I.G.H.T. had purchased ten shares of common stock with the intention of confronting Kodak at its annual stockholders' meeting, Arthur realized Kodak had chosen a location as far away from a large city as possible, making it difficult to draw demonstrators, let alone Rochester's black community some 300 miles away. In addition, Kodak had decided to hold its meeting not at a hotel, where demonstrators might have a chance to buttonhole stockholders in the lobby, but at a local high school. Arthur was fast learning the tricks corporations play.

When Arthur and his brothers pulled into the Hunterdon High School parking lot, where the demonstration was being held, they could not believe their eyes. Not only had F.I.G.H.T. brought some 350 demonstrators, another 350 had been mobilized from New York, New Jersey and elsewhere. The group from Rochester was predominantly black, while the other demonstrators were predominantly white. Arthur spotted a familiar face, though he could not place it at first. Then he recalled his talking with Daniel at length during one of the breaks at the Wappinger Retreat. Glad to see someone he knew, Arthur also wondered what motivated this white man to come to Flemington.

About six weeks earlier, in mid-March, the most intense period of Daniel's life was about to begin. Daniel had been invited by one of the national church leaders, who had been with Minister Florence during that New Year's Eve airport meeting, to be the sole organizer of people in the New York City area to support the F.I.G.H.T. organization at Kodak stockholders' meeting. How Daniel had been chosen he never found out, but he immediately threw himself into the task. He had talked on the phone dozens of times a day, driven a rented car sometimes a hundred miles a day, recruiting students, faculty and some townspeople from university and college campuses in New York City and suburbs, northern and central New Jersey, and eastern Pennsylvania. Daniel had visited each recruiting location several times, first meeting with campus ministers and other local leaders sympathetic to the civil rights movement, then returning a second and third time to recruit people to journey to Flemington, a town few even knew existed, to support an organization none had ever heard of. Daniel had been supplied with an American Express credit card for expenses by a department in the National Council of Churches, which had also paid for the rented car, but had not offered—nor had Daniel asked for—a salary for himself. Once he had recovered from the sheer terror of agreeing to take on such a gargantuan project, the thrill of possibly being a part of history-in-the-making was more than enough reward, or so he thought during the last weeks of March. Doubts mounted, however, as each minute became more nerve-wracking than the last with the calendar flipping rapidly toward April 25th.

The week before the stockholders' meeting, Daniel had driven the rented car along the precise route into Flemington and to the high school. He drew a map of the route, with landmarks along the way for each of the bus drivers to follow. Knowing the precise driving time, Daniel had made certain that his bus stayed at the head of the caravan of nine packed buses in order to set the pace and decide when to make pit stops, so that every demonstrator would arrived at the high school location well before the start of the stockholders' meeting.

Daniel busied himself with giving out hand-lettered placards to every fifth or sixth person descending from his bus. Greeting the demonstrators with a smile as each stepped onto the parking lot asphalt, Daniel thanked them. He had instructed captains on the other eight buses to do the same.

At first, white and black demonstrators remained in their own section of the large parking lot, not wary of each other, but uncertain what to do next. It was the Rev. Marvin Chandler from Rochester who walked from the group of black demonstrators to the whites, welcomed them, and invited them to join the Rochester contingent. It was then that Arthur, spotting Daniel walking toward the Rochester group, waved at him.

"Hey, what are *you* doing *here*?" each asked in unison, surprised to see the other. Not only surprised, but curious. Their mutual question implied another: "What journey have you been on, since we first met at that retreat just over a year ago, that has brought you to *this* place *today*?"

Each felt strangely compelled, as if entering a confessional for the first time, to unburden himself to the other. As if no one else in the parking lot mattered, they were drawn to each other by an overwhelming need to unlock and disclose a secret life they had kept hidden from family and friends, and even their closest comrades. Daniel looked into Arthur's face and saw an acceptance he had never felt before from anyone, except his grandmother whose own secret had disturbed his relationship with her. In turn, Arthur looked into Daniel's face and saw an innocence he could trust.

"It's been quite a year since Wappinger, hasn't it?" Daniel began.

"Yes, it has. I can't think of a year in my life that has changed me more," Arthur responded.

"That's for sure," Daniel continued.   "It's frightening what I've learned.   I'm certain now that the white power structure has co-opted and suppressed peoples of color in America and killed or imprisoned peoples of color in foreign lands either directly or through military support of dictators."

"I wholeheartedly agree," Arthur continued.   "I'll give you an example.   I almost puke whenever I see Lyndon Johnson on TV.   His Great Society is only designed to co-opt black leadership, and his Vietnam War is a way to draft blacks, and others, to kill browns, leaving whites a clear path to enlarge their imperialist reach, at home and abroad."

"I'm with you. I feel the same way. I hate Johnson.."

During their conversation, each came to realize that the other had selected different, but unexpectedly compatible, authors to read again and again, as if their books, now heavily underlined and highlighted, had become canonical texts, quoted whenever necessary.   As they shared more and more of their stories and attitudes, it dawned on both that Daniel's white radical and Arthur's black power positions were closer than they had ever imagined.

"No man is an Island,"

Daniel began to quote aloud quietly, almost to himself, recalling a poem he had once memorized.

"Entire of itself.
Every man is a piece of the continent,
Part of the main.
If a clod be washed away by the sea,
Europe is the less.
As well as if a promontory were.
As well as if a manor of thy friends or of thine own were."

Daniel stopped as he heard another voice.

"Any man's death diminishes me,"

Arthur continued without missing a beat.

"Because I am involved in Mankind.

And therefore never send to know
For whom the bell tolls,
It tolls for thee."

Both sat silent for a moment. They then turned to face each other, and smiled a knowing smile, heads nodding slowly.

The silence continued, hanging in the air between them, as the noise of idled demonstrators surrounded them. They then resumed comparing notes.

They realized how passionately each believed in following an authentic leadership, leaders who had been through the crucible of struggle, shoulder to shoulder with those whom they would lead. Names of what they considered fake leaders were tossed about, people who spoke charismatically to groups, but had excuses for not talking one-on-one to the powerful, saying the time wasn't right.

"Stokely Carmichael said that any organization seeking to lead a community must speak in the tone of that community," Arthur stated. "That's what Black Power means. We are going to use our own words, Stokely said, speak in our own language, not the words whites have put into our mouths."

"I know exactly what you mean," Daniel responded. "The other side of that coin is what Saul Alinsky called stooge groups. Watch out for them, Saul said, because they might look good on paper, their leaders boasting lots of members, but they represent no one. Their leaders just want to be in on the action, looking for an eventual payoff. They talk citizen participation, but just let even a few community folks try to get in the door of their bogus grass roots' meetings, and they'll cancel the meeting or change its location."

"And you know what? Stokely talks about black people defining for ourselves who we are. For hundreds of years we've let white people define who we are, lie about who we are and what we can do. Yeah, we're lazy, right, lazy enough to pick cotton from sun up 'til sun down, lazy enough to take care of our own family and then see our mothers take care of Miss Ann's family. I know what you're talkin' about when you talk about leadership. We've got so-called leaders who spend more time on how they can please the white man than how they can fight for the black man."

"You know, I've sat in the same room with representatives of welfare and poverty organizations and I've heard them, like Saul has said, assess local leaders using their own liberal, middleclass criteria, evaluate what is good or bad in the community according to their own code. They wouldn't know a natural, indigenous community leader if they tripped over one."

"Any leader that's a true leader must recognize that their power comes from the unified and collective strength of the community, Stokely says. Then true black leadership can not be bought off by white leadership with either patronage or prestige, and so whites will have to talk to the community's representatives in terms of real power."

"The power of the people. That's what it's all about. All power to the people. That's what Saul says, that's what Stokely says."

Everyone was standing around, waiting for the stockholders' meeting to begin. Arthur and Daniel moved to the edge of the parking lot, away from the idled demonstrators, and sat down on a curbstone.

During his short activist career, Arthur had already come to expect drama and excitement during the run-up to a demonstration, and then a good deal of boredom during it. Counting the number of demonstrators, buying next day's newspapers to see if there was any, let alone accurate, coverage, analyzing how the next demonstration could be organized to draw more people than the last—it was becoming all-too predictable. True, Arthur still loved to see the excitement in the new faces and voices swelling the ranks, the expressions of hope that this time the power structure would be convinced to alter course, but the excitement for him was fading more quickly now.

Daniel did not yet feel demonstrations were ineffective or a waste of time, but he had been in so many over the last almost one and one-half years that he, too, felt they had taken on a certain predictability. He had recently concluded there was not a big enough payoff for all the effort expended. He was questioning strategy and tactics, looking for more powerful means to bring the elite to the table, to force them to change.

Continuing their conversation, each began to see in the other the possibility of moving toward the next political plateau. Instead of sharing their own experiences and what they had learned, they continued to paraphrase their political mentors, as if Carmichael and Alinsky spoke for them, as if their mentors' words on paper were gospel, spoke for all activists, and perfectly described the enemy, without nuance or exception.

"White people always talk about giving black folks our freedom instead of, like Stokely says, what they're really doing is always denying us our freedom. Well it's time they learned that no one can give another his freedom. We've got to take it for ourselves."

"Man, are you right. I've finally come to realize that the only thing my people understand is power. They may cloak it in a rainbow of colorful ribbons. They may share the crumbs and fool themselves into believing it's a main meal, but in the end, wealthy white people erect all types of barriers to keep others outside their counting houses stuffed with the booty of centuries of grand theft.

"You know, I've seen something going on lately which, to me, is the height of cynicism. It's happening with organizations. Whites are electing or appointing blacks to positions of what would have been prestige positions long held by whites, creating all this theatre to look like whites are just bending with the times, doing the correct thing in the face of the civil rights movement, but what they don't tell the incoming blacks is that they've taken all the goodies and moved them someplace else, formed another committee or organization which really holds the power and purse strings, leaving those now black-led organizations weakened. And who gets blamed when they start failing?"

An hour after it began, having heard Kodak's board chairman announce that the company would not honor the December 20th agreement, Minister Florence walked out of the auditorium. Addressing the demonstrators in the parking lot, Minister Florence said he would lead a nationwide march to the Kodak headquarters on the June anniversary of the Rochester riot. Some took this to mean he was threatening violence against Kodak if the company did not accede to F.I.G.H.T.'s demands. Some other remarks were made, and the demonstration was over.

"Arthur, do you mind, and do you think your friends will mind, if I ride back with you to Cornell? I'd like to continue talking with you."

"No, not at all. We've still have lots to talk about."

As he walked back to his bus to tell the others he was not returning with them, Daniel was deeply disappointed that his six weeks' worth of intense organization had not persuaded Kodak to honor its agreement. Nevertheless, he was also energized by what he took to be Minister Florence's threat of violence. He remembered the thrill he felt when smashing the pane of glass in the Columbia University president's door. He had not only gotten away with it, Daniel had warmed to the idea of destroying more property as a protest tactic. He had often fantasized that his destroying symbols of power was a liberating exercise, signaling the Establishment that their symbols of power held no awe or mystery, but were only the gaudy trappings of an immoral elite intended to deflect the public's attention from their misdeeds and crimes. Waxing more and more arrogant as he had sharpened his focus on what he considered the vulnerable places in the Establishment's armor, Daniel saw himself smashing the display windows at Bergdorf Goodman's on Fifth Avenue, and burning tires at the entrance to the New York Stock Exchange before the opening bell to prevent employees from entering. He had often imagined the disguises, escape routes, and cover stories he would invent to explain why he was in his targets' neighborhoods, if ever questioned. Daniel now pictured a mass of black and white demonstrators descending in June on the Kodak headquarters, blockading all truck entrances for days, finding where the silver for making photographic film was stored, then threatening to degrade the silver by pouring acid on it unless Kodak hired the 600 blacks recommended by F.I.G.H.T.. Daniel felt so powerful, so in control of events and their outcomes, in his imagination.

Arthur returned to his car to ask his fellow passengers to wait for Daniel. He was troubled by Minister Florence's possible threat of violence. Arthur had heard Stokely and others repeatedly use the phrase "by any means necessary," and he had used it many times during tactical discussions with brothers at Cornell, but for the first time he confronted himself with its practical implications. Did he want to face criminal arrest by destroying private property? How could the public be made to understand the symbolism of such destruction as an act of political protest? He instinctively put his hand to his neck as he wondered whether such destruction would trigger a white vigilante reaction.

Daniel diligently spoke with each of the nine bus captains, to make sure they double-checked their rosters so that everyone who came to Flemington returned on the same bus. Then he walked toward Arthur's car, so very pleased with himself for a moment, having mentally crossed off the last entry in his extraordinarily long "to do" list begun six weeks ago. Daniel allowed himself to feel a moment of relaxation and accomplishment. And then, suddenly, he felt so very empty, the victory he had imagined having been denied him.

The four piled out of the Chevy and walked up the short flight of concrete steps into the stainless steel, shiny, brightly-lit diner. Arthur and his two schoolmates chose a booth just inside the door, along the row next to the large windows, so that they could keep an eye on their car. Daniel was unaware of the reason for their choosing this booth. He was simply content to be inside the familiar surroundings of a diner, here on Route 11 in downtown Whitney Point, seventeen miles due north of Binghamton. It reminded him of the diners back on Long Island.

About twenty minutes before, the urging of their empty stomachs had persuaded the three black students to abandon their plan to make Ithaca without stopping, except for gas. Arthur and Daniel had been discussing what Arthur called northern racism which, though less overt he said than in the South, was nevertheless just as oppressive and exploitative.

"No, no, I can't agree with you," Daniel had objected. "Sure, there are individual acts of discrimination, but black people can vote, can move practically anywhere they want in the North, can apply and get into excellent universities. You must see that, Arthur."

"I don't have to see anything, if it does not exist," Arthur had replied evenly. "There's a subtle paternalism in the North, and its aim is exactly the same as the Jim Crow laws and all the Bull Connors in the South, to keep black people believing they are inferior. If you want to make it in the North, you've got to play by the white man's rules and customs, and even then you'll always have to keep proving yourself, performing better than the white man at the white man's game, and if you succeed, do well in his world, then the white man'll change the rules of the game, just like that."

"Oh, I don't believe that. I had a wonderful Negro teacher, Mr. McMasters, in high school. He was idolized by his white students. And I would visit my Negro friends in their homes, and they and their parents made me feel very welcome."

"Did you ever invite your so-called Negro friends to your home?"

"Let me think. No, I never did. I don't know why. I remember one time after a Little League game, I asked my Dad if we could bring Prescott with us to the ice cream parlor we always went to after the game, but he said, no, he had to go straight home and work on something. I think it would have been OK with my parents to ask Preston to our home, but something always seemed to come up, so I didn't."

"Look, we're stopping at that diner up ahead. Just keep your eyes and ears open, and I'll show you what I've been talking about," Arthur had said.

The white waitress, pad in hand, approached the booth from the middle of the diner where the opening between the counters allowed her to enter and exit the kitchen. Daniel's and Arthur's backs were to her as she approached.

The waitress stood in front of the middle of the booth, turned to Daniel and asked him if he wanted separate checks. After a brief discussion among the four, Arthur said to the waitress that one check would be fine. The waitress continued to look at Daniel for confirmation.

"What would you like?" the waitress finally asked Daniel. Taking Daniel's order, she asked no one in particular, "And what do you boys want?"

When she left the booth, Arthur turned to Daniel, looking him straight in the eyes.

"Now you see why Ralph Ellison wrote the book, *The Invisible Man*! That waitress noticed us alright, but didn't want to see us, as individuals I mean. That's what I was talking about, Daniel. We're in what is supposed to be an enlightened region, not all that far from Albany, New York, and we could just as well be in Albany, Georgia."

When the meal was over, the waitress brought the check without anyone asking for it. She placed it in front of Daniel.

"Why did you do that?" Daniel asked the waitress.

"Do what?"

"Place the check in front of me. There are four of us at the table."

"But you asked for one check, and I just thought you'd be paying for everyone."

"First of all, it was my friend Arthur, here, who asked for the one check, not me. And second, why did you assume I'd be paying for everyone?"

"I don't know. Don't make a federal case out of it, I just assumed," the waitress said in a peeved tone.

182

"You mean you assumed because I was white and my friends are black that I could afford all this food and they couldn't?"

"No, no, of course not! How could you think that?" the waitress responded sharply. "Well, I guess I thought, well, it's a complicated bill, what with everyone ordering different items at different prices, so, well, there's a lot of figuring to do, and, well, look, you want more coffee?"

The waitress abruptly left the booth after re-filling near-empty mugs. While the other three laughed aloud, Daniel shook his head from side to side, smiling knowingly to show Arthur that he understood the lesson he had just been taught.

Arthur tallied each one's share of the bill, and then suggested each contribute whatever they wanted for the tip.

"You're going to leave her a *tip*?!" Daniel asked incredulously.

"You bet, and a generous one!"

"I just don't understand. She insulted you at every opportunity."

"No, no, let me explain. White people have been insulting us all their lives. It's second nature to them. Most of the time they don't even know they're doing it. But we're used to it. So, it's only an insult if we let it hurt our feelings or lower our self-esteem. Like I said to you before in the high school parking lot, we have long believed it's our mission in life to civilize the white man, teach them how to behave. True, we've really begun to grow weary of this monumental task, and we now really think whites like you should take it over, organize in your own racist communities, because it's now time for us to build up our own communities, without you, but still, here we are, in a diner, with a waitress who's been carefully taught all her life not to recognize the humanity of a black man. So, my mother always taught me, leave a big tip no matter how you are treated, much more than the waitress expects, so that you leave making a good impression because my race is counting on me to make these good impressions, but frankly, I don't know how long I can follow my mother's advice and stay sane!"

Arthur and Daniel were back on the road again, sitting, as they were previously, in the back seat while Arthur's brothers continued to take turns driving.

"Look, we need to be honest with each other, right?" Arthur began.

"Yes, of course," Daniel agreed immediately.

"OK, I think we agree on a lot," Arthur continued. "But, could we actually work together, I mean, say, over a long period of time? What I'm saying is, could blacks and whites ever work together to achieve freedom, for blacks, poor whites, anyone who is oppressed?"

"We agree that integration is not the solution," Daniel declared.

"Yes, we do," Arthur responded. "Even if integration were possible, the black community would not develop on its own terms, preserving its own racial and cultural personality. No, integration is intended to abolish the black community's own identity. No matter how often the media distorts and lies about the meaning of Black Power, this is the essential difference between integration as it is currently practiced and the concept of Black Power."

"OK, so while all this organizing by blacks in the black community is going on, what do whites do?"

"Here's an easy question for me to ask, and a damn hard one for you to answer and especially to put into practice. Can white activists stop trying to come alive using the black community as your caffeine rush, and be men who are willing to move into the white community and start organizing in white communities to oppose white power structures? Can you do that?" Arthur asked.

"Honestly, I'm not sure."

Daniel then told Arthur about some white male organizers he knew personally who had worked for several years in black neighborhoods, north and south, who were now more frequently hearing the loud cries for Black Power from young blacks in those neighborhoods as well as softer references to Black Power from older blacks whom the white male organizers knew as well as their own family. Daniel told Arthur that he had looked into the eyes of these white male organizers and had seen a distracted, almost glazed stare, as if these men willfully refused to absorb and adjust to what they were hearing all around them. It was as if these white males had been piloting an airplane, which once had lots of thrust, but was now stalled in mid-air, gliding without fuel to power their engines. It was only a matter of time before they crashed. All around them would witness the tragedy, but these white men, still focused on doing what they had always believed was still working, would never even sense their crash landing was happening."

"I've seen that glazed stare, too," Arthur responded, "in some liberal professors whose moral compass still relies on dead reckoning, but they don't get, as the world quickly changes around them, how condescending they now sound. And you know what? Politically active white folks need to find their own psychologists! We blacks refuse to be the therapy for white society any longer. We have gone stark, raving mad trying to do it."

Both fell silent. The car sped along Route 79 North as the sun began its final descent toward night behind the trees of Buttermilk Falls State Park. Arthur was the first to break the silence.

"Remember the waitress back at the diner?"

"Sure."

"Now, maybe what you and I did was a kind of dance around her racism, and maybe, after thinking about us, maybe she thought about her behavior, and maybe she might serve blacks differently next time, but maybe not, OK?

"Yes, I get you."

"But that pace of change, if it happens at all, is so slow. We cannot go one white person at a time. So we've tried non-violent demonstrations and sit-ins, and that's helped, but we're not being treated equally and fairly in the place where it really counts, in the marketplace, right?"

"That's right."

"So what is it that the white man really understands? You see it throughout the white man's history and even today?"

"You tell me."

"The power of the gun."

"Really?"

"Think about it. Land grabbed from native Americans at the point of a gun. Spaniards and Portuguese and English, French and German colonizing people at the point of a gun. Hitler's Panzer divisions, American soldiers in Vietnam's rice paddies, white police gunning down unarmed young black men, two crackers murdering Emmet Till. It's the only real kind of power whites understand. So, tell me, Daniel, do you believe blacks in America are entitled to the right of self-defense, just like every other American?"

"Absolutely."

"So do I. But what about blacks arming themselves and, for example, firing at police in the ghetto, like warning shots, or even hitting a few, so they get the message to leave us alone?"

"No, I don't believe that's morally right, or even practical."

"Well, I think we agree on that. But the big question remains, short of taking up arms offensively, what can be done to create a force powerful enough to convince whites, in the same measure as if they were actually staring down the barrels of guns held by black men, that they need to give up some of that political and economic power they so jealously guard?"

Arthur and Daniel talked for the next hour about the design of a grand political strategy and its accompanying tactics. They first reviewed the effectiveness of progressive strategies they both knew well.

Daniel began, "When folks want to mobilize pressure on decision-makers in the white power structure, we resort to putting together coalitions, don't we?"

"We seem to rely recently on that strategy a lot," Arthur responded. "But there are also a lot of pitfalls, aren't there?"

"Yes, a lot. For example, there is a lot of effort put into gathering names of organizations to sponsor, say, an 'Appeal to Conscience' about some issue or crisis, or to get those organizations to sponsor a demonstration and urge their members to picket," Daniel said.

"True," Arthur continued, "but these efforts have flaws, and are unsustainable over the long haul. For example, it takes precious time to contact enough organizations to make the public listing of them on a letterhead or in a newspaper ad or on a flyer—precious time to have enough organizational names to make a big impact."

"Exactly," Daniel continued. "And then there are the heavy-weight organizations which can really add lots of clout, but their internal decision-making process takes weeks, if not months, to decide to join the coalition, and sometimes they finally decide not to join."

"And you've got to wonder," Arthur mused, "when you see the same names of organizations, or their leaders, and the same names of well-known people appearing more or less again and again and again no matter what the issue or crisis. You can just imagine hearing a loud yawn coming from the white power structure every time a new newspaper appeal appears with the old rent-a-group names, or they receive a letter from the 'Committee To ...' or the 'Coalition Against ...' with the same sponsors, or some variation of the same sponsors, again listed on the letterhead."

Arthur continued, "And what gets me, nine times out of ten, is that only the name of the organization's leader appears, often with an asterisk saying that leader is representing only himself or herself, that they're not speaking on behalf of the organization, so you know there is not the strength and voice of the entire organization in the support of the appeal."

"Earlier, Arthur, you said these coalitions are not sustainable over the long haul, which means their pressure on decision-makers can fade even though the issue or crisis continues. I'll give you an example. We know that you have to take the time and effort to cultivate progressive leaders, but then the top leader's term of office, in some organizations, might only be a year. So you've got to repeat that same time and effort on the new leader who might finally decide he doesn't want to be part of the coalition anymore."

"That's right. And you know, in all of this strategizing, we've got to talk about 'power to the people'. How does the 'power to the people' fit into a Grand Strategy?"

Arthur and Daniel concluded that coalitions, as currently structured, could win a few concessions, but would not fundamentally force significant changes in the existing power relationships.

They then agreed that the bedrock basis for fundamental change would occur when multi-issue, community-based organizations led by authentic leaders were engaged in a regional and national network, creating powerful enough coalitions to bring whites to the negotiating table and keep them there.

"The community-based organization has to be multi-issue," Arthur argued. "When asked to support another group on a different issue, a single-issue group will only get involved if they see it will further their own self-interest. In addition, if a single-issue group's leader keeps urging the members to support this or that appeal for action, they'll wear out the members especially if those appeals do not strongly reflect the reasons why the member joined in the first place."

"I see what you mean, Arthur. So then, a multi-issue organization can call on only that portion of the membership, which is more likely to support action on one type of appeal, and another portion more likely to support action on another type of appeal. This way the entire membership will not be worn out. In other words, the multi-issue organization can structure itself to be flexible enough to respond repeatedly to calls for action at critical points in a variety of struggles."

"You've got it," Arthur responded, "but now we've got to figure out who actually decides which appeals are worthy of mobilization, and who decides what parts of the network are mobilized and for how long, and how is the success or failure of any action measured."

"I learned somewhere along the way that, often outnumbered by the cavalry in battle, native Americans moved their warriors from rock to rock, so that their gunfire, coming from many different locations, created the illusion of greater numbers," Daniel remarked.

"I think you watched too many TV Westerns!" Arthur joked.

"You could be right," Daniel agreed.

"But still, during key moments in a struggle where overwhelming pressure was needed to bring the white enemy to the negotiating table," Arthur offered, "we need to devise a strategy of concentric circles of influence being brought into play."

"OK," began Daniel, "let's say you bring together lots of community-based groups like we talked about. Let's call them network partners. After a lot of discussion among the partners, each would assign themselves to one or more in a series of concentric circles based on geography. Let's say one partner was solely based in a neighborhood, another was city-wide, and a third had regional participation. That would make three concentric circles of influence. Any number of concentric circles could be brought into play to create a force, which is concentrated, numerous, and sustainable enough to persuade whites to surrender some of their power."

"So how would it be decided which circle or circles would get involved in an action?" asked Arthur.

"Good question. Here's how I think it could work. It starts with the nature of the issue itself and then identifying the initial decision-makers who represent the powers-that-be. For example, if the issue was localized, like a policeman shooting an unarmed black teenager, initially the neighborhood network partner would act. But since we also want to outflank the initial decision-makers, the neighborhood partner would work with city-wide network partners. Once the mayor, chief of police, and police union leader get involved to protect the policeman, those city-wide partners would then join with county-wide network partners, once again trying to outflank the authorities."

"I get you," Arthur continued. "And if the city authorities reached out for regional allies, then the next concentric circle's network partners, say, on the state level, would get involved, as well as involving local partners from other cities."

"Yes, and depending on the issue and the players now involved," Daniel continued, "national partners with proven track records of supporting community-based organizations would act. It might even require an international action because some of those national organizations have overseas affiliates."

"OK, I can see how that works," Arthur responded. "But who decides to get the mobilization going? We know there is sometimes rivalry and jealousy among and even within the best organizations."

"One *elected* person."

"You're kidding!"

"No, not when you think about it," Daniel said. "Here's my idea. Think about all the executive directors you've ever known running non-profit, progressive organizations. They are *appointed* by their boards to that position. Board members have sometimes conflicting viewpoints, back different candidates. If the executive director wants to back a major action, he or she has their board looking over their shoulder, sometimes blocking it. The executive director always has to worry about the board's reactions, or he/she maybe out of a job."

"True," Arthur continued, "I've run across a lot of them who are caught between keeping their jobs and serving the constituency of their organization. And it's rare they buck the board. So much for power to the people."

"Precisely," Daniel responded.

As the sun set, Arthur and Daniel continued to discuss the critical question of where the seat of authority lay within their grand political strategy, and who occupied it. They both knew that "umbrella" groups, formed by old style coalitions to call coalition members into action, were cumbersome, sometimes slow to act due to leadership rivalries within the "umbrella" group. In addition, the umbrella group had virtually no money to carry out their joint decisions, relying on each coalition partners' meager staff, already overburdened, to take on additional tasks to get the entire coalition in motion and serve its subsequent needs. In a few coalitions, there was some money to hire staff dedicated only to the coalition itself, but these meager staffs were equally overburdened.

No, a new mechanism, powered by a different understanding of authority, was required, Arthur and Daniel agreed, but one organically related to the community-based network partners so that the mechanism itself would not become yet another regional or national bureaucracy, however small, telling local groups what to do.

"Here's how I visualize it," Daniel began again. "There would be a series of city-wide, then regional, and then national meetings of representative delegates from multi-issue, community-based organizations. Through workshops, speeches, informal meetings, lots of people would be getting to know one another. Not just by reputation, but by how they acted in those settings. Perhaps it would take a year for all these meetings to occur, but at the end, there would be a final national meeting for the purpose of electing one person for a one-year term. It would be a competitive election, with candidates on the same platform having to answer questions in an open forum from all the delegates. This elected-one would, in turn, appoint one person affiliated with each of the network partners to be a member of the Communications Network (CN), as this imagined organization would be called.

"The decision to call into action any coalitional partner from any concentric circle would be made solely by the elected-one. It is understood that the elected-one is in constant consultation with the CN members. The decision to bring into play any combination of network partners would be made also with the understanding that any partner asked must comply immediately and extend their actions as long as the elected-one required."

"I like this, but what happens after a year?" Arthur asked.

"Another national meeting, with another election. The same person can run again and be elected, but cannot serve unless at least one other person runs against him or her."

"OK," Arthur wondered, "are those members of the CN also the heads of community-based organizations?"

"Absolutely not," Daniel responded. "One of the more stubborn obstacles in the way of effective multi-organizational campaigns has been the dual role played by heads of organizations who also represent their organization in a coalition. It's not just this dual role that creates a huge workload beyond an individual's capacity. The dual role sometimes creates conflicts of interest between the leaders' two roles, not to mention rivalries among leaders. No, the elected-one appoints as a CN member someone known and respected by the community organization with which they are affiliated, but not its leader. The appointee is to be both in the flow of the community organizations efforts, and a two-way reporter/advisor between the community organization and the elected-one."

"So, to guard against creating any bureaucracy," Arthur continued, "I should think that the elected-one would also have a small budget, funded by the network partners on a proportional basis, with which he or she could hire a small staff devoted entirely to the day-to-day flow of information required to keep the Communication Network members well informed on developments. And a tiny board of directors, required only for incorporation purposes, receiving funds, and the obligatory annual meeting."

"I agree," Daniel said. "Therefore, the seat of authority would be the elected-one who would be in continuing consultation with members of the Network. Powerful partnership actions could be quickly launched, and, more importantly, sustained for the duration of the battle. In fact, several large-scale battles could be fought simultaneously because different parts of the Network could be engaged in different battles.

"As I see it, over time the CN members' primary allegiance would grow more and more to be to the other CN members, and less and less to the elected-one. That's because they would continue to meet in regional and national gatherings. In this way, CN members would have the independence and ability to measure results objectively. Such independent analysis is critical for success. Because they are comparing notes with one another to analyze what worked and what did not, as well as sharing uniquely new tactics and research, CN members will more rapidly discover vulnerable points of entry into the power structure's armor than traditional coalitions. CN members will also be able to repair quickly any weaknesses in their forces.

"Finally, the CN members freedom to circulate any analysis critical of the elected-one's decisions would provide the check on his or her power, as well as ammunition for anyone seeking that position in the annual election."

As the car turned right onto Dryden Road from Cornell Street, Arthur and Daniel were in high spirits. They knew their work, along with the work of many others in support of F.I.G.H.T., had brought TV cameras and print reporters to the high school parking lot and corridors, focusing the nation's attention on the hypocrisy of a highly regarded international company. They also knew so much more had to be done if Kodak or Dow or First National City Bank were ever to give up some of their power and control.

Arthur and Daniel at least now had their Grand Political Strategy, in theory at least.

CHAPTER 11 – CONFRONTATION (SUMMER 1967)

Burn, Baby, Burn, words and music by Jimmy Collier, 1966, written in response to the 1965 Watts' riot while he was living in Chicago.

This Land Ain't Your Land, sung to the tune of Woodie Guthrie's *This Land is My Land*. It was a favorite especially of "short-timers" in Vietnam who, after each verse, shouted "Short, Short, Short."

The Trailways bus from Ithaca rolled into New York's Port Authority Bus Terminal early the next afternoon. As the bus door opened, Daniel did not hesitate a moment. He ran to the Seventh Avenue subway, and boarded the uptown express to 125th Street. Walking the streets of Harlem again, not lowering his eyes as he passed its residents, Daniel headed for 63 Tiemann Place to the woman he thought he now knew well. He had no clue as to the secret life Christie was living.

Ever since last September's party in Baltimore after the radical research and action meeting, Christie had felt herself a different woman. Whether it had been the wine, rocking music or anonymity that night, Christie had experienced physical liberation for the first time in her life. Moving her body to the driving beat of almost every song, she had no concern as to how she looked to others. Centuries of breeding had fallen away. Self-consciousness had lost herself. It had been as if her clothes no longer constrained her spirit, but rather had untied themselves and fallen, unveiling an energy and excitement never experienced by her before. During the long evening, Christie had been neither herself nor anyone else, but a vortex of joy moving in space and time.

When Christie had returned to Morningside Heights, she attended as many parties as possible, always going and returning alone. Sharing the experience with anyone else, either on the dance floor or in conversation afterwards, distorted and diminished it, she had been certain. Christie had owned space and time, more comfortable in her body and self-assured in her spirit than ever before.

Now dating often, some had been "political," with young men in the movement. Others were "social," with young men starting their climb on the corporate ladder. She never, however, had gone dancing with any of them. Her "partners" at these dances, if such a word applied, had been young men and women spatially closest to her who, for a moment, had displayed movements with their heads, hands, or hips that acknowledged or were in syncopation with her own. Such recognition and validation, though frequent, had been short-lived. It was, however, enough for Christie.

On occasion, always deliberately with a different young man, Christie had permitted sexual intercourse, but not as herself. Unmarried physical intimacy had been the last sinful act still clinging to her orthodox Calvinist upbringing, or so she had thought. As the moment approached when she was entered, Christie had distanced herself from penetration by transporting her body outside the room to anywhere safe and wholesome. She had denied its power by imagining herself at a Sunday church picnic, squeals of pleasure arising from a little girl's enjoyment of licking an ice cream cone or feeling her father's hands around her waist, lifting her onto a pony. She had been determined to remain pure throughout.

The lobby front door to Number 63 had been carelessly left ajar. Daniel pushed it open and bound up the flights of stairs, two steps at a time. How familiar these steps had become since he had comforted Christie at the Retreat. Over the succeeding months, nothing had been agreed, or even ever discussed between them, about the status of their relationship, but as Daniel rounded the banister on the fourth floor, in anticipation of seeing Christie, the only person with whom he wanted to share his newly discovered grand political strategy, he experienced a rush of love for her never felt before. Out of breath from the swift climb, almost doubled-over by the sharp pain below his right rib, which he was massaging with his left hand, he paused on the landing. Soon, he straightened, smiling broadly. Such a sweet feeling, this love, as if a spring meadow were inviting him to lose himself in its fragrances, enticing him to shed "to do" lists, schedules, meeting agendas. He turned a corner on the landing and began to ascend the last flight to her door. Just then, above him, Daniel could hear Christie saying "good-bye" to someone.

Ephraim descended the stairway.

"What are *you* doing here?" Daniel snapped.

"Oh, nothing much. Christie and I get together to discuss ancient texts. She's learning Sumerian, you know, and I'm taking advanced Hebrew."

"No, I didn't know. She never told me you and she were seeing each other," Daniel replied, more to himself than Ephraim.

"Look, we should all get together for a party at my place, OK?" Ephraim said enthusiastically.

"Oh, OK," Daniel said half-heartedly.

No sooner had Christie opened her door than Daniel demanded, "What is that guy doing in your apartment?"

"Ephraim?"

"You know who I mean. I didn't know you were seeing each other."

"I'm not *seeing* him!" Christie explained, annoyed she was being questioned. "We're studying ancient languages. It's fun to share what we're learning."

"Is that all?" Daniel pressed her.

"I don't think it's any of your business. Why are you acting this way?"

"Never mind. Look, just never mind," Daniel barked, wheeled around, and headed away from the door.

"Why did you come by?" Christie called after him.

"Never mind, I said! It wasn't that damn important anyway," Daniel shouted as he quickly headed down the hallway. The stairs creaked with the weight of his bitter disappointment.

He sat on the steps of Number 63 for a long time. He felt as if the first roots of a new flower had been ripped from his heart. There they were, lying on the sidewalk in front of him, crushed underfoot by indifferent passersby. Bitterness then yielded to introspection as Daniel confronted himself about his behavior. Why had he been so possessive all of a sudden? Why was he so angry that she entertained people in her apartment without telling him? But then, why hadn't Christie told him about Ephraim? How many other visitors did she have? Oh, God, had he stayed the night?

Cooling off a bit, he asked himself what right did he have to claim a special relationship with Christie. He had assumed so much.

Still feeling rootless and empty, Daniel suddenly wondered if it had all been worthwhile, all this political running around, the endless meetings, the picketing. What had he really to show for almost two years? All this self-sacrifice, thinking of others all the time, what did it really come down to for him, his life, Daniel wondered half-aloud. Thoughts tumbled over one another, like drops of water in cascading mountain streams crisscrossing each other. Thoughts merged, then diverged, then merged again, mixing and separating so rapidly, providing no clear direction. Why so jealous? Had it all been worth it?

A half hour ago, he thought he knew his own saga so well. He was genuinely excited to share his newfound grand political strategy with the only person he thought he could trust with whatever he kept hidden behind his curtain. On the way upstairs, he had visualized Christie as being a part of every part of his life. A grand strategy coupled with blossoming love. Now, after coming back down, he was devastated. He could not trust her to be available to him whenever he needed her. Why did he feel he needed Christie? He could just keep bluffing his way through life, couldn't he? Did he really need anyone to love? Feeling desperately alone, he wondered now from where the strength would come to propagate his grand strategy. But then, why did he think he needed to be a radical activist at all? What's the use, why not give up? He was suddenly so tired, so very, very tired.

Daniel continued to sit on the steps. He thought back to the first time he had climbed them, reassured by the number 63 on the canopy that he was in the right place. Before that ascent, he now realized how much of his life had been one of obligation in exchange for emotional and physical comfort, praise and respect from others. He had traded good deeds, like campaigning for Eisenhower, for praise and, he chuckled to himself, an extra helping of mashed potatoes. Had his life really changed that much? Well, he chuckled again, not only were there no second helpings of mashed potatoes, there were no mashed potatoes at all! But had the fundamental motivation in his earlier life—obligation—been supplanted, he wondered? Or was there merely a new coin in his old realm of exchange?

Why was he running around non-stop, doing all those bits and pieces of what he was beginning to feel as political theatre? Was he still somehow obligated? To whom or what?

Daniel stared across Tiemann Place and down Claremont Avenue, for the first time in his life making the courageous attempt to separate out the hour-by-hour sheer motion of his life and all its tasks from the arc of their meaning. Complicating his self-confrontation were the many different versions of who he thought he was and what he was doing. He no longer trusted his own view of himself. To Christie, he appeared kind and gentle, yet to a university president he appeared a destroyer. To his mother and father he appeared a successful student, and yet to his professors he appeared an absentee. To the public, he appeared ebullient, self-assured, with much to offer and yet to any shop inspector he appeared to be out of goods. Who was he really?

Not getting very far in the pursuit of his truth on the steps of Number 63, Daniel went back in his imagination to a time of childhood joy and excitement, seeing himself playing touch football in the street outside his home. He saw himself take the snap, look down the block, then launch a long pass, watching the arc as it simultaneously moved forward in the air and spun rapidly on its axis. His daily political actions, he concluded, were the spinning of the football through time and space, each rotation, perhaps a bit wobbly, virtually the same as the last, sustained in flight by the force applied at the beginning, but destined to fall back to earth, no matter how high or how long the flight, pulled down by an unseen, millennia-old force. There was a second and equally important aspect to the pass itself, Daniel reasoned: its purpose. Its intent was to advance toward the goal, an imaginary line across the street marked at either end by lampposts. Although constrained by agreed-upon boundaries, made-up rules, precedents, and teammates' abilities, Daniel had relative freedom in the huddle to call the play. He chose each passes' intent.

Touch football, stickball, and other sand lot games, Daniel suddenly realized, were his childhood's antidote to obligation. More than anyone else's respect, he was earning his own self-respect through participation in these games. Of course he wanted to win, but the deepest satisfaction came when he played the game well. The choices he made, whether a cut-to-the-curb pass pattern or a low-outside curve ball, were ends in and of themselves, not means to delayed rewards from authority figures populating his world of obligation.

Or was Daniel fooling himself again? Hadn't he truly exchanged one set of authority figures for another: his parents for History, his high school teachers for Fairness, his coaches for Justice? Weren't his new authority figures just as expectant of loyalty, deference, admiration, doing well, never quitting, as the old ones? Wasn't the old mechanism of obligation still in full command? Wasn't he secretly yearning for some kind of delayed pay-off if he just kept doing what he was doing as well and as long as he could do it? Ok, yes, Daniel admitted, he liked praise from Christie, Jeff, and the others. But if obligation had never left his side, where was the physical and emotional comfort for doing his duty? The tangible payments for deeds well done? Where *were* the mashed potatoes?

Obligation or freedom? All these years, wasn't his shading the truth, even outright lying, *the* method Daniel used to carve out an area of relative freedom? How could anyone in authority nail the moving target he had become, pin him down to consistency? Eventually, even Daniel could not. Wasn't his anger a form of rebellion against obligations for which he saw no fairness in the exchange, no worthwhile rewards commensurate with the effort? If he now had relative freedom, did he need to shade the truth or lie any longer? In fact, did he still require, as Daniel had so doggedly believed in the past, a shop at all, with a public front and a private back?

Daniel was transfixed by new possibilities. He imagined himself occupying some territory, if only temporarily, akin to the street in front of his boyhood home, working out with his new-found relatives—his brothers and sisters--the boundaries, inventing the rules, testing precedents, and assessing his and his contemporaries' abilities. He did not know yet how his grand strategy—no, his *and Arthur's* grand strategy--would intertwine with territorial occupation, but he was certain he had discovered the way to sever himself from the old mechanism of obligation.

He also felt freed from a long-time gnawing doubt—that he was, in fact, a hypocrite. Daniel had always thought of hypocrites as people who keenly sensed their obligations to others, especially others hierarchically above them, uncertain if they were doing all the deeds required to earn the praise of and rewards from those equal or especially higher in status or authority. Hypocrites concealed, though not always consistently, their at-oddness toward those with whom they curried favor, giving off, unless they were extremely careful, muffled, discordant notes during the performances they gave to impress others. Not always reassured they were actually in favor, hypocrites sometimes overreached, convincing themselves that their stridency would surely gain the attention and favor of those above.

How could there be status and the currying of favor at the beginning of a move to new quarters, Daniel reasoned? What hierarchy could there be at the outset of a temporarily occupied territory? There is no one else, except those setting up the new boundaries, fashioning the new rules. No one else to impress with a show of fealty or gifts or deeds. New thoughts challenging old patterns, new visions of what could be, jockeying to replace memories of what had been. Daniel's mind was overwhelmed.

Or, should he, Daniel asked himself, just plain quit? Tell everyone to take a hike, he needed a long vacation from which he may never return? Hadn't he earned it? But, Daniel reflected, earned it from whom? He was not in the old world of obligation anymore. There was no one to give him the time off. Wasn't it now the same as his sand lot game? The game ended when everyone agreed to end it. And it certainly didn't look like anyone on the team, any of his newfound brothers and sisters, was going to agree to finish anytime soon!

The more he sat, thought, and experienced his new reality, the more he realized he had to ascend those stairs again. He did not know what he would say to Christie, but he felt compelled to say aloud something of what was going round and round in his mind, as if to lock in the seeds of this new reality.

The front door was closed tightly this time. Probably, Daniel thought, he had slammed it shut when he left. So, after hesitating, not knowing how she would respond, he rang the buzzer, and asked Christie if he could see her again.

Her enthusiastic, "Yes, yes, of course," followed by her buzzing him in, was a great relief. Daniel climbed the stairs again, slowly, grasping the railing firmly to steady himself. As he ascended, he soon walked more upright than before, stretching his body to its full height. In front of her door, before ringing the buzzer, Daniel paused, calm in the knowing that something inside himself had shifted and may have found fertile ground. Christie opened the door, smiling broadly.

"I'm glad you just didn't disappear," she said.

"Me, too."

One evening toward the end of June, Geoff, a fellow graduate student, phoned Christie to invite her to a movie. Christie learned during the conversation that they had an interest in common. While she had been doing research on South America, Geoff, along with Matthew, had focused on the United States' 1965 military intervention in the Dominican Republic to protect American sugar and other interests.

Geoff suggested he and Christie see Antonioni's "Blow-Up" with Vanessa Redgrave, which was opening on June 28th at the Embassy-72nd Street theatre. Christie, however, had been wanting to see Lelouch's "A Man and a Woman" with Anouk Aimée, which was in its 51st week at The Paris theatre on West 58th Street near Fifth Avenue.

After seeing "A Man and a Woman," they returned to Christie's apartment where Geoff unburdened himself about his decision to return his draft card to his hometown draft board in Richmond, California.

"Remember I told you I had applied to become a conscientious objector to the war?" Geoff began.

"Yes, I remember."

"Well, I originally thought being a CO would best express my individual opposition to the war. That status no longer appeases my conscience."

"I don't understand."

"Christie, the more I've researched the collusion of the American government and American multinational corporations, the more unsettled I am about a CO status, which still represents being part of the government's military system to protect American business making huge profits both overseas and through defense contracts."

"But you wouldn't have to fight anyone."

"Except myself."

Geoff reached into his back pocket and pulled out his wallet.

"Look at this draft card. It's government property. It represents the system, which forever handcuffs me to their regulations, their imperialism. It's not enough any longer for me to write letters, be on anti-war marches like the one where we met. These no longer jive with my deeply felt repugnance to what's being done in our name."

"What are you going to do?" Christie asked, hesitatingly.

"I'm returning this card to where it came from. And so that you'll understand, I'll read a part of a letter I've drafted, which I'll send with my card in a day or two: ' ... my feelings about the legitimacy of the Selective Service System have changed. I do not feel the state has the right to conscript or force citizens into military 'service' or 'alternative service'. I understand this attitude may lead to prosecution and rather severe penalties and feel I am prepared to face such.'"

Across America, there was a growing sense in the air that more was needed than protests. Persuasion, no matter how creatively presented, had produced only limited results, allowing the powerful and their haughty counselors far too much room to maneuver. A single person making the decision to write a letter, which could potentially bring the full weight of the government's prosecutorial powers to bear on him, was confrontational. Confrontation, in many forms, brought the powerful into the open, daring them to use their power to punish. Coaxing the powerful to come out from behind their corporate public relations' facades and distant estates might just expose some of their vulnerabilities, even immoralities, to full public view, and maybe, just maybe, demystify and deconstruct their authority, disgracing and weakening them in the process.

At first, a few dozen, then hundreds, then thousands across America decided to stand motionless, legs astride in the streets where they knew speeding trucks filled with the freight of frauds would hurtle toward them. A generation convinced itself it was "prepared to face such."

When Daniel's school year ended in May, he broke with his summer tradition. For nine previous summers, ever since his sixteenth birthday when he was legally allowed to work and be paid on the books, Daniel had had only one weeks' rest between his last day of final exams and his first day on a

201

full-time summer job. Now, he had enough money in his savings account from various school year part-time jobs to spend most of the summer any way he chose. After all, his rent was cheap.

He had lucked out in finding an apartment, with Norman whom he had driven to Lafayette Park, which had been previously occupied by another movement acquaintance in a rent-controlled apartment on West 106th Street. Each month, Daniel and Norman contributed $50 each to one money order, signed it with the previous occupant's name, and sent it to the unsuspecting landlord. Daniel could easily afford his half of the apartment rent for the summer while he visited an array of movement contacts meticulously recorded in his bulging address book.

His first travel destination, an altogether unlikely political choice, was Stuart, Florida. A schoolmate was fortunately driving all the way down I-95 from New York to his family home in Port St. Lucie. Three days after they started out, saying goodbye to his schoolmate, road-weary Daniel boarded a bus in Port St. Lucie, which, with connections, took him to Stuart. From the tiny bus station there, with sleeping and duffle bags in hand and sporting four days' growth of stubble, Daniel walked the half-mile, partly along Seminole Drive, to a small ranch house on the outskirts of town near Hoggs Cove, which eventually emptied into the Indian River. His grandmother opened the front door as if she had expected him even though he had not contacted her in advance.

> **Montaukett stands across the street, nodding slightly as the summer sun further burnishes her skin. She is not content. Talking to the wind, she praises the familial thread she feels between the two generations, but fears its fraying.**

Gra'ma had rented the house for the three summer months. She had saved her AT&T dividends for many years to afford this small luxury, but not enough to afford three months during the popular and pricey winter season. The owners were delighted to have it occupied while they stayed in their cool Maine summer home.

Pure love had existed between grandmother and grandson. Fixing tea and "jelly bread," as she had called her jam on toast, had been one of several simple pleasures they shared as often as possible. In fact, it was the repetition of simple pleasures, which had anchored their love for each other. Her reading the Sunday funnies to him as a young boy while enjoying hot cocoa in the winter. Rocking on the screened-in porch together during hot summer days when Daniel was a teenager, watching squirrels chasing each other around tree trunks.

"No thank you, Gra'ma," Daniel said softly, "I don't want jelly bread."

She was the only person who had fired Daniel's earliest childhood imagination by reading aloud tales of faraway places as he fell asleep. Her tales had been such a contrast to the next morning's restriction by parents who had not allowed him to leave the block on which they all lived. Perhaps her nighttime stories, Daniel had often wondered, were the seeds, which later bloomed as his hitchhiking treks.

"I don't want jelly bread," Daniel repeated, "not until we've talked."

"Talked? We always talk."

"No, Gra'ma, I mean really talk."

Daniel stood up, and walked to the other side of the small kitchen, gazing out the window. He bent over, placing both palms on the counter, and lowered his head.

"Gra'ma, you must forgive me. Last summer I opened your trunk."

"Forgive you for what? Daniel. I can't hear you clearly. Wait, I'll turn up my hearing aid."

Daniel's grandmother adjusted a dial on a small box clipped to her blouse.

"There, that's much better. Come back here to the table."

Daniel walked back to his side of the kitchen table, but did not sit down.

"I opened your trunk, in the basement."

"No, no, you were told you should never open my trunk. Your mother told you never to open it, remember?"

"I don't remember her saying that. Anyway, that's why I'm asking you to forgive me. I know I shouldn't have, but I did, and I looked inside and found something."

"Forgive you? Forgive you, when you violated me?"

"Gra'ma, I didn't violate you. I just looked inside. I was curious.

203

And I found a piece of paper, a death certificate."

"You should never have opened my trunk. You had no right. I want you to leave my house."

"Gra'ma, technically this is not your house, and—"

"Please get out."

"I've never seen you like this. I've wanted to ask you, for a whole year now, I've so many questions. Was Mathilda your sister--?"

"You're just as persistently mean as she was--"

"I'm not mean, you're the one who's being mean, telling me to leave."

"I'll say it again, get out," Gra'ma said firmly, without emotion, standing up and moving to the front door. She opened it, and turned away as Daniel passed by, bags in hand.

Daniel walked and walked, finally stopping at a coffee shop in the center of town. The coffee and danish he ordered waited in front of him as he stared out the window. He stayed until closing time, and then walked to the other side of town, found a vacant lot, and unrolled his sleeping bag at the back of it, behind some bushes. Each time he closed his eyes, he saw the open trunk lid and the pit of darkness below. The warm, moist air of a Florida summer night did not ease him to sleep.

The next morning, with the odor of wearing the same clothes for four days all about him, Daniel extended his arm and raised his thumb. The route to Tampa would hardly be as the crow flies.

He traveled south to the Fort Lauderdale area, then due west on the Tamiami Trail, then north past Naples. Taking this longer route south of Lake Okeechobee meant Daniel passed through the Everglades. Seeing marshland for miles and miles on either side of the highway was just the scenic tonic he needed.

A college acquaintance had invited Daniel to visit whenever he was "in the Tampa area." Normally Daniel would have ignored an invitation from an apolitical acquaintance, but the thought of a guest bedroom, a shower and home-cooked meals was too tempting to miss before pushing on to the uncertain digs of Southern Student Organizing Committee "comrades" in Atlanta, and after his grandmother's ice cold reaction.

Daniel entered Tampa late in the afternoon of Tuesday, June 13th, having traveled 340 miles in 8 hours since leaving Stuart. He had no clue that two nights before a riot had erupted. Neither Daniel, nor perhaps anyone else in America, could have anticipated that "Tampa" would be one of the earliest of 164 civil disorders that rocked the country during the first nine months of 1967.

It had been a swelteringly hot week. Daniel was glad to be in a centrally air-conditioned home, sitting around a dinner table laden with delicious treats. His college acquaintance's father, Mr. Francks, was a local corporate lawyer. Some of his clients were white small businessmen in and near the Central Avenue business district where windows had been smashed and stores looted, including a grocery and liquor store.

When dinner was over, Mr. Francks put his elbows on the table, his palms together in front of his chest, and slightly rested his chin on the tips of his fingers. He paused until he was certain he had everyone's undivided attention.

"I have lived in Tampa all my life. Until two nights ago, I really believed, and all my colleagues believed, we had good race relations in our town and I truly believed integration was working. Some of my good friends are Negroes. But I can *not* for the life of me understand this rampant hooliganism. Burning buildings for no good reason, looting stores, smashing windows. They are all criminals. Even the by-standers are criminals for not stopping it. Did you know that two of the stores belonged to clients of mine? They've been in business at their locations for over twenty years, each one near that Central Park Village Housing Project. They had many neighborhood customers. But did those savages care about my clients? Hell, no. My clients tell me they are never going to return to that neighborhood, never! I hope the National Guard keeps patrolling that neighborhood. Martial law is what those people need and deserve!"

Daniel sat silently as Mr. Francks continued to vent his anger. Despite all his activist experience, sitting at Mr. Francks' dinner table was the first time he had come face-to-face with what he took to be a bigot.

"Mr. Francks, you and your wife have a beautiful home here," Daniel said.

"Well, thank you--" Mrs. Francks replied.

"Wait dear, I think this young man has more to say," Mr. Francks interjected.

"I do. I know I'm a guest in your home, and, believe me, I appreciate being here, you can't imagine."

"But," Mr. Francks added.

"But, I am guessing you are far removed from the realities of those hooligans, as you call them, from their daily lives. I don't think you can picture, or me ever explain, the daily insults they experience."

"Ah, a bleeding heart liberal--"

"God, knows, Mr. Francks, I am *not* a liberal. Far from it. I will tell you this. Earlier this spring, Fisk University, Jackson State University, and Texas Southern University were harbingers of a black vanguard creating the sparks of revolution. And Tampa may just represent where it first caught fire!"

"Mother, we might either have a prophet in our midst," Mr. Franks responded, "or a young man who has smoked too much grass. What I do know is, my friends are out of business, and whoever put them out of business should be locked up!"

"Mr. Francks, I do not know what to say so you'll understand."

"There's nothing you can say."

As he was preparing for bed, Daniel reached into his duffle bag and took out a recently published book on Black Power, co-authored by Stokely Carmichael. Daniel had purchased the book after his long conversation with Arthur last spring. He opened it to where he had left off the last time, and read: "Because one thing stands clear: whatever the consequences, there is a growing—a rapidly growing—body of black people determined to 'T.C.B.'— take care of business. They will not be stopped in their drive to achieve dignity, to achieve their share of power, indeed, to become their own men and women—in this time and in this land—by whatever means necessary."

Daniel slept that night on the most plush mattress he had ever known, thinking how fortunate he was to be on the outskirts of what might prove to be America's Second American Revolution.

Another day's hitchhiking, this time 440 miles in 10½ hours, brought Daniel to Atlanta, home to several major civil rights' organizations and the largest Ku Klux Klan membership in America. Before leaving New York, Daniel had contacted Sharon in Nashville, reminding her of their ride to the Christmas Eve bombing pause vigil in front of the White House a year and one-half ago. He needed to get her friend Joyce's address and phone in Atlanta. Upon arriving at Joyce's apartment late on Tuesday evening, June 20th, Daniel learned that, earlier in the evening, a confrontation had occurred between 200 community protesters and 300 policemen following a community meeting. In response to the sound of a cherry bomb exploding, Joyce had heard, a policeman discharged a shotgun round, which killed a black by-stander sitting on a front porch and critically wounded a nine year-old black boy.

Daniel could not believe his good fortune again, to be so close to another conflagration, which could indeed ignite the Second American Revolution. Any revolution has casualties, Daniel rationalized, and so one death, however tragic, was an acceptable price to pay.

Daniel further reflected on his discussions with Arthur. He was struck by the idea that poor whites, organized by radical whites in their own communities, and poor blacks, organized by militant blacks in their own communities, could form a powerful alliance to start a revolution. This revolution would fundamentally break the power of the ruling class, Daniel calculated, and give the wealth of the country to the people for them to decide, democratically, how it would be divided and used for everyone's betterment. Moreover, he did not give it another thought when he heard that moderate blacks in Atlanta had gathered 1,000 signatures on a petition telling Stokely Carmichael, who had first been arrested there and then spoke at a community meeting urging revolution to liberate black people, to get out of the community and leave the local people to handle their own business. Daniel was so confident that the disruptions created by urban blacks had caused a crisis for those Negroes long accustomed to speaking on behalf of the entire black community, he dismissed the importance of the petition out of hand.

Atlanta's two days of rioting were actually ending the evening Daniel arrived. He spent the next day with Joyce and other SSOC members listening to their analysis of the causes of the riots, but his mind was elsewhere. He decided he could not continue traveling for the remainder of the summer. Relaxing and conversing with like-minded people around the country, sightseeing along the way, all seemed a luxury now, an immoral waste of time. Daniel had to make his way back to New York, to be with people he knew, to plan together in the wake of the start of the revolution. Nine days later, having stopped in Durham, Washington, D.C., and Philadelphia, Daniel was back in New York on the last day of June. Summer was just getting started.

One morning in July, a ringing phone awakened Daniel early. He had previously ignored such early calls, but these days, with so many political actions and reactions occurring so rapidly, he now took every incoming call. A distraught Reverend Randy Cain, calling from Newark, reminded Daniel that they had met at the Retreat and that his wife and Daniel had attended grade school together. The Reverend explained he was contacting people he knew, however slightly, to see if they could spend a day or two interviewing residents and writing up their stories of the recent riots in his city. Daniel agreed to come immediately. He was invited to stay with the Reverend and his family.

Rev. Cain and Dorothy lived with their two young daughters in a middle class section of the city. Daniel had never imagined Newark's population as ever having any non-poor residents, but here he was on a beautiful, tree-lined street far more upscale than the one on which he had lived in Babylon. Rev. Cain's church, however, was only a few blocks from the riots' starting point, at Belmont and 17th Avenues, where some of his current parishioners had once lived before moving to this upscale neighborhood. In fact, Rev. Cain was horrified to learn that a few of his middle class parishioners were among the looters, not only settling scores with white merchants who had gouged them in the old days with inaccurate scales, but also identifying with the young looters. Some in the black middle class understood that police violence, and the racism that sanctioned it, made no distinctions between the poor and the well off. This was Daniel's first taste of the complex currents swirling in what he had mistakenly imagined as a great divide between poor blacks and blacks who had succeeded in the white man's world.

Daniel arrived in Newark excited about seeing more evidence of the beginning of the Second American Revolution first hand. He heard what he took to be reliable reports that snipers, atop the roofs of housing projects and other apartment buildings, had been able to pin down police officers and National Guardsmen for hours. Daniel concluded that these snipers, obviously handy with rifles, must have been returning Vietnam Vets, using skills taught by the US Army against symbols of oppression back in their old neighborhoods. He was certain Tampa, Atlanta, and now Newark were the Lexington, Concord, and Fort Ticonderoga of his day. And here Daniel was, not just turning the pages of history and reading about past events, but smack in the midst of history, about to chronicle fresh pages first-hand—and hopefully to find ways to continue to make the revolution himself. Daniel was beside himself with anticipation. Could this be the start of a second "New Ark", a chance to redeem the history begun by Puritans on this same land in 1666?

More than two dozen whites and blacks had responded to Rev. Cain's plea for assistance. At a briefing in his church on the evening of Wednesday, July 19th, a full week after the start of the five days of civil disorders in Newark, Daniel learned that he would be paired with two young black men, going door-to-door inside and near the Reverend William P. Hayes Housing Project. It was there, on the evening of Saturday, July 15th, that two columns of National Guardsmen and state troopers joined city policemen to direct " … mass fire at the Hayes Housing Project in response to what they believed were snipers." Daniel fervently wished that he could meet some of these snipers. Of course he did not believe they would just come out and admit they were trying to kill the oppressor, but by asking draft-age black men if they had served in Vietnam, and listening carefully to their rhetoric, maybe he could guess which young men were in the vanguard. Maybe they would even take him into their confidence and teach him to fire a rifle!

At the briefing Daniel was overwhelmed by the statistics he heard. Twenty-five community residents had been killed, more than 1,000 had been arrested, and over 500 had been treated at local hospitals, from July 12th through July 17th. He could not comprehend how all that carnage could have happened in just five days. He also learned that a white fireman and white policeman were also killed. Politicians and others were quick to blame snipers, but the circumstances did not support these claims, as the two could have just as well been killed by official violence, Daniel was to learn later.

During the first evening of the riots, July 12th, demonstrators at the Fourth Precinct station building were protesting the arrest and beating of a Negro cab driver. Some 43 hours after the first bottle and rock were thrown at the Fourth Precinct, 3,000 National Guardsmen from all over New Jersey, plus 500 State Troopers, had joined 1,400 city patrolmen, a virtually all-white force.

Daniel could not believe what he was hearing. He just could not take it all in during this one briefing. Should he really be there at all, he now wondered? What had happened was so distant from his own experiences, his own reference points, how could he hope to do what was asked of him? Daniel did grasp that community leaders, dead on their feet from days and nights of trying to redirect the anger of many neighborhoods, wanted to detail meticulously how an occupying army had rained death, bodily injury, and property destruction on a significant portion of approximately 200,000 Negroes. The sheer magnitude of the events, and Daniel's feelings of inadequacy in the face of what was being asked of him, disturbed his night of sleep at the Cain's home.

> *A pool of blood. On the church floor. A figure looks around. Looks for an exit sign. Sees none. Looks behind, looks sideways, looks ahead. Sees only armed men in uniforms, everywhere. Soldiers, policemen. No sign of immediate exit.*
>
> *A priest or minister, with a stole draped around his neck, both ends hanging uncrossed down the front of his uniform.*
>
> *Figure stands. Everyone in his pew is standing. All walk to their right, turn left to walk up the aisle toward the priest or minister. Figure wants to leave the line. Cannot. Sees no exit sign. Sees pool of blood, expanding, straight ahead.*
>
> *Sees dead bodies everywhere in the choir loft. Shot. Blood draining. Into the pool.*
>
> *Figure is in front of pool. Priest or minister takes wafer. Bends. Dips wafer into pool of blood. Offers wafer to figure.*

The first individual interviewed by Daniel's team was Bernie Smart, fifty-two years old, who lived on the twelfth floor of one of the Hayes Homes' buildings, which was opposite the Fourth Precinct. Bernie stated:

"All these eight buildings you see around you, what we call the projects, were built about ten years ago to clear out the slums. If you ask me, they just made the slums vertical, each slum twelve stories high. These are hellholes, just like the slums I lived in this area before, only you can't see the garbage-strewn lawns or paint peeling off houses like before. They simply hid the hellholes behind brick facades. Now I'm not saying everybody didn't keep up their homes, like I'm not saying everybody in the projects don't keep up their apartments, but those that don't just drag down the spirits of those that do. And then, I'll tell you what. If the elevator *is* working, which is usually never, I take a deep breath before I step in, and I got to watch where I step, and hold my breath until I get off at the twelfth floor, 'cause of the urine. And you know, I like to read books. And so, when I have bought enough new books so that I need another bookcase, I've got to carry it up twelve flights of stairs because when I get home with it, the elevator's broke.

"You see that police station across the street? I don't want you to tell anyone this, okay, no one, but, okay, there are about one *thousand* people living in this one high rise slum building, and, okay, I cheered when one of them—I saw him—threw one of those Molotov cocktails and hit the wall high up on that goddamn police station, and we all cheered and cheered as we watched the flaming gasoline rolling down that wall. Those goddamn honky cops. They beat up that cab driver. John Smith's his name, busted his ribs. And for what? The cops said he was driving the wrong way on a one-way street. And then they found he didn't have a valid license. And those cops would've kept beating him if some of the folks didn't insist to the police that he be taken to the hospital. For driving the wrong way, you get beat up, broken ribs? In Newark, you sure do!

"That's right, I cheered. After the years and years of honky cops harassing us, acting as if every black person is a criminal until proved otherwise. We file complaints about harassment, but hardly any are fully investigated and practically none result in cops being disciplined or fired. And, yeah, the cops run those summer programs for our young folks, and they go to police and community relations training programs, but when it comes down to it, they don't care about the crime that happens inside our vertical slums. Oh, no, they act as if they're a private army hired to protect what's left of the white community in Newark!"

Daniel, for the first time in his life, felt the anger and desperation in the voice of an ordinary citizen. He was also cheered momentarily by Bernie's delight in the direct hit on the police station, but such a momentary "victory" could never, for Daniel, relieve the dread he felt about Bernie's daily life. As the elevator door opened for the interviewers to descend, Daniel stopped himself before walking into the car, to look carefully at the floor.

Daniel and his team next knocked on the door of Bessie Jeffries, thirty-eight years old, who lived on the second floor of another of the projects' eight buildings. Bessie stated:

"My boy is sixteen years old. He's wild sometimes. I don't understand him sometimes. But that first night, when all his friends were throwing bottles and rocks at the precinct station, my son was with me in our apartment. But then, around one in the morning, I couldn't find my boy. I don't know if he ran up 17th Avenue to Belmont or not, but I heard later that's when young people, teenagers and others in their early twenties, started smashing windows, setting off burglar alarms, and stealing things out of stores. It breaks my heart to think my son might have been one of them. He never said.

"I shop at a lot of those stores on Belmont. I knew they overcharged me a lot for that second-hand television set I bought, and I was tricked once by the tiny print in an installment agreement I signed, but not all those merchants are crooked. And now, even the honest ones are still boarded up with signs saying 'Moved'. I can't blame them, but where am I going to shop?

"And I'll tell you another thing. Yes, some of those boys' parents were looters, too, and other adults also joined in, folks who should know better, helping themselves to furniture and liquor and appliances. They said later they were owed these things, but I don't think so. They should've gone up to Belmont to stop those boys, 'cause it ain't right to take something that doesn't belong to you. So what, they got a brand new, free toaster, and now can't buy nothing else in this neighborhood!"

Daniel, again for the first time in his life, was face-to-face with an innocent person displaced by the revolution, if that's what had started in Newark. But as he walked to the ground floor, thinking of Bessie who must now shop outside her neighborhood, Daniel chalked it up to yet another price to pay for fundamental change.

Daniel and his team next went to Springfield Avenue to interview twenty-five year-old Jerome Bates who lived above a shop that had been looted on the second night of the riots. Jerome stated:

"I was in the crowd early Thursday evening outside the precinct. To tell you the truth, I figured the riot was over, having ended much earlier that day, maybe four Thursday morning when all you could see were lots of police patrolling the neighborhood and occasionally rousting any small groups of neighbors who dared to congregate. Sure, everyone was still angry, plenty angry about a lot of things, so I guess whoever thought of the idea to circulate flyers saying 'Stop! Police Brutality!' meant well in calling for a demonstration in front of the precinct Thursday evening. But I guess not all the community leaders were reading from the same script during the demonstration. One of them announced that, if we all went home then and there, a Negro would be promoted to police captain, a rank only held by white men. Even I booed, but I didn't throw rocks and bottles like some others. How could anyone think our anger, which was directed not only at the virtually all white and arrogant police force but also equally at the arrogant white society which hired that force, and at white store owners who gouged us, and at white banks which red-lined our neighborhoods so we couldn't get mortgages to buy homes--how could anyone believe the promotion of one of our people to a higher rank could satisfy anyone in that initially peaceful demonstration?

"And then, without warning, the doors of the Precinct open and out come police in helmets and riot gear, swinging their clubs, chasing and beating whoever they can catch, arresting and handcuffing as many as they can grab, and then beating some of those they caught while they're handcuffed, and dragging them to jail. You tell me if that didn't cause the riots which followed. Word spread quickly. The rioting was not only around the precinct, but here, three blocks away, all along Springfield Avenue, the main commercial area, and other neighborhoods. And not just looting. Some stores were set on fire, like the one below my apartment. You can still see the smoke and water damage done to my living room!"

Here was proof, thought Daniel, as he walked down the street, that when the revolution comes, current minority leaders, who have earned a conditional place in the white man's world, would be swept aside for leaders who come from the streets. The damage to Jerome's apartment would be a small price to pay for authentic leaders, Daniel concluded.

Daniel and the team were to visit three more individuals, and then return to Rev. Cain's church to report their findings. Their next stop was to interview Sharita Jones, a nurse at Newark's City Hospital:

"The hospital administration put us all on 12-hour shifts, there were so many being brought in. On Thursday night alone, the second night of the riots, we counted about 250 neighborhood folks. About fifteen of those were gunshot victims. So many had cuts and bruises from billy clubs or from falling down as they tried to get away from the police chasing them. My brother is one of the few, relatively speaking, black policemen, and he told me that, by Friday morning, five of our folks had been killed by police, and that 425 folks had been arrested. Now, he and his black policemen brothers did not participate, so all the shooting was done by white policemen. He thinks they just lost it. They became more and more violent which, in turn, got folks angrier and angrier, and smashing windows and looting got bigger and bigger. But I know one thing for sure. By early Friday morning, from everything me and my brother were hearing, the riot was petering out. Folks were exhausted. Folks had already wreaked their vengeance on storeowners whom they thought had gypped them.

"Yea, you know, I talked with as many people as I could, both in the hospital even though it was a nightmare there, and outside. I know another thing for sure. People also felt exhilarated. 'People felt as though for a moment they were creating a community of their own.' I guess it sounds crazy to an outsider, with people being shot at and arrested and all that, but for one long evening, folks were setting the pace in their own neighborhoods, controlling parts of their own neighborhoods where police were afraid to show themselves, setting their own rules, settling old scores they couldn't have settled before, establishing kind of like, however temporary, liberated zones. But as I said, by early Friday morning even that exhilaration was petering out. I firmly believe the riot would have ended at that point."

Daniel was cheered by this account of territory being established and held by the people. Just to feel the exhilaration of having power, of having control of territory, however fleeting it was, Daniel thought, that experience of liberation would never be forgotten. But was the human cost too high, he briefly wondered? He moved quickly on.

Daniel and the team next interviewed Willie Benson, a house painter, who had been sitting on his front porch on 15th Street when National Guardsmen demanded that everyone inside his home come outside:

"I was told to lie on the ground. The Guardsmen handcuffed me. And they beat me with the butt of their rifles and stomped on me with their boots. Then they searched my home and, after they left, I found they took $75 out of my aunt's pocketbook, and they also took a transistor radio and cigarettes.

"I found out later they crucified a lot of people. One man I know was awakened at night by his son by something happening in the street outside their home. The father and son walked down the hallway of their apartment. Even though they didn't go outside, policemen attacked them anyway, hitting the father on the head with their billy clubs until he was unconscious. He told me he had to have fourteen stitches. He also told me how hard a head he had because the billy club broke in two!

"I heard about a 10-year old boy who was riding in his family's car on Friday night, going to White Castle to get something to eat. The father slowed the car as it neared a barricade on Elizabeth Avenue, but the Guardsmen fired on the car anyway. The car was riddled with bullets and the boy was killed with a bullet to the head.

"If you have the stomach for it, I know of another boy, he was twelve, and lived on Fifteenth Avenue. His mother had sent him out of the house about midnight Sunday to put out some garbage. He was standing with another young man who sassed some National Guardsmen. Those soldiers fired at them, and killed the boy with the garbage."

As Daniel walked down the steps of the porch, he felt faint. The blood seemed to have drained from his brain, leaving him no exit from the horrible images Willie had evoked. The other team members steadied him, and suggested they go to a corner shop for some nourishment.

The final person interviewed that evening was Muhammad Al-Alachi, formerly known as Julius Blackburn. He had converted to Islam, but had been drafted into the Army despite his application for conscientious objector status, and had returned from Vietnam three months ago:

"Snipers? I'm sorry to disappoint you. The politicians and newspapers kept talking about snipers. If you believed them, there were snipers everywhere, shooting at firemen, policemen. But here's what I know. By early Friday morning, the Mayor gave up pretending he had everything under control. And there were a lot of white people in authority that wanted to 'teach us a lesson'. And then there were those claims by the police that snipers had been firing at ambulance drivers. How absurd was that? As much as I hate this white dictatorship called America, what conceivable reason would I have to kill ambulance drivers taking my people to the hospital!

"Maybe, just maybe, there were one or two folks on rooftops shooting down at cops. But I know this for sure. When that Governor Hughes declared there was an open rebellion in Newark and brought in 3,000 white Guardsmen Friday afternoon, and added another 500 white State troopers to the 1,400 mostly all-white city police force, suddenly their claims of the number of snipers rose dramatically. Why? Police thinking shots coming their way, thinking they're coming from snipers, when they're really coming from Guardsmen across the way. And the same with Troopers returning police fire, and National Guard fire, thinking it was coming from snipers. Officials said there was 'withering' sniper fire, but only one policeman and one fireman were killed, both under circumstances, which did not prove snipers were responsible. Besides, no so-called snipers were ever killed, or even caught and accused of shooting at cops or firemen. No, no, the riot was dying out on Friday when the Governor and others decided to occupy the ghetto and allow, if not encourage, hundreds upon hundreds of violent acts against our people and our property. Yes, our property.

"My cousin owned a dry cleaners. For no reason except that he's black and hung a 'soul brother' sign on his door, one night over the weekend troopers smashed his store windows and shot into the store. This wanton destruction of property by this white occupying army happened to maybe a hundred black-owned businesses. So you tell me, who kept the riot going?

"These Guardsmen didn't know what the heck they were doing. I'm sure some of them were scared. Unfamiliar terrain. Who was the real enemy? We had a tough enough time in Vietnam trying to figure all that out. But here are white boys from the suburbs trying to play soldier in our neighborhoods.

"On Friday night, with all that fire power fully deployed, ten folks were killed, about 100 suffered gunshot wounds, and 500 went to City Hospital, and at least another 500 were arrested. By Sunday night, another ten folks were dead, about 50 more had gunshot wounds, and an additional 500 were in jail. This wasn't, as some brothers and sisters think, a war. This was the brutal repression of an entire population."

That evening, before all the teams of interviewers met together, Daniel took a walk in Rev. Cain's neighborhood. How peaceful and manicured the homes and yards were, how orderly and respectful the few neighbors he saw seemed, thought Daniel. Which way would the people in this suburban neighborhood, middle class to the core, go should the revolution come? Revolutionists or counter-revolutionists? Or passive spectators? Although he was a suburban kid himself, he could not imagine the neighbors he knew would ever be revolutionists, unless, by some miracle, their faith in a future, where things got better for them and even better for their children if only they worked hard, was deposed. No, Daniel thought, that was a fantasy too far.

After each team had reported in, and a plan was set for the following day to put together and publish all the interviews, Daniel ended the evening in conversation with Rev. Cain and Alphonso Smith, a young black man who had grown up in Newark, and had lived for a year in Algeria.

"What do you think it all means, Rev. Cain?" Daniel asked.

"The first thing I've concluded is that no one can speak anymore on behalf of blacks. No community leader for his community, no national leader for all blacks. The second thing is, it was our communities, which were busted up, our communities where young mothers are trying to keep their small children safe, where old men are unable to get around, where young husbands and wives are trying to make a start. No one during the riots spoke for them, what they felt, how scared they were."

"With respect, Reverend," Alphonso said, "I see the riots differently. As destructive as they were, as chaotic and unplanned as they were, weren't the riots really a people trying to make their own history? What if all that anger, all that vengeance, were harnessed and then focused at systematically disrupting the points where oppressive power is exercised. Call it rolling black outs!"

"I can not accept that," Rev. Cain responded.

"In the last week," Alphonso continued, "the problems of urban Newark have received more media and political attention locally and nationally than all the marches and petitions put together. How much more likely would whites sit across from us at a real bargaining table, and cede some real power under threat of more rolling black outs!"

"I'm listening, but so far I'm not agreeing," Rev. Cain stated.

"I've also realized that black leaders, like yourself, Reverend, can play a significant role, but not in the way you might think. I've been thinking a long time about how political pressure can lead to significant change. But the riots have taught me something new. I'm certain now that any strategy must have two prongs, two groups who keep in close contact with each other, although publicly they deny that there is any contact between them.

"The groups are composed of two different types of people. Call the first group the Negotiators. These are well-known and respected members of the community, like yourself. They make public speeches, organize marches, collect petitions, and are also the ones who would eventually strike the deals with white authorities. These folks wear suits and ties. The second group, call them the Warriors, are the disrupters. They carry out, in highly creative fashion, attacks on symbols of white power, as well as on actual targets where white power is exercised. These folks wear dungarees and T-shirts, and maybe even masks sometimes. Despite widely different personalities comprising these two groups, methods are found for building trust between members of the two groups, knowing that neither group can bring about significant, sufficient, and sustainable change without the other. They coordinate their actions, the one above ground and the other somewhat underground. Publicly, the Negotiators condemn the methods used by the Warriors, but then use the occasion of the Warriors' attacks to focus attention on the issues. Disruptions, then negotiations backed by threats of further disruptions, create the environment for fundamental change."

"I understand what you are saying," Rev. Cain responded, "but it would, I think, take a particularly adroit type of leader to be what you call a Negotiator."

"I thought the revolution would sweep away all traditional black leaders," Daniel chimed in. "After all, haven't we seen the pace of events driven by people in the streets undercut the effectiveness, even legitimacy, of such so-called leaders?"

"Yes, Daniel, you are correct about the recent past," Alphonso responded, "but those are leaders largely unconnected with the streets, as you call it, and they sense they could lose the white man's favor if they can't control the streets or these newer, militant leaders. But, as I said before, if the Negotiators, including even some traditional black leaders, and the Warriors have already built a back channel of trust and communication and common objectives between them, a revolution can commence."

Daniel returned to New York, upset, confused, and sick at heart. Political action was no longer, as it had been for him he realized, carried out as an arm's length business. He had met people in Newark, face-to-face, who were deeply affected. He could not forget Bessie and all those boarded up shops around her, or Muhammad's cousin and his ransacked business, no matter how much he wanted to dismiss them as the price to be paid. These were the invisible victims of the escalating cycles of other victims' violent response to official violence and neglect.

Daniel was also struck by the calm and confident manner by which Alphonso had laid out his Negotiator/Warrior Strategy. He also thought about the Grand Political Strategy he and Arthur had fashioned. Both strategies were certainly sophisticated, Daniel thought, both could work, but what might be the unintended consequences, the unexpected forces let loose, which could potentially undermine their long-term effectiveness? Or could the two strategies be combined? Yes, Daniel concluded, merge the two strategies into one. But then, once launched, would a Bessie or Muhammad's cousin be harmed? Could they be protected, or, if not, could Daniel live with himself, knowing he had caused their harm? Daniel put a note in what passed as his calendar, to take a month or two off and think through how the combination of the two strategies would work, and how to avoid unintended consequences.

Events were outpacing Daniel's ability to absorb and react to them. Emotionally drained from his southern travels and Newark immersion, he had not been able to use the summer break for rest and reflection.

As late summer turned into early fall, Daniel was still certain that a well-organized, rapid response national Communications Network, coupled with the Negotiators/Warriors dual track, could take on the elite and win. Daniel yearned for a tranquil setting to work through the operational methods of such an ambitious national network and the moral questions raised by the Warrior track. But how could he ignore an upcoming gathering of the enemy in his own backyard? And so it was that the development and implementation of his Grand Strategy was this time, and for many more times in future, sacrificed for the Immediate Opportunity.

Daniel would shortly find himself in the midst of demonstrators dodging policemen on horseback galloping up and down Sixth Avenue.

CHAPTER 12 – DISRUPTION (FALL 1967)

I-Feel-Like-I'm-Fixin'-to-Die Rag, written by Joe McDonald, performed by Country Joe and The Fish, also known as *Vietnam Rag*, released in November, 1967.

Keep Your Eyes on the Prize, melody from the traditional hymn, *Gospel Plow* (aka *Hold On*, *Keep Your Hand on The Plow*), some lyrics came from the traditional hymn, others were added during the Civil Rights Movement by various performers.

"Hey guys, you're smiling," Daniel observed as Christie and Ephraim approached. "How did it go?"

"Really well," Ephraim replied to Daniel and Jeff. "And you?"

"Just great!"

The four were jubilant as they reconnoitered at ten o'clock, Tuesday evening, November 14th, on the corner of West 52nd Street and the Avenue of the Americas.

"Christie's aim got better and better," Ephraim affirmed. "She's ready for the Yankees!"

"You should have heard a passerby cheering when I hit the Morgan Guaranty sign!" Daniel added.

Flowing past the four, hundreds of demonstrators were walking down Sixth Avenue toward Times Square. Jeff stopped one of them, wearing a helmet, to ask what was going on.

"They've been galloping the horses at us. They didn't let us get out of the way. And coming at us on motor scooters, too. And you wouldn't believe how many pigs they have around the Hilton. We can't get close enough. Because the pigs escalated their tactics, we're re-grouping in Times Square. There's an Armed Forces recruiting booth there. Maybe we can draw the pigs down there, and then double back to the Hilton and outflank them."

Jeff and the other three declined his invitation to join, but wished him luck. They were headed instead for their favorite Orange Julius table to celebrate the success of their new strategy.

A year ago, Daniel and the others felt they had all the time in the world to make the revolution, but the quickened pace of external events and opportunities became an unforgiving taskmaster. Virtually no time for reflection. Or transition. Their gaining new information and experiences every week, if not every day, resulting in insights for new tactics and tasks, had its own acceleratingly disruptive pace. Disconnects had multiplied. Rapid change had meant repeated dislocations, altered physical, mental and psychological environments. Dislocation had also meant the constant need to set out new roots, which were hardly able to search for, let alone absorb, nutrients before the next dislocation occurred.

Daniel and the others could not realize how starved they were becoming. Quite the opposite. On this New York City corner, not two blocks from where many of the most powerful men in America—no, in the world— had dined together this evening, Daniel and the other three felt full of themselves.

The Fifth Avenue Parade Committee, a coalition of approximately 70 anti-war groups, plus the New York Regional Students for a Democratic Society and others had been planning what Liberation News Service called a "militant confrontation" during the Foreign Policy Association's (FPA) Fiftieth Anniversary celebratory dinner in the Grand Ballroom of the New York Hilton Hotel. Secretary of State Dean Rusk would be the featured speaker. Daniel and the other three, however, had agreed to experiment with a far different approach than the organizers of the demonstration outside the Hilton were planning. The four would serve the maw of the immoral war, the immoral *apartheid* system, the immoral imperialist web directly to the laps of these elite, and to their corporate front doors.

The four had embraced a new strategy and, in the process, had not fully understood the consequences to themselves. The new strategy had also fostered a new vocabulary. During one of their meetings, they had christened themselves "TUF", Tactical Unit of Four. This naming had been yet another moment of self-realization that the four were starting to move beyond being simply a group of individuals who met often. Each had been undergoing a more rapid transformation than in their earlier activist years, not only with respect to their individual consciousnesses, but also and especially in their beginning to solidify a group consciousness.

"I've just learned that the organizers of the Hilton demonstration are talking about throwing marbles under horses' hooves if mounted policemen charge them," Jeff had stated during an early October meeting of the four.

"That's certainly a more militant tactic toward the police," Daniel had responded.

"Look here, Daniel, no matter how much I'd like to see old imperialist Engelhard tarred and feathered, I'm sick to my stomach at the thought of horses breaking their legs," Jeff had replied.

"I agree with Daniel in general about coming up with militant tactics, certainly not that one, which seems a desperate act, but what is our overall strategy?" Ephraim asked. "We need a strategy first."

"Anyway, that's a tactic aimed only at the surrogates of the elite's power, not directly at the powerful themselves," Christie had offered.

"I can't believe how gently we treated Engelhard at the awards ceremony in Newark a year and a-half ago. We've got to come up with direct assaults on the enemy itself," Jeff had affirmed, surprising himself with the vehemence of his words.

In the old days, about six months ago, any confrontational tactics would have troubled Jeff because such militancy might preclude back-channel discussions leading to rational compromise. He had respected his father's method for settling disputes in the family by talking things out, seeing the other's point of view, each person understanding they may have to give up a little of what they wanted to get most of what they wanted, or, alternatively, coming up with a new approach on which everyone could agree. By now, Jeff had abandoned rational discourse as the means to move toward equality and justice. He had seen what he thought were compromises with the powerful used by them as stalling tactics, their way to avoid ceding real power. He also now viewed those wanting to pursue rational discourse as coming from positions of cowardice, their way of putting a toe into history's stream, and feeling good about it without leaving the safety of the shore.

"I agree with Jeff. I used to count on fairness as the bedrock of any strategy," Daniel had continued. "But all our radical research has shown that fairness is wildly impractical unless the means of distribution are adjusted so that all sides have roughly equal opportunity to compete with one another."

"And I once thought that the politeness and manners of the powerful also meant respect for others far less powerful, but it doesn't," Christie had added. "The powerful give respect grudgingly only to those who swim the same waters they do, and prove themselves successful combatants over time."

"I've learned the hard way that justice is not a set of abstract standards to be administered impartially," Ephraim had concluded, "but the result of who has the most influence to pass laws and write regulations."

Many plans of attack had been discussed during several TUF meetings. Daniel had especially wanted to make up for what he perceived as his cowardice when he had confronted Thomas Nichols in Baltimore. In the end, the plan they had adopted was bold, would take courage, and would deliver an unmistakable message.

The Liberation News Service dispatch, written by Michael Grossman of the *Washington Free Press,* distributed on November 11th, described the targets:

> "Their [FPA] membership principally consists of industrialists with more than a passing interest in events beyond our shores. They are men of the stature of Charles Engelheart [sic] whose Anglo-American Corporation controls 28 per cent of South Africa's gold production, 22 per cent of the uranium, 43 per sent [sic] of the coal, 57 per cent of the copper and almost all the diamonds. Another member is Ellsworth Bunker. Bunker has been Special Ambassador to the O.A.S. while he is also one of the leading stockholders of National Sugar Refining Corporation, the second largest sugar corporation on the east coast. During the crisis in the Dominican Republic, a prime producer of sugar, he was called in as Special Emissary to the Dominican Republic. He is now a Special Ambassador to Vietnam.

"On the fiftieth anniversary committee we find James Rogers, former Deputy Director of the O.S.S. [forerunner of the Central Intelligence Agency], past President of the Foreign Bond-holder Protector Council, and now Chairman of the Board of Operation Crossroads Africa, which, with the help of CIA funds, helps train future leaders for Africa; also Herald [sic] Linder, a large donor to the Democratic Party, who worked for the Department of State during the fifties and is now Chairman of the Export-Import Bank which is a main supplier of loans to Latin America; and George Brown, of Brown and Root Construction Company which receives Billion Dollar government contracts to construct air bases in Vietnam and Thailand—he is also a large contributor to the Democratic Party.

"Then there's Roswell Gilpatric, who is a partner in the largest U.S. law firm which specializes in representing military contractors. He recently served as Undersecretary of the Air Force, was a member of a Rockefeller study in the fifties which gave rise to the concept of the missile gap, and for a while chaired the board of Aerospace Corporation. While Deputy Secretary of Defense, he was involved in the critical decision to give the 7.5 billion dollar TFX contract to General Dynamics whom Gilpatric's law firm represents.

"Others include A. Kaplan of CIA fame, John Richardson Jr., President of Radio Free Europe, a recipient of CIA funds and an enterprise nurtured by Allen Dulles of the CIA, C.D. Jackson, Eisenhower's advisor on psychological warfare, A.A. Berle, Kennedy contact during the Bay of Pigs (also a long time sugar executive), and Nelson Eldridge, an officer of Chase Manhattan Bank and a heavy investor in South Africa.

"One of the association's projects has been to sponsor the printing of 'objective' basic pamphlets on foreign policy which are used in public schools.

"According to one of the organizers of the demonstration, 'the members of the association represent the corporate interests abroad which are at the root of American Imperialism—these are the interests U.S. foreign policy must protect, why revolutions must be put down, why Vietnam must be an object lesson to the people of the world.'"

For the first two years of their protest activities, each of the four had truly believed that the arguments for change, grounded in their values of fairness, mutual respect, reasonableness, and justice, would persuade powerful and wealthy people to see the light and change policies and practices. Facts, reasoned arguments, and practical solutions would win the day, they all had once deeply believed. The four had not viewed themselves as being "radicalized" during this leg of their political path; rather, they had spoken in terms of new tactics to accomplish prior goals.

No matter how "militant" the confrontation at the Hilton Hotel might become, Daniel and the others had now assumed it would be yet another street demonstration, marked this time by angrier placards and a more aggressive testing of the police lines. The four had come to suspect that these exercises to raise public consciousness about important issues were a cop-out. Instead of a strategy to win power from the elite, the four had now convinced themselves that many of their contemporaries were satisfied with just trying to win greater numbers to their side, and that, in a fuzzyheaded way, greater numbers would somehow turn the tide toward peace or majority rule or economic equality. The four had witnessed the growing numbers, but did not witness a commensurate change of policies or ceding power by the elite.

Their experiences had taught them differently. Letters-to-the-editor, letters to persons in governmental and commercial authority, hand-circulated petitions, meetings with elected representatives, and, if granted, meetings with corporate or government decision-makers had failed to achieve over time the demands for moral solutions. Sometimes they had expectantly interpreted a cosmetic alteration as a substantive victory, only to realize their mistake later when it was discovered that the immoral policy was still robustly in place.

Mobilizing larger and larger numbers, they had discovered, was time-consuming, and had its own share of internal problems. Money had to be raised, relationships among activist leaders had to be sorted out, disputes resolved, tactics agreed upon, texts approved. For large demonstrations, marshals had to be selected and trained to maintain the non-violent intent, knowing all the while small groups might either plan to break away, or spontaneously break away, to attack police. They had finally and recently realized that even the force of large numbers had not led to fundamental change in the dynamics of power. The Vietnam War raged on; majority rule in South Africa was no nearer; blacks were still second-class American citizens.

The four now viewed past tactics and the political assumptions on which they were based as naïve, a deliberate evasion from trying to fathom what it really meant to wrest power from an entrenched elite and truly change the course of history. The impact of both non-violent and militant demonstrations, no matter how many swelled the ranks or how many others sympathetically supported the goals, seemed perpetually sidetracked by debates with newspapers and the police about the correct count of demonstrators, or mired in a narrow-focused public hunger, fed by politicians, to dwell on any violence, however minor, which occurred during a demonstration. The public's focus followed the media's reporting, e.g., two policemen treated for minor injuries on the scene became the more important story line than another hundred US soldiers killed in Vietnam or another thousand children going hungry in America. In addition, radical research had uncovered the enormous extent to which the print and broadcast media were owned and interlocked with the very elite targeted by demonstrations. The activist message was either distorted or ignored by major media. Their own progressive publications reached only those, by and large, already committed to the struggle.

Research also revealed interconnected systems, which the powerful had created over time to grow and protect their empires. Now the four finally understood why their previous efforts, and those of a generation, had been mostly in vain. No strand of the extensive spider web of power and privilege could alter itself in a major way without negative consequences for every other strand. Each part of the web had to be protected, or at the most only one strand might be slightly modified to satisfy and deflate the pressure for change so that such pressure would not also target other interconnected strands.

Alongside their intellectual understanding, an emotional toughness was building up in the four. They no longer found any usefulness in being deferential. Perpetual frustration and anger also built up as they were reminded of the sharp contrast between their moral values and daily news stories. They became certain they had the best information on who their enemies were and how they protected themselves. They only required a new way to act. The four resolved to take a new stance, based on a process they would, in hindsight, call their "radicalization."

At first, the four sought out and found a few others who had advanced along the same path, creating an informal network within each of the larger groups with which they were affiliated. The fours' efforts focused on sharing with others what they had discovered and understood about the power elite, but as time went by, they realized what a painstakingly slow effort it would be to re-focus the strategy of any large liberal group. Although they had not felt superior to those groups, they did feel separate. The four finally decided that their identity as TUF, and what TUF alone decided to do, was far more important than any other allegiance.

As Daniel reflected on his own transition, he vaguely remembered from his high school history class that theologian Roger Williams had been perhaps the first to represent what had become the great American separatist tradition. Daniel also remembered that Williams' fifth child had been named Daniel. He smiled at the memory.

Christie and Ephraim checked into the Hilton Hotel on the afternoon of Monday, November 13th. The two were about to implement the first piece of TUF's new strategy.

"No, sir, it's my fault," Ephraim explained to the desk clerk. "In our eagerness to get married, I totally forgot to make a reservation for our honeymoon."

Christie proudly showed the clerk her wedding ring. The clerk was charmed by the young couple standing before him, and took their payment in cash for three nights.

"No, that's Ok, sir, we'll carry our suitcases," Ephraim responded to the clerk's offer to summon a bellman. Ephraim groaned slightly as he lifted the larger suitcase.

During their TUF planning sessions, Daniel and Christie had talked openly about Ephraim and her spending nights together in the same hotel room. Their evolving group consciousness had distanced each of them further from their past self-understandings and emotions, pushing them to uncharted and unfamiliar places. Each had needed the support and encouragement of the others to make the journey successfully. Daniel came round to the fact that, for the strategy to work, he had to set aside any feelings of possessiveness. As he watched Christie and Ephraim's joking and laughing about "acting married," he had worked on overcoming his jealousy, for the cause.

Once in their room, Christie and Ephraim unpacked their clothes, putting them in drawers and the one closet. Everything else in their suitcases remained inside, locked.

Christie at once felt self-conscious and shy as she hung her dresses next to his pants. Even that low a level of intimacy unexpectedly violated her upbringing. She could not imagine her father, let alone her grandfather, approving any part of this subterfuge. My God, she thought, remembering how she had proudly shown the desk clerk the wedding ring her father had given her mother, and then had given Christie as a family heirloom, my God, if father ever found out, he would disown me. Christie launched herself into a dozen tasks, fluffing the pillows on the twin beds, checking to see if the heater worked and hot water came out of the faucet, and more.

For his part, Ephraim realized, after a few minutes in the hotel room, how much of a loner he had been all his life, even as a member of a family whose parents had tried to impose communal traditions on him. It was one thing to entertain at a party in his apartment, Ephraim reflected, as he only had to chat for a few moments with each guest, spending the bulk of his time fixing food and drinks or cleaning up. Now, here he was, going to spend two days and nights with another human being and, of all things, acting out the fiction that they were married.

"They don't have a lot of hangers in the closet, do they?" Ephraim said, rapidly. "I thought for a luxury hotel they'd have lots of hangers, didn't you?"

"Yea, lots. But I can hang a few of my blouses on one hanger, and that'll leave more for you," Christie quickly responded.

"OK, thanks, I appreciate that. Ah, do you want to have the entire basin counter for your cosmetics," Ephraim called from the bathroom. "I can put all my stuff in a drawer. I don't have much."

"I usually don't have much, either, but, OK, I did have to buy some make-up I've never used before," Christie replied.

"I think I'll shave a little later, I mean, if that's OK with you, if you don't need the bathroom. I totally forgot to shave this morning."

"Yea, yea, that's fine. We've got to look the part, don't we?

"Look the part. I like that."

In the early evening, Christie and Ephraim left their room, and found their way to the Grand Ballroom. They delighted in finding there was no event scheduled, so they felt free to explore its cavernous dimensions. They imagined where the head table would be, noted where the Ballroom exits were, as well as the proximity of stairways to the Ballroom's entrance. They spoke in whispers. If a janitor or other hotel employee asked them what they were doing, they had agreed to say they were looking it over for a reception they were planning. Ephraim felt perfectly at home telling lies in aid of a moral cause, as he had done so often with his father, but Christie had only recently realized that once one lie was uttered, it would inevitably lead to another lie and another lie and another lie. She crossed her fingers, hoping so many lies would inevitably lead to the truth.

From their room on the 6th floor, Ephraim figured there had to be a way to get into the Ballroom proper. With so many dinner guests arriving about the same time, if they could find an inconspicuous way to join the Ballroom mob scene they pictured, then their formal evening clothes would be the ticket to the rest of the event. They discovered that there were other meeting spaces on the 3rd floor, such as the Mercury and Trianon ballrooms. That floor must also have a large kitchen area, they surmised, able to serve so many banquet participants. Christie and Ephraim continued their explorations, and finally found a way, using staircases only, to get from their room to the kitchen, which served the Grand Ballroom.

The next morning, Christie left the Hilton, walked up Sixth Avenue and across West 58th Street, past the Paris Theatre and into Bergdorf Goodman's. She had an air of confidence this time, as if she belonged in this luxurious store. This had not been the case a month earlier when Christie had made, in Nicki's eyes, a most strange request.

"Nicki, I want you to come with me to Bergdorf Goodman's," Christie had commanded.

"If you say so, but why?" Nicki had replied.

"I need an evening gown. I've never owned one. You have to help me pick one out."

"An evening gown? Wow. What's the occasion?"

"I can not tell you. And you can not tell anyone about the gown."

"Sounds like a lot of fun, though."

"Hardly. But if you can't promise me not to tell anyone, I'll find someone else."

"Hey, you're getting quite bossy, but I like it. Count me in. I promise."

At first, in the fitting room, Christie had difficulty figuring out how to put the gowns on, which Nicki and the clerk had selected. How could she reach that zipper in the back? Did they have different kinds of bras, which would not show underneath those bosom-revealing necklines? How would she ever be able to sit down? As before, Nicki had assisted her with each question and doubt, which were the same as Nicki had for her mother six years before when trying on gowns for her "coming out" debutante party in Pound Ridge. The more Nicki had reveled in revealing to Christie the secrets of allure and femininity, the more Christie had taken on the airs of a woman enjoying the pageantry.

Christie had told the store clerk that she would come back in two weeks to try on the gown after the alterations were completed, and then finally take the gown on the morning of November 13th.

Christie could hardly believe that she had next asked Nicki if they could go to the cosmetics counter, and search for an appropriate lipstick and other make-up to go with the gown. At first, as she looked into the mirror on the counter, she had laughed at herself so much she could not apply the sample lipstick. But then, steadying herself, she had thoroughly enjoyed the experience.

Also a month earlier, Ephraim had walked into Mr. Formal on West 18th Street near Seventh Avenue, and asked the store clerk about tuxedos. Not having ever worn one before, Ephraim had peppered the clerk with questions about the latest style, appropriate cuff links, color of the cummerbund. He had forgotten about the need for appropriate dress shoes until the clerk asked if he owned patent leather ones. Ephraim had been unaccustomed to being dressed in black, a color he associated with the rabbis and elders of the synagogue who seemed to wear nothing but black. How ironic that he would be wearing *their* color to carry out the plan, he had thought. He had also wondered more than once if Yahweh was not having a joke at his expense. After all, here he was, standing in front of a mirror as the clerk had checked the length of the jacket's sleeves, looking for all the world like one of the elite himself, growing steadily more comfortable with his new appearance. He had even decided, without hesitation, that he would have to have his hair cut, ponytail and all, to "business" length. He had rather fancied himself a Wall Street broker at the top of his game as he continued to admire himself in the mirror. Ephraim had given the clerk a deposit and said he would return in a few weeks to rent the tuxedo, all the accessories, and the patent leather shoes.

Over the next few weeks, in the middle of the night, Ephraim had boarded the #1 downtown train on the IRT Broadway/7th Avenue subway line at 86th Street, changed to the 42nd Street/Grand Central Station shuttle, and then took the downtown IRT-Lexington Avenue #6 train to Canal Street, had walked to East Broadway, and then entered his father's locked kosher butcher shop. Fortunately, Joseph had not changed the locks in all the years since he had given his son a key.

So that his father would not notice, Ephraim had filled only one or two Mason jars during each visit with some of the blood his father had drained from sheep and cows. Ephraim had been nervous during his first visit, scooping up blood, which his father, through years of training, had so carefully and ritualistically removed from these animals. During this and each subsequent visit, Ephraim had carefully followed his own ritual, making certain no blood dripped on the floor. Each jar top had been tightly closed. He had wrapped each jar in its own towel, and then set them inside a canvas bag lined with towels, so that the jars would not break if the bag accidently hit a solid object. He had remembered how respectful his father was toward blood, but Ephraim viewed this blood differently, as if it were the blood of soldiers. Each visit to the shop had made him more confident, overcoming fears of divine retribution, haughtily daring either his father or Yahweh to punish him, believing he was protected by his engagement in a great moral crusade. After his last trip to East Broadway, he had eight jars filled with blood, stored in his apartment's refrigerator.

During the weeks that Ephraim had been making his midnight visits to the butcher shop, Daniel had been busy gathering various materials, such as saltpeter, sugar, and baking soda. Mixing substances had always been a particular pleasure. For his tenth birthday, his father had given Daniel a chemistry set with which he turned water into different colors. But this time, his mixing substances would not be for self-entertainment.

On his apartment's stove, he had heated all three ingredients, adding more saltpeter than sugar, over a low heat in a pan. As the sugar had started to melt around the edges of the pan, the mixture was stirred continuously, and then the pan was removed from the heat for a moment, and placed again on the stove over an even lower heat. Blue dye had been added to some batches and red dye to others. When a batch of ingredients turned to liquid, Daniel had removed the pan from the stove to let cool.

How would these mixtures be delivered to their intended targets? Daniel decided the delivery vehicle had to be small and light weight. By chance, in late October, he had passed by a store selling costumes. He had thought about going to an up-coming Halloween party on campus, perhaps disguised as his favorite childhood hero, the Lone Ranger. He had entered the store, easily found a black mask, but then could not locate a holster whose belt fit around his adult-sized waste, or a cowboy hat, which did not look silly on his head. As he was going up and down the aisles of this toy and costume shop, Daniel had happened upon his delivery vehicle, and bought a dozen.

Daniel had poured small portions of the liquid through a hole he had previously drilled in each hollow, imitation golf ball. He had then covered each hole with adhesive tape, and packed up a half-dozen "blues" in one egg carton and another half-dozen "reds" in another egg carton.

While he had waited for Ephraim to come by and put the cartons in his "wedding" suitcase, Daniel was at first thrilled with his ingenuity. Leaning back in his one chair, with the fingers of his hands interlocked across his stomach, Daniel had felt again the immense ten-year old satisfaction of mixing substances, and seeing them change into something new and different. But then, as if an unseen hand had flipped a switch, Daniel found himself desperately trying to fight off the anxiety creeping into his mind, like a thief with a rapier. The thief had opened a wound underneath Daniel's armor of rationalizations--that the means justified the ends, that a great moral cause lent him a hero's cloak of protection against arrest or retribution. As Daniel would experience today and for months to come, anxiety would be a tricky foe. But for this fight today, he had parried the rapier's double-edge blade by picturing himself wearing the black mask to conceal his identity and using the silver bullets to slay his enemy.

> **Montaukett stands next to the stove, watching Daniel intently. She knows the dark side of a man's soul, from the avaricious raids visited upon her people by more powerful tribes to the North. She**

is sick of warfare. She sees in Daniel's disguised face and feels in his heart the conflicted soul of one in battle.

The four had decided to meet for their last planning session the day before the Foreign Policy Association dinner. Assuming a photo of everyone would be taken surreptitiously, they had agreed not to be together even in the vicinity of the Hilton on the 14th. More than that, some of their comrades were convinced that the FBI and CIA either had planted their own agents or had paid informants inside many progressive organizations and committees. Some thought they had spotted such plants. A few comrades had even been paralyzed by paranoia, seeing an FBI agent behind every lamppost. On the whole, however, the four and most others had simply accepted that their words and actions were being monitored by the government, and went about their business.

Meeting over lunch in Times Square at an Orange Julius, perhaps the only eatery they could afford in midtown, the four had figured Dean Rusk would probably be brought to the hotel a few hours before the dinner began, perhaps around 5 pm. They had decided they would not try to disrupt his entrance because that would focus attention only on the anti-war issue. Their strategy was to encounter the elite directly, and as a whole. Their message would be delivered at close range, not through leaflets or placards, or letters-to-the-editor, or hoped-for accurate media reports. Their message would be "global", highlighting many major injustices at once. The list would be long: Watts, Harlem, Vietnam, Cambodia, Dominican Republic, Cuba, The Draft, Racism, Capitalism, ROTC, union-busting, chemical-biological warfare research, Imperialism, Selma, Rochester, South Africa, Mozambique, Angola. The fiftieth anniversary guests were interconnected to all these injustices, TUF had concluded.

If any of the four had misgivings about their mission, they did not voice them now. Each had known that the success of their mission rested in the constant affirmation among themselves that it would succeed. Any doubts to the contrary had been squelched.

Inside their Hilton room, Christie and Ephraim were dressing. In turn, each used the bathroom to change into their formal attire. It was a nerve-racking experience for both of them, as they covered themselves with unfamiliar garments, adjusting here and tucking there. Would they even make it to the Ballroom? Would they be arrested inside? Would their parents visit them in jail? The anxious images piled up.

Christie applied her make-up slowly, trying to remember Nicki's instructions. This would be the very first time she would apply all the brush strokes to the bare canvass of her face. As she transformed herself externally, she felt slowly transformed inwardly. Yesterday's doubts were evaporating. She understood her mission more keenly than ever. The struggle, as she now called it, was overcoming her long-standing feeling of second-handedness that she had experienced in her parents' home. She was no longer her mother's daughter.

Ephraim was equally particular about getting his new appearance right. He adjusted the cummerbund several times, so that half covered his pants and the other half his shirt. He did and re-did the dress shirt's studs to make sure they were clasped correctly. He was pleased with himself that he managed the cufflinks without asking Christie's help. He thought of his grandfather. He was certain the old man would neither have approved of his mingling with the aristocrats, for whatever purpose, nor his looking, with short hair, all the world like one. But Ephraim liked what he saw in the mirror. He no longer felt helpless in the history of his own times.

Their rented car headed down Broadway, crossing Houston. Daniel and Jeff had pooled enough money to afford the 24-hour rate after Ephraim's flat refusal to borrow his father's car again. Passing through the heart of America's financial capital, they saw street names new to them: Pine, Nassau, Exchange, Maiden, Beaver, Pearl, Broad, John, Marketfield, Whitehall, Gold. How tightly packed were the buildings up against the sidewalks, Jeff marveled, almost forcing pedestrians into the narrow roadways. How chaotic the network of roadways, Daniel observed, intersecting at angles unheard of in midtown Manhattan, at angles only a drunken cow could have laid out. But these were, nevertheless, the arteries of the financial and legal barons of the world. These were also the arteries of the minions serving those barons high-up in their offices. Clogged on weekdays by pulsating activity along every artery, each vehicle, bicycle, cart or pedestrian missing every other at full gait by an eighth of an inch. Buses maneuvered tourists around impossibly tight corners, their guides pointing out George Washington's statue marking the site of New York City as the first capital of the United States, Fraunces Tavern, Trinity Church, New York Stock Exchange, World

Trade Center, South Street Seaport. For tonight, Jeff had put together a very different, hand-made "tour."

For their first ever foray into Lower Manhattan, Daniel and Jeff had decided to wear suits and ties. Neither had much in their wardrobes from which to choose. Their string ties were not quite the Wall Street business attire image they had hoped to achieve, but if each kept the button closed on his single-breasted jackets, perhaps no one would notice the odd pastel shirt he was wearing. Jeff had to borrow a pair of dress shoes, as his only pair was still back in his parents' home. Daniel did have the right shoes, as he kept a black pair in the original box, polished, to be used only for funerals.

Sitting next to Daniel's leg on the passenger side of the rented car was a Saks Fifth Avenue shopping bag and a box of rubber gloves. Two nights before, Ephraim had carefully poured blood from the Mason jars into balloons being held by Daniel, both wearing gloves purchased by Christie at a beauty supply store, not knowing if the surface of a balloon would capture a fingerprint. The two then carefully wrapped towels around and on top of the balloons inside the bag.

Ephraim and Christie had decided they would not take the elevator to the third floor for fear that, upon exiting directly into the Grand Ballroom, they would be faced with FPA staff checking invitations against the guest list. They counted on the fact that perhaps as many as 2,800 people would have been invited, the Ballroom's capacity for a banquet. They also assumed most of those 2,800 would be arriving around the same time, since many would come after work from offices in Manhattan. Others would fly up that afternoon on the Eastern Airlines Shuttle from Washington, D.C. into LaGuardia Airport, or arrive at the near-by Marine Air Terminal in their private jets. For those who had not had a chance to change into eveningwear, the Hilton provided suites and attendants to assist those not staying overnight in the hotel.

Ephraim marveled at the transformation standing next to him. He knew it was Christie, but where was the comrade of blouses and miniskirts? Who was this in a gown, with pearl necklace and earrings, pink high heels, deep red nails, and polished face? He gazed at a vision of an English lady, making her grand entrance at a ball during the London "season," regal and confident.

Ephraim was no less transformed in Christie's eyes. He stood more erect than before, with gleaming black hair to match his shiny black shoes, and everything in between perfectly attired, as if Ephraim had just emerged from a dinner party at J. Pierpont Morgan's Madison Avenue mansion sixty years ago. His shorter, polio-crippled left leg lengthened beneath the drape of the pants. The fingers of his left hand fully extended to adjust his cravat. Christie saw in Ephraim's image a gentleman and hugely successful businessman.

They continued standing side-by-side, alternatively looking at themselves and each other in the mirror. The longer they stared, the more they saw through their costumes to the persons underneath. Doubts crept back. The seams of their beautiful garments held tightly together the images of what they wanted to project, but their nerves were not knit together strongly enough to keep anxiety out.

"How do I look, Ephraim? Do you really think I'll fool them into thinking I'm one of them? Do you think my hair looks alright?" On and on went her questions.

"If my older brother ever got a glimpse of me. What would he think? Do you think he'd ever speak to me again?" On and on went his questions.

All that afternoon, each frequently thought, but could not say it aloud, that they could not go through with the plan. Each hoped the other would call it off. Now, as they continued to peer into the mirror at the new people they had chosen to become, they reassured the other how beautiful and handsome they appeared together. They forgot their uniforms of the past, Ephraim's torn dungarees or chauffeur's cap and Christie's cotton dresses or flats. It was as if they felt they were actors at the make-up table, building their characters from the outside in, choosing the style of nose or wig, which would instruct how the lines would be delivered. And so, the socialite and the tycoon left their room, walked down the hallway hand-in-hand through a door marked "stairway down."

The kitchen staff was too busy to notice the couple walking past them and through the swinging doors, still hand-in-hand, into the crowded Ballroom. The couple quickly moved to stand near a group of people chatting away with glasses in their hands. The tycoon asked the socialite if she wanted a cocktail, but *Christie* ordered him not to leave her side for any reason! The nearby group opened their ranks and invited the couple to join them.

236

"Hello, I'm Trent Alsop, and this is my wife, Emily."

"Are you related to Joseph—"

"No, no,--"

"So, did you travel far to come here tonight?" a female member of the group asked the couple, one of those innocent-sounding questions intended to ferret out one's social and financial *bona fides*.

"Yes, we did as a matter of fact," the tycoon responded. "We flew in from Prague a few days ago."

"Prague? How intriguing," the female member continued. "Were you there when the Soviet tanks crushed, oh what did the Czechs call it, oh yes, the Prague Spring? How intriguing. Let me go and find Harrison Salisbury—I just love his reporting in *The Times*, don't you?--and bring him over here, I'm certain he would *love* to chat with you."

"Oh, no, no," the socialite quickly interjected. "Please don't trouble yourself. Anyway, I've just seen an old friend from Paris across the room. I must see her before she gets away. Would you please excuse us?"

As they crossed the room, *Christie* pointedly asked, "What's this about Prague?"

"I thought I was picking a place which sounded great," *Ephraim* defended himself, "and nobody would have been from there. I forgot all about the Soviet invasion. I won't let it happen again."

"You better not. Try not to say anything about anything. Let them think we're above all their chatter," said the socialite, regaining her composure.

The tycoon and the socialite were by now in the middle of the main course. They had managed to avoid just about every question or topic which could have allowed the curious—and there were many—to pierce their armor. They actually found themselves enjoying the chatter around them, the quick-witted jousting and joking, the incessant remarks about private schools and inadequate maids.

But now it was time.

Rusk would speak after dessert. As previously planned, the four had not wanted their action to be interpreted solely as anti-war, so the Ballroom piece of the plan must occur before Rusk's speech. Everyone at their table was so enjoying the food and the banter. The couple was also drawn in, tasting new delicacies and listening to old family stories, even making up a few of their own. But it was indeed time. The socialite was becoming acutely aware of the six "blue" golf balls in her purse, and the tycoon of the three "red" golf balls in each of his two front pockets. Ephraim reached for Christie's hand, squeezed it slightly, and nodded. Not looking at anyone else around their table, the two slipped away and walked to an outer ring of vacant tables, waiting for guests who never arrived.

Pulsing with capitalist adrenalin during the workday, the Wall Street area was a virtual ghost town at night. Daniel and Jeff timed their "Tour of Imperialist Sites," as they called Jeff's map, to start an hour after sunset, and then finish in time to park the rental, which the two would return the next morning, close to the Hudson River in the mid-fifties, and walk to their rendezvous with Christie and Ephraim. Each balloon in the Saks Fifth Avenue bag was no larger than the hand, which would throw it. While the elite were schmoozing over cocktails and canapés at the Hilton, some of their corporate headquarters would be delivered an unmistakable message.

The first destination was 20 Pine Street in Lower Manhattan. Chemical Bank was a junior partner in the $40 million revolving loan to the South African government, Jeff had learned during meetings of the Committee on Southern Africa. It had been agreed between the two that Daniel would deliver the blood balloons while Jeff drove their "get-away" car. Jeff was somewhat relieved at this arrangement. As much as he disliked American banks lending financial support and credibility to an oppressive regime, he was surprised how structurally magnificent were the building exteriors he passed en route. He allowed himself a fantasy or two, walking with briefcase in hand into a marbled lobby, ascending in a private elevator to his penthouse office, of course *after* his imagined employer had withdrawn from South Africa.

At each site on the hand-made map, the maneuver was the same. Jeff drove slowly past the headquarters' front door while they looked around to make sure there were no security guards or passersby near the entrance. Then Jeff stopped the car. With one balloon in hand and both hands gloved, Daniel got out. Jeff then pulled down the street a few doors, stopped again, and waited for Daniel.

Approaching the corporate sign near the front door of their first target, Daniel looked through every pane of glass at or near the entrance. He was looking for any employees walking across the lobby toward the front door, and also for the normally large desk, usually at the back of the lobby, where a security guard might be sitting. If he spotted no one, or if a security guard seemed pre-occupied with a newspaper or a nap, he quickly stuck a pin in the balloon and squirted blood all over the corporate sign. If the sign were higher than he could reach, he threw the balloon at it. Daniel then walked at a normal gait toward the car, as if he were a late-leaving employee being picked up by a friend.

Daniel was ecstatic as he glanced back at the Chemical Bank sign, blood dripping from it, before opening the car's passenger door. He knew it to be a revolutionary act. No one outside TUF would ever know about it. No credit would be given, no praise from other activists. The act itself was all the gratification Daniel expected.

The next destination was Wall Street, on which Jeff's map showed seven corporate targets. Daniel was glad that his first toss on Pine Street had worked so well, because he would have to work quickly on this long street.

Number 120 Wall Street was the American Sugar Refining Corporation, the nation's largest, with extensive plantations in the Dominican Republic, which the Marines had invaded two years before to protect American economic interests and make sure a pro-US government was installed. Christie had reviewed the research on this target. As Daniel threw a blood-filled balloon at the corporate sign, he also meant it for the nation's second largest refinery, National Sugar, which also had extensive Dominican holdings.

Brown Brothers Harriman & Company, at Number 59, was a private bank, which, according to a government report in the 1930s, was among the largest stockholders in five of the ten largest American companies at that time. Robert Lovett, former Secretary of War under President Truman, was its current president. As Daniel squirted blood on the corporate sign, he felt peculiar pleasure in knowing, though their worlds were very far apart, that he and W. Averill Harriman had the sport of polo in common: Daniel as an avid fan going to Bostwick Field with his parents years before, and Harriman as an avid player in his youth. As he walked back to the car, Daniel relished the idea that he had now crossed paths with this influential political and financial player whose career was described, in a book Daniel had used for research, as moving from " … command post to command post … ."

Number 55 was home of First National City Bank, one of the South

Africa consortium loan members. Daniel took particular delight in hitting its corporate sign.

Kuhn Loeb & Company, at Number 40, was next. On this investment bank's executive committee sat Benjamin Buttenweiser, a member of the Foreign Policy Association. Manufacturers Hanover Trust Company was also at Number 40, a member of the consortium for the South Africa loan.

Morgan Guaranty Trust Company, at number 23, was part of the extensive holdings of its founder, J. Pierpont Morgan. Daniel was delighted to discover that a Morgan company was the investment banker for Eastman Kodak. In addition, its president, Thomas Gates, was Secretary of Defense under President Eisenhower. Morgan Guaranty was also one of the consortium of banks involved in the revolving loan to South Africa.

Bankers Trust, at Number 16, was another South Africa loan consortium member. The bank had become one of the "new tycoons" of the American economy by controlling huge pension funds, like AT&T's.

The final Wall Street target was Irving Trust, at number One, also a South Africa loan consortium member.

"This is going very well, isn't it?" Daniel said, less as a question and more as a statement.

"Yeah, great, but I can't wait to get it over," Jeff replied. "How many more do we have?" Jeff asked, pointing to the map in Daniel's hand.

"I wish we had chosen more sites, damn it. I didn't think it would be so easy. Anyway, maybe three or four more here, and then those in midtown," Daniel answered.

"Can't we just forget the midtown ones?"

"Look, we all planned this together. Christie and Ephraim, who have by far the toughest assignment, what would they think if we quit half-way through ours?" Daniel asked without waiting for a response. "Chase is next!"

One Chase Manhattan Plaza, a skyscraper completed six years earlier, was at the corner of Liberty and William Streets. Christie's research had discovered that Chase Bank was not only involved in a revolving loan, with nine other banks, to the South African government's Industrial Development Corporation, but Chase had also merged with the Standard Bank of South Africa. The new building also housed three high-power law firms, including Milbank, Tweed, Hadley & McCloy (Chase's main outside counsel), Davis Polk & Wardwell, and Cravath, Swaine & Moore. Daniel took particular delight in hitting Chase's sign.

To get to their next destination as quickly as possible, Jeff had mapped a route, which took into account many one-way streets. He continued on Liberty Street all the way to Maiden Lane, turned right onto Pearl Street, and eventually wound up at One William Street. Lehmann Brothers, an investment firm, had grown through financing large retail trade and department stores, and then took positions in major arms manufacturers, like General Dynamics. He remembered the phone conversation last July with Muller, a high school friend, and hoped Muller would hear of his corporation's blood-stained sign.

Jeff stayed on William Street, going to number 46 next. Daniel bloodied the exterior of Dillon Read & Co., which had floated bonds for the South African government in the 1950s.

Number 55 Broad Street, Goldman Sachs & Co., was the last stop on the Lower Manhattan portion of Jeff's map. Alongside Lehmann Brothers, Goldman Sachs had grown by financing the expansion of retail trade and department stores, orchestrating mergers to consolidate control of those industries. Daniel felt he was striking a blow for every Mom 'n' Pop store in America.

Jeff then headed the car south, down the West Side Drive, around the horn of Manhattan past Battery Park, and up the East Side Drive, exiting at East 42nd Street. He was headed for Park Avenue, where they would cruise by the headquarters of Middle South Utilities (at number 280) and Olin Mathieson Corporation (at number 460). But first, they stopped in front of 150 East 42nd Street, the Mobil Oil Corporation that had extensive holdings in South Africa. Seeing many more pedestrians on the sidewalks than they had anticipated, Jeff did not want to chance being caught. Even though Daniel told Jeff to drop him at Mobil's headquarters and park much further down the street, Jeff insisted that, if Daniel was caught, the FBI would trace his activities, and eventually all of TUF would be charged with some kind of conspiracy. Reluctantly, Daniel decided to end their mission.

After parking the rental car on West 54th Street near Eleventh Avenue, they walked toward the Hilton, ditching the remaining balloons and used gloves in various wire trash baskets along the route. Daniel kept vigorously patting Jeff on the back, emphasizing how overjoyed he was that they had not been discovered.

"Hey, I get it," Jeff protested after a particularly forceful blow on his back. "Yeah, we were damn lucky!"

"No, no, not luck, not luck at all," Daniel upbraided Jeff. "We were protected. Yes, I know it, protected. Call it fate, destiny, call it whatever you want. Don't you get it? No one came after me when I smashed the university president's window. And no one caught me tonight. As long as I keep moving, you know, like Muhammed Ali moves in the ring, nobody's going to lay a glove on me! Or on you, Jeff. Not on one of us."

In the Grand Ballroom, Ephraim and Christie separated, moving four or five tables apart in the outer ring of empty tables, so that, if one were spotted and stopped, the other might still be able to continue. Out of her purse and his pockets, they laid their golf balls on the table in front of them, covering them with a near-by scalloped napkin. Each waited. They hoped the other would go first. They waited more minutes, not daring to look directly at the other. They heard nothing of the din in the room. They sat motionless, each glued to the moment. Then, as if a switch had been flipped, each remembered the plan. They were to do it together, simultaneously.

Their hands trembled as they started to reach for the matchbooks, seeing the other do the same out of the corner of their eyes. Christie could barely re-open her purse. Ephraim's hand at first could not find the opening to his pocket at the top of his trousers. The room now seemed far quieter than when they left their empty dinner plates, quiet enough, each feared, that the entire ballroom would surely hear the striking of the matches. Ephraim started to perspire, but thought better of using the scalloped napkin to daub his forehead. Christie felt slightly nauseous as she saw a line of waiters exiting the kitchen with dessert trays held high, heading for the tables. Then she noticed the lights go down. At each table, a waiter lit a banana rum flambé, with the guests' attention fixed on the ritual.

The plan's next steps had been rehearsed verbally over and over at their meetings, but not the actual motions. The fingers of Ephraim's left hand started to curl back toward his palm as he reached for the matchbook. With his right hand, Ephraim placed the matchbook with great difficulty between his index and middle fingers of the left hand as they continued to curl toward the palm. He opened the cover with his right hand, then slowly moved his left thumb to hold it open. Suddenly, he remembered he had to remove the adhesive tape from the bottom of the golf ball, so he took one from under the napkin, placed it in front of him, and looked around. Relieved for the moment that the entire room seemed pre-occupied with receiving what he alternatively hoped would be their just desserts, Ephraim put the matchbook down and peeled away the tape. He then tried to re-grip the matchbook. His fingers closed into a fist. He pried them open enough with his right hand to re-grip the matchbook with his left.

Christie's hands were trembling so much now that, after several attempts to remove the adhesive tape from one of the golf balls, she was ready to give up. She looked across the empty tables to Ephraim struggling to grip the matchbook, and took heart. She could not let the team down.

Ephraim held the match with his right hand, and kept missing the striking edge or not applying enough pressure to cause a flame. His frustration grew. All his life his body had been an unwilling companion to the instructions from his mind, refusing at times to cooperate easily even for the most rudimentary of motions. He decided to quit for sure this time. He looked over to Christie, hoping she would see his pained expression and relieve him of saying aloud that they should just walk out. But she did not turn toward him. Ephraim saw she was intent on removing a piece of tape from the hole. He would have to soldier on.

As planned, out of the corners of their eyes, they confirmed with a nod that each now held lighted matches. They were then to throw the lit smoke bombs at the same time, one in the direction slightly to the left of the center of the room, and the other to the right of center. This would make the greatest initial impact, they theorized. Confusion would provide time to light and throw the remaining ten in an arc fanning out to the tables farthest to the left and the right, filling the entire Ballroom with blue and red smoke, bringing a teargas-like effect, felt by civil rights demonstrators, to the eyes and noses of the elite. Since they had not actually practiced lighting smoke bombs, Ephraim and Christie only hoped the smoke would be quickly released after the missiles landed.

Finally striking the match with his right hand, Ephraim dropped the matchbook and managed to hold the ball off the table with his left hand while the flame seared the bottom of the ball. He slowly transferred the ball from his left hand to his right, only to have the fingers of his right hand now curl around it. As he drew back his right arm, the fingers seemed to tighten even more around the ball, locking it in place, holding it captive, signaling they would not release their hold even when Ephraim tried to release the ball, his deformities revolting against an act which, if ever discovered, would certainly kill his father out of fear that the entire family would be arrested as traitors and sent to an American Gulag.

Ephraim quickly looked toward Christie, to tell her to stop. But he saw her stand up, cock her hand behind her head, and jump her body forward as her arm moved to release the golf ball. Without thinking, Ephraim stood, too. Let everyone see him, his body demanded of the assembled from a place deep within its patriarchal memory. Like Christie, he, too, threw the ball as far as he could toward its intended destination.

The two did not hesitate another single second. Their actions released all the anxiety in their minds. Ball after ball was lit and thrown. Ephraim's fingers on both hands cooperated; Christie's delivery gained fluidity. Relieved and overjoyed as the last golf balls left their hands, Ephraim and Christie turned their backs on the assembled, walked rapidly toward the main doors of the Ballroom as the lights came up again, imagining smoke would soon fill the targets' nostrils. They gained the safety of a stairway, returning to their room, undetected, where they hugged each other, changed into casual clothes, and left the hotel for their Sixth Avenue rendezvous point with Daniel and Jeff.

"You know, I don't give a damn what CBS, NBC or ABC broadcasts tonight on their eleven o'clock local news programs," Daniel said, as he sipped a frosted orange cream drink, his three comrades seated around the table. "For once, it doesn't make a bit of difference how they cover the Hilton demonstration. The powerful bastards already know, first-hand, what it feels like to be under siege."

"It's a great feeling, not to have to wait around weeks for a response, if they ever give one, from Chase Manhattan after delivering petitions, with hundreds of signatures, demanding it leaves South Africa," Jeff stated. "They heard from us tonight!"

"You know, when my article on the Rockefellers' interests in Venezuela is published next month," Christie said, "I'll still send it to Senators interested in changing hemispheric policy, but tonight we had more impact than my article will ever have!"

"I feel so good," Ephraim declared, "I'm going to have *two* franks!"

All four laughed heartily.

They knew their global message to the elite was unfiltered, undiluted, and unavoidable. True, they also knew they had crossed a line. They were not peaceful demonstrators anymore, going limp in the best civil disobedience tradition, willing to face the consequences, even if that meant a day or more in jail. They saw themselves as provocateurs, disrupting important gatherings, targeting property, using disguise and guile, as well as moving quickly out of an area, to avoid any consequences.

They could not know that only half the plan had gone well. In the Grand Ballroom, the lit matches had resealed the holes in the golf balls with melted plastic. The saltpeter mixture had fizzled for lack of oxygen. As some of the golf balls came to rest on their tables, a few of the dinner guests chuckled at the imaginative party favors.

Nor could the four have ever imagined, congratulating themselves over franks and frosted orange creams, that their desire to have an even grander victory would end dreadfully.

CHAPTER 13 – INSURRECTION
(WINTER/SPRING 1968)

Freedom Train, recorded by James Carr, written by Steve Bogard, Larry Rogers, Carl Wells, 1968.

Move on Over, words by Len H. Chandler, Jr., to the tune of *John Brown's Body* and the *Battle Hymn of the Republic*, 1966.

Like trees, the four went into a quiescent period during the winter. No visits home for Thanksgiving or Christmas. No more Pabst at the West End Café. No more marijuana. Perhaps an occasional party, but ginger ale only. Their social contacts dwindled to virtually none. Assignments were submitted on time, even Daniel's, but class participation dropped practically to zero.

On the surface, like any other winter, the cycle during which trees made sap, slowly turning to the sugar required for spring's showy green, was continuing. Appearances were deceptive, however. Beneath the bark, trees' bared exteriors concealed their preparation for one of Nature's grand revolutions. Also engaging in a similar phase of their political cycle, the four prepared for revolution. They were letting fall many of their exterior connections, just as trees let fall their leaves to preserve energy for other purposes.

As snow occasionally dropped its mantle of silence over the city, inside their rooms the four were busily reading and discussing Camus and Burke and Che and Jefferson and Samuel Adams and Franz Fanon and C. Wright Mills. They made excursions into Marx, Lenin, Trotsky, Goldman and Mao. Talking often with foreign students, the four gained as much insight as they could into the civil societies within Cuba, North Vietnam, and Algeria.

"The capitalists keep dangling hope in front of the public's eye," Ephraim observed. "The call it The American Dream. A few make it into the wealthy class, just to keep that dream plausible. For everyone else, the wealthy devise a hundred ways to nibble away our money. A new fee here, a subway fare raise there, selling us on our having to have a new super-duper this or that."

"Acquisitiveness," Daniel continued, "capitalism is organized for the purpose of the people making more and more purchases. Then the elite and their mouthpieces sow fear, fear about communists, militant blacks, the Viet Cong, so much fear that you crave comfort food, comfort things, guns to protect yourself, politicians who tell you what you want to hear."

"My God," Christie asked, "do you mean my mother was right all those years ago, about not giving in to fads?"

"I don't know about that," Ephraim responded, "but I do know that we've got to identify our own bourgeois activities and attitudes, and rid ourselves of them. We must live simply, detach ourselves from their capitalist dragnet."

"What we do when we are together also has to be what we do when we are apart," Daniel observed. "We support each other here, become more disciplined, so we can also be disciplined when we're not together."

"I agree," Jeff added. "Our strategy meetings can be far more focused than they have been. And, to help each other to change our habits and routines, I suggest we have shorter meetings, but more of them each week."

The others agreed with Jeff, and all four decided that Daniel should come to each meeting with an agenda based on topics suggested between meetings.

Without fanfare or self-promotion, TUF decided in February to become a cell of disciplined revolutionaries. Week after week, the four were creating a new universe for themselves within their own bubble.

Honesty within; fabrication without. It became their motto. To anyone coming in contact with any of the four, their words and actions were "normal," blending right in with the prevailing tone, frictionless, though they often conducted themselves in a subdued, placid manner. Their external communications raised no hint of the sap they were creating and storing beneath their bark.

Even when their strategy persuaded them to meet with other groups, they often successfully imposed their discipline on what would have been a meandering conversation by sitting at different places around the table, supporting each other's efforts to keep the discussions on track. They were often successful at steering decisions toward ones on which they had agreed in advance.

Of course, they had bought *The New York Times*, *The New York Daily News*, *The New York Post*, and *The Washington Post* the next day after the Foreign Policy Association dinner, to see if any of their actions had been reported, however inaccurately. They had not totally disregarded the influence of establishment publications, or the CBS Evening News with Walter Cronkite and NBC's Huntley-Brinkley Report. They were still a bit hooked not only on these medias' power to influence public opinion, but also, as it were, had hoped to read their next day "notices" after their Hilton and Wall Street performances. Nothing had appeared, however, in any paper about the smoke bombs at the Hilton or blood balloons in Lower Manhattan. Obviously the FPA luminaries had suppressed the story, the four concluded, not wanting the public to know that their hotel celebration or financial sanctuary had been invaded.

TUF had discussed going with their story to *Liberation News Service* or the *Underground Press Syndicate* or any of the mushrooming individual underground newspapers, like the *East Village Other*, *Los Angeles Free Press*, *Berkeley Barb. The Paper, The Rag, The Inquisition, Fifth Estate, The Oracle*, or the *Seed*. Even if they used pseudonyms, however, the four had agreed that it would draw too much attention too early to their burgeoning revolutionary strategy.

During the winter and into spring, they rarely returned social phone calls, and stopped writing newsy letters. Friends faded away, not knowing what to make of their subdued behavior. Were they depressed, friends wondered? Had someone died in the family? The four never said. As the fog of the obligations of friendship lifted from their daily lives, they more clearly perceived TUF's day-to-day objectives and cohesiveness.

248

Through the course of its meetings, now as many as four per week, TUF was consciously and deliberately becoming a collective. Any sense of hierarchy, whether based on age, experience, gender, intelligence, or any other differentiation was to be exposed, challenged, and then eliminated. Each was equal to the other, meaning that all opinions were honored and thoroughly discussed, all decisions were unanimous, and each person was equally responsible to insure that every decision was implemented, even though different members might assume different tasks. Each one was to feel responsible for the fate of everything discussed, agreed, acted upon, and reported back to the collective.

As in winter, when all the leaves have fallen and the branches of different varieties look the same, the four shed, or tried to shed, their individual differences. The only personality that existed inside the meeting space was the one formed by the incessant polishing of the collective's style, through discussions and agreements. As time went on, nothing personal was expected to survive within each member's daily routine. It was as if nothing else was supposed to happen within the meetings or between meetings that was not collectively discussed and agreed.

"Honesty within; fabrication without."

In addition to the TUF meetings, however, Christie was attending another regular meeting, unknown to the other three. A women's group had formed three months earlier. Christie had faithfully attended every weekly meeting during which women simply shared stories about themselves, their relationships with family, and with men. She felt for the very first time she had found a group in which she could just be herself. Perhaps Christie might use all her talents and energy toward women's liberation, she considered, but for now she kept those thoughts to herself.

Jeff was attending a different kind of meeting, though not regularly, also unknown to the other three. He was not certain he belonged with the men who met weekly, though he liked them, and felt more and more at ease with them.

Each TUF member was quite animated with the other, even humorous, when conversing one-to-one. The same vitality also existed whenever three of the four met informally, apart from their official collective meetings, which were held only when all four were in attendance. But whenever the collective gathered, whether once or four times a week, virtually every time an invisible blanket was felt to be thrown over the proceedings by some inexplicable hand. That same hand then flicked the switch on an invisible exhaust fan, which proceeded to remove most of the oxygen from each participant's brain. Moving through molasses would have been easier for the four than moving through the agenda. These activists' lethargy stayed for the entire meeting, lifting only at the end as they walked out as suddenly as it had descended in the beginning.

"Why do I feel so tired?" Ephraim finally found courage to ask at one meeting in early April. "I don't feel tired before I get here."

"I feel the same way," Jeff responded. "Sometime I feel like I'm Sisyphus. After we've agreed on what I am to do at a meeting, I push that rock up the hill a few feet, really feel good about accomplishing a few tasks, and then, when I'm here at the next meeting, and we're figuring out what's next to do, I feel like the rock has fallen back to the ground and I'll have to push it up again, over and over. I don't ever feel that I finish anything! I'd like one day to feel the relief and satisfaction of actually finishing something for good. I'm drained when we're all together."

"But look," Daniel reasoned, "maybe we feel this way because we're doing something new. Like beginning an exercise routine. Our revolutionary political muscles are adjusting to the new regimen. It'll only be a matter of time until they're in shape. You'll see."

The other three nodded unenthusiastically.

"I hope so," Christie interjected, "but a lot of times when our meetings start, I'm suddenly overwhelmed by the sensation and weight of both the tasks I didn't finish from our last meeting and knowing that I'll have even more tasks to do as a result of this meeting. Will this feeling of being constantly overwhelmed ever end? Sometimes I feel like I'm on my last nerve."

"I'm with Christie," Ephraim added. "It's like my energy evaporates soon after a meeting starts. I feel as if I'm in a sauna, the fog of steam everywhere, causing me to feel logy, even sleepy."

The four came to the conclusion over time that the Movement must replace the tactic of disrupting single events with a more encompassing and sustainable direct action. After all, they had experienced the limits of protests, petitions, letter-writing, peaceful placard-waving demonstrations, sit-ins and teach-ins. Surface accommodations had been made by the powerful, but that was about all. Even when the risk of being arrested and serving a jail sentence had become much greater with more aggressive tactics, like disrupting a speech, smashing a lock to access government property as a symbolic act of destruction, or blocking military recruiters from talking to prospective volunteers, the changes sought had rarely occurred.

The four also came to understand that they must prepare fully for whatever strategic targets they chose. After much discussion, TUF finally decided their own Morningside Heights University would be the first target. Their burgeoning strategy required that no accessible tentacle of the ruling class' power would go unconfronted, undisrupted, or unoccupied. The four would organize others not just to control the street for a few hours of what they had affectionately nicknamed "the touch football tactic." They intended to seize control of an entire area for days, if not weeks, and own the entire field. Their pamphlets, research papers, statements, press releases (if any), interviews, would write the historical narrative this time, not the elite's public relations departments or media outlets.

Morningside Heights University (MHU) had an international reach, which appealed to the four. Its International Fellows Program gathered graduate students from different departments once a week to sit at the feet of such guest lecturers as current and former Secretaries of State, top government advisors on foreign policy, elite historians, and other well-placed dignitaries. Its journalism school graduated would-be reporters likely to interpret US and world events for Americans. Graduates from its departments of law, medicine, engineering, theology and many others were as likely as not to be future influencers, if not decision-makers, on local, national, and international policies.

MHU was also a massive force in New York City's real estate market. It owned not only the large campus housing its educational, administrative and some dormitory facilities along a stretch of four undivided city blocks, but was owner of 192 residential properties as well as owners of the land under the mid-town Rockefeller Center complex and the downtown World Trade Center area, including Trinity Church, and the very recent owner of an entire block in the Wall Street area and a large tract in Rockland County, as well as portions of a West Side area running from 125th to 135th Streets. Instead of smashing the glass in the university president's door, Daniel now fantasized smashing the entire university by bringing its workings to a halt.

The four met at any hour of the day or night. Each became very familiar with the other—speech patterns, ticks, snack preferences, ideas, fallback arguments, clothing choices. Meetings developed their own routine, including each of the four always sitting in the same place, talking in the same rotation. The familiar became so familiar that, despite the gravity of their discussions, a certain boredom crept into their midst.

During several meetings in mid-April, Ephraim began to notice, and then wondered, as he tried to focus on another of Jeff's oft-repeated points, why Jeff was exactly ten minutes late to almost every meeting, despite Daniel's upbraiding Jeff for his tardiness. What was Jeff doing to cause him to be chronically late?

Jeff's tardiness became such an obsession with Ephraim that he decided to find out why it occurred. One day Ephraim went to Jeff's dormitory, and waited around the corner at about the time he guessed Jeff would leave for the meeting. In fact, Jeff did leave thirty minutes before the meeting, in plenty of time to make the scheduled start. Ephraim had no clue what he was looking for, but in his mind he had concluded Jeff was up to no good. Not wanting to raise suspicion about his pre-meeting surveillance, Ephraim followed Jeff for a few blocks, and then hailed a cab to arrive at the meeting on time. Jeff was indeed ten minutes late again.

His second surveillance attempt paid off. Ephraim saw Jeff leave the dormitory in time to make the meeting, but ten minutes later he saw Jeff ring the buzzer of a basement apartment, wait, and then be let in by a male. About ten minutes later, he saw Jeff emerge from the apartment, carrying a small envelope, which he soon stuffed in an inside jacket pocket. Ephraim then hailed a cab as Jeff continued to walk in the direction of the meeting. Ephraim was there when Jeff arrived ten minutes late.

A few days later, before TUF's next meeting, Ephraim again witnessed Jeff leaving his dormitory to get to the meeting on time, and then saw him stop at the same basement apartment, go inside for ten minutes, and reappear with another small envelope in his hand. Ephraim then waited for Jeff to disappear around a corner, and walked down the stairs to the apartment. He saw the name "Sean Constable" next to the buzzer. Was this the same Sean who had ridden in his father's car, and wanted to turn back after pissing on his pants, during their trip to Lafayette Park?

Ephraim had to be sure. A few days later, he stood across the street for several hours when a male finally went down those basement apartment stairs, put a key in the lock and entered. Ephraim waited a few moments, crossed the street, and buzzed. He scampered back up the steps, pulled his hood around his head, and waited at the edge of the ground floor railing where he could see anyone walk out of the apartment. His stealth was soon rewarded, as he recognized Sean. Ephraim had not seen his face all that clearly on the way to Washington, since Ephraim sat in the passenger seat and Sean in the back, but he could not forget Sean's grimace as he passed him repeatedly on the vigil circle in Lafayette Park, or the mouth which uttered curse after curse on the return trip. Was Jeff receiving some kind of payoff from this creep, Ephraim questioned? Was Jeff working for somebody? What was he up to?

As the unelected "chairman" of the four, Daniel was determined to set an example on how to run a meeting efficiently and productively. In the beginning, Daniel wrote in time limits for each topic on the agenda he had typed. He allowed these limits to be extended only if the discussion had not yet produced a decision. He noticed, however, that discussions sometimes went around in circles, with individuals just repeating points they made earlier, but with more emphasis. Other times he felt discussions meandered because everyone had clearly come to understand that decisions were followed by the assignment of tasks, and everyone was reluctant to take on more work. Daniel then tried to enforce the stated time limits in order to keep the discussion focused and end with decisions and task assignments.

After a few weeks, Christie was distressed by discussions being arbitrarily curtailed after a set time by Daniel. She was additionally upset by Daniel's insistence on "calling the question" whenever any of the others tried to extend the discussion. She felt disheartened by signs of Daniel's growing autocratic style. It contrasted sharply with the egalitarian style of her women's meetings. She sensed that even discussions that repeated things needed time to breathe, for each to take in fully what the other was saying and truly understand it, so that any decision made was grounded not just intellectually, but emotionally. She finally confronted Daniel, and was surprised, and pleased, to be joined by Jeff. Ephraim said nothing. Daniel reluctantly gave in to this small revolt within their revolutionary collective. The four then agreed they would not by governed by the clock, but by their own consensus as to when the discussion should end.

Although at first excited about being in TUF, and taking on the identity of a revolutionary, Jeff wondered if his political actions now might hinder his chances for a professional career later. He was taken by all the criticisms of capitalism expressed at their meetings and in their readings, but he also wondered how much of his association with TUF would be exposed in the future and hurt his chances for a financially successful life? Jeff also knew he could not simply walk out on his comrades. They were more than just political allies. They were even more than friends. Jeff relied on them as he had relied on his family when growing up, for praise and re-assurance and belonging. And yet, he asked himself, was he making a mistake by identifying so closely with TUF? And was he doing the right thing by agreeing to be Sean's errand-boy in exchange for Sean's taking Jeff into his confidence about a business Sean wanted to start?

On March 27th, a small student demonstration demanded the severance of all university ties from the Institute for Defense Analysis (IDA). It had been reasonably assumed by the demonstrators, based on research, that IDA, whose chairman was also a university trustee, had approved classified military contracts in part aimed at the prosecution of the war in Vietnam. Some Department of Defense contract recipients had also been university employees. In response to this demonstration, the university placed the activist student leaders on disciplinary probation. This series of events, not dissimilar to many others happening across America, nevertheless provided the spark, which set aflame the passions of almost the entire MHU student body.

To the outside observer, the political cyclones, especially in March and April, seemed to appear suddenly, spend their force, and withdraw just as suddenly. The conditions creating and supporting their appearances, however, had been nurtured for years, like a gardener learning season after season how better to enrich the soil to support the plants. It took a special kind of weatherman, however, to predict accurately when the conditions were ripe enough for a cyclone to touch down.

Confrontations with the Administration grew in size and seriousness, with activist students having the advantage of swifter internal communications and public pronouncements than the tortoise-like Administration's consultative apparatus. In the strongest signal to date of the students' increased level of determination to effect change, 200 students, led at first by student chapter leaders of the national University Movement and student leaders of the campus Afro-American Association, occupied Burr Hall on April 23rd. As the first evening of occupation rolled into the early morning hours of the second day, Daniel was thrilled to learn that the black students, now aided by black power leaders from the surrounding community, had persuaded the white students to leave Burr Hall, claiming that they were not revolutionary enough. The black students and their supporters also redefined what a "coalition" was. Blacks would no longer stand for alliances led by whites, but would rather first define the issues and tactics for themselves, and then determine what, if any, would be the whites' support role. It was on-the-ground confirmation of what Daniel had learned during his parking lot conversation with Arthur a year ago.

At first, the Burr Hall occupation caught TUF by surprise. All their radical research, discussions of strategies and tactics, analyses of interconnected corporate, university, and military interests—all their research had distanced them from the everyday ebb and flow of student life. TUF moved quickly, however, to insert itself into the rapidly unfolding late April cyclone. As four other buildings were soon occupied, each TUF member chose one of those buildings and joined the occupiers. Their goal was to effect a coordinated, single-voice channel through which all the occupiers would speak.

> **On the high ground near the north end of Morningside Heights University, four Original People dismount from their horses. Preparing their camp, they know they will remain in the area for days. Montaukett, Anishinaabe, Lenni-Lenape, and Munsee review their plan for hours.**

Through now months of conversations among themselves, TUF had known that their first order of business was to secure the perimeters of the occupied areas. They also made certain no one else, besides students, remained behind in their buildings. Knowing that they had to gain recognized leadership positions early on by setting an example, each chose a few of the other occupiers to join them in dragging desks and chairs to block exit doors and lock first floor windows. Once all access points were secured, each TUF member found other occupiers to scavenge for first aid kits, toilet paper rolls, and even food, which may have been stashed away by professors and administrators. In addition, blankets, pillows, sleeping bags, transistor radios, portable phonographs, guitars and other personal items were brought into the five buildings by supporters, some of whom joined the occupiers.

The four were energized by their clear-headed focus on what needed to be done and their ability to lead others to accomplish unambiguous tasks. That chronic condition of tiredness during their previous meetings, of having the oxygen taken out of the air, disappeared immediately as they moved freely inside their occupied buildings.

Even in these early hours of organization, Daniel felt he had won. The boundaries were established. The designated field of play was defined. Inside the field, Daniel glowed with an anticipation of creating "the people's rules." He was within a liberated zone he and his teammates had created, an area no longer governed by either parents or authority figures acting *in loco parentis*. He had shaken off the long hand of precedents, unwritten codes of conduct, tradition, even law itself.

Daniel walked around *his* field, pulsing with the openness of his immediate future. He even entered the classroom where Professor Schwinn taught. Daniel sat in the professor's chair. He paced the front of the room, as if lecturing the professor. Now it was *his* room. Schwinn was banished, his authority having been usurped. As day after day passed, Daniel obsessively returned to this classroom, to regale in his triumph.

> **Montaukett stands in a corner of the classroom, day after day, watching Daniel. Each day, Montaukett calls to Daniel from across the room, attempting to calm him.**

Daniel gloated to himself that now he can do whatever he wanted inside this classroom.

Montaukett returns to the high ground.

In Madison Hall, Jeff led by example to solve the need for a continuous supply of food. In the first day, most of the occupiers' cash, which they had brought with them, ran out. Pizza deliveries also ceased because some student athletes, strongly opposed to the disruption of *their* campus by left-wing freaks, had forced the delivery boys to run a gauntlet of hecklers who additionally impeded the boys' forward movement with feigned football blocking and tackling maneuvers. Jeff snuck out of Madison Hall, and spent hours talking with supporters of the occupation, organizing a roster and scheduling food deliveries to each building, with supporters paying for and delivering the food.

> **Anishinaabe follows Jeff as he walks the campus, indicating to Jeff, by pointing his finger, that Jeff must leave campus and attend the meeting of men. Anishinaabe knows Jeff's enjoyment during these tribal gatherings, and of the rituals forming over the last month.**

Jeff slowed, believing he sensed someone directing him. He turned his head, but did not see anyone. The tasks he still needed to accomplish before returning to Madison Hall crowded out his intuition.

Anishinaabe returns to the high ground.

Christie and Ephraim were equally busy in their chosen buildings that first day, setting up watch teams, which would report what they saw outside their perimeters, so nothing could take them by surprise. In their respective buildings, Jefferson and Franklin Halls, the two also selected runners who would sneak out every hour to canvass the university, especially the student newspaper office, to read the temperature and get the news of what was happening on the rest of the campus.

> **Lenni-Lenape enters Jefferson Hall, and stands next to Christie. She whispers, reminding Christie is to time to go to her meeting of women. Lenni-Lenape knows how much Christie enjoys the sharing of stories without men present, and how much Christie feels she can just be herself.**

Christie paused, straining to hear. She was certain she heard an unfamiliar

257

voice near her, but the noise in the Hall finally masked it.

Lenni-Lenape returns to the high ground.

Munsee moves closer to Ephraim, as he listens to Ephraim question a runner who returns with news of an anti-strike group active on campus. Munsee taps Ephraim on the shoulder.

As Ephraim walked with the runner over to a group of occupiers, he brushed off his shoulder, as if something were on it.

Munsee returns to the high ground.

"I can't believe this has been so easy," Daniel stated at one of their early meetings.

"Yes, it feels like we're finally making a revolution," Ephraim continued. "And there's no doubt we're in the vanguard. We're setting the pace."

"We've got a lot more to do, though, let's remember that," Jeff added. "I was really surprised the administration cancelled all classes, all of them. Wonder what they're up to?"

"Forget about them," Daniel countered. "We've got to strengthen the occupation. Then we can dictate the future because we can establish our own rules and regulations inside our own territory."

The four felt the power shifting toward them. They were more determined than ever to have all the occupiers speak with one voice in continuous defiance of the administration's calls to end the university shutdown.

TUF had engaged in so many practical and visible activities that each member became well known to the occupiers in their respective buildings. They had met physical needs, defined some procedures for safety, set up areas to protect and distribute food, laid out some common sense proposals on sanitation. All of these activities had resulted from their planned and coordinated strategy to gain an influential position on the looming larger issues of deciding the occupiers' demands, including amnesty, and how the disruption could be duplicated elsewhere on campus. TUF yearned to have

PASSING THROUGH (The Sixties)

its new sense of power, and that of the occupiers, solidified and expanded.

The tensions that had been previously building among the four, especially between Ephraim and Jeff, and between Christie and Daniel, were submerged in the euphoria of being at the center of history-in-the-making. They could not believe how lucky they were, in the right place at the right time, with the right strategy to make a revolution. Everything they had experienced in their short activist careers had, they were certain, prepared them for these momentous moments, this historic opportunity. They were ready, they were confident, they were unconcerned in the heat of battle about any adverse consequences. On the contrary, each was certain they were protected, protected because their cause was just, because history demanded this next turn of the wheel, because moral outrage at abuses by the powerful created its own shield.

The thrill and excitement of the first twenty-four hours, the ecstatic feeling of actually taking over a building and replacing its normal activities with the setting up of an encampment, were replaced in the second day by the occupiers' continuous discussions.

On Day Three TUF faced a fundamental problem. What was "participatory democracy," really? It had been loosely defined by anyone invoking the concept as a decision-making process in which people effected by an issue not only would voice their opinions, but also would have the opportunity to effect the decision, and vote, if necessary. The concept had been tossed around so often for so long, but rarely applied.

During the occupation, the populations inside each building kept changing a bit every few hours. Some left for a while and returned, others left for good. New arrivals stayed only a few hours, others stayed for good. What did today's vote, based on the occupants at the time, mean when tomorrow's vote, based on a somewhat different set of occupants at that time, reversed or modified today's vote? Since conditions and information were changing rapidly both inside and outside the liberated zones, how could yesterday's decision possibly bind today's occupiers? How often would a decision be reviewed, or issues be re-debated? When was it timely to discuss the need to reach a new agreement because conditions underpinning the previous decision had, in fact, changed? Were participatory democracy and political chaos first cousins in disguise?

Another major problem had also developed. The occupiers in

Madison Hall, drawn to that building because some of their science classes were formerly held there, were less "radical" than students occupying the other four buildings. It eventually became obvious that the administration was working hard to peel away Madison Hall from the other buildings, and to end that occupation peacefully. How could TUF prevent this age-old divide-and-conquer strategy, and keep "a single voice" going?

TUF members had met every three hours in Christie's carrel during the first evening and throughout the next two days and evenings. (How fortunate the library was open twenty-four hours a day, they had joked.) Meeting now on the morning of Day Four, each carried the largest sized coffee they could afford from the local delicatessen.

Calling the meeting to order, Daniel rummaged through his school bag looking for the agenda he was convinced he had hand-written only a few hours earlier. He stared and stared inside the bag, cursing the darkness, which stared back at him. When Jeff suggested they forget the agenda, Daniel looked at him with narrowed eyelids, as if Jeff had just uttered a treasonous remark. Ephraim joined Daniel in challenging Jeff's loyalty, but his muttered and meandering accusation, something about how Jeff had better watch out whose buzzer he rang or he would be in a lot of trouble, was met with puzzled expressions. Daniel finally jotted down a few phrases on a piece of paper and declared the meeting open, again.

"We've got a lot to talk about, but little time to do it," Daniel began. "We'll each report in about our buildings, then, then, hold it, I wrote it down, oh yes, we've *got* to talk about our demands. People keep demanding to know what our demands are, funny that, demanding demands, don't you think?"

Silence.

Daniel took a gulp of coffee, scalding his mouth, but seemed not to notice.

Christie looked at the desk in front of her, highly conscious of the three others' close proximity. Her eyes would not stay focused on its flat surface, but rather darted around, catching the contrasts of color and light on forms and clothing. What is happening to me, Christie wondered. I'm not on any drugs, I haven't taken anything, ever, so why is everything pulsating around me, she questioned. She could hear and understand the muffled voices of the other three around her, but it was as if through a fog of fatigue that she heard them. Sensing the voices had stopped, she felt it must be her turn to speak.

"Yes, I agree that the demand for amnesty for all those threatened with disciplinary probation must be unconditional, but, make no mistake, I have to define amnesty, I mean amnesty can not mean only, I mean not only mean," she faltered and paused, not sure of what she had just said or where her mind was taking her, and then, without looking up, Christie said slowly and distinctly, afraid of each word, "*Do I sound crazy to you?*"

"No, no, no," Daniel said quickly, too quickly to be taken by Christie as any reassurance about her sanity. "I think we make all six demands non-negotiable. After all, we can hold out for a lot more days, food is holding up, I got a few hours' sleep last night, more than the night before, did anyone else get any sleep, we can stick it out and-----"

"-----Yeah, yeah, you're OK Christie, no problem, just fine," Jeff interrupted, "but how are we going to get our washing done, we still haven't organized the washing and this is a huge problem, and I can't keep asking my roommate to bring clean clothes, but the laundromat costs so much, so-----"

"-----Washing! You're talking about washing when we've got the whole world looking at us," Ephraim interrupted. "You're changing the subject again, aren't *you*! Daniel was talking about the demands. We must, absolutely must, add a few more, like reducing tuition. If we've got them by the balls, and they haven't been able to convince the people in Madison to end their occupation, so we're still as strong as ever, though I do worry, I see police coming straight at us, tear gas, water cannon, vicious dogs, with their guns drawn -----"

"-----Stop it, Ephraim," Daniel ordered, raising his voice, "we're not making any progress, and we've got to get back to the buildings, so let's summarize what we've agreed on, and-----"

"-----We've not agreed on anything," Jeff interjected, "except I think we've definitely agreed on amnesty being non-negotiable. That way they'll have to wipe the slate clean, officially forget anyone had ever trespassed or damaged even a little bit of property, expunge our actions from the record, that we shut down-----"

"-----There you go again, Jeff," Ephraim interjected, "who the hell is worried about trespassing. Anyway, those buzzer friends of yours'll help you, won't they Jeff, won't they, *admit it*."

"What are *you* talking about-----"

"*We are getting nowhere,*" Christie declared, emphasizing each word as she clenched her fists on the desk and tried to steady herself.

"-----I wonder," Daniel interrupted, in a shaken tone, "we've been at this for what seems like centuries, I just wonder, do we *all* sound crazy?"

The meeting ended without agreement on anything. The four drained their coffee cups, and left them on the desk alongside a large empty bag of potato chips.

Meeting on the evening of Day Five in Christie's carrel, each now carried a large thermos of coffee and set it with meticulous care on the floor. A pizza was devoured quickly, along with a 64-ounce bottle of Pepsi.

"We have just got to get the janitors and cleaning people and all the cafeteria employees involved," Ephraim intoned. "Can you just imagine when they go out on strike, it'll just cripple the university. Faculty will have to decide if they'll cross the picket lines and-----"

"Wait a minute, wait," Daniel interjected. "We can talk about that later, when we get to it on the agenda."

"All we have to do," Ephraim continued without acknowledging Daniel's request, "is support their grievances. Higher wages, better working conditions, more benefits."

"But won't that raise our tuition?" Jeff questioned.

"Hey, come on, knock it off," Daniel pleaded. "We've got lots to cover, it's all on the agenda I passed out, so let's get started."

As Daniel tried to keep discussion focused on the order of the agenda topics, Christie remained silent. More numb than silent. Her carrel had been a refuge during the last two years, just she and her research. She had come to understand, more profoundly and disturbingly than the other three, just how powerful and resourceful the elite were. Torn now by her loyalty to this increasingly fractious collective trying to create a revolutionary movement and her sinking feeling that it would not succeed, Christie exploded:

"Let's bomb them all to kingdom come!"

"What?" Daniel asked.

"Bomb who?" Jeff asked.

"Now?" Ephraim asked.

"I don't know what I'm talking about anymore," Christie said softly.

"It's this pain inside my head. I can't think straight with this pain inside my head."

"You want an aspirin?" Jeff asked kindly.

"No, not that kind of pain. I just thought, maybe if we blow up the world, this pain will stop," Christie said softly.

"Ok, I don't think we're getting anywhere, *again*," Daniel barked.

"You know what I'd like to be doing right now," Jeff mused, and, without waiting for an answer, "I'd like to be on my horse galloping across a meadow with butterflies rising up-----"

"My God, Jeff, there you go *again*," Ephraim observed, more in resignation than anger.

Daniel bent down slowly toward the floor, gripped the base of his thermos tightly, straightened up, and placed the thermos slowly on the desk in front of him. Now not aware of the others, as if he would fall mute were his attention drawn to them, he slowly turned the red cap, unscrewed it, and set it gently next to his thermos. He removed the top, carefully lowered the mouth of the thermos to the lip of the cup, and poured a full measure. But he did not drink. He merely watched as the rippling coffee became still in the cup, his eyes drawn to its serene surface.

Everyone else fell silent, afraid where their tumbling thoughts were leading them, infrequently glancing for a second to see if Daniel were still looking at his coffee, and then quickly turning inward again. Oceans of thoughts and memories were passing through each of their minds. It was as if each had become untethered from a source of stability.

A voice came through, seemingly from another world.

"Are you OK, Daniel?" Jeff asked.

"Uh, yes, er, why do you ask?"

CHAPTER 14 – WHIRLWIND (MAY-AUGUST 1968)

Nkosi sikelel' iAfrika was the South African people's national anthem, having been first composed in 1897 as a hymn by a Methodist school teacher, Enoch Mankayi Sontongga. It became synonymous as a defiant protest against *apartheid*, and was sung throughout the country. The first verse comes from the original people's anthem, while another verse comes from the national anthem of apartheid governments. Both verses (and others) became part of the official South African National Anthem after the election of Nelson Mandela as president of the Republic of South Africa.

Like a python seemingly asleep in the warmth of May's late afternoon sun, the line of soon-to-be graduates, standing almost motionless, stretched for three lazy blocks to the doors of Riverside Church. Parents and relatives stood beside familial figures gowned in royal blue with ill-fitting black mortarboards perched precariously atop their heads. Hushed conversations up and down the well-formed line filled the time before the dignified procession, led by deans and faculty robed in varied and splendid colors, was to commence. Today, Tuesday, May 21st, would be the first of the graduation ceremonies staged by Morningside Heights University this spring. Solemnity, the ingrained tone of respect for this venerable rite-of-passage, awaited the soon-to-be graduates just inside the sanctified doors.

The graduation line was ordered by the alphabet. Christie stood near the beginning of the line, with her father, grandfather and two parishioners. In the next block stood Daniel, still in disbelief he had earned enough credits to be in line, with his mother, father, and sister. Much further back, Jeff stood with his father, mother, and three of his seven siblings. Four blocks further south, seemingly a world away on this august occasion, a political cyclone, which had previously touched down in late March and April, was gathering force again.

Fifteen, perhaps twenty minutes slowly unfolded, consumed by comments on how beautiful a day it was, how far away one had finally found a parking space, where a family might go for a celebratory meal afterwards. So many parents had dreamed of this day, their child's final gateway into adulthood. Parents basked in the warm sun, knowing their own career and personal choices had led to this moment. The vacations not taken, the luxury items not purchased, the extra hours worked by husbands and the relatively recent jobs taken by wives to earn more money for their offsprings' tuition, room and board. It had all been worthwhile, as spouses exchanged knowing glances with each other. These proud parents were certain their children would have the key to unlock a better opportunity in life than their own parents had given them.

It would be the last diploma, the ultimate symbol of completing their educational marathon, the soon-to-be-graduates thought they would ever need in their lives. Suits, ties, and dresses would soon be taken to the cleaners in preparation for job interviews. Part-time jobs to earn extra money for movies and snacks would be cast aside for "real" jobs to pay the rent. "Going steady" would be exchanged for marriage, or separate ways.

As if it had been in hiding until this very moment, the cyclone touched down again, this time at the southern tip of the python's tail. Sneaker-clad, dungaree-wearing runners, who had sprinted up those four blocks from the main campus, delivered the news to the soon-to-be graduates at the very back of the line:

"Burr Hall is occupied again!"

The news undulated along the entire length of the snake, one small section at a time, stopping the last bits of idle conversation in mid-sentence, royal blue gowned soon-to-be graduates doing a literal about-face, one after another, after being tapped on the back by the newly informed classmate behind, looking southward down the disintegrating line, stepping off the curb into the street, expecting to see and hear more clues to confirm what they had just learned, like many more dungaree-clad students running down the street toward Burr Hall, or police sirens echoing in the canyons of Broadway and

Amsterdam. All that the now maybe-soon-to-be graduates saw, however, were the confused faces of their classmates. "Burr Hall is occupied again!" was repeated up and down the ragged line. Anxious chatter rose in volume. Parents and relatives, suddenly abandoned, continued to look forward at the sanctified doors, hoping they would open quickly and, as if by magic, sweep everyone inside a calm and reassuring interior.

Many of the students had not only been supportive of the student strikers who had brought Morningside Heights University to a standstill for eight days in April, a large number, many known to Daniel, Christie, Jeff, and Ephraim, had also occupied campus buildings, causing official classes to be cancelled. But what should these students do today? Was this another revolutionary moment? Was history calling them to action even on their graduation day? They looked for signs from each other, and from the street below, as to what to do next.

Again and again, as the cyclone proceeded slowly up the line, it ripped into some familial ties, restored only for the sake of this occasion, leaving parents to question why their off springs were so agitated and distracted. Some sons and daughters tried to explain their going from protest to resistance to revolution, an arc, which they had left unexplained for the last three years, but gave up, the gulf too wide. Other students assured their parents, falsely, that they were thinking only about getting their diploma. A few others ignored their parents' questions, even commands, leaving their "place" in line, as Daniel readily did, running to find Jeff and Christie.

"Where is he going *now*!" Rebecca declared.

"I hope not far," Edwin said, soothingly. "We've waited so long for this day, I'm sure nothing will spoil it."

"Yes, it has been a long time. Remember when we thought we couldn't even afford to send him to college, and now he's about to get his graduate degree?" Rebecca reminisced.

"All too well. Now he can find a good job and settle down," Edwin hoped.

"I wonder what he's doing now, though," Rebecca asked the universe more than her husband.

As Daniel walked toward the front of the line, a classmate called out to him.

"I just returned from Paris," Bridgette began, "where I participated in a march of 20,000 students, teachers and others because the administration closed the University of Paris at Nanterre and the police took over the Sorbonne."

"You told me you were going home after your last exam," Daniel recalled.

"Yes, it was so exciting. The French workers are spontaneously taking over factories in support of the student protests as well as demanding the ouster of President de Gaulle, over the objections of their unions' leadership."

"I had read about that," Daniel said. "Is it true that the April student occupation of university buildings here in New York added to the inspiration which fueled the French students' actions?"

"Yes, it is true."

Daniel also learned that Bridgette had visited American soldiers, living in Paris, who had deserted in protest against the Vietnam War. She had heard of some 25 living throughout France, a smaller number in Switzerland, and many more in Sweden, the only government that gave them money, housing and other benefits.

Daniel continued to walk toward the front of the line to find Christie and Jeff, but then he spotted Carlos, whose home was in Mexico.

"Oh yes, things are heating up in Mexico, too, just as in France," Carlos stated. "The student movement is growing throughout universities and vocational schools."

(This fall, Carlos would return to his home where, on October 2nd, he would be wounded by police and then arrested during what would be called the Tlatelolco massacre of students and other protesters, along with bystanders, during a peaceful rally of some 10,000 people in Mexico City.)

Daniel found Jeff, who then left his "place" beside his family, and both found Christie, who also left her "place" beside her father and grandfather. They moved yards away from all the others to consult with one another.

"But what if this news about Burr Hall is only a rumor, a false rumor," Jeff wondered. "How can we get confirmation?"

"I kept looking down the block where the runners came from, but didn't see anything else," Christie remarked. "But I can't see one of us going over there, checking it out, and then coming back. The line might move by then."

"I don't think anyone would run over here with false information, do you?" Daniel said. "We've got to act. We've got to get involved, at least see for ourselves."

"My family has come thousands of miles to be here, but somehow I think my father would understand why I had to join the occupation," Jeff began.

"My parents are just happy I'm getting a diploma, so I can smooth it over with them later," Daniel rationalized.

"My Grandfather would never understand, but I don't care," Christie continued.

"So, here's what we'll do," Daniel concluded. "We'll go back in line, and stand with our families until the line starts to move, and then we'll break free, join up together, and head for Burr Hall. Agreed?"

"Agreed."

"Agreed."

The three returned to their places beside their families.

The graduation line started to move, step-by-step, toward the just opened doors of the church. Sighs of relief from parents were audible. Each of the three, however, asked their families to forgive them. They could not now participate in an archaic ceremony. They hoped their families would understand, but in the face of history summoning them to action again, they explained, they could not, even with all its enticing pageantry, sit through the hypocrisy of being awarded its symbol of completion by an institution they sought to bring down. Stunned, their families watched as their beloved children ran down the block, royal blue gowns flapping in the whirlwind they were creating, mortarboards falling to the ground.

Daniel, Christie and Jeff were giddy with excitement. They had not only freed themselves from a traditional ceremony made meaningless by their direct actions in the weeks previous, but they were also re-ignited by the cyclone they thought had died at the end of April. As soon as they reached their dormitory rooms to change, Daniel called Ephraim.

"The revolution is back on!" Daniel shouted into the phone. "Meet us at Burr Hall."

TUF found a vacant classroom after entering Burr Hall. The transition from graduation line to occupied building had been so swift that none of the four could think through what to do next until they all had talked as a collective.

"OK, OK, here we are," Daniel started out. "Obviously no time to make an agenda. What's the first thing we've got to do?"

"Got to find who the leaders are," Ephraim offered. "Have to know why they re-occupied this building."

"No, no," Jeff countered. "We've got to make sure the perimeter is secure. Remember how fluid it was in April."

"Then we should split up. Ephraim, you find out who the leaders are and Jeff--"

"I disagree," Christie interrupted. "The last time we occupied buildings, the women wound up doing all the drudge work. This time--"

"Christie, we can't solve every problem all at once," Daniel interjected. "Let's not forget who the enemy is. The administrators and trustees."

"No, Daniel, I think Christie is right," Jeff declared. "We can't tolerate oppression inside the struggle to end oppression."

"That's very noble sounding, Jeff, but not very practical," Ephraim added.

"Look, there's lots we have to do, all at once," Daniel said, "but maybe I should make an agenda, and we'll go one by one."

"There's no time for that," Ephraim countered. "I'm certain this time the administration will call the cops, and--"

"Oh, God, we've got to get to the Dean and reason with him before we're all arrested," Jeff pleaded.

Christie had by now moved her chair back from the small table around which the four were sitting. She stared across the room, at nothing.

Jeff stood up, walked around the table, and whispered something to Christie in her ear.

"Thanks for that, Jeff," Christie remarked softly.

"Oh, here we go *again*," Ephraim ranted. "What is Jeff plotting now? So, are you *ever* going to tell us why you were always late to our meetings?"

"Please, let Jeff alone," begged Christie.

"We're getting *nowhere*," Daniel declared.

"Maybe that's the only thing we can agree on," Christie concluded.

"We must have order," Daniel pleaded. "Discuss our priorities in an orderly manner. Now, let's go back to the first question. What do we do first, what's our first priority, the thing we want to do first?"

"You're rambling, Daniel," Jeff cautioned. "And I can't even think straight. The stress is too much. I think this is all a mistake. I should never have left my parents and the graduation."

"How *dare* you!" Ephraim said, firmly. "Who the hell do you think you are, trying to bust us up?" his voice growing louder with each word.

"Stop it, stop it," Christie interjected.

"Yes, Christie, you tell them," Daniel affirmed. "Now, let's get back to the first question. What do we do first, our first priority? We must have order."

"Can't we take a break?" Jeff asked.

"So, you think the Algerians took a break against the French, or Fidel took a break against Batista?" Ephraim demanded.

"Order, we must have order."

The sun set behind rows upon rows of sturdy apartment buildings. This particular May evening remained balmy. Near campus, evening shoppers mixed with strollers, both dressed in summer-light attire, anticipating more casual days ahead.

On campus, outdoor lights were deliberately turned off. It was the time of the new moon. The campus was darker than it had ever been before. Joy, spontaneity, exhilaration, enthusiasm--all fully evident during April's occupations--vacated the campus during Tuesday evening's re-occupation. It was as if, with students and others marking time both inside and outside Burr Hall, the wheel of history was clamped, unable to move forward or backward.

At either end of the walkway leading to the red brick quadrangle, students had erected fifteen-foot high barricades at the only two entrances remaining to the main campus. They had piled up fences, chairs, tables, benches and anything else they could find. Although the intent had been to prevent police from entering campus, the barricades effectively prevented all those inside the campus from leaving. Milling around on the quad in the middle of campus, the four were in the midst of three hundred or so students who sought to protect the building's entrance. The chanting in support of those occupying Burr Hall died down.

The police entered the campus, after removing the two massive barricades. They stood around the perimeter, unillumined, shadowy figures, marking time. The clock moved not at all out of fear as to what would happen next.

It was now an hour later, just after midnight. The police had not moved from the entrances, some forty yards away, or from the perimeter. The students continued to mill around. Not talking or chanting, just marking time. The mere presence of the police sucked the air out of their determination. It was as if a human fence had been installed, demarcating the ground under the protesters' feet and a small adjacent area in front of them as their territory, and everything beyond the fence containing all they opposed. The protesters' will to use the territory left to them for cursing the administration had evaporated. For the first time in years, the students viscerally knew in their gut that their freedom of movement had been circumvented, contained, and curtailed.

It was just after one in the morning. The police had not moved. The students had stopped milling about. Everyone stood still. Nothing was said by anyone on either side.

Late in the night, Ephraim came to Daniel. With his right hand, he pointed to his left hand.

"I can't straighten my fingers at all. As soon as we got here on the quadrangle, my fingers clenched. They've locked. It's like a force over which I've no power. I'm anxious, Daniel. Really anxious. If the police come, they'll have dogs, I'm sure of it. I can't run very fast, not with my crippled leg. I could be trampled. I want to stay. You know that. But I can't."

"What? You want to leave?"

"We've been through a lot, but—"

"You can't leave, *not now*. What, are you crazy?!"

"I'm just going to stand over there, on that sidewalk, over there where people are watching, on the other side of the quadrangle, you can see it from here, so if the police come, I won't be hurt. Daniel, I can't be hurt!"

"You can't leave. We're TUF. We stick together. You're just a little nervous. So am I. But look how brave you were at the Hilton. You can't let us down."

"I'm sorry, I'm really sorry." Ephraim said as he started to move away, "I've got to think of me."

"Go, Ephraim, get the hell outta here. Stab me in the back, why don't you! Go, take solace, see if I care."

Ephraim left.

Later in the night, Jeff came to Daniel. He put a hand on Daniel's shoulder.

"I can't chance it. I'm very sorry. If the police come, they'll arrest us for sure. I can't have a record, I just can't. It was spoil my chances. And I could be raped in jail. I've read about that happening. I want to stay. You know that. We've been through a lot, but—"

"What, not you, too! What the hell's happening here? *No, no, I won't allow it.* We go back a long way. You've got to stay."

"I'm not as tough as you."

"What are you talking about? Are *you* crazy, too? Look what guts you had when we were driving around Wall Street—"

"I'm going to stand over there, on that sidewalk, over there where people are watching, on the other side of the quadrangle, so if the police come, you know I can't stay. I've got to think of my future!"

"Go, get the hell outta here, Jeff. Two less won't make any difference. Go, take security, see if I care."

Jeff left.

Later still in the night, Christie came to Daniel. Christie took Daniel's hand in hers.

"My Grandfather would just die if he ever found out I was here. I can't chance my name getting in the papers or the university sending me a letter at my father's home, saying they revoked my diploma. I'm very sorry, really."

"Oh, God, no, not you. We began together. Remember that first night, in your apartment, you were the one who got me started in all this. Remember? You can't—"

"I want to stay. You know that. I know we've been through a lot. But—"

"Don't turn your back on me, please, Christie, don't desert me."

"I'm going to stand over there, on that sidewalk, over there where people are watching, on the other side of the quadrangle, so if the police come, you know I can't stay. I just can't hurt my family anymore!"

"Go, Christie, get outta here. Three less won't make a difference, damn it. Go, take sanctuary, and see if I care."

Christie left.

Later, as he looked across the quadrangle to try to see the three on the sidewalk, Daniel felt strangely validated, the righteous one withstanding the fiery furnace. He had deliberately cut himself off from family because he could not explain to them, let alone justify in their eyes, his path. He had severed himself from any thought of personal gain. He had cut himself off from the traditional society around him, challenging every authority figure. Now his closest comrades had deliberately cut themselves off from him because they could not take the heat, he assumed. In some deep recess of his being, he sensed he would always be alone, unrelievedly alone. As he looked around the darkened campus, at *his* playing field, the resurrected zone of liberation inside which his dreams had been activated again, Daniel felt strangely euphoric, again so pleased with himself. That's all he knew he needed to live. He looked on what he had created and saw it was good.

> **Montaukett stands next to Daniel, a single
> tear rolling down her left cheek. She looks
> around, as if expecting someone.**

Daniel watched as Christie talked with a group of young women on the far side of the quadrangle, and Jeff talked with a group of young men, and Ephraim talked with Patricia. The three all seemed so very far away now, as if Daniel never truly knew them, as if they had passed through his life without really touching him.

Daniel now realized the police had formed a semi-circle, six deep, across the large red brick quadrangle. Immediately behind Daniel were some of the stone buildings of the campus. He looked quickly in every direction. There was no exit.

The police raised their plastic shields. With their batons, they hit their shields one loud blow, in unison, the sounds of silence broken and scattered by a thunderclap. Then the police walked ten paces toward the students in the center of the semi-circle. The police stopped. They did not move. They waited an eternity. Then they raised their batons again, struck another loud blow against their shields, walked ten more paces toward the center, and stopped. They were now only ten yards away. The protesters' self-defined playing field, where earlier in the evening they thought they had been able to write the rules, was cut in half.

The sergeant raised a bullhorn: "You are all under arrest. We do not want to hurt you. Surrender peaceably." The police struck a third loud blow against their plastic shields and walked to the edge of the students, and stopped. No one moved a muscle. No one. The air held its breathe. The moon was not in the sky.

Daniel stands without motion, his eyes straining to see beyond the darkness, to see if Christie, Ephraim, and Jeff are still there. He sees nothing. He hears nothing. He grieves for all those around him who will be taken away to jail. He imagines them, one by one, being escorted or dragged to the waiting vans. Such brave comrades. Daniel knows he will not be touched. He is protected. An unseen force will keep him safe, he is certain. The loss of all his comrades, in one evening, weighs on his soul. He is without status now, even state-less. No one to praise him. No one to act with him.

Daniel feels a new loss. He sees the police tearing down the front of his shop, removing all the walls, taking away all the props he uses to negotiate the world around him, tearing the curtain to shreds, exposing that there is no back of the shop, not even the records of his faults he thought were there, nothing. Daniel is soaked with grief. It drips from his forehead, arrests his heart and takes it prisoner. He is paralyzed. He stares without life in his eyes, and recognizes nothing.

Hearing his mother's voice calling him to dinner, Daniel smells the aroma of hamburgers sizzling in their juices on the stove. He watches his mother mash the potatoes.

Daniel heard a scream, which pierced the night air, and tore it asunder.

"Kill *me*, kill *me*."

He wondered what anguished soul cried out, begging to be relieved from all of his burdens.

"Kill *me*, kill *me*," Daniel screamed for a second time.

Others in the crowd followed. "Kill *me*." "Kill *me*." "Kill *me*."

Not in unison, not a chant, only a few souls.

Unique, distinct, individual pleas to be erased.

With terror forming the words in his throat, Daniel offered himself up to the enemy. No more room to maneuver. Implacably, relentlessly, inexorably, his choices had given him no quarter either to return to his old world of obligation or continue in his new world of freedom. He was trapped.

Daniel screamed for the weight of building the new America to be lifted from his shoulders. His piercing prayer was his plea to be released from the burden of the history he and others could not now create, and from the anguish of the guilt his failure produced within him.

> **Montaukett, Lenni-Lenape, Munsee, and Anishinaabe stand around Daniel. Each extend both hands, palms up, to welcome him to their circle. Daniel is unable to feel their presence.**

TUF never met again. Individual members met on occasion, especially Ephraim and Christie, but the four never met again as a collective. If Ephraim or Christie or Jeff ever thought about all of them getting together again, his or her mind did not take that thought very far, preferring instead to avoid the memory of the mental anguish experienced during their last meetings. Each of the three, in their own way, was trying to move on.

Jeff returned to Austin, riding horses whenever he could, and avoiding Sally. Christie returned to Hopewell, occasionally coming to Manhattan to be with Ephraim. Only Ephraim of the three had plans. He became a full-time chauffeur, saving his money for the possibility of going to Israel to work on a *kibbutz*. He told Christie he wanted to work with his hands and further the socialist movement, both of which the *kibbutz* represented for him.

Daniel did not immediately go home to Babylon. He could not face his parents. How could he convince them of his reasons for suddenly leaving them on the graduation line? How could he explain his activist actions over the last almost three years, which had caused him to choose Burr Hall instead of them? Even if he could make them understand, he knew they would ask what had happened to him on graduation evening.

Again and again, he pictured how Jeff, Ephraim, and Christie had walked away from him, how the police had closed the space between themselves and the demonstrators, how he had inched his way along the sidewall of Burr Hall. As he recalled how some demonstrators had gone limp and allowed themselves to be carried off and arrested, Daniel again saw himself sneaking away, crouching low, hiding behind bushes and then other buildings, until he found an unguarded exit to the street. How could he tell his parents about his cowardice?

Instead, Daniel remained in his apartment, going out only to buy food. He kept imagining a fall meeting of TUF, when he hoped all four would be together again, a gathering of the collective at which Daniel imagined he would feel as he had in those earlier days, making the agenda, chairing the meeting, at the height of his power again. Just as quickly as he imagined his restoration, he imagined its disappearance, members making excuses why they could not attend, the feeling of betrayal permeating his mind. His spirits sank. In early June, Daniel watched the recurring scene on television of Robert Kennedy being murdered in a hotel kitchen. He watched it again and again for days, just staring at the screen, not reacting, just staring, as he had done following Martin Luther King, Jr.'s murder two months earlier, two recurring nightmares from which he could not escape.

"You've got to get out into the sunshine," his roommate, Norman pleaded. "It's a beautiful day. Take a walk. For heaven's sake, you can't stay indoors all your life."

"Leave me alone."

"I wish I could. Look, I'll get you some razor blades if you don't have any," Norman offered.

"Leave me *alone*."

"You've got to take care of yourself."

In mid-June, Daniel rallied himself to go to the Registrar's office to get his diploma. He knew his savings were running low, so he bought a newspaper on the way home, but only to look at the Help Wanted ads, and nothing more. As he called prospective employers and received a few encouraging responses, his confidence began a slow recovery.

Daniel managed to call Christie once on the phone, but her grandfather's cold voice, as if Daniel were to blame for her missing the graduation ceremony, discouraged him from calling again. He thought of calling Ephraim, wondering if one of his parties would cheer him up, but somehow he never got around to making the call. He had not known that Jeff had returned to Minnesota, thinking he was still in New York. TUF could get together again, Daniel fantasized, and he'd find a way to forgive them. Just wait until fall, TUF will rise ..... he could not complete the thought.

In early July, Daniel had been sent by a temp agency to work nights cleaning a multi-floor law office in midtown. Once he mastered the routine, he liked his not having to think about what to do next. Repetitive tasks started to rebuild a sense of accomplishment. The night's quiet appealed to him, too. The few other overnighters often invited Daniel to join them during breaks. He enjoyed their laughter and animated conversations, though he understood not a word. As the nights went by, Daniel began to use his mornings to read books, visit museums, or stroll the neighborhood. He felt better.

Daniel thought about all the people he knew—his family, classmates, activists—but, one-by-one, he eliminated all but Gra'ma as someone with whom he had once felt completely safe and reassured. He recalled their earlier times together, he as a young child with his head on her lap in the back seat of the family car, returning home after a visit with relatives. He yearned for that closeness again, and hoped whatever secret she had would not again provoke her anger. He needed to mend the rift between them.

One day in early August, Daniel told Norman:

"I must see my grandmother. I can't stand the distance between us. You know, she actually put me out of her house the last time!"

"Why did she do that?"

"I don't know the real reason, but I've got to find out."

"Maybe you'll also find out a few things about yourself."

Daniel did not call in advance, afraid this time his call would distress her, and she would find an excuse not to see him. He notified the temp agency he was quitting the cleaning job, and packed his old duffle bag for the 1,200 mile journey to Stuart. This time he left the sleeping bag in his apartment. He hoped he would not need it.

As the Greyhound bus passed through Lincoln Tunnel and proceeded south on the New Jersey Turnpike, Daniel looked back across the Hudson River at the office buildings in Lower Manhattan. For a moment, he thought about the blood-filled balloons, which he had thrown. As he passed the Turnpike overhead sign for Exit 14, he thought of Rev. Cain and the riots in Newark, Tampa and Atlanta. Passing Exit 10 on the Turnpike, he thought of the bus caravan to Flemington for the Kodak stockholders' meeting, and the conversation with Arthur on the ride to Cornell. As he passed the exit for downtown Baltimore, Daniel thought of the confrontation at the Methodist Church, and how, he thought now, he had not treated Julius, the chauffeur, very well. As he changed buses at the Greyhound Terminal in Washington,

D.C., Daniel remembered his exhilaration at driving students back and forth to the Lafayette Park vigil. He knew his life had been changed by that first anti-war meeting, and the unpublished letter-to-the-editor, which had caused him to attend.

As the bus sped southward, Daniel questioned whether or not he had made any difference at all over the last three years. What had changed? The escalation in Vietnam continued, poverty remained an American way of life for tens of millions, *apartheid* remained entrenched, and progressive national leaders, black and white, were dead. The powerful had made only surface accommodations here and there. What if he had been more extreme, Daniel wondered, throwing Molotov cocktails at the corporate signs or raising money for African liberation movements to purchase weapons? As he watched the gentle, verdant southern Virginia hills out the window, he doubted that, if he had pursued his "what ifs," they would have made a fundamental difference. All he knew was that he wanted to remain some kind of radical activist, that he wanted to re-unite TUF, but now Daniel also knew he had somehow to go about life differently. He had no clue how he would start, but he knew he had to find a new path.

It took Daniel an hour during the early afternoon to build up his courage to knock on the front door of his grandmother's house. He took a few steps backward and waited for the door to open. He had prepared many first things to say, but when the door did not open, he knocked again, louder this time. Still no response. He waited. It was August, alright, he thought. She should be here. What if her dividends had dramatically decreased, and she couldn't afford the house rental this year, Daniel wondered. What if she had fallen, and was in hospital? He waited.

> **Montaukett, Lenni-Lenape, Munsee, and Anishinaabe stand together on the pebbled shore. They walk across the yard and around to the front of Gra'ma's house. They see Daniel sitting in a wicker chair on the front porch, and know that Daniel does not yet see them.**

Another hour passed as Daniel rocked back and forth, facing the other side of the narrow porch. Then he heard a wheel squeak behind him.

He turned to see his grandmother slowly pushing a cart half-filled with groceries. Her arms opened to receive her grandson as he ran toward her.

"I thought you'd never come," Gra'ma said.

"Me, too."

As Daniel emptied several plastic bags filled with fruits and vegetables, he noticed a large number of oranges and a cantaloupe.

"Mr. Antonioni, the green grocer, gave me the cantaloupe. For free. He's a nice man."

After putting the food away, Gra'ma asked, "Would you like some jelly bread and a cup of hot tea?"

"I sure would."

"While I'm fixing it, please call your parents. I know they don't know where you are. They call me every few weeks, to see how I am, but also to see if I've heard from you."

"I'll call them, I will, but not today. I have to think what to say to them."

"Just as long as you call them while you're here. And, do not think too much about what you will say. Let it come naturally."

Gra'ma looked frailer to Daniel than during last summer's visit. Knowing she was eighty-eight, he wondered how much longer she would have for them to enjoy their rituals together.

"How long are you going to stay this time?" Gra'ma asked.

"Well, I really don't have a schedule. Would a few days be alright?"

"Of course. Stay as long as you wish. It's nice to know you are not on a schedule this time. You need a rest, eh? You don't look so good."

"I didn't think it showed."

"Maybe not to everyone, but to a grandmother, it shows. We'll have an early dinner, then you can have a long night's sleep. After all, it's not like we have much night life here," she said, laughing.

The next morning, Daniel said he felt much better, and that he would call his parents in the evening, when he knew his father would be home from work.

After breakfast, when the dishes had been cleared, Daniel gave his grandmother a present.

"A picture frame. How beautiful. But there's no picture in the frame. But it's a beautiful old frame. I like it. Thank you."

"I think it's the right size," Daniel remarked, softly.

"The right size for what?"

Daniel hesitated, and then said, "For the photo, your photo, of you and, I guess, your sister, the photo in the steamer trunk."

Gra'ma looked intently at the frame for minutes, as if the pewter finish, with its garland of flowers etched around the matte, did indeed complement her old black-and-white photo. She began to cry.

"You're not angry with me, Gra'ma, don't be angry with me," Daniel pleaded.

"No, not with you," Gra'ma managed through her tears. "I've been angry with me for so many, many years."

"I bought the frame in an antiques shop in Greenwich Village. I wanted it to look as old as your photo, as if you'd always had it in a frame. Why are you smiling?"

"First, your gift is so thoughtful. Second, I remember Greenwich Village well. As a teenager, I used to sneak out at night and go to the Village, just to walk around and feel its life and vibrancy."

"Gra'ma, is that your sister, Mathilda, in the photo?"

"Yes, it is. We were both so young in that picture. She was three and I was eight."

"I remember you had a scowl on your face in the picture."

"I certainly did."

"Do you remember why?"

"I guess it's time you knew. I did not think I would ever be telling you, but your gift is so beautiful, so thoughtful."

She paused, wondering where to start.

"I have to take you back to Zurich. The Gens family lore, a myth actually, is that I came to America alone, when I was seventeen, and married Papa a year later. My coming to America alone is not true. It was a convenient white lie. That way, a lot of things did not have to be explained. They could be forgotten."

"You did marry Papa?"

"Yes. He saved me. I was eighteen. But a lot had happened before. Here is the truth.

"I actually came through Ellis Island to New York City, from Zurich, sailing from the port of Southampton, England, when I was three years old, with both my parents and that steamer trunk. We lived in the Yorkville section of Manhattan. My father died when I was ten. I remember so fondly his telling me stories about the Alps, and the cows with bells around their necks so he could find them when it came time for milking. When I was very young, he would put me on his shoulders whenever we went to a parade. It was just the three of us, until two years after we arrived in America. Mathilda was born then. I resented her. After a few years, my father was telling the same stories to my sister. They were *my* stories. And he put her on his shoulders. I had to be on the ground, so I could see only glimpses of the parades."

"There was a doll in your trunk, with bright yellow hair."

"Yes, that doll. I hated it when Momma took my doll and gave it to my sister, saying I didn't need to play with dolls anymore."

"So where is Mathilda today?"

Gra'ma paused. Her eyes teared again.

"Do you remember your mother saying to you, let the dead bury the dead, when you mentioned the trunk at Thanksgiving dinner?"

"Yes, I do, and I thought it a very strange response."

"Your thoughtfulness about giving me a frame to hold my past, and listening to me talk about it, is, I hope, finally about to make your mother's wisdom come true.

"I was an only child for five years. I had my parents' full attention. I had crossed an ocean with them. Then, for the next five years, my father seemed to ignore me. At times, I hated my sister, especially after my father died. That's also when mother gave Mathilda my doll.

"Every day after school, I had to walk to my sister's school and walk her home. Then I had to stay with her, fix our dinner, because my mother worked the second shift at a shirt factory. I couldn't be with my friends after school, or go out during the evening.

"One day, when I was fifteen, I was fed up having to care for my sister. That evening, Mathilda refused to eat what I had cooked. I yelled at her, then locked her in our bedroom. I was so upset, I left the apartment, just to get some fresh air, I felt so cooped up. I came back about two hours later, and knocked on the bedroom door, but there was no answer. I thought she must be asleep. I started my homework. Later, I unlocked the bedroom door to make sure she had changed into her night clothes before falling asleep, but she was not in the room. To my horror, she must have fallen out of the open window. We were ten stories up. I went down to the ground as fast as I could, and some people who were milling about told me an ambulance had picked up a young girl who was lying dead on the ground. The spot was directly below our open window. I went back to the apartment, so guilt ridden, to wait for my mother to come home."

"Oh Gra'ma, that is so *terrible*."

"I slept in that bedroom, night after night, looking at that window before falling asleep and again when I woke up, wishing my sister would come back through it. I still don't know if it was an accident, maybe she leaned too far out, or if she fell on purpose. I'll never know, but the guilt and shame are the same, either way. I just kept looking at that window."

"You said Papa saved you?"

"I was so desperate to leave that bedroom, when, two years later, I met Papa at a Swiss Club dance. I fell so deeply in love with him. I knew part of that love was from wanting to live somewhere, anywhere else. He was such a good man. A year later we were married. I was eighteen and he was twenty. He took me away from that bedroom.

"I'll put the photo in your frame as soon as I go back home, and display it on my dresser. I feel so much better now that you know. "

At mid-afternoon, over jelly bread and hot tea, Daniel said, "Giving you the picture frame is part of my recovery, too."

"Recovery? Recovery from what?"

"Recovery from me."

For the next three hours, Daniel told his grandmother about his activist years, beginning with the request to write the letter-to-the-editor. She listened intently, asking questions only for clarification as Daniel revealed his secrets, causes, anxieties, actions, recent feelings of loss and depression. He left nothing of importance out.

"I want very much to continue as a radical activist, but I don't know how," Daniel concluded. "I feel wounded, and I don't know how to move on."

"Wounded. That's a very good word. Some wounds never heal on their own, like mine about Mathilda's death, until you helped me today.

"Let me ask you this. You told me about the heart-to-heart you had with yourself on the steps of Christie's apartment, but that seems to be the only partly honest conversation you had with yourself. Am I right?"

"Could be."

"Let me tell you what I feel. I do not agree with you that you think you just burned out, ran out of gas, as you put it earlier, however much you feel that way. No, there's more to it than that. It seems to me you never made the time to breathe deeply."

"*Breathe?*"

"Let me go on. Your sharp response to that word tells me that you hear it from a narrow perspective. And you reacted from that perspective. Notice this. You did not pause, you did not take the time to allow a different understanding, and therefore reaction, to come through you when I said breathe, did you?"

"I don't follow."

"Let me try another example. It's hot outside today. Say you were at the shore. You walk toward the ocean, still feeling hot. After entering, you swim, or just stand, covered by the cold, buoyant water of the ocean. Don't you feel invigorated, better than before you went into the water? That cold water, such a contrast to what you felt before, gives you enough separation from the heat to allow refreshment."

"I should go to Jones Beach often?"

"If you want, but I am talking about finding various ways for you to restore you to your self. You see, my grandson, when you gave me the picture frame, I looked at it for a long time. In a way, the buoyant, cold water was rushing through my mind, filling it with so many wonderful, and some tragic memories. As I cried, I realized in an instant that guilt, anger, shame are like barnacles. They need to be scraped off our souls. I have mistaken them all these years for who I am, and today you allowed me to swim in the cold water, and get back in touch with my self."

"We're going to have to talk a lot more about breathing and cold water. But what do I do about TUF?"

"I truly do not believe you have to heal yourself before you can help others. But I also do not believe you can ignore healing yourself *while* you help others. You can do both. For now, my advice is that you do not re-unite with your three friends. Possibly never. If you try to re-unite now, you will find yourself back on the same path, which took you farther and farther away from your self. Your shop, which you told me about, with its curtain separating the public from the private, has a fundamental flaw. That flaw is you. You, with all your baggage, passed back and forth through that curtain. You might have gained some relief from the public, but not from yourself. You need to find a balance. Find a pathway, which leads to broader perspectives, refreshing contrasts, and base your external actions on your fundamental self. I suggest you need to find your own pathway to peace, inside you and within the world around you."

"Sounds like a lot of work."

"Or, a lot of play."

"That would be nice."

After dinner, Daniel phoned his parents. He told them where he was, and that, after returning to New York in a few days, he would call them again. He said he wanted to come to Babylon for a weekend, and tell them all about his last three years.

Early the next afternoon, when Daniel awoke from a long sleep, he said: "I feel a lot better, Gra'ma. Thank you for helping me."

"And I thank you for helping me."

They looked into each other's eyes, and smiled.

> *Daniel glances out the back kitchen window. He believes he sees three women and a man, all in one canoe. He believes they turn to look at him, smiling, each raising their right arm, bending at the elbow, with palms facing Daniel. Daniel smiles.*
>
> *And then, they are gone.*

PASSING THROUGH (The Sixties)

Endnotes

Chapter 1

Page 8: "No, not really. We went to college together, in Connecticut. But no, he wasn't really my friend." See *Finding Pete: Rediscovering the Brother I Lost in Vietnam*, by Jill Hunting (Middletown, CT, Wesleyan University Press, 2009). Peter Hunting and I were fraternity brothers at Alpha Delta Phi, Wesleyan University. *The New York Times* article concerning Peter's death appeared on November 13, 1965, p. 3.

Chapter 2

Page 11: " ... words and music by Guy Carawan, Eve Miriam, and Norman Curtis ..." *Sing for Freedom: the story of the Civil Rights Movement through its songs*, edited and compiled by Guy Carawan and Candie Carawan (Bethlehem, PA, a Sing Out Publication, 1990), p. 40. This is an invaluable compilation for an understanding of the power of "freedom songs" in the context of specific events during nine years (1960-68) of the Civil Rights movement. Lyrics and music for 102 songs, thumbnail histories, and historical context are included.

Page 22: "Then, as if a collar around his neck were violently jerked by someone next to him, ..." The hypnic jerk is a well-documented involuntary movement which can occur when someone is about to fall asleep. Professor Fred Coolidge, University of Colorado, has postulated that apes, who had to remain in trees during the night to escape predators in the distant past, may have developed this "jerk" to keep themselves from falling asleep and off their perch. Listen to "Radio Lab," a segment titled "Still Hanging On," broadcast on NPR, May 1,2016.

Page 23: " ... Arthur Goldberg, the US representative to the UN." *Minutes*, Southern Africa Committee, National Student Christian Federation (NSCF), December 17, 1965, 3 pages. A PDF of these Minutes can be found in Michigan State University's African Activist Archive Project library. http://africanactivist.msu.edu/document_metadata.php?objectid=32-130-432.

Page 23: " … only the fifth meeting of the Committee on Southern Africa." See PDF, "*Minutes*, Southern Africa Committee, NSCF, October 22, 1965," in Michigan State University's African Activist Archive Project library. http://africanactivist.msu.edu/document_metadata.php?objectid=32-130-421

Page 24: "The minutes from the previous meeting had been distributed." This description of the "minutes" represents a composite of *Minutes* from Fall 1965 meetings of the Southern Africa Committee, NSCF, all available in Michigan State University's African Activist Archive Project library. http://africanactivist.msu.edu.

Chapter 3

Page 38: "The long trial had ended with the settlers' defeat." Wikipedia, British Colonial History, Hopewell, New Jersey, at http://en.wikipedia.org/wiki/Hopewell,_New_Jersey.

Page 43: " … how canvassers and teachers were needed that summer in Mississippi." I am indebted to Bruce Watson's book, *Freedom Summer: The Savage Season That Made Mississippi Burn and America a Democracy* (New York, Viking Penguin, 2010), for the extent of his detailed research. All my references to Smith College and Mileston, Mississippi, are based on his depictions of actual events. See especially pp. 20, 148, 178, 189, and 221.

Chapter 4

Page 54: " … at the top of his lungs in Mt. Zion Baptist Church." See Carawan, Guy and Candie, *ibid.*, p. 62.

Page 59: " … some from Louisville, Kentucky, were discussing how to counter the attacks on them by anti-communist organizations." See "'People Have Had to Learn to Live with Us' …: The Bradens and SCEF 20 Years Later," by Bill Patterson, *The* (Louisville) *Courier Journal,* April 2, 1972. The Southern Conference Education Fund (SCEF) was often accused by its strident opponents of being a communist organization.

Pages 59: " … volunteers in support of a black agenda rather than bringing their own 'project' with them to implement." The Student Interracial Ministry (SIM) launched the Southwest Georgia Project, based in Albany, Georgia, in the summer of 1965. Created by students at Union Theological

Seminary and assisted by the Rev. Charles Sherrod, SIM's aims were instructive for many active in this period, no matter what their religious background. Other institutions could be substituted for "the Church" mentioned below, and other professions for the "clergy," in this "Student Interracial Ministry Report, Summer 1966," by Ed Feaver, 10 pages. (The report is part of the "Robert E. Maurer Papers" in Michigan State University's American Radicalism library.)

1) to force seminarians out of their conventional manner of living, and out of their intellectual ivory tower theological security
2) To work in SW Ga for the purpose of educating ourselves; helping to develop local leadership; and making a direct attack upon the racial separation of the US
3) To engage seminarians in the economic, political [,] social issues for the purpose of discovering how these relate to the Church.
4) To attack the established manifestation of the Church in the South and the confining image of the clergy.
5) To work with and not for the people in SW Ga. This meant, among other things, that SIM people would not identify themselves as a unit, "SIM" bringing a project to SW Ga; but would rather identify ourselves as volunteer workers with the SW Ga Movement."

Page 59: " ... Michigan State University Group in South Vietnam and its relation to pacification programs." "The Professor, the Policeman and the Peasant," Part I, by Martin Nicolaus, reprint from *Viet-Report*, detailing Michigan State University Group in South Vietnam, February 1966, 6 pages. The reprint is part of the "Robert E. Maurer Papers" in Michigan State University's American Radicalism library.

Page 59: "He had defended Nelson Mandela and others at the Rivonia Trial in 1964." "'Bram' Fischer on Trial," *South Africa Bulletin*, published by the American Committee on Africa, No. 5, March, 1966. The *Bulletin* is part of the "Robert E. Maurer Papers" in Michigan State University's American Radicalism library.

Page 59: " ... as Dillon, Read & Co., Lehman Brothers, Kuhn, Loeb & Co., Goldman, Sachs—in a book ..." The book is *The Empire of High Finance* by Victor Perlo (New York, International Publishers, 1957).

Chapter 5

Page 68-69: "'After all, we've been working mostly on campuses and in poverty communities, and we've found ourselves mostly cooperating with religious, peace and civil liberties groups, but ...'" The August 24, 1966 issue of *New Left Notes* contains brief descriptions of the workshops to be conducted during the Student for a Democratic Society's National Convention, Clear Lake, Iowa, August 27-September 1, 1966. One workshop was titled, "Working with Liberal Organizations," the description of which provides part of the basis for Paul's "introduction". The flow of the workshop in this chapter, however, is fictional, combining elements from various student movement conferences at the time. The titles of the other eleven workshops listed earlier in the chapter, however, are taken directly from the SDS National Convention's line-up.

Page 70: "' ... to find young men in their midst, to recruit as potential draft resisters.'" Information for this statement came from "Crossing Borders: The Toronto Anti-Draft Programme and the Canadian Anti-Vietnam War Movement," a Master of Arts in History thesis by Matthew Roth for the University of Waterloo, 2008. See http://uwspace.uwaterloo.ca/bitstream/10012/4108/1/Matthew%20Roth%20M A%20Thesis.pdf.

Page 70: "He said he had helped to set up the JOIN Community Union's first storefront office in Chicago ..." JOIN's office was established in April, 1965. A rent strike was organized in May, 1966. See *New Left Notes*, Volume 1, No. 32, August 24, 1966.

Page 71: "'... to create federal legislation for affordable and safe housing.'" Peter Countryman had founded the Northern Student Movement (NSM) in 1961 at Yale University. The demonstration mentioned was on February 15, 1964. See "Harlem's Rent Strike and Rat War: Representation, Housing Access, and Tenant Resistance in New York 1958-1964," by Mandi Isaacs Jackson, page 10, at https://journals.ku.edu/index.php/amerstud/article/viewFile/2942/2901

Page 72: " ... envisions a new communist movement creating a mass party of the working class." The first full term of the Free University was from November, 1965, to February 1966. See http://www.fermentmagazine.org/Bio/newleft3.html
Lyn Marcus was later, and better known as, Lyndon LaRouche. According to Edward Spannaus, Lyn Marcus was teaching at the Free University during the

Fall, 1966, term. See: http://www.crmvet.org/vet/spannaus.htm. (The Wikipedia entry for Lyndon LaRouche cites that he did not start teaching there until 1967.) Spannaus was a long-time LaRouche associate.

Page 77: "'But then, at a break, I left with the girl I had brought with me so no one would suspect I was a homosexual.'" See "Out of the Closet: A Gay Manifesto," by Allen Young, *Ramparts* Magazine, November 1971. Young details the sexism he experienced both outside and inside The Movement. A copy of the article is part of the "Robert E. Maurer Papers" in Michigan State University's American Radicalism library.

Page 80: " ... to work on the Freedom Election in the fall of 1963 ..." See Watson, *ibid.*, especially the Prologue.

Page 81: "'Don't just stand there, do something!'" In May 1967, the University Christian Movement published a 6-page collage of some of the articles which had appeared following its creation on September 6, 1966. Many of the phrases which described the hopes and ambitions of that nationwide student movement appear in the statement of "reflection" read by Al. However, it should be noted that the Wappinger Retreat is a composite of conferences held in 1966, and is not an attempt to re-create the UCM conference held at McCormick Theological Seminary, Chicago, Illinois, September 4-9, 1966.

Page 82: " ... burned their draft cards on the steps of a courthouse in Boston." This event occurred on March 31, 1966. See http://en.wikipedia.org/wiki/United_States_v._O'Brien, in which the burning of the draft cards and subsequent court cases are described, including the decision handed down by the Supreme Court.

Chapter 6

Page 84: "'... and have not obeyed the voice of the Lord our God by following his laws, which he set before us by his servants the prophets.'" The Book of Daniel, *The Holy Bible*, Revised Standard Version (New York, Thomas Nelson and Sons, 1952), p. 930.

Page 88: "*William listened intently as WBAI in New York City broadcast an appeal by Bertrand Russell on this Monday, July Fourth, at five in the afternoon.*" I am indebted to Ken Blackwell, Treasurer, and Tom Stanley, Librarian, Bertrand Russell Society, for a digital audio copy of Bertrand

Russell's "Appeal to the American Conscience". The text, issued on June 18, 1966, can be found in Russell's *War Crimes in Vietnam* (London, George Allen and Unwin Ltd., 1967), and published in the United States by Monthly Review Press, New York. The "Appeal" was also published in *Clare Market Review*, an independent student publication, London School of Economics, July 1966. WBAI, the New York-based station of the progressive Pacifica Radio network, may have been the first to broadcast the audio version of the "Appeal" in the US. At least one of those broadcasts occurred on July 4, 1966, at 5pm (EST), according to its program guide. Russell and Alfred North Whitehead wrote *Principia Mathematica*, a three-volume seminal work in mathematical logic.

Page 92: "Running to catch up to a small group of students heading toward First National City Bank two months ago, ..." In a letter dated January 8, 1967, four students from Union Theological Seminary wrote to its chairman, John Irwin, and members of its board of directors, concerning the nature of the relationship between the Seminary and First National City Bank's participation in a loan consortium to the South African government. The letter recalls student body members " ... withdrawing personal funds *last spring* [italics added] from First National City Bank ... ". The letter is part of the "Robert E. Maurer Papers" in Michigan State University's African Activist Archive Project library.

Pages 97-98: Quotations are from Russell, *ibid.,* pp. 116, 117, 120, and 123.

Page 102: " ... *The former, a student at the University of Kentucky, ... * " See *New Left Notes*, published by Students for a Democratic Society, August 24, 1966, p. 8. This newspaper is part of the "Robert E. Maurer Papers" in Michigan State University's American Radicalism library.

Page 105: " ... trying to distance themselves physically and emotionally from their parents' Orthodox culture and religious rituals—and their poverty." See *The Tribes of America: Journalistic Discoveries of Our People and Their Cultures* by Paul Cowan (New York, The New Press, 2008), pp. 212-14.

Chapter 7

Page 108: "*Ain't Gonna Let Nobody Turn Me Round*, adaptation of a traditional song by members of the Albany Movement." Carawan, Guy and Candie, *ibid.*, p. 62-63.

Page 112: " ... were part of a movement engaged in tedious, old-fashioned research. These 'radical researchers' had ferreted out primary sources, ... " At this time and in the months ahead, the best sources on the power of US multinational corporations were hearings held and reports issued by US House and Senate committees. These major government sources were:

"Interlocks in Corporate Management," A Staff Report to the Antitrust Subcommittee (Subcommittee No. 5) of the Committee on the Judiciary, chaired by Emanuel Celler, March 12, 1965, U.S. Government Printing Office, 1965, 270 pages.

"Economic Concentration", Hearings before the Subcommittee on Antitrust and Monopoly of the Committee on the Judiciary, United States Senate, September 12, 13, 19 and 20, 1966, Part 5, Concentration and Divisional Reporting, chaired by Philip A. Hart, Chairman, U.S. Government Printing Office, Washington, 1966, 300 pages.

"Control of Commercial Banks and Interlocks Among Financial Institutions," Staff Report for the Subcommittee on Domestic Finance of the Committee on Banking and Currency, House of Representatives, chaired by Wright Patman, July 31, 1967, U.S. Government Printing Office, 1967, 96 pages. Patman's subcommittee had earlier published a report, "Twenty Largest Stockholders of Record in Member Banks of the Federal Reserve System," in 1964.

Perhaps the most famous series of published hearings on the concentration of corporate power in several industries were held by Senator Estes Kefauver during his chairmanship of the Senate's Antitrust and Monopoly Subcommittee from 1957 until 1963. Senator Kefauver had largely finished the draft of a book, *In A Few Hands: Monopoly Power in America*, based on his extensive Senate hearings, when he died in August, 1963. Staff members of his Subcommittee then added additional material and completed the book (Baltimore, Penguin Books, 1965).

Page 112: "Large, white cardboard, poster-sized sheets of paper were spread on several long, rectangular tables arranged side-by-side-by-side." The Baltimore radical research participants would have had access to numerous reference materials during the summer of 1966 on which to base the information they presented. Listings and descriptions of these reference materials (and many more) would later be published in two important guides for "radical research": (1) *N.A.C.L.A.* [North American Congress on Latin America] *Research Methodology Guide*, first appeared as a two-part series in

VIET-*REPORT* magazine (January 1968 and April/May 1968), and later combined and revised into a single NACLA publication, 19 pages; and (2) *The University-Military Complex: A Directory and Related Documents*, compiled by Michael Klare, published by NACLA, March 1969, 61 pages.

Some of the many documents available for the Baltimore meeting participants would have included, but would not have been limited to, the following: annual corporate reports, 10-K corporation filings with the Security and Exchange Commission, university catalogues, *Who's Who in America*, *Who was Who*, *Hearings* before the Subcommittee on Antitrust and Monopoly, Senate Committee of the Judiciary, conducted by its chairman, Senator Estes Kefauver (1964-66), *Directory of National Associations of Businessmen*, *Directory of American Firms Operating in Foreign Countries*, *Research Centers Directory* (Gale Research Company, 1965), *Industrial Research Laboratories of the United States* (Bowker Associates, 1965), *Directory of Department of Defense Information Analysis Centers* (Office of Naval Research, 1965), *Technical Abstract Bulletin* (Department of Defense Documentation Center), *Research and Development Directory* (Government Data Publications, Inc.), *Aerospace and Defense Research Contracts Roster* (Bowker Associates), *Air Force Research Resumes* (Air Force Office of Scientific Research), *100 Companies and Their Subsidiary Corporations Listed According to Net Value of Prime Contract Awards* (Department of Defense). All these and many more were detailed in the two NACLA publications cited above.

"Radical research", an early component of "The Movement", rapidly gained in importance from 1966 onward. Not simply an academic exercise, "radical research" was also known as "action research," pinpointing targets for demonstrations and other tactics to effect change.

Page 112: "B. Johns Hopkins University." In 1966, Johns Hopkins University was #1 of all US universities in the total dollars ($50,394,000) of Department of Defense contracts, according to the Department of Defense, *500 Contractors Listed According to Net Value of Military Prime Contract Awards for Research, Development, Test and Evaluation Work, Fiscal Year 1966*, cited in *N.A.C.L.A. Research Methodology Guide*, May 1968, p. 13.

Page 113: "a. National Brotherhood Award." Eisenhower did not actually receive the National Brotherhood Award until November 22, 1966, presented by the National Conference of Christians and Jews meeting in Baltimore. See *The View From Here*, a bi-monthly journal by Grenn Whitman, Vol. 1. No. 6,

November 24, 1966. All issues of this journal are part of the "Robert E. Maurer Papers" in Michigan State University's American Radicalism library.

Page 116: "' ... Olin started preparations at the Badger Plant to manufacture ball powder, which is used in the Army's M-16 rifles for fighting in Vietnam.'" Olin Mathieson would manufacture 99,985,600 pounds of ball powder from May 1966 through May 1975 at the Badger Plant. http://en.wikipedia.org/wiki/Badger_Army_Ammunition_Plant

Page 116: "' ... making it the 5th largest US chemical company with corporate headquarters moving to New York City.'" See http://en.wikipedia.org/wiki/Mathieson_Chemical.

Page 117: "' ... presumably to help persuade Milton Eisenhower, whose brother, Dwight, was President of the United States at the time, to serve as University president.'" In 1972, the University president's home was renamed the Nichols House in honor of Thomas Steele Nichols. http://webapps.jhu.edu/jhuniverse/information_about_hopkins/about_jhu/chro nology/index.cfm

Page 117: "'It consisted, in part, of stones from all states, three federal territories, six continents and various Holy Land sites, all for the commemoration of Methodism and Christian brotherhood.'" See http://www.baltimorecityschools.org/domain/1587.

Page 117: "' ... and the National Republican Committee's treasurer during the first two years of the Kennedy Administration.'" See http://www.nytimes.com/1995/04/17/obituaries/spencer-truman-olin-executive-for-olin-corporation-dies-at-96.html; and also, http://en.wikipedia.org/wiki/Spencer_Truman_Olin.

Page 118: "'The Lab [Applied Physics Laboratory] was first located in a rented garage with its 'used car' sign left in place as camouflage.'" See http://webapps.jhu.edu/jhuniverse/information_about_hopkins/about_jhu/chro nology/index.cfm.

Page 119: "' ... Washington Center for Foreign Policy Research, created in 1957 by the Johns Hopkins University's School of Advanced International Studies.'" It was renamed the Foreign Policy Institute in 1980.

Page 120: "' ... he [Milton Eisenhower] was also a successful fundraiser for Johns Hopkins, especially from the Rockefeller and Ford Foundations.'"

Encyclopedia of World Biography, at
http://www.bookrags.com/biography/milton-eisenhower.

Page 121: "" … echoing Dwight Eisenhower's famous dire warning about the military-industrial complex …"" On January 17, 1961, in a farewell speech to the nation three days before the end of his Presidency and after fifty years of public service, Dwight Eisenhower warned:

"This conjunction of an immense military establishment and a large arms industry is new in the American experience. The total influence -- economic, political, even spiritual -- is felt in every city, every State house, every office of the Federal government. We recognize the imperative need for this development. Yet we must not fail to comprehend its grave implications. Our toil, resources and livelihood are all involved; so is the very structure of our society.

"In the councils of government, we must guard against the acquisition of unwarranted influence, whether sought or unsought, by the military-industrial complex. The potential for the disastrous rise of misplaced power exists and will persist.

"We must never let the weight of this combination endanger our liberties or democratic processes. We should take nothing for granted. Only an alert and knowledgeable citizenry can compel the proper meshing of the huge industrial and military machinery of defense with our peaceful methods and goals, so that security and liberty may prosper together."

See
http://www.americanrhetoric.com/speeches/dwightdeisenhowerfarewell.html
and also http://www.ourdocuments.gov/doc.php?flash=false&doc=90.

Page 126: "Some sang out enthusiastically as Stevie Wonder's version of 'Blowin' in the Wind' played." These four songs were, respectively, numbers 2, 4, 5, and 9 on *Billboard's* Top Ten chart for the week of September 3, 1966.   http://www.billboard.com/charts/hot-100#/charts/hot-100?chartDate=1966-09-08.

Page 134: " … recalling the old days when nineteenth-century industrialists like Thomas Winans, then one of the wealthiest men in America, … " *The New York Times*, June 11, 1878.

Chapter 8

Page 136: "*Oh Freedom*, adaptation of a traditional song by members of the Student Non-violent Coordinating Committee." Carawan, Guy and Candie, *ibid.*, p. 74-5.

Page 141: "Daniel saw hypocrites everywhere." See The Book of Matthew, *The Holy Bible*, Revised Standard Version (New York, Thomas Nelson and Sons, 1952), chapter 6, verses 1-6 and 16, for one of the best descriptions of hypocrites.

Page 144: "In fact, the university board member was IDA's chairman." See *Who Rules Columbia?*, prepared and published by the staff of the North American Congress on Latin America (NACLA), 1968, p. 25, and its 4-page insert which provides the corporate ties of Columbia University's board of trustees.

Page 145: "He had heard about Morningside Heights, Inc. ... " Reading all 40 pages of NACLA's *Who Rules Columbia?* provides a fascinating insight into the many non-academic roles played by Columbia University within New York City, nationally and internationally.

Page 148: " ... the biggest investors in Middle South are all in Boston, like Harvard University and State Street Investment Corporation ... " See "The Mississippi-New York-Boston Axis," my 16-page unpublished paper, August 1, 1967, circulated to members of Project CN, a national organization dedicated to social change. Also, see 2 undated, 2-page memos from Ted Seaver, executive director, Michael Schwerner Memorial Fund, Inc., based in Jackson, Mississippi, describing various connections among Middle South Utilities, Mississippi Power and Light, and its New York and Boston shareholders, sent to Rev. Isaac Igarashi, executive director of Project CN. These documents can be found in the "Robert E. Maurer Papers" in Michigan State University's American Radicalism library.

Chapter 9

Page 155: "The older, full time chauffeurs, in a class by themselves, ... " See my as yet unpublished book, *I'm Circling: The Life and Times of Manhattan's Chauffeurs*, for an explanation of the difference between "drivers" and chauffeurs" in the for-hire industry. This definitive work traces the for-hire industry back to 1605 in Hackney, an "inner borough" within the City of London.

Page 158: "He poured each a cup of wine." See "A Radical Haggadah for Passover," by Arthur Waskow, *Ramparts*, April 1969, pp. 25-33. I have borrowed liberally from the recitation of this Haggadah, but have kept its spirit.

Page 160: "' ... and then the government resorted to a show of force to crush opposition to its policies, only then did we decide to answer violence with violence..'" *The Guardian* newspaper, April 22, 2007, quoting the text of Mandela's defense statement on April 20, 1964, during his and other defendant's trial on charges of sabotage.

Page 162: "We are about to drink; may our wine give us joy for the work ahead!" See "A Radical Haggadah for Passover," by Arthur Waskow, *Ramparts*, April 1969, p. 33.

Chapter 10

Page: 165: " ... as one speaker would put it, 'tune in, turn on, drop out.'" Timothy Leary, who coined the phrase, and Richard Alpert (later known as Ram Dass) were two of the speakers. The *Berkeley* Barb published a cover drawing of Lyndon Johnson dressed as Timothy Leary with "Turn Off, Tune Out, Drop In", a parody of Leary's mantra, written across Johnson's chest (Vol. 5, No. 9, sometime in 1967). "Volume 5" may have been misleading, since this underground newspaper was only founded in August, 1965.

Page 170: " ... Cleage was telling blacks to stop worshipping a white Jesus." Glanton Dowdell was the artist who painted the "Black Madonna", unveiled in the sanctuary of the Central United Church of Christ in Detroit. The text of the Easter Sermon, "Call to a Black Ecumenical Movement," preached by the Rev. Albert B. Cleage, Jr., opened with these words: "For nearly 500 years the illusion that Jesus was white dominated the world only because Europeans dominated the world. Now, with the emergence of the nationalist movements of the world's colored majority, the historic truth is finally beginning to emerge – that Jesus was the non-white leader of a non-white people struggling for national liberation against the rule of a white nation, Rome. ... The Nation, Israel, was a mixture of the Chaldeans, the Egyptians, the Midionites, the Ethiopians, the Kushites, the Babylonians and other dark peoples of Central Africa." This sermon can be found in a 3-page document, issued by his church, in the "Robert E. Maurer Papers" in Michigan State University's American Radicalism library.

Page 172: "' Alinsky and Minister Florence liked the name F.I.G.H.T. for a new, black community organization to confront the local giants.'" "Kodak, FIGHT, and the Definition of Civil Rights in Rochester, New York: 1966-1967" by R.D.G. Wadhwani is an excellent and well-researched article, *Historian*, Volume 60, Issue 1, first published online, October 9, 2007, at http://onlinelibrary.wiley.com/doi/10.1111/j.1540-6563.1997.tb01387.x/pdf.

At that time, I had recently been engaged (January, 1967) by the National Council of Churches' Eastern Field Operations to contact, encourage and transport demonstrators from New York and New Jersey (primarily) to support FIGHT during Kodak's annual meeting in Flemington, NJ. I first met Minister Florence at LaGuardia Airport in early January, driving him into Manhattan for a meeting with national church executives, when he shared his making, as I recall, a hobbyhorse, for his children's Christmas. Documents related to FIGHT and the stockholders' meeting can be found in the "Robert E. Maurer Papers" in Michigan State University's American Radicalism library.

See also "Franklin Florence's Collections," 1962-72, Department of Rare Books, Special Collections and Preservation, River Campus Libraries, University of Rochester. http://www.lib.rochester.edu/index.cfm?page=882.

Page 173: "After all, it had only been eight days since Kodak had broken the agreement for which Florence had hailed the company's 'vision'." See Wadhwani, *ibid*, p. 66.

Page 176: "' ... killed or imprisoned peoples of color in foreign lands either directly or through military support of dictators ...'" It may be hard for anyone not following the events of the day during the Sixties to understand how many dictators across the globe were receiving financial (either military or other aid) or political support—or both--from the United States government. Here's a partial list: Pinochet (Chile), Stroessner (Paraguay), Amin (Uganda), Marcos (The Philippines), Smith (Rhodesia), Vorster (South Africa), The Shah (Iran), Kai-shek (Taiwan), Onganía (Argentina), Castello Branco (Brazil).

Page 176-77: "'Because I am involved in Mankind.
And therefore never send to know

for whom the bell tolls,
It tolls for thee.'"

Commonly referred to as "No Man Is an Island," this was a section of a prose work by John Donne titled, "Meditation XVII," within his larger work, "Devotions upon Emergent Occasions". Parts of "No Man is an Island" are quoted both by Saul Alinsky in his book, *Reveille for Radicals* (Chicago, University of Chicago Press, 1946), p. 23, and Stokely Carmichael in his book, *Stokely Speaks: Black Power Back to Pan Africanism* (New York, Random House, 1965, 1971), p. 76.

Page 177: "'We are going to use our own words, Stokely said, speak in our own language, not the words whites have put into our mouths.'" Stokely Carmichael's actual words were: "An organization which claims to speak for the needs of a community—as does the Student Nonviolent Coordinating Committee--must speak in the tone of that community, not as somebody else's buffer zone. This is the significance of Black Power as a slogan. For once, black people are going to use the words they want to use—not just the words whites want to hear." Carmichael, *ibid.,* p. 18. First appeared in *The New York Review of Books,* September 1966.

Page 177: "'They talk citizen participation, but just let even a few community folks try to get in the door of their bogus grass roots' meetings, and they'll cancel the meeting or change its location.'" See "Citizen Participation and Community Organization in Planning and Urban Renewal," a speech delivered by Saul Alinsky, Executive Director, Industrial Areas Foundation, to the Chicago chapter of the National Association of Housing and Redevelopment Officials, January 29, 1962, 14 pages. A copy of the speech can be found in the "Robert E. Maurer Papers" in Michigan State University's American Radicalism library.

Page 177: "'We've got so-called leaders who spend more time on how they can please the white man than how they can fight for the black man.'" Stokely Carmichael's actual words were: "We're not lazy. We are the hardest working people in this country. We are! The trouble is we are the lowest paid and the most oppressed and the most exploited people in this country. In this country, yeah! We're not lazy people. If you ride up and down the Delta in the South today, you will see black people chopping and picking cotton for two dollars a day while white folks sit on their porch, drink Scotch, and talk about us. We're not a lazy people. It is our mothers who take care of their own family and then go across town to take care of Miss Ann's family. So you should get that out of your mind. We're not lazy. We are a hardworking, industrious people. Always have been—our sweat built this country. Built this country." From a speech delivered by Stokely Carmichael, then chairman of the Student Nonviolent Coordinating Committee, to students at Garfield High School, Seattle, Washington, on April 19, 1967. The full text can be found at http://www.aavw.org/special_features/speeches_speech_carmichael01.html.

Page 178: "'They wouldn't know a natural, indigenous community leader if they tripped over one.'" Saul Alinsky's actual words were: "Since representatives of formal [welfare, poverty] agencies judge leadership according to *their own* criteria, evaluate what is good or bad in the community according to *their own* standards, and understand life in the community only when interpreted according to *their own* code or standards—it is crystal clear that they don't know the meaning of indigenous leadership, let alone the identity of these natural leaders." Alinsky, *ibid.*, pp. 91-92.

Page 178: "'Then true black leadership can not be bought off by white leadership with either patronage or prestige, and so whites will have to talk to the community's representatives in terms of real power.'" Stokely Carmichael's actual words were: "A leadership that is truly 'responsible' ... must be developed. Such leadership will recognize that its power lies in the unified and collective strength of the community. This will make it difficult for the white leadership group to conduct its dialogue with individuals in terms of patronage and prestige, and will force them to talk to the community's representatives in terms of real power." Carmichael, *ibid.*, p. 42. First appeared in *The Massachusetts Review*, September 1966.

Page 178: "'All power to the people. That's what Saul says, that's what Stokely says.'" Saul Alinsky's actual words were: "If we strip away all the chromium trimmings of high-sounding metaphor and idealism which conceal the motor and gears of a democratic society, one basic element is revealed—the people are the motor, the organizations of the people are the gears. The power of the people is transmitted through the gears of their own organizations, and democracy moves forward." Alinsky, *ibid.*, p. 70.

One of the slogans of the Black Panther Party, founded in 1966, was "All power to the People." One of the inspirations of the Party was the Lowndes County [Alabama] Freedom Organization organized by Stokely Carmichael who would later be named as Prime Minister of the Black Panther Party in February 1968.

Page 179: "'We've got to take it for ourselves.'" Stokely Carmichael's actual words were: "Now we want to move ... to the concept of denying one one's freedom. And this is very, very important because white people have assumed that they're God; that they can give somebody your freedom, and so if they don't like the way you act, they won't give you your freedom. But now what you have to get crystal clear in your minds is that nobody gives anybody their freedom. People can only deny somebody their freedom." From a speech delivered by Stokely Carmichael, then chairman of the Student Nonviolent Coordinating Committee, to students at Garfield High School, Seattle, Washington, on April 19, 1967. The full text can be found at http://www.aavw.org/special_features/speeches_speech_carmichael01.html

Page 184: "'No matter how often the media distorts and lies about the meaning of Black Power, this is the essential difference between integration as it is currently practiced and the concept of Black Power.'" Stokely Carmichael's actual words were: "Even if such a program [integration] were possible its results would be, not to develop the black community as a functional and honorable segment of the total society, with its own cultural identity, life patterns, and institutions, but to abolish it—the final solution to the Negro problem." "The fact is that what we must abolish is not the black community, but the dependent colonial status that has been inflicted upon it. The racial and cultural personality of the black community must be preserved and the community must win its freedom while preserving its cultural identity. This is the essential difference between integration as it is currently practiced and the concept of Black Power." Carmichael, *ibid.,* p. 39. First appeared in *The Massachusetts Review*, September 1966.

Page 184: "'Can you do that?' Arthur asked." Stokely Carmichael's actual words were: "The question is, can the white activist stop trying to be a Pepsi generation who comes alive in the black community, and be a man who's willing to move into the white community and start organizing where the organization is needed? Can he do that?" Carmichael, *ibid.,* p. 51. First appeared in a speech delivered at the University of California, October 1966.

Page 185: "'We blacks refuse to be the therapy for white society any longer. We have gone stark, raving mad trying to do it.'" Stokely Carmichael's actual words were: "And that's the real question facing the white activists today. Can they tear down the institutions that have put us all in the trick bag we've been into for the last hundreds of years?" "Let them [whites] find their own psychologists. We refuse to be the therapy for white society any longer. We have gone stark, raving mad trying to do it." Carmichael, *ibid.,* p. 52. First appeared in a speech delivered at the University of California, October 1966.

Chapter 11

Page 193: "It was a favorite especially of "short-timers" in Vietnam who, after each verse, shouted "Short, Short, Short." From *The View From Here*, a newsletter by Gren Whitman, Volume 1, Number 18, June 18, 1967, p. 3. "Short-timer" usually referred to a soldier in Vietnam approaching the end of his tour of duty.

Page 201: "'I understand this attitude may lead to prosecution and rather severe penalties and feel I am prepared to face such.'" From the June 30, 1967, letter sent by Fred Goff to Local Board #30, 1322 Nevin Avenue, Richmond, California, from his then home in New York City. This letter, which also contained a xerox of Fred's draft card, can be found in the "Robert E. Maurer Papers" in Michigan State University's American Radicalism library.

Page 205: " ... that Tampa would be one of the earliest of 164 civil disorders that rocked the country during the first nine months of 1967 ... " See *Report of the National Advisory Commission on Civil Disorders* (New York, Bantam Books, March 1968), p. 6. Subsequent descriptions of riot scenes and consequences in Tampa and Atlanta are taken from this remarkably candid and detailed document, which was popularly known as the Kerner Commission Report.

Page 206: "' ... earlier this spring, Fisk University, Jackson State University, and Texas Southern University ... '" There had been riots on or near each of these university campuses in the spring of 1967. *Report of the National Advisory Commission on Civil Disorders*, pp. 40-41.

Page 206: "' ... to achieve their share of power, indeed, to become their own men and women—in this time and in this land—by whatever means necessary.'" *Black Power: The Politics of Liberation in America,* by Stokely Carmichael and Charles V. Hamilton (New York, Random House, 1967), pp.184-85.

Page 207: " ... which killed a black by-stander sitting on a front porch and critically wounded a nine year-old black boy." *Report of the National Advisory Commission on Civil Disorders,* p. 56.

Page 207: " ... to get out of the community and leave the local people to handle their own business." *Report of the National Advisory Commission on Civil Disorders*, p. 56.

Page 208: " … made no distinctions between the poor and the well off." Except where specifically footnoted, statistics and other descriptions of the Newark riots come from the excellent book, *Rebellion in Newark: Official Violence and Ghetto Response*, by Tom Hayden (New York, Random House, 1967). Evidence for middle class participation in the riots can be found on pp. 31-32.

Page 209: "' … in response to what they believed were snipers.'" *Report of the National Advisory Commission on Civil Disorders*, pp. 67-68.

Page 210: " … how an occupying army had rained death, bodily injury and property destruction on a significant portion of approximately 200,000 Negroes." *Report of the National Advisory Commission on Civil Disorders*, p. 57. The Kerner Commission estimated the total Newark population in 1967 as 400,000, with 52% Negro.

Page 213-4: "'About fifteen of those were gunshot victims.'" Hayden, *ibid.*, p. 35.

Page 214: "' … so all the shooting was done by white policemen.'" Hayden, *ibid.*, p. 45.

Page 214: "' … for a moment they were creating a community of their own.'" Hayden, *ibid.*, p. 32.

Page 214: " … a house painter … " Hayden, *ibid.*, p. 94.

Page 215: "' … he had to have fourteen stitches.'" Hayden, *ibid.*, p. 95.

Page 215: "' … the boy was killed with a bullet to the head.'" Hayden, *ibid.*, pp. 80-81.

Page 215: "' … and killed the boy with the garbage.'" Hayden, *ibid.*, p. 81-82.

Page 216: "'Officials said there was 'withering' sniper fire …'" Hayden, *ibid.*, p. 40.

Pages 216: "'This wanton destruction of property by this white occupying army happened to maybe a hundred black-owned businesses.'" Hayden, *ibid.*, p. 49.

Page 216: "'By Sunday night, another ten folks were dead, about 50 more had gun shot wounds, and an additional 500 were in jail.'" *Hayden, ibid.,*   p. 48.

Page 217: "'... weren't the riots really a people trying to make their own history?'" Hayden, *ibid.*, pp. 69-72.

Chapter 12

Page 224: "' ... these are the interests US foreign policy must protect, why revolutions must be put down, why Vietnam must be an object lesson to the people of the world.'" "Here's Your Opportunity to Dine With Rusk and the Warmakers!", by Michael Grossman, distributed by Liberation News Service, November 11, 1967, 2 pages. There is a "menu" which leads the release, featuring "Yellow Peril Pate, Red Menace Mousse, Chopped Charlie, Napalm Nougat Flambe".

Page 227: "As Daniel reflected on his own transition, he vaguely remembered from his high school history class that theologian Roger Williams ..." Roger Williams first separated himself from the "corrupt and false" Anglican Church to become a Puritan in England, moved to Plymouth in 1630, and then founded a colony called Providence Plantation (Rhode Island) in 1636 after being forced out of Salem, Massachusetts, on charges of heresy and sedition. Unlike the King of England, Williams purchased the land for his colony from the Narragansetts. Having studied a few native American languages, he wrote a book primarily on an Algonquian language. He was also an advocate of fair dealings with native Americans. Providence was the first tract of land in modern history where religious liberty and a "wall of separation" between church and state were practiced. It became a haven for persons persecuted for their religious beliefs (Baptists, Quakers and Jews, especially). The colony was governed in civil matters by a majority vote of the heads of households. A law, though short-lived, was passed banning slavery. Williams' radical example was testament to the core of the best in the American spirit. See http://en.wikipedia.org/wiki/Roger_Williams_(theologian).

Page 231: "On his [Daniel's] apartment's stove, he had heated all three ingredients ..." This recipe can be found at About.com, part of *The New York Times* company, under the title, "How To Make a Smoke Bomb," by Anne Marie Helmenstine, Ph.D., specifically at: http://chemistry.about.com/od/demonstrationsexperiments/ss/smokebomb_2.htm.

Page: 234: "He no longer felt helpless in the history of his own times." Paul Rockwell, in "The Columbia Statement" adopted by the Columbia chapter of Students for a Democratic Society on September 12, 1968, made two statements concerning the relationship between "helplessness" and "history." "We felt helpless in the history of our times," and "It was only through struggle that we could overcome our helplessness." See *The University Crisis Reader: The Liberal University Under Attack*, Volume I, edited by Immanuel Wallerstein and Paul Starr (New York, Random House, 1971), pp. 24 and 25.

Page 239: "Brown Brothers Harriman & Company, at number 59, was a private bank, which, according to a government report in the 1930s, was among the largest stockholders in five of the ten largest American companies at that time." *The Empire of High Finance*, by Victor Perlo (New York, International Publishers, 1957), p. 94.

Page 239: "Robert Lovett, former Secretary of War under President Truman, was its current president." *Who Rules America* by G. William Dumhoff (Englewood Cliffs, NJ, Prentice Hall, 1967), p. 99.

Page 239: " … Daniel as an avid fan going to Bostwick Field … " Bostwick Field, in Old Westbury, Long Island, was created by Dunbar Bostwick and two siblings so that the aristocratic sport of polo could be enjoyed by the "populace." I watched many polo matches at Bostwick. See https://en.wikipedia.org/wiki/Dunbar_Bostwick and http://www.nytimes.com/2006/01/28/sports/othersports/28BOSTWICK.html?_r=0.

Page 239: " … Daniel relished the idea that he had now crossed paths with this influential political and financial player whose career was described, in a book Daniel had used for research, as moving from ' … command post to command post … .'" Dumhoff, *ibid.*, footnote on p. 21.

Page 240: "Bankers Trust … had become the 'new tycoons' of the American economy by controlling huge pension funds, like AT&T's." Dumhoff, *ibid.*, pp. 53-54 footnote.

Page 240: " … but Chase had also merged with the Standard Bank of South Africa." See "An Appeal to the People of New York Banking at First National City and Chase Manhattan to Investigate Their Involvement with Racism in South Africa," published by the American Committee on Africa, on the occasion of the December 9, 1966, action to close accounts at those banks.

This flyer is part of the "Robert E. Maurer Papers" in Michigan State University's African Activist Archive Project library.

Page 241: "Lehmann Brothers, an investment firm, had grown through financing large retail trade and department stores, and then took positions in major arms manufacturers, like General Dynamics." Dumhoff, *ibid.*, pp. 183-84.

Chapter 13

Page 246: "*Move on Over*, words by Len H. Chandler, Jr., to the tune of *John Brown's Body* and the *Battle Hymn of the Republic*, 1966." Carawan, Guy and Candie, *ibid.*, p. 307.

Page 248: "Nothing appeared, however, in any paper about the smoke bombs at the Hilton or blood balloons in Lower Manhattan." *The New York Times*, November 15, 1967, front page. The reporter was Homer Bigart.

Page 251: " … and the very recent owner of an entire block in the Wall Street area and a large tract in Rockland County, as well as portions of a West Side area running from 125th to 135th Streets." For a detailed review of Columbia University's massive influence and ownership in New York City's real estate market, see *Who Rules Columbia?*, prepared by the staff of the North American Congress on Latin America (NACLA), published in 1968 by NACLA, 36 pages. See especially the sections on "Historical Perspective", "The Real Estate Establishment," and "Appendix: Columbia's Real Estate Holdings."

Chapter 14

Page 266: " … brought Morningside Heights University to a standstill for eight days in April, …" I participated in only a few events of what was known as the "Columbia [University] Strike". This chapter is not a fictionalized attempt to render its story. In writing this chapter, however, I did consult a number of sources which detailed and analyzed the "Columbia University Student Strike". From Tuesday, April 23rd through Tuesday, April 30th, a total of eight days, five buildings on the Columbia campus were occupied by students and others. Then on May 21-22, one building, Hamilton Hall, was re-occupied. I was present outside Hamilton Hall when the police moved in to clear the demonstrators.

Page 267: "'The French workers are spontaneously taking over factories in support of the student protests as well as demanding the ouster of President Charles de Gaulle, over the objections of their unions' leadership.'" Eventually in May, 1968, more than ten million French workers, comprising two-thirds of the workforce, would defy their own leadership by continuing to strike in support of the students' demands and expansion of their own rights. The resulting nationwide protests actually drove President de Gaulle from France, albeit for one day, during which the country did not know his whereabouts. See http://en.wikipedia.org/wiki/May_1968_in_France.

Page 267: " … had visited American soldiers, living in Paris, who had deserted in protest against the Vietnam War." See copy of a letter written to me by Larry Cox, then a (Presbyterian) Frontier Intern living in Paris and aiding deserters, and a "Dear Friend" fund raising letter from "The Second Front," giving an address in Paris to which funds might be sent. Both originated in 1968 and are now a part of the "Robert E. Maurer Papers" in Michigan State University's American Radicalism library.

Page 267: " … the Tlatelolco massacre of students and other protesters, along with bystanders, during a peaceful rally of some 10,000 people in Mexico City." Although figures widely vary, it has been documented that 44 persons were killed by the Mexican authorities during a demonstration in the Plaza de les Tres Culturas in the Tlatelolco section of Mexico City. See http://en.wikipedia.org/wiki/Tlatelolco_Massacre.

PASSING THROUGH (The Sixties)

About The Author

Robert Erwin Maurer

I was born eighty-three days after Japan attacked Pearl Harbor. For my first eighteen years, I lived in my parents' home in Rockville Centre, on Long Island. I graduated from Wesleyan University with a B.A. in English, and then Union Theological Seminary with a M.Div. graduate degree. I also earned a Diploma in computer programming from The Chubb Institute.

For nineteen years (1965-1983), I served multiple non-profit advocacy organizations, committees and publications, as follows:

Columnist, *The Grain of Salt*, official Union Theological Seminary student newsletter (1965-66)

Member, Union Theological Ad Hoc Committee on South Africa (1966-67)

Administrative Assistant, Foundation for the Arts, Religion, and Culture, Inc. (1966-67)

Founder and Editor-in-chief, *"Christianity and Revolution"*, an unofficial magazine published at Union Theological Seminary (1966-68)

Member (1966-69) and Chair (1967-68), Southern Africa Committee, University Christian Movement

Advisor, World Student Christian Federation, on its "Banks Campaign" (disengagement from South Africa) (1967)

Attendee, Social Change Project (Chicago Consultation, "From Caste to Black Nation: What is Church Policy to Be?"), (1967); Member, National Project Committee, Division of Christian Life and Mission, National Council of Churches (NCC) (1967); Attendee, Conference on Economic Power and Responsibility, NCC (1968); Member, Strategy Board on Race as a Factor in US Foreign Policy, NCC (1970-71)

Volunteer, Eastern Field Operations, National Council of Churches, organizer, demonstration in support of F.I.G.H.T at the Kodak stockholders' meeting, Flemington, New Jersey (1967)

Executive Assistant, Communications Network, Inc., the organization formed by Rev. Isaac Igarashi after he left NCC's Eastern Field Operations (1967-69)

Chairman (elected), Steering Committee, Youth Participants' Assembly, Fourth Assembly, World Council of Churches (Uppsala, Sweden, 1968)

Delegate, World Student Conference, World Student Christian Federation (Turku, Finland, 1968)

Member, North American [Advisory] Committee, World Student Christian Federation (1968)

Liaison to Organizations, National Citizens Committee Concerned About Deployment of the ABM (1969)

Finance Committee Chairman, Africa Research Group (1969)

Editor-in-Chief (aka Strategy and Planning), *motive* Magazine (1969-71)

Staff Member, Cuba Resource Center, then Chairman, Cuba Resource Center Council (1971-73)

Writer, *American Report* newspaper, published by Clergy and Laymen Concerned (1972-73)

Recruiter and Supervisor, volunteer harvesters, New Communities, Inc., largest black-owned farm in the United States, founded by Rev. Charles and Shirley Sherrod (1972-74)

Founder and Executive Director/Secretary, Committee to Recognize Guinea-Bissau, then organizer and MC, American People's Recognition Ceremony (1973-74)

Editor, *People and Systems*, published by Friendship Press, National Council of Churches (1974-75)

Published articles in *Christianity and Crisis*, *The Christian Century*, *Hispanic Historical Review*, *Encore*, and others

Conference Consultant and Newsletter Assistant, Child Welfare League of America, Inc. (1974-76)

Attendee, "Alternative Marketing Organizations and Third World Producers", Noordwijkerhout, The Netherlands. One of two participants from the USA invited by the Dutch government to meet with leading Third World cooperative producers and their European marketing agencies. (1976)

Founder and President, Pancontinental Exchange, Inc., a "fair trade" organization concentrating on African products (1976-79)

Deputy Director for Program (and acting Executive Director), Amnesty International USA; delegate to annual AI International Council Meetings in Bad Honnef, Leuven, Vienna, Montreal, and Rimini (1976-83). Amnesty International was the 1977 Nobel Peace Prize recipient.

In more recent times, I have been a chauffeur, a limousine account manager at The Plaza Hotel, a student of computer programming, IT recruiter, career services supervisor, home security salesman, and a caregiver in a group home for developmentally disabled adults.

All have provided ingredients for a literary stew.

Robert E. Maurer
May 2, 2016

www.PassingThruTime.com